I0818159

ANDREW P.
WESTON

THE IX

EXORDIUM OF TEARS

WWW.THEPERSEIDPRESS.COM

Perseid Press
P. O. Box 584
Centerville, MA **02632**

Exordium of Tears

First Perseid Press Edition, 2016
First Perseid Pres Kindle Edition, 2016
First Perseid Press ePub Edition, 2016
First Perseid Press Hardcover Edition, 2016

A Perseid Press Original

Cover art: Roy Mauritsen
Cover image © Perseid Press 2016
Cover design: Roy Mauritsen
Book design: Sarah Hulcy

Trade Paperback edition ISBN 13: 978-0-9964289-9-6, ISBN-10: 0-9964289-9-2
Kindle Digital edition: ISBN-13:978-0-9968982-1-8, ISBN-10: 0-9968982-1-2
ePub Digital edition ISBN-13:978-0-9968982-0-1, ISBN-10:0-9968982-0-4
Hardcover: ISBN-13: 978-0-9964289-8-9, ISBN-10: 0-9964289-8-4

Published in the United States of America

10 9 8 7 6 5 4 3 2 1

SPQR

Serovak Pluserak Qen Rhomanax

(For Security Prosperity and Rhomane)

ACKNOWLEDGEMENTS

To the team at Perseid Press, who encouraged me to take the idea far beyond what I'd first imagined.

TABLE OF CONTENTS

PART I

"...by the dawn's early light"

—*Star Spangled Banner*, Francis Scott Key

Prologue

Parked in geostationary orbit above a lifeless world, the vessel was a testimony to cultural and technological innovation. Sleek, vast, and lethal, she hung like the Titan she was; a leviathan sleeping amid a sea of infinite possibilities. Myriad stars bore witness to her majesty, and although each one glittered fiercely, none could lift the invasive chill leaching like death through the very constitution of her bones.

Within, a petrified forest of metal, fabric, and thermoplastic polymers slumbered.

Here, a coffee cup perched precariously on the edge of a counter, its flash-frozen contents discarded and forgotten long, long ago. There, a simple paper notebook hung suspended in the void above a set of stairs, as if waiting for the moment gravity would send it on its way toward the deck below. Between them, an ornate pen spiraled lazily by, captive to inertia, doomed to bounce endlessly back and forth between the bulkheads until an outside force intervened to stop its lonely, acrobatic sojourn. An all pervading hush dominated, enveloping the interior in a resonance that was absolute. As it had for hundreds of years now, time dragged on inexorably. . .

A sophisticated-looking device situated close to the main communications array suddenly illuminated, and a series of complex glyphs fluttered silently across the gap in the air above it. Soon the space was filled with blazing icons curling around one another in a never-ending Möbius loop, until its phantom cursor came to rest in the bottom right-hand corner, blinking rapidly, awaiting further instructions.

Adjoining speakers squawked to life. A burst of static followed, signaling the receipt of a compressed data package. Then everything went blank, the process halted as abruptly as it had begun.

Silence reigned once more.

Bip—bip—bip—bip—bip—bip.

A larger console activated, and a cluster of master codes appeared within the display. As each cipher scrolled down the screen, it triggered redundant systems that had lain dormant for an age.

Lights winked on. A background hum lifted above the electronic chatter. A subtle vibration ran the length of the craft. Floating objects crashed to the floor and lay still. Empty halls and corridors thrummed with growing potential. Interior illumination dulled to a soft background radiance.

Psssssssssst!

A hissing sound issued from the vents as pressure seals primed and engaged. Oxygen circulated once more.

A lotus-petal graphic flowered within the main holo-emitter, folding outward to be replaced by an overlapping series of ship's schematics that quickly expanded off screen. One by one, oscillating star charts cascaded. Soon, the control center was awash in glittering green, scarlet, and royal blue phosphorescence.

"Arden home world located," a female voice intoned, "security codes authenticated."

"Caution! Time sensitive parameters breached."

It sounded as if the entity was arguing with herself.

"Scanning for updates . . ."

"No fresh data available. Security protocol Coralin alpha-one, initiated. Homing beacon, activated. Full systems check. Accessing . . ."

"Internal sensors, online. Life signs, absent. Monitoring . . ."

"Emergency pods, present and intact. Anomalous energy signature detected. Isolation protocol instituted. Self destruct sequence prepped . . . Stand by."

"Listing primary networks showing as fully functional. Life support, gravity core, weapons grid, deflectors, shields . . ."

"Propulsion diagnostics now complete. Maneuvering thrusters, sub-light engines, and rip-space drive standing by . . ."

"Security protocol Coralin alpha-one confirmed. Cold systems start in . . . Three, two, one. Primary burn commencing . . ."

At the rear of the behemoth nearly two miles away, a series of ruddy glows ignited deep within the bowels of the injector outlets. Power levels intensified. As they did so, the shimmering maelstrom divided to fill four giant nacelles.

With infinite grace, the huge cruiser moved out from the planet's shadow cone. As she broached the solar penumbra, the sparkling iridescence of her matte black exterior flared as an ancient coating of rime blasted away into space, adding a shower of miniature diamonds to the gauze of eternal midnight.

Her speed increased, and she received a final signal.

Within minutes the vessel was gone, leaving behind only gravitational eddies resonating out into the void forever.

*

Ten hours and fifty light years in the opposite direction later, the onward transmission reached its mark. A dormant entity sparked to life, and once again a prolonged and complex group of ship's systems came online.

Although similar in appearance, this craft was even larger than her sister, and had clearly been designed for one thing. Death.

Vector control skirts as wide as a sports stadium flared in response to the cataclysmic energies now thundering toward its main booster nozzles.

The colossus punched forward. As it did so, panels on its exterior surface shimmered, and the destroyer faded from sight.

Now invisible, it adjusted trajectory and set a course for home, four hundred and twenty trillion miles distant.

Chapter One

An Honest Day's Work

*(3 months later. Post re-genesis—
11 months & 2 days)*

The day was unmercifully hot. Stripped to the waist, men bent their backs and went about their labors with an eagerness that filled the meadow with the irregular, muffled beat of metal on soil. Every now and then someone caught their shin or toe instead of their intended target, and a barrage of cursing filled the air with colorful metaphors.

None of these distractions intruded on the world of Marcus Brutus, former Prime Centurion of the Ninth Legion of Rome—and more recently sub-commander of the Ardenese city of Rhomane.

As was his custom when engaged in monotonous physical tasks, Marcus became an automaton. Lost in a cadence of his own making, he allowed the rhythm of his exertions to detach his mind and transport him back to a time only three years previously, when he had basked in the limelight of achievement and success.

The eradication of Gallic insurgents who had disrupted major supply routes for months. A commendation from Emperor Hadrian himself. His promotion to Triari thereafter.

A sad smile creased his lips.

If only I could have realized my dreams there and then. The district of Lugdunum was prime real estate, especially the villages clustered along the Saône River. I could have built a house there, close to the forest and away from the rest of civilization. Found myself a woman. Settled down. Spent my twilight years getting old and fat . . . and overrun with children.

His smile broadened into a grin.

"Happy about something?" an unexpected voice enquired.

"I . . . I'm sorry?" Marcus stammered, caught by surprise. "What did you say?"

Marcus allowed his eyes to re-focus and discovered Searc Calhoun standing above his trench, a bottle of chilled water clutched in one hand.

Searc was leader of the Vacomagi clan, part of the Caledonian army that had ambushed the Ninth Legion back on Earth and inflicted heavy casualties before fate intervened and snatched them all away to Arden. Former enemies, the two men were now close friends who enjoyed each other's company.

"I asked if you were all right," Searc repeated, "you looked to be a million miles away there."

"A million miles away?" Marcus snorted. "I'm afraid I was a lot, lot farther out than that."

He snatched the bottle from his companion's grasp and took a long deep pull.

Realizing what Marcus was alluding to, Searc couldn't resist the opening.

"Och . . . dreaming of the ass-kicking we gave you back in Callie, eh? Lucky buggers. I'd have loved to stick your head on a pike and drink a blood-toast to your dearly departed ghost." He paused to spit on the ground. "Bloody aliens and their interfering sprites, they spoiled a good ruckus."

"That they did, my friend. That they did." Marcus handed the bottle back. Shielding his eyes against the glare of the sun, he countered, "Anyway, what makes you so sure your uneducated rabble would have won? I think the Architect may have done you a favor."

Around them, clansmen and legionnaires alike began hooting and hollering as the good-natured jesting became more personal. Joining in, several interrupted their chores to brandish hoes and picks at one another in mock anger.

"We could always reenact our little shindig, here and now," Searc offered, "just you and me. I've got a score to settle, remember, after the tragedy of our last bout."

The mood spread and soon a small crowd gathered in a loose circle to watch what had become a regular feature between the two warriors.

"Yes, that *was* a rather good tussle, wasn't it?" A hint of steel entered Marcus's gaze. As he climbed from the pit, he stretched his sore limbs. "Especially as I evened the score with a most skillful maneuver that put *you* flat on your face."

"Skillful? Bloody lucky it was —"

A shadow flickered across the ground and everyone looked up.

Resplendent in midnight-green plumage, a chiraff spiraled lazily down from the sky to land in a nearby tree. A male, it was clearly on the hunt for a mate, for it cocked its head to the gathered throng below, strutted to the end of the branch, and puffed out its chest for inspection.

A flash of topaz-blue and royal purple stood revealed.

"Who's a pretty boy then?" someone shouted.

"I wonder if it tastes good?"

The bird ignored them, continuing to flex and pose like an Adonis so his colors were displayed to their best effect.

"Nervy little sod, that's for sure!"

A few whistled and stamped their feet. Others whooped and cheered the interloper on. In reply, the chiraff threw back his head, and fluted birdsong filled the glade with musical bliss.

His query was answered by a warbling echo, and everyone stopped to watch as a female appeared from the dense foliage of a nearby tree. Swooping low, she glided across the intervening gap and alighted near her would-be suitor.

They called back and forth for a few moments, whereupon the male skipped closer, spread his wings wide, and commenced bobbing up and down. The female, obviously impressed, issued a little chirrup of pleasure before both disappeared in a flurry of feathers and leaves.

"He's got all the right moves too!" Searc cackled. He slapped Marcus on the shoulder. "Talking of which, how are things coming along between you and your new lady pilot friend?"

The highlander flashed his eyebrows outrageously, much to the amusement of those nearby, who tried to suppress their giggles.

"Who, Angela? Very good. She'll be back any day now, and has asked if I'd consider opening up some free time so I can learn more about flying one of the smaller cargo shuttles. She thinks such a skill will enhance my standing on the council."

"Enhance your standing? Not good enough as you are? Well, well, well." Searc pulled a face and addressed his audience. "We all know who wears the trousers in *that* relationship, don't we, lads?"

A smattering of lewd comments rang out from tribesmen and soldiers alike. Marcus bristled and his eyes narrowed.

Searc edged closer, alert for any sudden moves: "But then again, I don't profess to be an expert on the wiles of women. Fey creatures." He shivered. "I mean . . . there must be something seriously wrong when they have a fine, augmented Highland specimen like me to choose from, and yet they go and pick someone like you. My God, man, even with the enhancements, you're a long streak of Roman shite."

This time the bystanders' laughter was loud and raucous. Their competitive mood rekindled, the gathered men closed in, and the catcalling began all over again.

The two leaders squared off and circled one another, searching for an opening.

"I'm looking forward to this." Marcus cracked his knuckles. "I'm going to teach you *why* a lady prefers intelligent conversation, sophistication, and good looks over some drooling, interbred, tartan-clad halfwit."

"I'm eager to learn, laddie," Searc quipped. "And don't worry, I shan't rearrange your new face *too* much. After all, your girlfriend does drive some rather large thingamajigs. I wouldn't want her to go parking one on my head in revenge now, would I?"

Once again backs bent to the earth in effort and sweat, but this time it had nothing whatsoever to do with an honest day's work.

*

Chief Medical Officer Patricia 'Pat' Frost adjusted the magnification of the holographic manipulator with a dexterity matched by few. When the latest batch of eggs came into focus, she began the delicate ministrations that would see them safely embedded within the lining of the artificial womb, ready to engender the latest in a new generation of children. Provided by the woman after whom this wing was named—Ayria Solram—Pat took her time to ensure everything was just right.

Excellent, the uterine wall has adopted the revised pH values without a hitch, so we won't have to jiggle the intervillous placenta or villi around this time. And the amniotic sac has molded nicely to the chorionic plate. No danger of displacement whatsoever.

Although she had a fine team of nurses and sentinels supporting her, Pat knew the first few weeks following an in vitro induction always presented the greatest risk. She was also keenly aware that the future was riding on her shoulders. Because of this, she still insisted that *she* be the one to complete the final insertion . . . Just in case.

I can't help it. It doesn't feel right, leaving something so important to someone else, or to machines . . . No matter how sophisticated they are.

Exhausted, Pat pushed away from the amplification console and pinched the bridge of her nose. Despite her fatigue, she felt a huge sense of pride and personal satisfaction. To refresh herself, she grabbed her mug from a nearby table and downed the last of her now cold coffee. Then she raised the cup high in salute.

There you go, Ayria. Another clutch of babies to carry on your name and ensure your light never fades.

The Ark, buried deep in the earth beneath Rhomane, contained the genetic heritage of the entire Ardenese race. From this colossal storehouse, the colonists could take whatever they needed to rebuild a devastated world. However, while the Horde Masters had provided the life force to initialize the re-genesis protocol, a viable fleshly host was necessary to activate it, for the newly formed codex required living tissue with which to bond.

In a heroic move, Ayria Solram had sacrificed herself to ensure the sequence would be completed. Her gesture hadn't been in vain, for the transmutation of her tincture had resulted in the generation of a new triple-stranded DNA helix. And over the months since it was released into the atmosphere, something incredible had happened.

Pat held up her hand and looked at the miracle that was her body.

Her fingers were slightly longer than before, and the flesh had adopted a darker tone, as if she'd spent her life in the sun. And yet her skin hadn't wrinkled at all. In fact, she looked as young and fresh as she had in her twenties. A glance toward the metallic surface of a nearby monitor revealed the recent development of an aquamarine cast to her eyes. She was also a few inches taller, something that both amazed and frightened her when she pondered just how far the process might go.

How many times will I have to change my wardrobe?

The adaptation went beyond the superficial, for Pat also *felt* different, a simple truth that the Architect and its myriad scanners must have also witnessed, as evidenced by recent revelations.

Sophisticated Ardenese technology had the benefit of a seven-millennium head start on the most advanced knowledge held by refugees brought from Earth. Much of it had been designed so as to blend with its surrounding environment when inactive. In itself, not a problem, for it revealed an aesthetic representative of their hosts' cultured way of life.

Originating from the year 3229, Pat had been part of the third intake and no slouch when it came to knowing her way around electronic components, or recognizing the signs of redundant technology.

Nevertheless, everybody was taken by surprise when, ten months ago, whole new areas of Rhomane had inexplicably opened up. Residents of the city had gone to sleep as usual, only to wake up the following day to discover hidden doorways now open, revealing concealed facilities or even whole new sublevels.

The hospital wing Pat now occupied had been part of the process which proved the evolving emergence of Ardenese DNA within the human genome.

We're hybrids now, Pat realized. *The Architect recognized that fact and granted us access to wonders that not only helped us cope with the transformation, but paved the way for the resurrection of full-blood citizens . . . or whatever it is they've now become.*

She thought of Ayria again as she strolled to the far end of the facility where the eldest fetuses were housed.

At nine months old, the single girl and two boys were plump and pink. Smiling, they wriggled energetically within their fabricated, amniotic world as if sharing a private sibling joke. And although engendered outside a normal biological context, they appeared none the worse for the experience.

As Pat surveyed the various aspects of the labyrinthine ward, her soul swelled in heartfelt appreciation.

We've got so much to be thankful for. This provision has promoted something that eluded our sharpest minds back on Earth; the full cultivation of tissue outside the living organism. And the artificial womb is a marvel of prophylactic ingenuity. Without it, I doubt we'd have been able to counter the hurdles resulting from the addition of Ardenese genoplasm. It's taken longer to bring the embryos to term than we originally anticipated, but by this time next month we'll have our latest additions to goo and gaa over.

She studied their hard-charts with interest.

Yes, the addition of the Ardenese strand prolongs gestation by about a month. Maybe a bit longer . . .

Then she caught sight of the clock.

Oh hell! I'm late.

Hurrying to her office, Pat activated the main computer and called up the latest information on some very special in-patients. Locating what she sought, she transferred their statistics onto her info-tablet and made her way to the department's transporter pad.

"Resurrection hall."

The response was immediate.

The air warped and Pat found herself within a vast darkened chamber. She smiled, for the view always reminded her of a night flight she had enjoyed a long, long time ago, when she had landed at Hillary Clinton Starport.

She had been welcomed home by a series of flashing blue beacons. Strung out along the tarmac like the tentacles of some cosmic jellyfish, they had guided a ship full of weary travelers toward the warming embrace of the main terminal, lost in the distance amid a sea of phosphorous red and yellow radiance.

Today a similar sequence of winking azure diamonds flickered in the darkness. Only here, the lights perched atop a protracted line of standing screens, arranged in uniform ranks along the very center of the room. Cushioned treatment platforms sat on either side of the consoles, where an army of extraordinary people lay sleeping, bathed in the rosy glow of muted instrument panels.

Each figure wore a simple metal coronet and matching wristband, made from what looked like platinum. Pat knew from personal experience that these halos were this very minute downloading vast amounts of data directly into a multitude of minds.

A very effective method of instruction. The Architect accomplishes in weeks what it would have taken the subjects hundreds of years of life experience to acquire . . . or in this case catch up on, while their tissue samples slept in deep storage.

Sizzling balls of light zipped through the air overhead, or hovered like wraiths above prone figures, creating a dizzying crisscross of after-images in the ether.

One materialized in front of Pat.

“Greetings, Doctor Frost. How may I assist you?”

“Hello, Architect, I’m only dropping by. I just need to touch base with Penny before I submit the latest projections for this week’s meeting. Do you happen to have the latest figures?”

“Estimates now indicate sufficient source material for a total of sixty-eight thousand, four hundred and ninety-three subjects.”

“So degradation *did* manage to soil the DNA samples?”

“I’m afraid so. The relentless struggle against the Horde resulted in a critical diversion of power from a number of crucial systems over a protracted period. Sadly, containment issues were inevitable.”

“Do we still have sufficient biodiversity to establish a viable population nucleus?”

The brilliance of the orb dimmed as it ran several computations.

“Latest algorithms indicate a ninety-eight point three percent probability of success. We are fortunate for the additional phylogenetic potential provided by the human advent, otherwise . . .”

The sentinel let its implication hang.

“What about the chromosomal redundancies?”

“Completely drained. As you are aware, things had reached a perilous juncture by the time the Architect brought the Ninth through. If not for their achievements, we wouldn't even have this many."

"Hmm. We'd better make the best use of the legacy we do have then." Pat gazed across the room toward her assistant, recalling the reason for her visit. "Look, I'll make sure this aspect is given special priority, and see if there isn't some way we can come up with a strategy to ameliorate the situation."

"Thank you," the sentinel buzzed, "I will do likewise."

It snuffed itself out of existence, and Pat made her way across to the nurses' station. Sitting at the desk, Doctor Penny Frasier, a xenobiologist from the year 3060 and a specialist on the Horde for the past fourteen years, worked with a female patient. Equipped with a diadem similar to those worn by the rest of the catatonic throng, she was manipulating a number of ghostly symbols hovering between her hands. Penny's circlet possessed additional blinkers to cover the eyes. Even so, she was aware of her colleague's presence, for she held up a finger as Pat approached. Without looking up, she murmured, "I take it the Architect gave you the latest news?"

"Yes, he did," Pat replied, concern in her voice, "I just hope we haven't gone through all this for nothing—"

"Hang on. I'll talk to you about that in a moment . . ." Penny's movements became more urgent. "Almost finished . . . got it!"

Penny pressed a holographic button in midair, and her headband flashed. A corresponding gleam pulsed from the bracelet worn by the woman on the bed immediately next to the console—a woman nearly seven feet tall.

Pat glanced at the female patient and noticed her wristband had blushed green.

"That's another one out of the way," Penny sighed. She removed her equipment and stood up. "Induced reanimation is almost complete for the second wave. When the council gives the go-ahead, everybody here can be revived."

"How are Sariff and Calen doing?"

"Absolutely fine." Penny gestured and led Pat over to a couple of adjoining cots on the opposite side of the hall. Upon them, two familiar figures reclined, oblivious to the world. "As with everybody else, they've been made aware of the adaptations applied to their bodies to compensate for the addition of human DNA. They're a remarkably resilient people and took the news in their stride. That's why I'm proposing both they and the surviving members of the Senatum be among the first to be awakened. Their example will provide the returning populace with a sense of familiarity and hope."

"Good idea. Actually, that's part of the reason I'm here. The memorial is fast approaching, and Saul has asked all department heads to include the latest updates in this week's conference. He wants the opportunity to pick through our current state of affairs to ensure he has some blindingly good news to lift everyone's spirits." Pat shook her head. "Unfortunately, with what I've just heard, that's going to prove difficult. I dread to think how he'll take the news of the loss. We were counting on—"

"*Well*," Penny interjected, a telltale smile creasing her face, "that's what I wanted to mention. I found out about the attrition rate earlier this morning, so I did a little research."

"And?"

"And I think I might have discovered a solution. Come and look."

Penny ushered her friend across to a command station, sat her down in the only chair, and said, "Population viability analysis, Frasier alpha one."

The screen bloomed to life, and a series of graphs and tables flowed into being.

Pointing to them, Penny explained: “As you’ll appreciate, we need to ensure a sufficient degree of variation to avoid reduced biological fitness caused by inbreeding depression. We were cutting it fine as it was, but now . . .” She shrugged. “So, I wondered how we might improve genetic variation.”

“Improve it?”

“Yes. I came up with this.” Penny paused to enlarge a series of flowcharts and diagrams. “I started with the impaired bio matter for those subjects lost in stasis. Do you see? While there’s insufficient mass to regenerate an entire being, we might be able to utilize what’s left to boost existing reproductive strength. And if we use the artificial womb to insert a small variation in each chromosomal packet, not only can we target and purge any phenotype carrying deleterious recessive alleles, but we can supplement the natural genealogical coefficient.”

Pat was thrilled. “And can you do this with all the samples?”

“I’m afraid not. So far the estimates are running at seventy to seventy-three percent. But it’s far better than what we originally faced. Of course, once we factor in the living population, and the augmentation each race has been blessed with since the combining of our genomes . . .” She grinned. “Well, we’re game on.”

And if they accept my proposals for the artificial engendering of dizygotic twins, we’ll be able to increase the chromosomal profile even more.

Jumping from her chair, Pat hugged her companion fiercely.

“It’s a miracle. Oh, well done, Penny, I won’t feel like such a pariah now.”

“What can I say?” Penny beamed with evident pleasure and placed an info-crystal containing her recommendations into Pat's hand. "Miracles are my specialty and all in a day's work."

Pat accepted the proffered gem gratefully and promptly headed for the transport pad. "Sorry Penny, I'm already late as it is. I'll let you know what they say . . . though I'm sure there won't be any problems. We've come too far to let things slip through our fingers now."

Minutes later, Pat found herself in the main arterial corridor of the medical wing. So excited was she that she had to force herself not to run.

At last! A definite step in the right direction. I've been living in a shadow for so long people tend to forget who I am. Perhaps they'll start to take me seriously now?

On the way out, her attention was drawn to the large golden epitaph adorning the main entrance. She stopped to admire it.

In memory of Ayria Solram.
Who gave her life so that Arden might live.

Pat allowed her fingers to trace over the words inscribed on the plaque. She suddenly felt deeply ashamed of her self-centered mood.

And here's me thinking I'm sooo clever. When you cut to the chase, we only have this chance of a new beginning because of Ayria's foresight and sacrifice.

Suitably chastened, Pat completed the rest of her journey deep in thought.

Chapter Two

Leopards and Spots

As the patrol approached the clearing, Jake Rixton, First Lieutenant of the Fifth Company, Second Mounted Rifles Cavalry Unit, raised his hand and held it steady. Those nearest him immediately halted, waiting patiently for the command to filter back along the column. Eventually, the entire platoon stood ready, concealed and waiting just within the tree line.

Even though they were equipped with covert radios, his men preferred to stick with what they knew, and relied on hand signals unless a dire emergency arose.

In the months following the release of the re-genesis matrix, the Fifth had been deployed doing what they did best: long-range reconnaissance. Ever cautious, Saul Cameron had wanted eyes on the ground to confirm what satellite imaging had already indicated. That the Horde threat was finally over.

At first, their missions were confined to the vicinity around Rhomane and the plains of the Sengennon Strait. But as it became increasingly obvious the long war of attrition had finally ended, the extent of their ranging had increased and now included assignments like this month long-security sweep out into the wilds.

Their current brief involved the physical check of inoperative way stations, dotted throughout the area between the Shilette Abyss mining colony and the Esteban basin, deep in the heart of the Tar'e-esh Forest. Because such facilities had been hermetically sealed during the siege, there was a remote possibility they might contain the odd ogre that had been shielded from the restorative effects of the new bio-energetic template. Such brutes would not only be ravenously hungry, but prone to levels of savagery that would make them even more unpredictable than the colonists were accustomed to.

To cover more ground, Captain Houston had divided the company in two. While Jake scoured the terrain south of the Esteban Sea, their commander took Jake's counterpart, Second Lieutenant Wilson Smith, and ventured north.

They had parted company fourteen days ago, and so far their task had been monotonous and incident free.

Let's hope it stays that way.

Jake leant forward in his saddle and listened. Birdsong filled the air with the contrasting twits, hoots and trills of innumerable contenders as each tried to stake a claim over its own little kingdom. Their challenge was answered by unknown critters that squeaked and squawked as they scampered about the undergrowth.

Jake felt reassured by their presence. He edged forward a few feet and scanned the glade.

Lazy sunlight slanted down through the foliage to the south, creating hazy contrasts of brightness and shadow. Squadrons of gaily painted butterflies cavorted through the air, engaged in imaginary dogfights that captured and then held his attention. Lush grass gently swayed in a breeze.

And there, in the center of the meadow, like an angry pimple marring the contours of an otherwise unblemished face, stood a pyramid. At thirteen feet in height, it reminded Jake of the monolith within the Hall of Remembrance, for the structure was seamless and made of the same richly veined rock as the Reverence itself.

He glanced toward the top of the construct. The telltale nimbus was missing.

Its power source has depleted. Or been drained.

A flash of beige and blue on the opposite side of the clearing caught his eye.

Jake stiffened, only to relax as the form of Wilson Smith on horseback materialized out of the gloom.

The two officers nodded at each other, and Jake gave the signal to assemble. Over his shoulder, he murmured, "Sergeant Williams, take one section and circle left. Move up from the south. Corporal Spencer, two section and yourself are with me. We'll go right, and ride in from the opposite direction."

They moved out from the trees and skirted the edge of the glade. Following standard procedure, Smith's men adopted a similar maneuver. A few minutes later, both platoons came together, whereupon they filed toward their destination in double columns. As they approached, Jake noticed second platoon appeared to be missing a number of men, Houston included.

"Lieutenant," he said, by way of greeting, "did you run into trouble?"

Smith tipped his hat in salute.

"No, sir, everything's been as blissfully tedious as usual. We haven't encountered a single soul. Apart from a couple of facility checks, we've had nothing to do."

"So where's Captain Houston?"

"Is he not with you?" Smith appeared genuinely surprised, and scoured the faces of the men opposite him. "But he said he would cut down to join you after he'd checked out the abandoned structure."

"Abandoned structure?"

"Yes, we ran into it the day after the patrol split. It didn't look like a way station, or any other building we've seen so far. This was—how can I explain it?—like a squat block of concrete. I got the sense it was fortified in some manner, as if it was an old military outpost. Something about it intrigued the captain, so he picked a few men and decided to stay behind to see if he could break in and check it out."

"Where was this?"

"On the slopes of Quirian Hill."

"Quirian Hill? Why were you so far out?"

"Do I really need to explain my uncle? We all hoped he'd be a reformed character once Permian Hasanem vacated his mind. You know, learned from the experience and mistakes of a wiser soul." Smith shrugged. "Turns out, he can still be . . . quirky."

Jake reflected on what he knew of Houston's former ghostly "tenant."

Permian Hasanem had been captain of the Shivan-Estre, an advanced Ardenese starship whose engines had malfunctioned centuries before the first refugees arrived from Earth. Still in flux after exiting rip-space just outside Rhomane's environs, the craft had impacted the lydium barrier surrounding the city and somehow blended with the nature of its construct. Unbeknown to anyone, this freak occurrence had created what was believed to be the first-ever mutation of normal DNA into the creatures that eventually became known as the Horde. However, due to the dense molecular composition of the walls, the transformation had arrested, leaving Hasanem suspended in limbo, bereft of a corporeal form and driven to the edge of insanity. Until James Houston had unwittingly provided a conduit back into the land of the living.

Having taken control of Houston, Hasanem became an essential player in the truce established between the human and Horde communities. And true to his word, once peace was achieved, Hasanem sacrificed his existence and simply faded into oblivion.

More's the pity. We all begged him to stay and take the place of that useless sack of skin. Jake shook his head. *The world's a cruel and unjust place.*

He was struck by a sudden notion: "Hang on a second, so who stayed with the captain?"

Smith thought for a moment. "Joe Stevens, Harvey Walton, Chris Spence, Johnny Ward, and a few more. Why?"

"Oh, call it a hunch . . ."

Of course he'd ensure to choose a handful of the pack that remained loyal while he was incapacitated. Guard dogs, eager to do their master's bidding. His "something's not quite right" bump began to itch. *But what's he up to? And why didn't he report in on the radio?*

Aloud, Jake added, "And you didn't think that strange?"

"Well . . . no. He's always been unpredictable. And since his mind was screwed with, we've all seen how prone he's become to odd behavior . . ."

Everything went still, as if a chill blanket had suddenly descended over the entire area: the background chatter of birds and other creatures fell away; the wind died. The only sounds to break the silence were the uneasy whickers and snorts of spooked mounts.

Jake pivoted on the spot, hand going to his gun.

"Relax!" a familiar voice called from the clearing's edge. "It's me. Jesus H Christ, what's the matter with everyone? I leave you girls alone for a few days and everyone gets wound tighter than a preacher's britches."

Captain Houston and his small group of men emerged from the undergrowth. To Jake's eyes, they appeared grim and not in the least bit relieved to be back among friends. Something about them put him on edge, and he noticed how their horses shied under their guidance, as if being forced to brave unseen hazards.

As the last trooper rode out, Jake saw a riderless colt on a lead rein behind him, with something large strapped across its back.

"What happened?" Jake snapped, sounding angrier than he intended.

"Not that I have to explain myself to you, Lieutenant," Houston drawled, "but we ran into a spot of bother. Atticus fell and broke his neck."

Not one of his cronies . . . Interesting.

"Was this up at the bunker you found at Quirian Hill?"

Houston turned to regard his nephew, and a shadow crossed his countenance that carried a sense of contempt and barely suppressed rage. Then it was gone.

"Yes, that's right." Houston continued as if nothing untoward had transpired. "It turns out the upper stairwell was being used as a nursery by a nest of firefangs. Nasty bastards at any time of day or night, and more so when you disturb them around their young. Bolted from their hole like a rain of arrows and caught Atticus by surprise. His mount reared, and he fell, landed badly."

At the mention of firefangs everybody tensed. A few men muttered out loud.

Looking much like a cross between a rattlesnake and a cottonmouth, a firefang was an aggressively fast pit viper known to stand its ground when threatened. Confined to the region of the Tar'e-esh, its bite always proved fatal, and its victims usually died screaming in agony unless an antidote could be administered within minutes.

In spite of the bad news, Jake wouldn't allow himself to become distracted.

But Smith said the place was sealed when they found it? How would snakes have managed to get in? He glanced toward the younger officer and could see Smith studying his uncle closely, as if he didn't know what to make of the man before him.

There's something odd going on here.

"So Atticus must have been your radio man then?" Jake asked.

It was Houston's turn to look baffled. "I'm sorry?"

"I said, I take it Atticus was your radio man? It would explain why you've been out of contact for so long without employing an emergency beacon?"

That same veil of darkness clouded Houston's face again. Seeing the captain's reaction, Stevens, Walton, Spence, and Ward closed around their commander. Despite being in the company of men they had served with for a number of years, each exuded an air of menace.

What the hell? I'd better diffuse this situation before things get out of hand.

"Mind you, I can see your point," Jake announced loudly. "The walkie-talkie got smashed, and there was nothing you could have done for the poor guy anyway, especially as we're so far out from Rhomane. It'll have to wait until we get back."

Houston blinked, and the tension faded away.

"Thank you . . . Lieutenant. You're quite right. He died instantly, so we went ahead and completed a thorough search of the outpost. Afterward, I decided it best to make our way here, to the midpoint rendezvous. I tell you what, while your platoons check out the way station, I'll use one of your uplinks to contact headquarters and give them a full intel package of our situation here, and see what they'd like us to do with Atticus."

Looks like I'll have to wait until we get back, too. No problem.

"Great idea . . . but may I make a suggestion, sir?"

"Go on."

"Why don't Lieutenant Smith and I complete the breach for a change? Show the men how the drill's should be done?"

Houston considered the request.

"That would be ideal. Please proceed."

Jake leapt from his saddle and signaled to the younger man.

I'll have to make this quick, but at least it'll give me an opportunity to sound him out. Hopefully, I'm just being paranoid.

As they circled the edifice to locate the doorway, Jake whispered, "First chance we get, we need to talk."

"That's funny," Smith grinned. "I was just about to suggest the same thing."

*

Specialist Joe Stark led the assault group toward their target. Situated in the foothills on the outskirts of Floranz, archives suggested this abandoned facility was once a storage depot for aqua-generator energy cells. Heavily damaged during the initial Horde purge, recent scans had confirmed that one level in particular had escaped destruction, and was, therefore, a possible security risk.

Armed with Heckler-Koch G40As, Joe and his commandos had been dispatched to check and, if need be, sanitize the area before sealing it.

Behind him, Sergeant Andy Webb, and Corporals Richard 'Fonzy' Cunningham and Stu Duggan stood prepared. They signaled their readiness to breach.

Although the layout was still fresh in his memory from the repeated run-throughs they had completed back in Floranz, Joe brought up the internal schematics of the building and meshed them to the optical overview of their HUDs.

Most of the structure lay below ground, with only one access point. Good news for them, for this ensured a narrow route of approach. While chokepoints were usually avoided, this time the arrangement would work in their favor because nothing could get out without passing them first.

As they closed on the outer hatch Joe issued final instructions, and the familiar tingle of impending action infused his senses with a heightened state of awareness.

"Switch to internals. Active camouflage engaged. Set eye patches to rotating frequencies, with sonic primary. Weapons hot. Good hunting, gentlemen."

Andy and Stu sprinted ahead to take up positions on either side of the entrance. Fonzy followed and, swiftly but methodically, examined the integrity of the door.

"Seal looks intact," Fonzy announced. "Stand by . . ." He removed a black box from a pouch on his belt and placed it against the smooth metal frame. Four red lights blinked on. A faint electronic ticking could be heard as the LEDs pulsed back and forth along the readout bar. Gradually, each one turned green.

Phffft!

"Locks disengaged." Fonzy altered his grip and looked toward Joe. He nodded. "Opening on three . . ."

As Fonzy prepared to count, Joe unclipped a small orb from his harness and stood ready. Designed to incapacitate ogres, the orbs employed a triple-tiered defense. A microgravity pulse to disrupt esoteric thresholds; a hypersonic disruptor to confuse the senses; and an iron sulfide solvent mist to discourage frontal assault.

"Three, two, one . . . Now!"

Joe tossed the flash-bang inside and everyone stepped back, just in time to avoid the concussive blast issuing from the gap.

A flurry of activity followed as Andy, Stu, and Fonzy peeled inside, one after the other, weapons ready. Joe was hot on their heels, delivering a calm and measured commentary as he went for the folks back in the control center.

"Stairwell accessed. Area is clear and free of obstruction . . ."

Not for a long time had anyone had passed this way, and as Joe faded into the darkness, his infrared and ancillary sensors took over. Within a few steps, he discovered how stale the air was. He glanced at the info-screen strapped to the inside his forearm. Despite his concerns, however, the readout indicated the mixture of gases read well within safety limits.

For now. I'd better keep an eye on that in case toxicity levels rise.

"Thirteen steps until split landing. Thirteen more until primary gantry. Blueprints of this outpost are confirmed accurate so far. No sign of hostiles. We are now approaching the first tier in standard formation. Wait . . ."

Joe and Fonzy lingered to provide cover while Andy and Stu checked the only room on that floor. Bread-and-butter stuff for experienced operators.

Flash-bang, pause, weapons to the shoulder, rapid entry, back to back, opposite arcs, friend or foe . . .

"Clear!"

"Clear!"

Like a well-oiled machine, the team descended to the next floor, where they employed the same procedure again. And again. Over and over, down and down, one after the other, until after more than five minutes of high intensity repetition, the final level came into view.

"Control, this is alpha-one," Joe announced. "We have gained the basement area. Substructure appears intact. There are signs it may still be powered by emergency backups. Wait . . ."

They stepped out into the vestibule of a pristine passageway. Lights blinked on overhead and cascaded along the corridor toward a heavily armored door twenty yards away.

Joe surveyed their intended path. A series of barely discernible flagstones covered the floor. Unusual, for the

Ardenese normally dressed the internal halls of their fortified structures with seam-free embellishments. He noted the parallel grooves running along the top and bottom of the walls on both sides.

A rail system perhaps? Movement and pressure activated?

Joe waited for his enhanced optics to confirm his suspicious. Sure enough, they detected a concealed energy source near the far end of the passage.

Gotcha!

He tapped Fonzy on the shoulder and pointed.

"Active defense grid ahead. Isolate its command frequency and shut it down."

Fonzy dropped to one knee and produced a device much like the radar guns used by twenty-first century police officers to catch speeding motorists. To it, he attached the same black box he had used earlier.

Once assembled, Fonzy aimed the contraption along the hall, activated its scope, and gave a quick thumbs-up.

Next to him, Andy selected a spare magazine from his ammo-pouch, leaned forward, and slid the casing along the decking. No sooner had he done so than the interior illumination dimmed, and a metallic girdle detached itself from the distant doorframe. Running flush to the wall, it slid toward the waiting soldiers.

A prickling sensation crawled across Joe's skin. A concentrated mesh of crisscrossed beams flashed into existence between the brackets to form a network of coherent light.

Nobody moved.

"Deploying countermeasure," Fonzy warned.

The blazing web swooped closer.

A background hum intruded, rising in pitch until it hurt the ears. A sizzling retort filled the air with dancing sparks, and the laser grid blinked out. The panels ground to a halt.

"Robot sentry deactivated." Fonzy declared. "We're safe to proceed."

Everyone moved forward together.

As they passed the inert sentinel, Joe eyed it dubiously.

"That thing's not going to switch back on, is it? I'd hate to think we don't have a clear line of retreat in an emergency."

"Hang on a moment." Fonzy stopped by the collars and took a few moments to squeeze a small block of putty against each of the ground-level rabbets. Having done so, he then inserted a cigarette-sized metal tube into both slabs. He pressed down hard on the protruding tips, and a soft blue glow indicated the moment each detonator armed. "Now we're okay. If the apparatus does move again, the CX-4 will make sure it doesn't get very far."

"Excellent," Joe replied. "Let's get this job finished. Stay sharp, we won't know what's in there if it turns out the warehouse is still full of aqua cells."

Scooting forward once more, they arrived at their objective.

The final gate proved seamless. Like the walls, it was made from lydium, and Joe knew they couldn't force their way through. Fortunately, only a simple keypad and retinal scan security pod still barred their way.

Fonzy examined the setup and took out his box of tricks again. Andy and Stu shuffled to one side and completed a series of equipment and ammunition checks.

"The Architect downloaded several old ciphers into my database," Fonzy murmured, "along with the ocular imprints of the previous command staff, so I should have this open in a jiffy."

Joe turned back to cover the corridor and seized the unexpected opportunity to give himself a once-over as well. He didn't have long. A prolonged *buzz* sounded, quickly followed by a loud *clunk*.

"Heads up!"

The huge door swung silently inward under its own weight. The blackness within seemed to leach out into the corridor.

Joe stepped across the threshold and scanned the interior.

The storeroom was a soldier's nightmare. At over a hundred yards wide and more than twice that long, multiple aisles branched away from a main access corridor. Every one of them was stacked floor to ceiling with rack upon rack of packing cases and assorted boxes; a veritable maze of blind spots, and hidden nooks and crannies. Even the advanced photosensitive capabilities of Joe's HUD failed to illuminate some of the darker corners.

"What do you think, Boss?" Andy enquired.

Joe considered his options.

Too many unknowns. Too many variables.

"Are there any residual energy readings?" he asked. "And if so, where?"

Fonzy stepped up and waved the radar gun backward and forward a few times. He studied the readout and jutted his chin toward the northeast quadrant.

"That way, a hundred and sixty, maybe a hundred and seventy feet. Levels are low, but indicative of depleted cells. If there are any mutants about, they'll be congregated in that vicinity."

"Why?" Andy chipped in. "Surely you're not thinking we go in there?"

"Nooo . . . but I *am* thinking of going fishing." Joe produced a thermos-type flask from his kidney pouch. He held it up. "I took the liberty of visiting the quartermaster before we set out. Remember, if any strays have been holed up in here, they've had to exist on low grade dross for nearly twelve months now. They'll be famished. *This* contains a gram of pure berydium, a highly energetic, short-lived isotope. Once I crack the seal it'll only last for ten to twelve seconds before it breaks down entirely, but that'll be sufficient to flush our soul-sucking fiends out into the open. Of course, once they're roused, we can expect a rather focused reaction . . ."

He let the thought sink in.

"Is everyone ready?"

Three affirmatives rang back.

"Right . . . Fonzy, you're with me. When I deploy the bait, we will cover the hatch and ensure nothing escapes. Andy, Stu, you'll be the main fire team. Take up position over there, behind those containers. Overlap your arcs. If the Horde are here, they'll come fast and they'll come hard. Take them out. If you experience any stoppages, don't hang about. Use a micro-singularity grenade and get your ass back here. We will cover your retreat. If one of you has to withdraw, the other will follow immediately. No one gets left behind. Is that clear?"

"Yes, sir," they chorused.

"Right, you know the drill. Set active-cam and motion diffusers to maximum."

Joe hunkered down by the doorway, watching through his HUD as the team got into place. They went still, blending into their surroundings as if they didn't exist.

When he deemed everything ready, Joe entered a three digit code into the pad on the lid of the canister. As a digital readout started counting down from ten, he tossed it along the gangway, and fixed it in his sights.

Tsssssst!

The lid cracked open.

They waited . . .

And waited . . .

Is that bloody thing working? They assured me —

Crash! Crash! Crash!

What the fuck?

Joe couldn't prevent an electric jolt from surging through him. He peered into the far reaches of the chamber, alarmed to see several distant storage shelves toppling. Closely ranked, each tier smashed into the next in line, falling toward him like oversized dominoes.

"I've got movement!" Fonzy snapped. His announcement made Joe jump again. "Sixty yards out and converging on us from all sides. Signal's clean."

"No shit?" Joe glanced toward his fire team's position. "Andy. Stu. You're safe where you are, but it's going to get a little loud. Don't be surprised if one or two things bounce over your hea–"

"I'm not just talking about the metalwork," Fonzy said. "They're fifty yards out."

"Contact!" Joe warned. "Coming straight at us. Hold your fire until they've swarmed the isotope. Fonzy? Give us an indication of numbers."

"At least two dozen."

Two dozen? Shit!

"Guys, change of plan. Too many to deal with all at once. Fall in on me and we'll hit them with —"

Booom!

A colossal fireball erupted from the center of the warehouse. Joe threw himself to one side in an effort to avoid the wash of searing light and heat thundering his way, but he was caught by an invisible fist and smashed back against the wall.

Air exploded from his lungs, and the room about him shook. He saw stars, as overwhelming pressure threatened to rupture fragile capillaries.

"Report!" he yelled above the din.

Although his ears were ringing, Joe heard a guttural roaring from somewhere in front of him. It got louder and louder with each passing second.

Head spinning, he dragged himself into a sitting position and looked up. Only then did he notice the bottom of his coveralls were on fire.

How in the . . . ?

He beat at his legs with his free hand. Pain lanced through his shoulder with every movement. Ignoring it, he continued searching about in hope.

"Andy? Stu?"

The area where they had been concealed was now a pile of twisted metal and burning debris. Of his colleagues, there was no sign.

Fuck! What the hell happened?

"Report!" Joe yelled again in growing desperation. "Assault group, sound off!"

A smoking heap of clothes and charred flesh lay on the floor beside him.

Fonzy?

The background shrieking got louder.

Confused, Joe wiped his face and raised his weapon. His hand came away covered in blood. An odd feeling of detachment trickled over him as he blinked repeatedly, trying to make his eyes focus. Waves of dizziness consumed him. Mesmerized, he peered into the growing inferno.

Was it alive? It acted as if it had a mind of its own. In some places flames warped and contorted in on themselves before disappearing into shadow, but in others they flared into incandescent effigies, possessed of terrifying horns, talons, and fangs.

Horde!

Joe fumbled for his grenades and came up empty. The cruel inevitability of his situation struck home.

They must have been stripped from me in the blast . . .

. . . ah well.

The nearest ogres spotted him and howled. An angry skein of midnight-blue and orange passion skittered through the pack's combined essence.

Somehow, Joe found the presence of mind not to panic, and set about methodically checking his surroundings. He was rewarded by the sight of Fonzy's G40A, discarded on the floor next to the still-open door.

Oh no you don't!

He came to an instant decision.

Grabbing the additional weapon, Joe leaped to his feet and staggered toward the hatch. For a moment, he considered simply running and shutting it behind him on the way out.

Leave no one behind . . . or nothing!

Instead, he put his back to it and heaved. With infuriating slowness, the door swung to and slammed shut. The reassuring sound of a vacuum seal engaging sighed above the ruckus.

Satisfied, Joe took a deep breath and turned to face his death. He flipped the switch on both guns to full automatic.

"What are you fuckers waiting for," he teased, "an invitation?"

With a final howl of rage, the wall of monsters collapsed on him, and a blistering hail of bullets met their charge.

The world went black. Joe's perspective shifted, as if he were floating on a sea of liquid dreams. An ethereal voice far off in the distance intoned, "Simulation terminated. Nervous system, disengaged. Consciousness restored. Cerebral and biorhythms returning to normal."

His vision swam. Joe turned his head to find Andy Webb hovering in the foreground. Behind him, the multi-paneled walls of the holographic training dome came into view. Further sensations intruded until Joe realized he was lying on a soft divan, a metal coronet clasped about his temples.

It was a VR replication?

"Well, would you look at that?" A smile creased Andy's rugged features. "It seems we have another hero fit to join the ranks of the elite."

Joe sat up. "You mean I've finally made it?"

Andy turned to look up at the people gathered in the observation window. Among them, the officer in charge of the newly formed Special Forces Directorate, Lieutenant Sam Pell, stared down, a calculating look in his eyes. The slightest nod of his head provided the answer.

"It looks that way," Andy replied. "You led well, kept your head, and continued to think laterally despite extreme pressure." He grasped Joe by the hand and helped him to his feet. "But best of all, it looks like you've overcome your natural tendency for self-preservation at last. That's why we insist the final exercises are conducted here. Your perceptions are altered so deeply, you think and act as if the incident were real. Hell, you've been in there enough to know by now. To you, they *were* real. You were a team leader on a Special Forces unit tasked to safeguard an installation. The sensors indicated that when the shit hit the fan, you instinctively acted to ensure the Horde wouldn't survive, even though it would cost you your own life." Andy slapped Joe on the back. "Just the kinda guy we need. Who said a leopard couldn't change its spots?"

Joe felt an overwhelming surge of pride, and was surprised by the lump that unexpectedly formed in his throat.

Bloody hell! Don't start getting all weak in front of your new sergeant now.

Fortunately, Andy didn't appear to have noticed.

"Walk with me, the boss wants a word before you go for your psyche evaluation. Looks like you might just have time to meet the rest of the team before we put you to work."

What work?

Chapter Three

A Dark and Hungry Dawn Arises

(Several days later)

As was his custom, Stained-With-Blood sat cross-legged on the floor of his room and rocked gently backward and forward. The remains of his tomahawk, Heaven's-Claw, rested lightly in his hands, a reassuring anchor to a world he no longer inhabited. Reciting an ancient mantra, he soared free of restraint and allowed the welcoming embrace of the vision quest to entice him toward revelation.

Although he was no dream-walker, Snow Blizzard, elected chief of all the tribes, relaxed before his old rival in a similar posture. Eyes closed, his chin slumped forward onto his chest. But there was no danger of him sleeping, for he too had joined his voice to the primal song now weaving its way through the texture of space and time.

Around them, elders representing the Blackfoot, Cree, Lakota, Sioux, and Apache nations sat in a circle. Fourteen strong, they looked on with respect, adding a melodious counter-harmony that swelled into the ether . . . and beyond. Despite the numbers, this setting remained intimate, for Snow Blizzard had recently completed his courtship rituals and sought Napioa's counsel before his wedding to princess Inuck-Shen.

Otherwise known as Small Robes, Inuck-Shen was eldest daughter of Blooded Chin, chief of the Blackfoot. Over a year before, she had been presented to Snow Blizzard in prejudice, as a gift to unite the Cree nations and end the unrest that threatened to tear their people apart.

However, following their passage to Arden the two had gotten to know each other better, and had fallen in love. True to their traditions, Snow Blizzard was now asking for direction from the Creator, to ensure the union would be blessed and fruitful.

An experienced shaman, Stained-With-Blood blended easily into the fabric of his heightened consciousness. He knew Napioa would reveal his purpose in his own due time, so while he waited patiently for the vision to gain its own momentum, he seized the opportunity to take in details of his newly materialized surroundings.

He found himself within a lee atop a wide, thickly-wooded plateau. The trees thinned as they neared the precipice edge, providing a place of comfort and tranquility.

Before him, the panoramic vista of a broad and majestic canyon stretched into the distance. Bathed in the unsullied radiance of a gibbous moon, each feature of its weather-beaten cliffs was up-lifted and inscribed in intricate detail.

The vault of the heavens folded out into an ocean of endless possibilities. Despite the presence of such a bright luminary, the diamond-studded haze of the cosmos blazed with clarity and hope.

Stained-With-Blood smiled and let the timbre of the occasion fill him.

In response, the ground shook, and a ring of standing stones sprouted up from the earth to one side. As he studied their formation, twigs and branches cracked in the forest behind him. A throaty snarl rumbled out of the shadows and a grizzly bear ambled forth from the thicket, a fat juicy salmon clenched in its jaws. The bear was tall; Stained-With-Blood judged it close to five feet at the shoulder, and weighed over eight-hundred pounds. The creature bore him no ill will, for as it passed it paused to lay the fish at his feet before continuing sedately on its way into the center of the henge. Once there, it reared up on its hind legs, extended massive paws toward the moon, and roared.

The hairs along the back of Stained-With-Blood's neck stood up, and he watched in wonder as the bear's call was answered by a piercing shriek.

A speck appeared against the otherwise pristine countenance of the lunar disc. Tiny at first, it grew rapidly as it approached with the undulating grace of one born to flight. Soon, it grew into the unmistakable profile of a great horned owl.

Swooping low, the owl circled the glade once before alighting silently upon the capstone of one of the megaliths.

A tufted head swiveled round on an impossibly flexible neck, and luminous yellow orbs solemnly regarded Stained-With-Blood. It batted its lids in a fetching way, and called to him.

"Ho—ho—hoo. Hoo hoo!"

The universe held a deeper meaning to the first peoples than anyone else, for they believed it home to much more than inanimate objects. Everything was a product of Napioa and, as such, alive with design and hidden purpose. All served a function in the greater scheme of things, and the enlightened amongst mankind must devote themselves to its understanding. Therefore when the bird spoke, Stained-With-Blood sat forward, concentrated, and noted specifics that would help him unravel the mystery of what he saw.

The owl signifies insight will be needed, for distrust still lingers in the hearts of some. Fortunately, the great healing power of the bear will ensure such guidance is forthcoming, for by its strength will this union bring lasting peace to our people.

He paused to count the blocks forming the monument.

Seven? Excellent, for that represents continued learning and growth, something in which Snow Blizzard must set an example if he is to unite all the factions.

Next, Stained-With-Blood noted that the obelisk on which the night hunter perched stood taller than all the others.

It's set to the north? Hmm . . . We are blessed, for it means wisdom will predominate. Perhaps Snow Blizzard will put aside his pride and —

His deliberations interrupted by an occurrence at the far side of the chasm, he peered across and watched as the sides of the nearest escarpment began to shiver. Boulders and rocks along its length shook free, skipping and bounding down the slope like runaway freight trains. Crashing into the abyss below, they threw up billowing clouds of debris which littered the ground in swathes of rose and orange dust. The distinctive tabletop of the mesa elongated, squeezing upward to form an impressive peak. Around it, clouds thickened, and the entire summit was transposed into the image of a magnificent bird of prey.

Appearing to be a cross between a phoenix and an eagle, it was wreathed in an electrum of fire. A cacophony of tympanic majesty pealed forth from its wings, and lightning bolts flashed from its eyes.

A thunderbird!

The apparition disappeared in an instant. Still, Stained-With-Blood sprang to his feet. In all his years this was the first time he had ever witnessed the manifestation of the legendary guardian of truth. Seeing such a totem now must mean that what was to follow would be of extreme significance. He wanted to move toward the edge of the clearing to get a better view, but before he could do so he heard something large pushing its way through the undergrowth.

A gigantic wolf emerged from the tree line. Grizzled and gray, obviously well past its youth, it yet bore itself with a grace and dignity belying its years. Atop its head sat a raven, which eyed Stained-With-Blood with suspicion.

A tingle skittered down his spine: both creatures were held in awe by the Cree. Long revered as the bearer of magic, the raven was thought to transport the energy of messages to those in need of new perspective. Its manifestation alongside the wolf—synonymous with the presence of a great teacher—reemphasized something of vital importance about to take place.

But how could such portents relate to the betrothal? Surely they can't . . . eh?

The shaggy great hound altered course to circle Stained-With-Blood repeatedly. After it had done so a half dozen times, the raven hopped down and did the same.

Stained-With-Blood glanced at the floor where they had trampled the earth to mud. Paw- and claw-prints now littered the soil with distinctive signatures. When he looked back up, both creatures were gone. An elderly warrior stood in their place.

Napioa!

Despite his age, the Creator was powerfully muscled, standing proud and tall, a king among lesser beings who would always pale in his company. Incorporating elements from his familiars, his flowing midnight-blue hair had long streaks of gray, a feature adding an air of wisdom to his already majestic aura.

"Come," he instructed, "there is much to see."

Napioa turned on his heel and made his way into the ring. Walking up to the bear, he bowed low as if according it a degree of respect, and invited it to sit with him. As they hunkered down, Napioa also gestured to the owl, which glided down from its vantage point and took up a position between them.

Stained-With-Blood maintained a respectful distance, listening as the Old Man spoke in the original tongue of the first peoples. Complete and reverent, it was a language of nature and of spirit, containing a depth and power that could be seen and touched as well as heard.

If he could have chosen one word to describe it, he would have said mesmerizing, for its inflection made him feel both lightheaded and peaceful.

He was stunned when both creatures answered their Creator, for each voice possessed a cadence that was almost musical. The conversation became animated, as if various strategies were being explored. Although he tried to pay attention and gain clues from their behavior as to what was going on, Stained-With-Blood found himself lulled toward sleep. Soon, he was dozing in a state of contented reverie.

A firm hand shook him awake.

Stained-With-Blood experienced a moment's panic over his faux pas, and then felt acutely embarrassed. He needn't have worried, for the Old Man appeared amused by his momentary lapse.

"Fear not, dream-walker," the Creator assured him, "such puissance is not for mere mortals. That you were able to follow as long as you did was remarkable. Just as well, for I fear such fortitude may be needed in the days ahead."

Before Stained-With-Blood could ask for clarification, Napioa turned and led him toward the lip of the bluff.

Pointing up into the night sky, he asked, "Tell me, shaman, what do you see?"

Stained-With-Blood looked out into the inky depths of space. The new constellations were familiar to him, having been carefully recorded over the past year on a brand new astral chart. Before he realized what he was doing, he listed them in his mind.

Kosan, friend of children and lost wayfarers. The Great Rhobexi. Alloran, charging across the firmament on a mission of mercy. Ateshnath, the mighty hunter. Bright Angule, Ix walker. Spenat, the farmer's companion. The Dancing Kooni. He Who Does Not Move at the pole. The Council of Twelve . . .

Hang on, something doesn't look right.

His gaze skipped back to the cluster that formed the Council. He counted the stars again to make sure he hadn't made a mistake. Then he scanned the heavens above him, in case unexpected mists had occluded the object of his scrutiny.

Nothing, it's clear as far as the eye can see.

"An elder is missing," he gasped aloud.

"Indeed. Such a tiny, seemingly insignificant matter, is it not? After all, there are trillions of flames burning brightly throughout my garden. Some might be forgiven for thinking the consequence of such a loss is trivial. And yet, observe the magnitude of our dilemma should we fail to take appropriate precautions . . ." Napioa waved his arms, and the moon wheeled through the air to set behind the mountains in the west. To the east, an ethereal roar signaled the approach of the sun. "Behold the day of our future's end."

Stained-With-Blood studied the horizon as indigo blooms leached upward into the glittering blue-black expanse. Quickly staining crimson, it showed him the earth's blood being encapsulated within the air itself. The process accelerated and spread, diffusing through lilac, orange, and then peach, kindling burnt umber promises upon coals of twilight passion. High in the atmosphere, clouds gathered, fluffy and pink, providing a surefire promise that a new dawn was almost upon them.

He leaned forward in anticipation. A flare announced the moment the tip of the solar disc breached the skyline. Everything blushed a deep rosy-gold, and the sweeping backdrop of the canyon lifted free.

All was not well, however, for the only part of the luminary to appear healthy was the corona. Its surface looked dull, as if Stained-With-Blood were viewing it through the filters he had seen employed by the pilots of Rhomane's flying craft when they were in space.

As he watched, he was horrified to see the star darken to black. Then it started devouring everything around it. Rocks, mountains, forests, and plains. Rivers, lakes, seas, and oceans. The whole world distorted, and his perspective rushed to keep pace.

Next, he found himself above the monstrosity, looking down into a well of never-ending hunger. Time ceased to have any meaning. The heavens wheeled, and the dark jaws continued to feed. The more the anomaly consumed, the more its malignant influence grew. Soon, its presence reached throughout the farthest reaches of the galaxy.

It is an abomination.

The air shimmered, Stained-With-Blood staggered, and everything was as it had been before, except for Napioa, whose mien now sparked with barely suppressed passion.

"Such a threat cannot be tolerated, for it is voracious and all consuming." He gripped the Cree warrior by his arms. "Do you understand what needs to be done?"

Before Stained-With-Blood could reply, the Old Man's eyes blazed brightly and the plateau faded away. He received the distinct impression that he was falling, as if descending through a medium that didn't really exist. But he wasn't worried. It was all part of the process of returning to the physical plane.

As had happened so often in the past, Napioa's words echoed in his mind.

Do you understand what needs to be done?

Stained-With-Blood was perplexed. As normal sensation returned, he reviewed the events he had just witnessed to ensure he hadn't missed anything of consequence. Then he compared the vision's import to the knowledge he had acquired since arriving on Arden.

Do I understand what needs to be done?

A frown creased his face.

Previous direction of this nature related to the Horde threat. But they no longer exist. So what in —

"Is something wrong?"

He blinked his eyes open to find a concerned-looking bridegroom staring at him. Stained-With-Blood reached out to reassure the younger man.

"Fear not, Snow Blizzard, your union with Small Robes appears to have Napioa's blessing, but the specifics of what that involves must wait . . ." He turned to face the gathered elders. "We have more serious matters to discuss."

Chapter Four

In Loving Memory

The cavern's vaulted interior resonated with silence. More than a hundred yards wide, it was a natural feature etched from living rock by the slow and patient attrition of running water over thousands upon thousands of years. As time passed the wellsprings ran dry, and the chamber gradually drained. Once barren, the cavity lay undiscovered for millennia until explorers from a faraway world happened upon it during their initial surveys prior to colonization.

Recognizing its value, those adventurers adapted the character of the gallery to suit their own purposes, transposing its simple grandeur into a wonderland of startling complexity and delight.

Yet even this transformation had been a long, long time ago, and for many years now the facility remained abandoned.

Although subdued, illumination was still afforded by a swarm of ethereal holographic constructs. Cunningly arranged along the cavern's outer circumference, each device glowed like a nebula, interpenetrating the multitude of surrounding workstations and hanging screens in a baffling display of technological wizardry and twinkling constellations of colored light. Of unknown purpose, these nevertheless had been rigged to serve the mechanism dominating the cavern's center.

Here, a circular dais more than twenty yards across rose from the floor. Above it, a pair of gleaming U-shaped collars hung suspended in midair. Each measured over fifty feet in length and were positioned so that their open arms bowed toward each other. Within the expanse of their embrace, a tear challenged the authority of spacetime itself. Appearing much like a DNA helix, it slowly revolved around its own axis, warping reality to its will. A gentle breeze flowed toward the rent from each of the cavern's exits, betraying the presence of a subtle vacuum.

Blip—blip—blip—blip—blip!

Harsh in the silence, a warning tone blurted from one of the control stations closest to the feature. Two adjacent projectors flickered to life. As their emitters focused on a condensed shimmering fog of ionized gas, a series of complex equations appeared. The beams intensified, and a stream of translucent symbols scrolled down the misty page.

"Anomaly detected," a voice announced. "Please stand by . . ."

Background generators kicked in. A steady whine signaled the buildup of impressive potential.

"Target recognized and locked. Quantum tunnel initialized. Temporal sheath established. Safety overrides engaged . . ."

An oscillating tone added deeper counterpoints to the coalescing energies. Underlying vibrations increased dramatically. Static sparks jumped out to scratch at the invisible plane lurking between the brackets. Lightning flashed, once, twice, then the void yawned wide and a tornado of warped sensibilities bloomed forth in a churning bore that somehow encompassed both pelagic and volcanic attributes.

"Gateway activated. Spectral sensors primed. Data retrieval will commence in three, two, one . . . Downloading."

A surrounding halo of ancillary equipment lent its weight to the process, and by its light hitherto unnoticed features of the chamber stood revealed.

Unlike the rest of the control center, a large area along the western periphery was free of equipment. Desks, cabinets, tools, and scanners occupying that zone had been smashed to pieces and thrown to one side to make room for the assortment of power cables trailing along the floor and into a wide pool of gelatinous goo.

The air above the mucus shivered gently, as if wallowing in the heat of a welcome zephyr. No sooner had the wormhole stabilized than the undulating curtain flared into a confusing amalgam of Orphic contradiction. Strontium-red passion vied against a well of midnight gloom. Magnesium-silver flares rushed to counter all-consuming darkness. And finally, neon-blue tendrils of scorching hot plasma contended the threat of everlasting obscurity. Such was the frenzy of the outburst that the atmosphere itself bristled, and nearby metallic objects clanged together as they became magnetized.

Had anyone been present to witness the event, close observation would have revealed why such a thing had occurred, for hidden at the very edge of the visible spectrum, a nest of nightmare apparitions languished in hibernation. The commotion had disturbed their repose and triggered an instinctive reaction. Roused to the verge of consciousness, their glittering fangs snapped imaginary necks. Steaming talons twitched toward phantom aggressors. Huge great jaws opened, and piercing howls joined together in a cacophony of spine-tingling complaint. Several pairs of eyes fluttered open and in that instant, an overwhelming sense of barely suppressed rage and rabid hunger flooded the cavern with the promise of certain death.

"Cycle completed," the same automated voice intoned.

The combined resonance of multiple stations shutting down droned through the gallery.

"Geodesic anchors retracted. Astrophasic tracking nodes disengaged. Gravity locks will be released in three, two, one . . . Mark."

The humming swarm abruptly cut off.

"Returning to passive-scan mode. Info-packet prepared. End run . . . Execute."

The hovering screens went blank, and the control room was thrown into darkness once more.

Deprived of the source of their agitation, the beasts' emotions cooled, and they were soon lulled back toward slumber. The energized cloud hovering above the ectoplasm continued to ripple awhile longer, but it too eventually subsided into inactivity.

All was as it had been before, except that now, a brooding, heightened state of watchfulness pervaded the ether.

*

Sam Pell led his team of commandos up the outer stairwell in single file: Not for them the cosseted luxury of transporter pads. At times like this, when a visit to one of the tallest spires in Rhomane was necessary, they utilized the occasion to maintain their outstanding level of fitness.

Round and round they went, higher and higher.

As they neared their three-thousand-foot pinnacle, their destination, Sam forged ahead so he could admire the view.

He lingered by the first open view port he found and allowed his gaze to rove outward, from the city walls far below, across the vast sweeping plains of the Sengennon Strait, and on to the ruddy escarpments of the Garnet Mountains.

The sun was setting, and its flickering departure made it appear as if the entire cordillera was being scourged with burning coals.

But it was just an illusion. Chill winds sweeping down from the distant massif proved a boon at this time of year, for as everyone had discovered, high summer on Arden was stiflingly hot.

No wonder she loves it up here. It's bloody breathtaking.

He inhaled deeply and suppressed a shiver.

And it does *make you feel as if the very gut-rock of the planet is reaching out to embrace you and make you feel welcome . . . exactly like she said.*

As his men closed the gap, Sam leaned out of the window and craned his neck. True to form, Jayden McDonald was out on her balcony, doing what she liked best at this time of day.

"Aha! She's in, then?" Andy Webb noted as he came panting round the corner.

"Yup. No excuses. Like it or not, today we're getting in."

Sam waited until Sean Masters, Fonzy Cunningham and Stu Duggan had caught up, and then led the way to the final landing.

They clustered around the entrance and Sam couldn't help but notice how his crew of battle-hardened veterans mumbled and fidgeted nervously as he buzzed the intercom.

Look at them. They've faced some of the deadliest foes in existence, yet they're shitting themselves at the prospect of her bawling us out. Je-sus, get a grip!

The sound of someone approaching filtered through from the other side of the door. It opened slowly, filling the corridor with the diffuse natural radiance of gold and burgundy light.

"Surprise!" they all chorused.

"Hi, Jayden," Sam said. "We thought it about time we came and paid our respects to Alan . . . If you don't mind, that is."

He noted the dark circles around her eyes.

She's still not sleeping properly.

Referring to her disheveled state, Sam added, "I see he's still keeping you on your toes?"

"Tell me about it," she muttered. "He had me up all last night with a bad stomach. Then, as soon as dawn broke, bam! Out like the proverbial light. Pat assures me it's a natural part of the process he's been through. But I wish things would hurry up and settle down into a normal routine. I need to be getting on with something useful, instead of playing nursemaid all the time." Jayden sighed. Stepping back, she ran her fingers through her hair, and made an obvious effort to remember her manners. "I'm sorry. Don't stand out there in the corridor. Come in, come in. He's not long woken up, so by all means, go and say hello."

Her visitors didn't need to be asked twice. Familiar with the apartment's layout they made their way through the lounge, across the dining area and down the hall. Stopping outside the door, they knocked once and entered.

Curtains were drawn, lending a subdued atmosphere to an already cool interior. A wide variety of pictures and stencils adorned the walls, each depicting the silhouettes of tanks, armored personnel carriers, and mobile cannons.

Military jets and helicopters from around the world hung from the ceiling, while above the crib a mobile comprised of assorted toy rifles spun round and round under the ministrations of long chubby fingers.

As one, everybody crowded forward.

The infant in the cot let out a squeal of delight as soon as he saw them. A gummy smile split his beatific face, and stumpy little arms and legs began pumping furiously in energetic excitement.

"Ah-da! Ah-da! Da-da-da-da-da!"

The small group of hardened killers broke out in a rousing serenade of *oo-goohs* and *aa-gaahs*. Then, when they couldn't contain themselves any longer, down went the bed sheet and up went the nightshirt. A cherubically plump tummy was then subjected to round after round of inevitable but melodic raspberry blowing.

The baby's shrieks of glee were deafening.

Despite the obvious differences caused by the inclusion of Ardenese DNA, Sam was struck by a familiar glint of steel in the piercing gray eyes of the child below him.

Re-genesis protocol or not, you still look much like your father . . .

He glanced across to the dressing table where a rare picture of Alan 'Mac' McDonald stood in pride of place. Taken not long after he had started dating Jayden, it showed the two of them enjoying a picnic, close to the citadel limits of the arc of death. Both looked happy and relaxed, without a care in the world.

We still miss you, brother. Such a tragic waste . . . and you never knew about your son.

Dark memories threatened to sour the occasion. Doing his best to snap out of it, Sam leaned across the bed and joined the festivities.

"Who's a big strong boy, then? Who's my big strong boy? Show me your war face, go on. Show me your war face." Sam leant in closer, grimaced, and made his eyes bulge by way of example. "See? Can you do that? Can you?"

A look of intense concentration etched its way across baby Alan's features. Letting go of everything else, his hands shot out and inquisitive fingers grabbed Sam's bottom lip.

"Cleber boy. So much more intelligent thab your dabby. And bhetter looking, too. He wab a very ugly bugger. Phank goodness you take aphter your mubby."

"Mhu-muh. Mum—mum—mum-uh," the baby chortled. Then, almost as if he'd experienced an afterthought, "Bu—bu—bug—bug-gurr."

Everyone froze, not quite believing what they had heard.

Good grief, only three months old and already on the verge of talking?

Unfortunately, Jayden had been listening in. She was on them like a ton of bricks.

"Right, everybody out. I've told you before, he's extremely precocious. I'll not have him listening to barrack room talk like that. Next thing you know, the first child born here in hundreds of years will go down in history as a foul-mouthed street urchin. They'll blame it on bad parenting of course, when nothing could be further from the truth. Go on, out!"

Clucking like a mother hen, she shooed them from the room and toward the exit.

Sam thought it best not to make an issue of their gaffe.

"My apologies, Jayden, of course you're right. That was entirely my fault. We're all still coming to terms with the changes the re-genesis matrix wrought and we need to be more cautious around those it might have affected more intimately." He stopped to give her a brief hug. "Look, there was another reason we stopped by today. We've thought of a way you can get back on the horse, so to speak, and do something useful. I think you're gonna like it, because it factors in Alan's special circumstances with your particular skill set."

Jayden's eyes flared, and the corner of her mouth twitched.

Gotcha!

"Tell you what, we'll leave you in peace for now, but I'll give you a call later tonight, and run it by you to see what you think. Okay?"

"Yes, okay. Thank you, Sam."

As she closed the door quietly behind them, Sam was struck by a sudden thought.

That's the first time I've seen her smile in a long, long while. Hopefully, what we found on our last trip should change that.

Chapter Five

Chinese Whispers

The assembly hall doors closed automatically as the last of the department heads filtered outside. Looking on from above, Commander Saul Cameron couldn't quite believe his luck. He checked the clock.

Ten minutes early. Wonders will never cease. Now, if only the rest of the high table meeting goes as planned, perhaps I'll get a chance to fit in a round of golf and . . . eh?

He scanned the auditorium below, surprised to see that Stained-With-Blood and Snow Blizzard were still there. During the forum, they'd sat off to one side and kept themselves very much apart. But now everyone had gone, both men had moved down to the speaker's dais, clearly having something on their minds they wished to share.

Even though they have every right to be here, they don't usually concern themselves in the everyday affairs of state. I wonder what they're up to?

He caught Mohammed's eye and drew his attention to the waiting chieftains.

The vice-commander noted his concern and summoned a sentinel. After he'd spoken to it briefly, the glowing orb divided in two and the secondary segment swooped down upon the warriors and engaged them in conversation.

Saul was distracted by movement behind him. The curtain swished aside and Marcus Brutus, the officer commanding what remained of the Ninth Legion of Rome, strode onto the upper gallery. His face was a mass of discolored bruises.

Ouch! The Caledonians must be improving their game.

"Been playing soldiers again, Sub-Commander?"

Marcus smiled and took his seat next to Saul.

"We come from simpler times. Now that we have no natural enemies to speak of, my men chafe for something to keep them occupied. Searc's too, if truth be told." He gestured to his swollen visage. "*This* is but a distraction to engage them and keep them focused. Something I'll gladly continue setting an example in." He leaned closer. "That's why I suggested we only partially automate the farming process. It not only gives idle hands something to do, but field husbandry is an essential skill everyone needs to learn. You never know when all these shiny machines might break down. If you don't know your pulses from your palms, or your roots and tubers from your fruits, we could all end up starving on low quality mush."

"Well, you'll be glad to know the market gardening side of things is proving popular among the masses. We've had forty-four new plot applications. Forty-four. Goodness knows where we'll find the space. Next thing you know, we'll be holding village fetes and country fairs, and awarding prizes for the largest podrom or sweetest kiish." Saul couldn't resist a little dig. "And seeing as how you're so keen, I thought you might like to be chief judge? You'll get to wear a special badge, and have the opportunity to fight each of the winners in turn."

Marcus looked suddenly engrossed, and for a moment Saul thought he might be seriously entertaining his proposal.

"Create a green ring . . ."

So quiet was his voice, Saul wasn't sure he'd heard his compatriot correctly.

"I'm sorry, what was that about a green ring?"

"If you're wondering where the space will come from to meet the demand for plots, just create a no-go area around the city. Keep a space of, say, a mile or so out from the walls exclusively for those who want to learn traditional farming methods. The automated stuff gets done by machines anyway, so it won't matter that they have to trundle out into the Strait to start processing."

Of course, it's so simple! "But that's . . ."

Before Saul could finish his reply, Mohammed encroached on the conversation.

"My apologies for the intrusion. You're not going to believe this, but Stained-With-Blood and Snow Blizzard might have something pertinent to add to the last items on our agenda today. In view of the nature of their concerns, I've asked them to hang around so they can explain it in person. You'll see why when we get there."

The last *items?*

Intrigued, Saul glanced down, only to find the braves studying him closely. Stained-With-Blood met his gaze and raised the stunted shards of Heaven's-Claw toward him. The gesture made Saul uneasy, for the tomahawk was made of meteorite metal, and here on Arden that substance was indicative of dark portents and hidden peril.

Of all the people in this godforsaken place, the Native Americans are the ones least prone to panic. If something's got them spooked enough to come forward, only a fool wouldn't listen.

"That's okay Mohammed," Saul replied. "Marcus and I were just gassing. But seeing as how everyone is here, I suppose now would be as good a time as any to get going. Would you be so kind?"

Mohammed retrieved the ceremonial gavel they used on such occasions. He rapped it sharply upon the smooth stone surface of the embellishment running along the outer edge of the command tier. Once. Twice. Three times.

Everyone fell quiet.

Once he had their attention, Mohammed meshed his image into the main display screen and opened the meeting.

"Ladies and gentlemen, thank you for coming. We have a short but important program today, only four items. However, you might want to save any celebrations for another time. The last two will cause quite a stir. You'll see why when we get there.

"Before we go any further, I've been asked to remind you. The memorial of the re-genesis event is only two weeks away. By then, the first of our survivors will have emerged from stasis. So we need to make sure all departments are fully apprised of who they are, what they do, and perhaps most importantly, where they lived. It would be embarrassing to have a member of the Senatum turning up at his or her lost home only to find it overrun with human hybrids. Ensure each of your section chiefs is given a copy of the list so that any necessary juggling can be completed well ahead of time."

Mohammed turned toward the officer in charge of the city's administrational affairs, Rosa Sophia. "Rosa? I take it everything is in hand?"

"It is. I already have teams assigned to checking and cleaning the addresses you just mentioned. All will be ready for occupation within a few days. I also took the liberty of instigating a deeper background check on each of our candidates. You know how it is with politicians. They do love their second homes or weekend retreats. If it's in the database, I'll find it and have everything shipshape and ready."

"Nice one. And have you finalized the recommendations for the memorial? Anything you can do to ease the transition will be welcome."

"I still think it better to extend the celebration over a period of one week. The Hall of Remembrance is vast, but if we try to fit everyone in at once, it'll detract from what the occasion is all about. People need time to reflect on what the sacrifice meant to them personally. You can't do that in a crowd. We also need to consider the feelings of our newly revived returnees. Being forced into a mass of total strangers, even ones who pulled off a miracle to save your race, is bound to be traumatic. Anyway, my recommendations are included within this report." She held up an info-crystal. "Look it over and let me know."

"Thank you, Rosa. I'll do that as soon as the meeting is over."

Mohammed turned to face the rest of the command staff.

"Okay, now that's out of the way, let's get on to the first item proper on our agenda. Healthcare overview. For that, I'll hand you over to our Chief Medical Officer, Doctor Patricia Frost. Pat, I understand you have something special for us?"

Pat pushed away from her desk, came to her feet, and activated her medi-pad. Everyone could see she was barely able to contain her excitement.

"Indeed I do." With a flourish, she projected the image of three fetuses onto the main holo-screen. Floating within a sea of artificially engendered amniotic fluid, each looked robust and healthy, if somewhat larger than a normal human newborn.

"These are the first of Ayria Solram's babies to come to term. As you remember, she donated her ovaries into the care of the Architect, on the understanding that her eggs be harvested to produce future offspring. Her wishes fit in perfectly with our strategy to increase the spectrum of our population whilst ensuring the survival of Ayria's bloodline.

"The two boys and little girl you see here were fertilized by volunteers from her own people. We did this as a courtesy during the initial process to promote as pure a Cree strain as possible, bearing in mind the obvious augmentations resulting from the addition of Ardenese bioplasm to everyone's DNA . . ." Pat altered the image to show four successively younger generations of infants. "However, as you can see from the examples here, these juvenile embryos contain strands from across the full spectrum available to us."

She cut the images and replaced them with several comparison charts.

"From what we have been able to determine, the eldest specimens will be full term in fourteen days' time, that's a total of five weeks longer than a normal human gestation period. We surmise this will be the norm in the future as we initiate our full program of artificial and natural hybridization."

Full program? Natural births? Saul was caught by surprise. *So that must mean . . . ?*

He expressed a concern that had been on everyone's mind recently.

"Hang on, Pat. Are you saying there *are* sufficient numbers of us to boost the population nucleus sufficiently to avoid, er, what was the term you used to describe it, inherited flaws?"

"The proper term is reduced biological fitness caused by inbreeding depression. And yes, I am. Look at this."

Pat brought up two comparison diagrams, and placed them side by side where everyone could see them clearly.

"Up until recently, we thought we might have weathered the storm only to face the prospect of a slow and gradual demise through degenerative attrition. The table on the left shows what we thought we might be dealing with. A bittersweet pill if ever there was one. Too few of the refugees from Earth survived the Horde, and too many specimens within the Ark were contaminated —"

"But now?" Saul insisted.

"Penny came up with the brainwave of incorporating the impaired bio matter from those subjects lost in stasis to improve overall genetic variation —"

"Wait a minute, you've lost me now," Saul said. "I thought you said those samples were contaminated? Spoiled. Unfit for use?"

"Yes, they are, *if* you're hoping to complete the full regeneration of an Ardenese subject—or the new hybrid version, at any rate. *But*, if we utilize the essence of what's remaining at the molecular level, and use it to enhance our existing reproductive strength, we get this . . ." Pat shuffled the second diagram to the fore and enlarged it. "A boost in the diversification coefficient by over sixty percent."

Bloody hell!

But Pat hadn't finished. She added another layer to the chart and expanded it.

"Now look what happens if we also adapt the artificial womb so that it inserts a small variation in each chromosomal packet . . ." In reply to the looks of confusion displayed by some of her audience, she explained: "Think of it as a similar process used in nature to produce fraternal or dizygotic twins. Such twins are offspring born of one pregnancy that developed from ova released from the ovary simultaneously, and fertilized at the same time. A strange and wondrous event, for such siblings can possess totally different genetic profiles. Exactly what we need to alleviate our predicament. If we put a similar bio-package into two different eggs at the same time, it'll double the chromosomal profile with each passing generation. Inbreeding depression will become a thing of the past, especially if we also target any recessive genes that might act to our detriment, whilst boosting those phenotypes giving us an advantage."

Pat projected the amended results of the successful implementation of such a program.

The room fell silent. All heads turned expectantly toward Saul.

"Pat, this is great news. But some may view it as provocative. I want Penny and yourself to run a whole battery of further tests to ensure the viability of your proposal prior to a public announcement. Before we start tinkering—or letting the populace in on the fact that we have been tinkering—we've got to make sure we know what we're doing, and anticipate any moral objections people might fling our way."

"And we'll need to involve our returning friends," Mohammed chipped in. "Don't forget, the collective *we* just got a whole lot bigger. The re-genesis matrix has seen to that."

Good grief, he's right . . . That reminds me.

"Pat, talking about absent friends. We gave you a green light a few days ago. Have you set a date for the first revivals yet?"

"Yes, I was going to mention it following the meeting, but seeing as you've asked . . . After discussing things with Sariff and Calen, we thought it'd be prudent to resuscitate all members of the Senatum at the beginning of next week. They'll remain in the comfort of the hospitality suite for a few days, getting up to speed with all the latest developments, and then we can start introducing them to everybody."

"I see . . ." *So quickly?* "Will they feel up to it, do you think?"

"Things have been much simplified since the city's power reserves returned to pre-Horde levels. We have sufficient energy to run the Architect at full strength now. That means we've been able to generate an avatar for everyone deemed ready for awakening. Much of the hard work has already been completed via holographic interface, and of course, Sariff and Calen have been with us throughout to help smooth out the odd wrinkle. As have the former Horde leaders, Buer and Caym. What a blessing in disguise *they* turned out to be, I can tell you. One or two of the elders were proving particularly stubborn. They're not like you scientific types; they weren't fully cognizant of the full implications of the re-genesis protocol in relation to the hybridization of our two cultures. You ought to have heard them, prattling on about preserving the sanctity of their race from outside interference. Until our erstwhile monsters sat them down, that is, and explained exactly what would have happened if not for the crude and inexperienced *interference* of the upstart interlopers."

"And how are the former Horde members?"

"Better than anticipated. Because of their warped genetics, it took longer to fabricate a template on which to build their new bodies. But now we've sorted out how to do it, their bioplasm seems remarkably robust. Even the least of them will be taller, stronger, and more resilient against the effects of aging and injury. An interesting conundrum. I can't wait to see what else about their heritage might be enhanced, especially when we include them in the gene pool."

Now there's a possibility I hadn't considered. And a timely one, considering . . .

"Keep me apprised on that." Saul had an idea. "In fact, set up a meeting for me, would you? Both avatars at the same time, I need to discuss something with our erstwhile enemy that might prove . . . beneficial."

Saul stood up so he could address the entire high council. “And the rest of you, keep what you’ve just heard under wraps. It’s not to be discussed away from this room. You’ll see why later.”

He held the gaze of each member present to reinforce his point.

Satisfied, Saul retook his seat. “Sorry about that, Pat. But it needed to be said.”

“No worries from me. I’d finished my little presentation anyway. Although related, all this additional stuff was going off subject.”

Mohammed gained his feet. “In that case, we’ll move on to the second item on today’s schedule. City Defenses. Sub-Commander De Lacey, I believe you have a short announcement for us?”

“Thank you, Mohammed, yes I do.”

Shannon De Lacey, an athletic-looking woman and former soldier from the year 2202, didn’t bother getting up. She merely craned her neck and raised her voice. It was enough to demand attention, for everyone was aware of her famous temper.

“A quick reminder about the state of the city wall. We’ve been forced to leave the barn door open since the Horde breached the outer defenses during their assault last year. Some of you might think it’s not a problem, seeing as there’s no one left to fight. But I don’t like it. Rhomane’s defenses are *my* remit. The barrier is there for a reason, and needs to be restored. Anyway, I won’t go on about it—for now—but as a member of the high table, I want it on record that as soon as Calen and co. have had time to find their bearings, they are to be petitioned to assign some Ardenese scientists to show us how to operate the lydium manufacturing center. As you know, when the re-genesis matrix spawned the additional alien strand within our own genetic profiles, hitherto inaccessible sites opened up to us. One of those was the state-of-the-art complex that generates pure fermionic matter. But of course, even with all the nanobots we have swimming about inside us, *we* haven't had a clue how to utilize the damned place. A shocking oversight we need to rectify as soon as possible."

Saul glanced at Mohammed and pursed his lips.

I wonder if she's somehow got wind of the latest intel?

Shannon turned to study Saul, narrowing her eyes. Her fingers drummed loudly on the arm of her chair.

Of course she bloody well did.

Saul coughed to hide his exasperation.

"Considering the last two items we're about to discuss, that won't be a problem at all." Saul turned to one of the hovering constructs. "Sentinel, please seal the assembly hall. Level two shielding, with confidentiality fuzzers."

"Level two lockdown initiated," the orb intoned. "Privacy screens, activated."

A shimmering blue curtain rippled into existence, and expanded to encompass the auditorium. Once everyone was safely enfolded inside it, the shell turned opaque. Saul felt a tingling sensation crawl across his skin.

Good, let's get this show on the road.

"You might be wondering why the precautions," he announced. "Well, let me tell you. Since the re-genesis matrix saturated the planet, things have been in a gradual state of flux. From what I've been told, this topsy-turvy emergence of our new hybrid way of life will continue until a natural balance is achieved after two, maybe three generations have passed. All well and good. However, we also know how skilled the Ardenese were at sealing their installations away. I mean, we've only got to remember what happened here in Rhomane to have that fact rammed home where the sun doesn't shine. Whole new levels suddenly opened up and surprised us. At least here, everything was relatively safe behind the protection afforded by the lydium barrier. The same couldn't be said for Cumale, Floranz, Locus, Genoas, Napal, and Elan. Six major cities, each with its redundant infrastructure . . . and goodness knows what else.

"So over the past year we took it upon ourselves to integrate the capabilities of the Global Satcom Net, the reemerging way station grid, and our ever expanding squadrons of drones. They were combined to provide a thorough network of scans that, by and large, have helped us confirm which areas might be safe enough to install a small colony, under the protection of a centuria of Marcus's men. As an added safeguard, we also had Sam's Special Forces guys conduct a room to room on the spot check, in each of the cases that were deemed suitable. You know me. I leave nothing to chance, and no matter how sophisticated our equipment might be you still can't beat boots on the ground. I wanted to make sure nothing unwelcome had gotten itself sealed away in the dark and forgotten about. It transpires my caution was justified . . ."

Saul manipulated the main display and brought up a number of stills captured by a helmet-cam. In them, a confusing mass of multicolored light and dark patches looked as if they'd been blurred across the smeared image of a dirty lens.

Referring to them, Saul explained: "To help you appreciate what you're looking at, I'll ask Sam Pell to talk to you. Sam?"

This is where I light the blue touch paper . . . and duck!

Sam Pell made his way to the end of the tier closest to the main monitor.

"Not to cause too much of a stir," he stated, "but we found a little pocket of Horde ogres buried deep within a hidden research station outside Napal a few weeks ago. Nothing to panic about. It's something we thought might be possible, given how airtight certain Ardenese posts can be, but a shock nonetheless when we eventually found them —"

"A few weeks ago?" Shannon De Lacey barked. "Why are we only finding out about this now?"

Sam glanced toward Saul.

This should be interesting.

Saul gave a barely perceptible nod, and Sam continued.

"Part of our ongoing operation over the past year has been the progressive clearance of each of Arden's main sites. We started with Rhomane and Genoas here on Kirban, and then worked our way through Elan and Locus over on Orianne, the other northern continent. Two months ago, we turned our attention south. The most interesting spoor we encountered concerned a few instances where our mutant friends had starved to death. As you know, if they leave off feeding for too long, their essences wane and simply bleed back into the ether. A very slow and pa–"

"Hang on," Shannon said. "You mean to say you'd discovered evidence of a Horde presence *prior* to the images you're showing us?"

"Yes, that's correct. Somehow, they'd found their way into some compounds that were ultra-secure, got sealed in or trapped, consumed everything in sight, and slowly wasted away."

A hush descended. Saul saw the sub-commander's face flush a slightly darker shade. She leaned forward in her chair, one fingernail rapping loudly against the armrest.

Here it comes.

"You didn't think such evidence might be indicative of further security issues?" she spluttered. "And why the fuck wasn't this brought to us sooner?"

"What I think is neither here nor there," Sam replied without a hint of embarrassment. "Because of the sensitivity of what we were doing, the missions were compartmentalized, 'need to know.' One thing we can't afford at times like this is Chinese whispers doing the rounds, even from those at command level."

The drumming stopped and Shannon's finger remained poised in midair.

Saul grimaced as the two stared each other down. *Any moment now it'll click she wasn't included within the mission statement.* In an attempt to ease the tension, he called out, "Please continue, Lieutenant, and emphasize the intelligence you think you might have stumbled across."

Miraculously, Shannon folded back into the comfort of her chair and looked away. Saul recognized the posture. He'd seen it on many occasions before when an angry sub-commander had worked herself into a stew, only to ambush him on the way out of a meeting.

She'll be on me like a rash the moment this is over.

Sam must have had a death wish. He watched Shannon closely until she glanced back toward him, whereupon he gifted her with a smile and a cheeky wink. Only then did he resume his delivery as if nothing had happened.

"As I was saying. In the older cases I mentioned, all the subjects were dead. What I didn't get a chance to highlight is a possible correlation between incidents. Remember, our patrols were conducted in tandem with high resolution, ground penetrating imaging run from Rhomane control center. It was a natural process for us to begin here, and follow with an operation across the Shilette Abyss at Genoas. Elan and Locus came next, simply because of their proximity across on Orianne. Although it might seem obvious, none of the cities situated in the northern hemisphere appear to have suffered the presence of displaced ogres."

"Is that because most of the Horde were drawn *here*, do you think?" Ryan Davies, the training coordinator, suggested. "We did theorize most of the enemy migrated toward Rhomane as it was the only bastion able to withstand their assault."

"I can understand your thinking," Sam countered, "but you'd be wrong. You're being deflected from the point."

"Which is?"

"Temperature. I don't blame you for missing it. I remember Mac mentioning to you once how unusual we SBS guys are as killers. Although we're trained to be highly aggressive when the need for violence arises, we're also schooled to notice details, minute particulars that others might overlook or fail to spot. Tiny insignificant pointers that can make all the difference in a confrontation. Or, as in this case, during a seek-and-recovery mission."

"Recovery?"

Ryan's outburst caused everyone to jump up and start speaking across each other.

"Let him finish," Saul yelled, "we're just getting to the good part."

Sam waited for the noise to subside before drawing their attention to the stills.

"Like I said, I don't blame you for missing it, because we almost did too. In fact, had we not helped in the insertion of the new colony down in Napal, we might still be swimming about in the dark. Just look at the pictures."

Sam clicked a handheld control, and the screen split into a multitude of exterior shots of the city environs. Several started playing audio, and a spine-tingling threnody of moans filled the hall with the sounds of Mother Nature's complaint.

Snow, as fine and as white as grains of dust, was whipped into dizzying vortices by keening banshee winds that worked their way into every available nook and cranny. Pressure ridges as huge and as perfectly formed as actual waves etched the landscape in frozen depictions of a surfers' paradise. Icicles large enough burst a small planet cascaded from glittering battlements in rainbow profusions of fire and ice.

"'Frosty' doesn't do it credit, eh?" Sam announced to his suddenly subdued audience. "A definite no-go area for brass monkeys if ever there was one . . ." He took a bow to lap up the smattering of titters expressed by one or two onlookers who got the joke immediately. "Although it's not as bad as this all the time, you've got to remember, Viléth is the southernmost continent on Arden, and seventy percent of her landmass exists in a permafrost environment. Napal is situated outside that zone, but as you can see, her winters are harsh. Anyway, two weeks ago we helped insert a colony there and went through our usual routine of searching through every office, suite, and complex. Look at this . . ."

Click.

The interiors of three separate facilities were depicted. A battery room, a large storage depot, and a main relay hub. Each looked empty until Sam added a filter across the images. Then it looked as if someone had tried to take photographs, only to spoil them in each case with an accidental double exposure.

"*That* is what it looks like when a Horde entity fades. Do you see how they leave a blemish across the normal fabric of reality? It's as if they distort it, until any evidence of their hyper-energized state has frittered away. A strange phenomenon we'd only encountered in two other locales, as I mentioned, and *both* of those were in Floranz. Now, Floranz and Cumale are situated within the continent of Asten. While Cumale borders the equator to the north, Floranz sits firmly within the southern temperate zone. She's much colder."

Sam enlarged the pictures on the screen.

"It was at this point I started to make the connection. Mind you, even then I wasn't quite sure, until we saw this . . ."

Click.

A pristine white landscape appeared.

"Outside the city, we stumbled across a research facility where, amongst other things, they were studying plate tectonics and planetary core thermodynamics. As you can see, we nearly missed it because the entrance was buried beneath five feet of snow. In any event, it was very secure, and very deep. Took us a bloody age to get down there, and when we did, we uncovered the subjects you see here on these images."

Click.

The confusing maelstrom of multicolored lights and shadow returned.

"They had secreted themselves away with a tidy little food source. Liquid setrium-4, a highly radioactive isotope. We thought they'd be quite boisterous from the word go, but we noticed a difference almost immediately. Remember, the Horde are mutants, with warped sensitivities that crave fresh stimuli and never-ending reservoirs of vitality. But what happens to many forms of energy if they become super-cooled? I'll tell you: While some are boosted into superconductors, others, like setrium-4, become viscous. Sluggish. And in this case, although a highly nutritional source of sustenance, it caused each of our candidates to fall into what they call hybernat, a condition very similar to suspended animation. Why? We think ingestion of this substance creates a new thermodynamic phase we've never encountered before, and renders them passive. Think of it as a form of nucleation. In any event, we didn't have to use any of our new tech to subdue them. And after they were encased within gravity sheaths, we trundled them aboard the *Tarion Star* and transported them here where they've been immersed within the healing balm of the matrix."

Click.

Several images showing waist-high silver canisters appeared.

"As you can see, we recovered the full stockpile of liquid setrium-4, as I think it might present us with a tactical advantage in the future as we expan–"

"I'm sorry, *in the future*?" Shannon piped up again. "I thought the threat no longer existed or you had it contained? Or are you now telling us we've suddenly discovered a whole new enemy to fight?"

"I'll answer that one," Saul cut in, "seeing as it looks as if it's time to fill in the gaps in your knowledge."

Everyone turned to look at their commander. In turn, Saul glanced down toward Stained-With-Blood and Snow Blizzard.

Ah well, it looks like that round of golf's gonna have to wait.

Chapter Six

A Broadening of Horizons

"*Promulus* now on final approach . . ."

"Where are you?" Jake Rixton yelled into the mouthpiece of his radio. "I can't see you yet."

"We're three miles out, due north of your position."

Jake shielded his eyes and peered into the distance. About him, those who had overheard the transmission adopted similar postures. Although it was high summer, the weather had worsened over the past few days, and the winds screaming down from the Caglioso and Erásan massifs were frigid and laced with malice.

The *Promulus* was only a small diplomatic liner, so Jake wasn't too concerned none of his men had spotted her yet. In the past, she had been utilized by the former First Magister as his personal shuttle. Lately, the *Promulus*, together with the *Tarion Star* and *Seranette*, had been used extensively on a wide variety of missions across the planet.

Flying fascinated Jake. Nevertheless, he much preferred the idea of keeping his feet firmly on the deck . . . or in the stirrups.

Poor Atticus. He doesn't have much choice about the matter.

A poignant thought struck home.

Still, at least he'll be home by nightfall. The rest of us need to resupply and spend nine more days in the saddle.

"Got her!" Wilson Smith crowed. His hand shot out, pointing to a growing speck on the horizon.

Around him, men clustered in anticipation, glad that their fallen brother would soon be on his way. The only ones who didn't look pleased were Houston and his cronies: Joe Stevens, Harvey Walton, Chris Spence, and Johnny Ward. They had recently been joined by Joseph Mitchell, Second Platoon's sergeant.

Jake watched them out of the corner of his eye as the craft drew near, hanging back in the shadows like a coven of witches.

"Makes you wonder what they're up to, doesn't it?" Wilson murmured.

Realizing his fellow officer had sidled up beside him, Jake turned.

"I don't know what to think," he admitted. "Atticus hurt himself weeks ago. Why wait all this time to fly his body out of here? I know they said the radio got damaged, but it's been four days since we met back up. Are you telling me Rhomane didn't have a ship available to do a quick mercy dash before this?" The two men watched the select group brooding in silence. "Resupply mission or not, there's definitely something going on. They've been like a bunch of ghouls since they got back. Staying out of the sunlight as much as possible, not letting anyone near the body, treating it like it's their own personal property. The men have noticed it too and are becoming increasingly uneasy in their presence. And their horses? Have you seen how they tend to shy away? That's not normal . . ."

"Hmm," Wilson agreed. "Since our chat back at the way station the other day, I've tried to broach the subject with my uncle on several occasions. I must admit, I do believe he's shutting me out."

By now, the *Promulus* was close enough that its distinctive aquiline shape was easily distinguishable. Jake remembered why they were here, and snapped his fingers.

"Heads up!"

Corporal Nick Spencer had been waiting for the signal. Putting his heels to his mount, he trotted forward a few yards and lit a flare. A thick billowing swathe of smoke piled high into the air, providing the incoming crew with an indicator of wind speed and direction. As the brume cleared the top of the canopy, however, the stiffening gusts scattered the marker far and wide.

But it was enough.

"Thanks for the beacon," the pilot's voice declared, "but we've been watching you for some time now on thermal imaging. ETA, twenty seconds."

Of course you have.

"Twenty seconds," Jake called. "Square everything away and make ready. When it lands, form two lines and stack the provisions over there, just in front of the tree line."

The *Promulus* closed the intervening gap with alarming speed. The one thing that always impressed Jake about Ardenese spacecraft was how silent they were. Despite his best efforts, he couldn't hear any engine noise whatsoever.

It's like the damned thing doesn't exist.

The craft plummeted toward the ground, and several riders backed away in alarm. They needn't have worried. When the liner came level with the treetops, its forward momentum arrested, and it pivoted around on a dime so its rear hatch was pointing toward them.

Still protected from the elements by a crawling skein of power, the *Promulus* edged the final few feet to the ground. The exo-web cut off. Only then was Jake able to discern a faint hum and the smell of ozone where the landing struts had singed the long grass.

A door lowered, and the troopers dismounted. Surging forward, they began collecting their supplies. Two technicians in flight coveralls ambled down the ramp. Jake recognized one straight away, as he was built like the proverbial outhouse and sported a distinctive purple and green plaid bandana instead of the traditional protective headgear usually worn by the crews.

"Lachlan Underwood, is that you?"

Only twenty-three years old, Lachlan was the eldest son of Kohrk Underwood, and one of the few Venicome to have survived the Horde assault of the previous year.

"Aye it is, and as ye can see, I'm still dreaming o' being the first highlander to fly one o' these newfangled contraptions." He lingered on the gantry to caress the already cool metal. "A dream, some might think, but one I fully hope to realize some day."

"Rather you than me," Jake admitted. He suppressed a shiver. "Could you imagine a squadron of these things piloted by you and a bunch of your half-crazed cousins? I don't know what would be worse: facing that; or facing a bunch of Horde armed with nothing but my flaccid pecker."

The two burst out laughing and shook hands. Lachlan abruptly sobered.

"I hear we're giving a lift to one o' yours who had a run-in with a firefang? Nasty business and a terrible waste o' life."

"Tell me about it." Jake ushered the younger man to one side. "Especially as the circumstances of the death don't ring true. So, what have you heard?"

"Heard? Nothing. We got a call this morning from fleet headquarters saying we were to bring your supplies to this location, and pick up a fatality for the return trip."

"Hang on. *This morning*?"

"Aye, that's right."

Jake glanced across at Wilson Smith, who had remained nearby. Then he caught sight of Houston and his cabal, who were studying the exchange closely.

Sneaky fuckers. I'm on to you . . .

"Wilson," Jake called, "give me a hand to grab some ammo, will you?"

Jake turned back to Lachlan. "Quickly, take us inside and show us where the stores are kept. I need to ask a favor."

Cool as a cucumber, the highlander turned on his heel and led them into the hold.

"So what's up?" he asked. "I can see something's got ye all hot and bothered."

"I don't have time to explain," Jake replied, "but both Wilson and I believe there's more to this death than meets the eye. You know Houston. He's out there with the fairies at the best of times. But lately his behavior's been even more bizarre. And now it's starting to spread. I don't know if it's some form of infection they've picked up, but I suspect there might be a connection, especially as Atticus died over two weeks ago, and —"

"Two fucking weeks!"

"Shhh, keep the noise down. Yes. Houston used some pathetic excuse about a broken radio. But the patrols met up four days ago. Four days. It's almost as if our venerable leader didn't want anyone to see the body until . . . until . . ."

I'm missing something.

They stopped by an internal hatch, and the ground crew handed them several boxes of adapted ammunition.

Jake was growing desperate.

"Lachlan, is there any way you can quarantine that body? Keep it separate until someone qualified and in protective gear gets the chance to give it a thorough once over?"

"Aye, there is, but what do I tell the flight officer?"

Jake wracked his brains and had a moment's inspiration. "Pilots are a cautious bunch. Just tell him this is a *Pandora* moment. After what happened last year, he should understand what that means. In the meantime, I'd like to grab a spare long distance radio. Just in case. Let your captain know I'll try to update him as soon as I can. Once you're back in Rhomane, go and see Marcus or Sam. They have the ear of the commander. He'll know what to do. Tell them I suggest we end these patrols early, or Atticus might not be the only one coming home in a bedroll."

They emerged back into the glare of the midday sun to discover Houston had edged around to where the supplies had finished being unloaded. Apparently, he had tasked three of his lapdogs to bring the body inside the ship.

Lachlan smoothly intercepted them as they approached:

"Good day to ye, lads. If you'd be so kind as to place our wee man over *there*, in the isolation booth? Ship's protocol and all that. We don't want anything nasty turning our stomachs, do we, especially if our package isn't fresh?"

He ushered them toward the chamber. Despite his smile, it was evident his request was not to be argued with. They obeyed after only a moment's hesitation.

"That's the ticket. And don't ye worry. We'll take good care of him, and see him safely home."

With so much attention being drawn to them, there wasn't a thing Houston's lackeys could do. Once the seal of the booth had engaged, Lachlan escorted the group from the ship and waved them a fond farewell. To those looking on, he made it appear as if he was sorry to see old friends go.

Jake was impressed. *Oh, very clever!*

Lachlan stepped back and spoke briefly into his throat mike.

The rho-field engaged once more, and the craft lifted away.

"Ye all have a lovely patrol now," Lachlan called down. He winked at Jake, and turned away as the rear hatch closed behind him.

Within seconds, the *Promulus* was a dot on the horizon.

Shame, I'd have loved to —

"Don't just stand there milling around," Houston snapped, "get those damned supplies sorted and let's be on our way."

His gaze bored into Jake and Wilson.

"Wilson. When your men have stowed everything you need, you're with me. We'll wind up our patrol by heading north, toward the Trechlan Gap. Once we're past the Caglioso Mountains, we'll swing round toward the city. Rixton? You and your men proceed west immediately. After you've crossed the Rhomane to Genoas highway, head north toward Boleni Heights. Wait there and we'll meet up and ride in together."

Something about the way Houston spoke made Jake's skin crawl.

Yeah, but how many of us will be left by then?

*

Jayden McDonald sat quietly sipping a cool effervescent beverage. She looked on as Doctor Kara Anders slowly manipulated the controls of an elaborate device.

"Thank you so much for helping us with this." Kara smiled warmly. "What with baby Alan being the first child born here, it means a lot to see him in action and witness how he takes to the educator. I'm sure his input will allow us to calibrate the machine more precisely so that we can achieve the best results for those who will follow."

Between them, little Alan McDonald had been placed on a pile of soft cushions in the exact center of a circular platform. Around the outer edge of the play area, four telescopic arms were positioned in such a way as to fold in on each other to form a dome. Bright pinpoints of light shone from probes at the end of those attachments. Inside, Alan giggled and gurgled contentedly as he interacted with a small furry rodent with a long fluffy tail. The delicate creature looked like a cross between a chipmunk and a miniature lion tamarind monkey, and seemed fascinated by its larger playmate. After cavorting wildly between Alan's legs, it scurried up one arm, across his back, and down the other side so quickly that it was hard to keep track of its movements. Eventually, it tired and stopped to sniff at Alan's ear with loud, panting snuffles. A tiny pink tongue probed inquisitively along the child's lobe and neck, causing him to squeal in delight, whereupon the fluff-ball exploded into a further frenzy of activity, bringing yet more gales of laughter.

Jayden couldn't help but smile.

"I've seen those on holo-clips. What are they called?"

"It's a chin-ta. They're extremely intelligent, and from what we've learned, many families living in rural districts would encourage them to come into the house as they're rather good at keeping insect pests at bay. They're only just starting to show their faces again, so it's a sign of things returning to normal."

"Dinta. Dinta," Alan chortled, waving his arms excitedly in the air.

The chin-ta bared its teeth, clapped its miniscule paws, and chattered a loud reply before skittering off the mat. No sooner had it passed the limits of the play area, however, than it disappeared from sight.

"Dinta?"

Alan froze. His bottom lip extended and an intense look of concentration creased his brow. A vortex of swirling lights coalesced in the air before him. This solidified, and another furry beastie appeared, this one with a rotund little body, large round eyes, and beaverlike teeth. It saw the child in front of it, bobbed up and down, and let out a piercing "squeeeeeee."

Alan whooped with delight, and started stroking his new friend.

"A guinell!" Kara enthused. "Oh, that's rather good. Have you been showing him pictures of the native wildlife?"

"I've no choice, I'm afraid," Jayden replied wearily. "As you can see, my boy's rather precocious and has a voracious thirst for stimulation. He's already started forming words, and if he doesn't know the real name of something, he'll label it with his own tag until he learns otherwise."

"Really? And he's what? Three months old?"

"Three months and a score of wizened old Buddhas. Pat tells me it's the effects of the Ardenese strain. I was about nine weeks pregnant when the re-genesis matrix worked its magic on us and, well, you can see the results. He's exhausting," she glanced at the device, "although with machines like this, I might get a chance to rest my brain for once."

Her professional curiosity roused, Jayden leaned forward to examine the control unit.

"You say Sam and his team found this particular contraption in a complex outside Cumale?"

"Yes, that's right. From what we've ascertained so far, Cumale was responsible for the implementation of Arden's educational curriculum. A program that commenced in the womb, ran through pre-school, and on into what we would call university level. Quite remarkable, really. They developed this little gem just before the siege began, so it gives you an idea of their level of sophistication."

"What is it, exactly?"

"We call it the psi-tutor. The sentinels have been helping me get to grips with its basic operation, but from what I've been able to fathom, this educator was devised to stimulate creativity within infants."

"Creativity?"

"Yes, this early version helps children concentrate and focus their thoughts sufficiently to recreate an image of what's on their minds. It can also be adjusted to measure and enhance intellectual capacity. Evidently, regular use strengthens the areas of the brain used for both conscious and subconscious functioning, and encourages them to mesh."

Jayden was stunned.

"Are you saying this thing turns the child's own imagination into an illusion?"

"More. You've seen the way each simulacrum interacts with the host. And *this* is only the kindergarten version. The addition of the Ardenese bio-sequence into our DNA has already resulted in a cognitive jump of over twenty percent. As you're seeing, for infants it's much higher. The more they use devices like this, the greater their scope and range. By the time they graduate, our children will have an average IQ of close to two hundred."

Jayden turned to stare at her son.

He'd gone abruptly quiet, and now she could see why.

A life-sized image of Mac's profile hung in the air before him, every feature, every line and scar captured in heartrending detail.

"A-dah! A-dah!" Chubby little hands reached out for an embrace that would never come.

"Da-duh! Da-duh!" Alan became more insistent, his movements more pronounced.

A knot tightened in Jayden's throat.

"Is that . . . ?" Kara whispered.

"Yes." Jayden's voice was hoarse. "Mac died before . . . Alan never met him, of course. He's just seen photographs and listened to vidi-clips of his father speaking at meetings . . ."

"Adah, adah dada . . ."

"Evidently, that was enough for him to—" Jayden silently cursed her own weakness and coughed harshly. "I'm sorry. It still catches me sometimes."

Kara leaned across and placed a gentle hand on Jayden's shoulder. She squeezed.

"Would you like to join Alan in the simulator?"

"What?"

"I said, would you like to join your son? It's quite all right. You don't have to get all the way in. Just lean over so that the probes can scan your brainwaves, and form a neural net between you. The Architect tells me that's part of its function. It helps parents and children bond and work together. And, of course, at times like this . . ."

The construct wavered as Jayden bent across the threshold and cuddled into Alan from behind. Once they had relaxed, the image returned, bolder and brighter than before, and with a solidity that made it look as if the man himself were before them.

Mac looked down, his eyes flaring wide in evident pride.

"Hello, young man. Are you looking after your mommy for me while I can't be there? I'm sure you are. Now, you be a good boy. Grow big and strong. I love you more tha–"

It was no use, she couldn't hold it together.

The image faded and Jayden fought down the urge to cry. She struggled to compose herself, and when she looked, she was amazed to find her son staring into her eyes. A solemn, knowing expression clouded his little face, and his gaze seemed to bore into the depths of her soul.

Another rainbow helix formed in the ether. When it settled, Jayden was stunned to see herself within a make-believe scene, embracing the hero she had dared to love. Between them, little Alan hung contentedly in their arms.

With a beatific smile, her baby son reached up to touch her face.

He did this?

"Momma. Dadda. Alhun. Luh, luh . . . Luhve."

Tears spilled, and flowed like rain down her cheeks.

"Mummy, daddy, Alan, love," Jayden repeated.

She hugged Alan fiercely, and began rocking him backward and forward. Lost in a mutual world of grief and solace, it took Jayden a moment to realize someone was stroking her hair. It felt as if the person was trying to soothe her fears. She peeped out through swollen, puffy lids, and was shocked to see that the image of Mac had gained an alarming substance.

And it incorporates a predictive element!

Kara's mouth was agape. Wide-eyed in shock, her attention kept flicking between the phantasm and the emitter nodes of the simulator, which were blazing like miniature novas.

"I didn't know it could do that," she hissed.

"Well, you do now . . ."
The scientist in Jayden seized the unexpected opportunity..

Chapter Seven

Need to Know

The chamber was buzzing.

Saul moved from his position to the exact center of the top tier.

"Right, it's time I laid some cards on the table." He fixed Mohammed with a determined look. "Architect, would you please have Calen and Sariff join us? I don't mind if it's their simulacrums or a mind-linked avatar. Either will do."

While he waited, Saul ignored everyone else and entered a complex series of codes into his info-pad.

"Are you sure about this?" Mohammed murmured. "Until the *Helexia* gets back we won't know for sure if the —"

"It's now or never. You know I trust every member of our team. It's gone against everything I stand for keeping them out of the loop. Well, no more."

A gentle thrumming indicated the moment Calen and Sariff materialized on the command level.

"Saul, Mohammed," Sariff announced. "We were woken from hyper-sleep and asked to download into an ersatz as a matter of urgency. Is everything well?"

Aha, they're the real thing.

"It will be soon, First Magister. After I've updated my people with some much needed background information."

Both leaders stared at the commander. Chancellor Calen was first to respond.

"I see," he muttered. Then he sighed. "It was bound to come out sooner or later, I suppose. Oh well. C'mon Sariff, we'd better tuck ourselves out of the way and let him get on with it."

They moved off to take seats next to Ephraim Miller.

Saul picked up the gavel and hammered the tabletop until a hush descended across the room. When he had everyone's attention, he began:

"In the months following the activation of the re-genesis protocol, certain things changed. Some you were aware of, others you were not. As the people taking the lead in the reestablishment of life across Arden, Mohammed and I were approached by the avatars of the Senatum. The revelation of what the Horde actually were affected them deeply. Not only had their greatest tragedy nearly caused their own extinction, but it now provided them with an opportunity to atone, for it was clear the bio-matrix would also work on the mutated essence of those who were once Horde.

"However, Calen and Sariff were privy to certain information that was never shared. As events are coming to a head, I'll reveal some of that information to you now."

He activated his pad, and an extensive picture of the Scutum-Centaurus and Sagittarius arms of the Milky Way appeared. Each had Ardenese subtitles underneath, reading Pessian Spur and Ularan Spur respectively.

"The intelligence I'm about to share stems from the fact that the Senatum had been aware for some time that not all the Kresh made it to Arden."

A palpable shock radiated around the chamber.

"Don't get me wrong. While most appear to have joined the exodus from their source in order to pursue the fleeing colonists, certain individuals held back. Exact numbers are unavailable. However, eyewitness accounts and recordings made over that period reveal the actual figure will include what *we* call Horde Masters, as well as their underlings. Many seem to have buried themselves away to await oblivion. As for the others? Your guess is as good as mine."

"So give us a conservative figure," Shannon said. "How much of a threat do they present? And by threat, I don't mean only to us here on Arden."

Saul glanced toward Sariff and Calen.

Calen adopted a thoughtful air, and reached across to a control interface. He tapped a few buttons and the image of the Milky Way shifted to show a magnified area containing thirty steady green lights and a single red one.

"These are the colonies," he began, "with Arden, represented by the crimson beacon, partway along the Pessian Spur. From what I am led to believe, the plague broke out *here*, on Exordium."

One of the dots along the Ularan Spur winked on and off.

"Once the problem was recognized, the infection quickly spread to Latinus Prime and Illumina . . ." two more lights began blinking, "for they were the first to respond to calls for aid. You will note how tightly clustered that region is. This is no coincidence, for each of those planets was devoted to highly classified research and development projects. They were protected by the Verianda Nebula, an area saturated with rogue black holes. You must understand, we were at the height of our power; the sciences we delved into there were extremely vigorous. The very latest of engine designs. Weapons that could shatter worlds or destroy suns. Devices that could alter structures at the molecular level, or mutate DNA. Ah, the ignorance of the self-absorbed and mighty."

Each of the highlighted green discs started pulsing.

"What you see here is a rearguard action fought over fifteen months. Twelve thousand years of civilization gone."—he snapped his fingers—"just like that."

Calen's eyes came back into focus as he turned to face the sub-commander. "You asked for numbers, Shannon De Lacey, and an assessment of the threat they represent. Our best guess would be that less than a hundred Kresh survived on each planet, if that; by now they would have stripped all life bare and starved. In addition, as the war dragged on, certain protocols were put in place to ensure any remaining technologies were drained to the point of depletion. We did what we could to assure that the enemy couldn't use them as a source of sustenance."

Shannon wasn't satisfied. "Buuut? I can tell by your face there's something else."

Calen's eyes narrowed. "Very well. Because of the nature of the experiments undertaken on Exordium in particular, and the speed with which the Kresh spread to Latinus Prime and Illumina, no clear picture ever emerged as to their actual strength or deployment on those colonies. As I mentioned, that area is protected by the Verianda Nebula. Time dilates throughout the whole region. Simply put, while the enemy may have withered and faded elsewhere, it is entirely plausible they remain numerous at those particular locations."

"Aha!" Shannon crowed. "Is *that* why you wish to atone?"

"I'm sorry?"

"Is that why you wish to atone? Saul mentioned that your realization of what the Horde actually are—creatures of your own making—affected you deeply. You nearly wiped yourselves out. Is *that* why you've all been working so hard to increase the Special Forces team? Has it been your plan all along to expand what Sam and his boys have been doing, so you can retrieve as many of your lost brothers and sisters as possible before it's too late?"

Calen smiled. "Very astute." He glanced along the tier. "Yes, it's true. We do want to assist our cursed brethren in any way we can; we've gone to great lengths since the re-genesis event to manufacture a much larger supply of the bio-matrix. We are close to fabricating a suitable delivery method too, by which we hope to seed the atmosphere of every single lost colony. Of course, once we do so, a certain hurdle remains."

Most of the command staff, especially those who weren't in on the secret, looked puzzled. Except for one . . .

"Exordium!"

All heads turned toward Marcus. "You don't know how many you're going to find there," he continued, "or indeed, what kind of resistance to expect. For we now know the Horde—sorry, the *Kresh*—are not mindless savages. If they have ascended through the spheres of enlightenment, some might be in a position to wreak havoc with the machines lying on their very doorstep."

Calen's face creased in delight. "You are correct, Marcus Brutus, and I freely admit, this news frightens me. Exordium means 'origins,' and the place from which our greatest achievements—and our deepest sorrow—originated presents us with a conundrum. Do we try to help, knowing we step into gravest danger, or do we simply quarantine the area and forget they ever existed?"

"Actually, it's got a lot harder than that," Mohammed interjected. "Sorry to butt in, Calen, but you might have noticed Stained-With-Blood and Snow Blizzard waiting patiently in their seats? They have something to say, and I've got a feeling that when you've heard it, you'll realize we don't have any options. Well, except one . . ."

Mohammed gestured toward the waiting braves. "Gentlemen?"

Stained-With-Blood nodded to his companion and stood to face the command staff:

"Four days ago, as is our custom, I sought Napioa's guidance in council regarding the forthcoming wedding of Snow Blizzard and Small Robes. All started as it should, and I was granted clear and unambiguous direction to ensure the union will bring blessings to our people. However, as the trance developed, the Creator chose to appear in the combined guise of wolf and raven.

"You must understand that among the Cree the raven has long been respected as the bearer of magic and heavenly portents, while the wolf represents the presence of the greatest wisdom. If this were not alarming enough, Napioa's arrival was heralded by an extremely powerful totem for our people: the Thunderbird, guardian of truth. Thus forewarned, I took steps to clear my mind and prepare for what was to come.

"The Creator showed me the celestial hunting grounds where Ateshnath, the mighty hunter, tracked cloven-hoof, the Great Rhobexi, and where Bright Angule, Ix walker, now resides. As I watched them at play, I noticed the Council of Twelve meeting, as is their wont, to preside over the heavenly arrangement. Something went wrong, for before my eyes, one of the twelve was consumed. The Old Man was quick to reveal the consequences of letting such a travesty go unanswered, for the sun rose mutated beyond recognition. As it flew high, it darkened and swallowed all things. Mountains, valleys, forests, and plains. Oceans, rivers, lakes, and seas. Nothing survived. Even after all life had been consumed the beast still hungered, for it turned to the stars for sustenance."

Stained-With-Blood stepped forward.

"In the past, such visions heralded the presence of those we call Horde, and their relentless march of conquest. Indeed, upon arrival in Arden, both Ayria Solram and I were forewarned by many such episodes. Following our great victory, however, my dreams remained untroubled. Until now. Today's meeting has only reinforced my certainty as to why such dark thoughts plague me again, for it explains the urgency of Napioa's final warning. As he left me, the Creator said, 'Such a threat cannot be tolerated, for it is voracious and all consuming. Do you understand what needs to be done?'" The aged shaman raised Heaven's-Claw high. "I ask you the same thing. Do *you* understand what needs to be done?"

Saul shot to his feet. "Yes, we bloody well do."

He fixed the braves with a stern look. "I know we haven't seen eye to eye in the past, especially when it comes to your dream-walking practices. But I'm not stupid. Too much water has passed under the bridge for me to dismiss your beliefs as mumbo-jumbo. After the events of last year, I promised myself I'd take any future warnings seriously. And I'll honor that today.

"It's obvious you were walking the Ix. That's what the Kresh call it. That's what Angule—a being I greatly admired and respected—called it. While there, you received a warning from Napioa. God. A higher entity. Call him what you will. I for one am going to listen to that warning, for the sun was obliterated and a world consumed. It's clear we face a cancer that will spread into the cosmos. That such a portent should come now . . . well . . ."

"And you're going to take this seriously?" Shannon was aghast.

"Damned right I am." Saul turned to face the rest of the command staff. "C'mon, think about what we've been talking about today. Only a select few were in on it. Most of you weren't. Stained-With-Blood certainly wasn't and neither were any of his people. Don't you think it odd they received a warning, *now* of all times? Especially as their revelation ties in with one or two other little snippets we've got tucked away."

"Oh, this gets better and better," Shannon responded. "Such as?"

"We all remember how the emerging DNA within us opened up new and previously undiscovered parts of the city. It's old hat now, but what you might not realize is that there were also a number of security subroutines hidden away, deep within the CIC mainframe awaiting reactivation —"

"Hidden subroutines? Pertaining to what?"

"How can I put this?" Saul struggled for an easy way to phrase what he must say. "Do you recall how difficult the Serovai was when we first encountered her on board the *Arch of Winter*? We all thought she was a pain in the ass. But she wasn't. Serovai was just fulfilling her nature. Her very name is based on the Ardenese word for security. Anyway, it transpires the Architect had similar safeguards built in, ready to activate if the right circumstances arose. Well, guess what. They did.

"When the new parts of Rhomane were revealed nearly seven months ago, certain information was brought to our attention. You don't know about it because it was marked 'eyes only—OIC and First Officer,' and related to a compartmentalized intelligence network stored separately from the main critical applications and bulk data processors. The system architecture had been designed to hybridize, and sequester the files in a fragmented form within several floating virtua-centers. The Architect itself, the Global Satcom Net, and Se'ochan's haze-cloud. One of the first things the initial download led to was the discovery of several intact starships; the frigates *Paladin* and *Dark Falcon*, and the heavy corvette *Helexia*."

"So that's how we discovered them so easily?"

Saul could almost see the cogs turning in Shannon's mind. "That's right. And although each vessel possessed its own AI matrix, which could have posed a major obstacle to getting them online, the Architect's new parameters allowed us to adapt each of them to function under the Serovai's standard operating procedures. Something that simply wouldn't have happened before."

"So how does this relate to what we're discussing today?" Shannon demanded. "Or Stained-With-Blood's vision, come to that?"

"I'm just getting there."

Saul manipulated the controls of the main work station and a picture appeared, depicting an incredibly sleek craft. Measuring some six hundred and sixty feet long by eighty wide, there were no external features to distinguish her full capability.

"This is the first time many of you will have seen the *Helexia*," he said, "a corvette-class starship that has proven a blessing in more ways than one. We simply don't have the manpower to go gallivanting off exploring the universe, but the *Helexia* only requires a complement of fifty souls. That's why we've been using her so much while the rest of our fleet remains parked in orbit. Once the population grows sufficiently for us to utilize them, we will. But until then, this corvette remains our go-to girl —"

"We already know this, Saul," Shannon said, "and she's due back any day now, having completed the first test runs of the new Slingshot-cum-Slipstream propulsion systems devised by Calen and Brent Wyatt. What's your point?"

"My point is . . . *that's* what you were supposed to think."

The room fell silent. So silent you could have heard a pin drop.

Saul was quick to fill in the details. "To be fair, yes, the *Helexia* has been trying out the new engine design, and by all accounts it's gone very well. But we knew it would, for that system had been bench tested in the labs prior to the Horde invasion. What you don't know is that there was another reason she was sent out on trails at that particular time. The *Helexia* was also checking *this* out."

Saul pressed another button and the monitor jumped to show an oscillating wave pattern. It was accompanied by a static burst that sounded very much like a rapid series of high-pitched beeps and warbling squawks.

"Is that a compressed data package?" Ryan Davies had closed his eyes and was leaning forward in his chair. "It is, isn't it? Extremely refined, so that it reduces white noise and amplifies the redundancy coefficient, but it's a terra-bundle, nonetheless."

"Well done." Saul addressed the room. "What you're listening to is a deep space communication sent in reply to a zone-wide broadcast issued by Rhomane CIC almost seven months ago. From what we can ascertain, the invitation went out following the recognition of the Ardenese DNA sequence within the human genome."

"And when did this reply come in?" Ryan Davies enquired.

"Just three months past. It was highly encoded and originated from the Verianda Nebula —"

"Oh really?" Shannon piped up. "The Verianda Nebula, you say?"

I might have guessed Shannon would make the connection.

"Yes, that's right. As cover, we chose a handpicked crew so we could maintain the pretext of testing the new Slipstream systems. In reality, the ship's company was also perfect to investigate the source of the transmission and, if necessary, carry out any retrieval."

"Retrieval of what?" she pressed.

"I think it'd be better if I just showed you."

Saul flipped a switch, and a stunning medley of shots filled the holo-screen, each portraying a two-mile-long leviathan from a number of angles. The matte black hull bristled with gun turrets, torpedo and missile ports, and myriad other antennae that clearly defined her sole purpose.

"I didn't realize the *Arch of Winter* had been sent out as well?" Shannon gasped. "When did she leave? Who's piloting her and why?"

"That's not the *Arch of Winter*," Saul said. "Calen, will you do the honors?"

"Thank you, Commander." The Chancellor took up the explanation: "Ladies and gentlemen, when we instituted the Avenger program we wanted to incorporate a fully independent, mission essential, self-sustaining environmental system into our existing fleet. Although capable of carrying nearly five thousand passengers and crew for protracted periods without any support whatsoever, they are fully automated and can be operated by a self-aware AI construct specific to each craft.

"This is the deep space cruiser *Chariot of Spring*, the second of four Avenger class long range exploration and patrol vessels designed and built at the Exordium shipyards. Despite her close proximity to the source of the initial Kresh outbreak, we are fortunate that her AI matrix, Coralin, remained fully functional."

Calen's laser pointer highlighted the various features of the Titan before them.

"As you can see, her dual point, defensive and offensive main photon batteries, laser backups, and Menta accelerators are fully deployed. We are informed that her silos and tubes carry retrofitted Excalibur torpedoes, Phoenix tactical strike missiles, and Sparrowhawk interceptors. She possesses a full complement of escape pods and standard shuttlecraft and, as with the *Arch of Winter*, has a reserved launch-and-retrieval pen for a standalone EMT shuttle. Apart from her near-depleted rip-space drive, she's shipshape and ready to go. And in that, we are lucky. As the last of her line, she had only just finished her trials at the time of the outbreak, and was manned by a skeleton crew."

"What happened to them?" Rosa called out.

"Scans show an anomalous energy signature down near the main engine room. We think there's probably a nest of Kresh hidden away in there, slowly bleeding the core dry. I'm afraid the people on board didn't stand a chance. It also explains why it took us so long to recover the *Chariot of Spring*. In the event of a catastrophic emergency, Coralin was programmed to take her into a dark cloud nebula, the Well of Souls, to await retrieval or destruction. She had to get there on sublight thrusters."

"So let me get this straight." Shannon interjected, keen to emphasize her point. "You're quite happy to bring a ship here that contains an unknown threat? Are you sure that's wise?"

"It's essential," Saul retorted, "because of the opportunity it offers us." He stood, pacing up and down so as to make eye contact with everyone present.

"Think about the things we've discussed today. First, we've been finding isolated pockets of Horde on Arden itself. Only a few, true, but enough to support Calen and Sariff's concerns about the possibility of larger numbers throughout the colonies where the re-genesis matrix was never deployed. Second, we've stumbled across the existence of something that can incapacitate our soul-sucking friends and render them comatose: Setrium-4. A remarkable discovery, for it will help realize the Senatum's dreams of recovering the lost colonies, and undoing the harm they unleashed upon themselves . . . and us in the process. And finally, just as all the pieces seem to be coming together, we get wind of a ship that contains a den of Horde from the very place the infection started. A location that's been cut off from us until now. I shouldn't need to emphasize how important that is. They'll be like a band of 'patients zero.' Among the very first Ardenese people to mutate, and a source of possible hope . . ." Saul stared around his gathered people. "That's why I'm taking Stained-With-Blood's warning seriously. It tells me that if we do nothing, a new threat will emerge that might not only sweep *us* away, but the rest of the galaxy too. That's how grave this situation is. Who knows what technologies these Kresh might be able to utilize? We simply can't take the chance by sitting on our collective asses."

"So basically, you want us to embark on some huge rescue quest?"

Shannon's statement caught everyone by surprise.

"It looks that way, yes." Saul regarded his sub-commander closely. "But what other choice do we have?"

Still unconvinced, Shannon leaned forward. "You *do* know this will probably end in tears . . . right?"

Chapter Eight

Whatever This Is

Jake Rixton came awake with a start and caught his breath.

For some reason his heart was pounding like a freight train running on too much steam. He tried to open his eyes but found his lashes stuck together with rheum. Cursing silently, he raised his fist and rubbed. His skin felt clammy. He wiped a film of perspiration from his brow.

What the hell . . . ?

He shivered despite his proximity to the camp hearth.

Blinking his lids open at last, he peeped across the clearing where they had chosen to bed down.

Ancient and brooding, sweeping branches arched overhead, blocking out most of the moonlight. Someone had been remiss. The fire had been allowed to burn low and by its embers dim glow, the clearing had become a confusing patchwork of undefined gloom and shadow that only hinted at the maze of hidden paths and tangled traps within.

Jake could barely make out the hazy outlines of his off-duty section tucked up tight in their bedrolls.

He took a further breath and listened, waiting for his night vision to adjust and for the darkness to reveal its secrets.

Apart from the occasional nickering of the horses, or sputtering fagot within the fire, nothing stirred. Not the men who were supposed to patrol the camp itself, not the roving picket farther out. Even the cevils—tree crickets similar to cicadas that festooned the trees in this part of the Tar'e-esh Forest—were silent.

Where are the damned sentries?

His sense of foreboding increased, and Jake's hand subconsciously edged toward his carbine lying snug against his side.

Crack! The retort of what sounded like a branch snapping rang out like a rifle shot.

Why are the lookouts not issuing a challenge?

He glanced across to the command post, where two troopers were supposed to sit and monitor the radio, along with other defensive equipment.

Both seats were vacant. A couple of spilt plates and upended cups lying on the grass showed the soldiers had dropped their meal to respond to something.

But what?

Snap!

This time the sound came from behind him.

Someone or something is definitely snooping about out there.

Jake spotted movement within the bushes. He rolled from his blankets, weapon in hand, and shook the feet of the man nearest him.

"Sergeant Williams. Stuart?"

A deep muffled cough fought its way clear of a sleepy

throat.

"Huh?" His lips smacked together loudly. "Jesus, who crept up and took a dump in my mouth?"

"Forget that. We have a problem. Rouse the men. Do it quickly and quietly."

Deep within the undergrowth, a glint of amber light on metal caught Jake's eye. He trained his gun on the target and strained to distinguish what it might be. Sadly, whatever it was soon became lost among the ranked boles parading off into the distance.

Williams returned from waking the men. "Sir, what's going on? Where are the guards?"

"That's what I'd like to know. Look." Jake pointed out the missing radio men. "Isn't Corporal Spencer meant to be on watch?"

"He is, yes. Lawrence and Bennett are supposed to be with him."

Now he was on his feet, Jake could see a little farther than before. His gaze fell upon a smashed laptop computer, the one his sentries were meant to use to monitor the mobile shield wall and motion detectors. The transceiver lay beyond it, disconnected, wires cut.

About him, the sight of the section standing-to did nothing to ease his discomfort. Although only a matter of seconds had passed, it felt as if everyone were wading through a quagmire of slow-motion frustration.

Flashlights clicked on and additional lanterns lit, penetrating the gloom but creating stark contrasts between light and dark. The reassuring sound of weapons being cocked rang out.

About bloody time.

"Sergeant Williams, form everyone into four-man teams. I want the first group here, patrolling the outskirts of the camp.

They are to stay in sight of each other at all times. Another will check on the horses and supplies. Equip two more with radios, and send them in opposite directions. They are to scour the outer perimeter immediately, and work toward our roving pickets' positions. If they find anyone, they're to call for help first. They mustn't get sucked in, no matter how urgent the situation might seem."

"And the rest?"

"They can remain with us at the control post. I'm going to get the radio up and running and call in some assistance. This crap needs to stop —"

Someone staggered out of the underbrush on the other side of the clearing and fell face down on the grass.

A wash of flashlight beams converged on the same spot, followed by a line of muzzles.

"Nick," Sergeant Williams called, "is that you?"

Jake rushed forward, and recognized an officer's sword grasped in one bloody fist. The other hand clawed repeatedly at the ground. The shoulder strap identified the mystery soldier as a second lieutenant.

"Wilson?" he gasped. Jake's gaze bored into the woodland about them. "What the hell are you doing all the way across here? Are you alone? Is anyone else out there?"

A thousand questions bloomed simultaneously. And all would have to wait. Even from a distance, Jake could see something was wrong. The man on the ground was panting desperately, as if in excruciating pain. His scalp was a mass of sores; his hair had thinned and grayed. Even his skin looked emaciated, as if all vitality had leached from his bones.

Wilson? Is this really you? "What the fuck happened? Talk to me, man."

A circle of men crowded in. Jake waved them away.

"Keep watch on the forest. Whatever did this might still

be out there."

He turned to his second. "Sergeant Williams, get that damned wireless back online and call for help, fast. I don't —"

Something clutched at his tunic and Jake was pulled forward.

He glanced down, only to recoil in horror. The thing below him had once been a young man in his early twenties. Now, Jake found himself staring into the cataract-tainted eyes of a decrepit at death's door.

"I'm sorry," Wilson Smith mumbled, "I couldn't . . . I didn't realize what was . . ."

His feeble voice trailed away.

Jake lowered his head in an effort to hear what his stricken friend was trying to say. He wrinkled his nose in distaste.

Good grief, what has he been eating? His breath stinks as if his insides have rotted. Even his teeth have yellowed. How is this possible?

"Get the first aid kit," Jake hissed toward the nearest trooper. *Like I could do anything about this anyway.* "And then call Rhomane on that bloody radio."

"I'm so thirsty," Wilson gasped, "so tired."

"Someone fetch me a canteen, quickly."

Jake couldn't tear his eyes from the dying man. "Who did this to you?"

"I can't . . . Oh Jake, I'm so sorry it's you."

"What do you mean, you're sorry? You've got nothing to be sorr–"

The wasted husk beneath him leaped up and grabbed Jake by the back of his neck. Wilson's other hand slammed against Jake's chest and bony fingers dug deep into his flesh.

"I can't help it. *He* did this to me."

Did what? Who —?

Excruciating pain tore into Jake's heart. No matter what

he did, he couldn't shake free. All the strength was draining from his body.

He screamed and lurched backward. Jake's eyes snapped open, his perspective abruptly changing. Drenched in sweat, Jake found himself sitting upright in the middle of a camp, surrounded by a mixed throng of his soldiers and Roman legionnaires. Bathed in the combined light of the fire and a string of solar-powered lanterns, here everyone looked relaxed and in the best of health.

Wilson? Where . . . ?

"Are you all right there, my friend," Marcus Brutus enquired from the opposite side of the clearing, "you look like you've had a fright."

Jake ignored the question and spun out from beneath his blankets. He saw rolling plains silvered by moonlight. Undulating away from his position at the edge of a small copse, the curving hills led toward the twinkling lights of the Starport and Boleni Heights in the distance.

Nearer, the roving picket rode by, accompanied by mounted sagittaria. Closer yet, someone played a gentle tune on a harmonica.

It was just a dream.

A hand on his shoulder made him jump.

"Jake? Is everything all right?"

He suppressed a shiver and turned to find Marcus by his side.

But it was so real . . .

"What are you doing here, Marcus?"

"Responding your request. We'd have arrived sooner, but the command staff had a meeting that dragged on all day and well into the evening, much longer than anticipated. Imagine my surprise when the doors opened and I found young Lachlan Underwood outside. He's not a lad to panic, but he was quite vocal in expressing his opinion regarding your concerns. Do you know, he waited more than three hours for the gathering to close to make sure he caught both Sam and me?"

"So? What do you think?"

"In the light of recent events, we're inclined to pay close attention to anything out of the ordinary. Sam and his boys must prepare for an assignment, so I took it on myself to check the body you sent back. Not a pretty sight and definitely unusual. We don't like unusual at the moment, so I've got Flavius and another centuria making their way toward the Caglioso Mountains as we speak."

"For goodness sake, tell them to be careful. There's something off about Houston lately. Something odd. It's not only spooking the animals, but his men as well. And it seems to be spreading. One by one, others are going down with whatever infection they're carrying. Advise Flavius not to drop his guard for one moment." Something in the way Marcus held himself made Jake suspicious. "What is it? What's wrong? Don't tell me there have been more casualties already?"

"That's just it, Jake. The drones were able to lead us here to your exact location because your life-signs showed up from miles away. So far, we haven't found any trace of our elusive Captain Houston."

Jake's blood ran cold. *But there are over forty of them.* "You did receive my update though," he stressed, "so you're looking in the right place? The other platoon is due to come out of the northern Tar'e-esh in the vicinity of the Trechlan Gap. After they passed the Caglioso massif, Houston said they would swing west and come in to meet us via the Trident. They should be well into the Sengennon Strait by now."

"Yes, we got that. But as I said, there's nothing between here and the northwestern fringes of the forest. We've checked." Marcus shook his head. "There's a lot for us to think about at the moment, Jake, and this distraction is the last thing command needs. Can you think of any reason why they might have veered off? Perhaps they're investigating something?"

Or Houston is up to his tricks again?

"And not update us on the radio? I made sure Wilson had an additional comms set in case anything unexpected came up." Jake could feel bile fighting its way up from the pit of his stomach. "No, you mark my words. Houston and his cronies will have something to do with this, whatever 'this' is, and it won't be good for anyone."

"Then we'd better make our way back to Rhomane with all haste. Despite the many unexpected activities we find ourselves engaged in this night, I took the liberty of sequestering the *Tarion Star* to ensure we all get home safely. Once there, we'll use the satellite net to help us sort this mystery out."

I somehow doubt that . . .

"Good idea. Let's crack on. The sooner we get started, the sooner we can see what sort of crap Houston is pulling now."

*

A determined voice teased at the fringes of her awareness.

As much as she wanted to disregard it, Va-ákil of the Praeturium Tier found she couldn't. The irritation called to her in a way that could not be ignored. It tugged and it worried and it nagged. So much so that the vast reach of her subconscious mind was forced to release its hold on the ultimate bliss that was the Well of Fractal Probabilities.

An existence incorporating the utmost quixotic fidelity, the Well encompassed the infinite magnitude of reality within a single sphere of purest complexity. Not everyone possessed the fortitude to withstand such an amalgam of disparate contradictions. And yet her brethren endured, for it was the only place they had discovered in which they could hope to survive intact, given the circumstances.

With a growing sense of exasperation, Va-ákil submitted to the influence of the mundane once more, and watched as the spiraling scale of the cosmos around her reasserted itself.

Time resumed its inevitable march toward oblivion and a pulse of anger swelled from the core of her being. Her aura blazed, and twelve concentrations of blinding luminosity flared about the crown of her massive head. The surge continued, and the fabric of Va-ákil's essence became wreathed in purple and violet majesty, revealing the grandeur of her station and the tiniest glimpse of the terrible potential residing within.

Her outburst washed across the receptors of the slumbering Prátors, Lega'trexii, Tribuni, and Praefacti nearby. Regardless of their station, each had no choice but to tolerate the bitter frustration radiated by their queen. True to their nature, they responded in kind.

Ill-defined parameters ignited, creating a confusing mass of boiling shadow and luminous clarity. Within, a horrific array of spectral horns, fangs, and scythelike talons were revealed. Etched in fire and blood-curdling savagery, the prospect of imminent violence multiplied a thousandfold, and the interior of the vast chamber trembled to a subsonic resonance verging on catastrophe.

Despite her agitation, Va-ákil had no wish to see her subjects waste themselves in pointless expression, especially as their current arrangement had helped them prevail far beyond the normal span of their underlings. Therefore, the sixteen-foot-tall monstrosity that was the Kresh monarch made haste to detach detached herself from the maelstrom of impending disaster. Having done so, she stood to one side, listening.

The fomenting cauldron of malice subsided into one of brooding acceptance.

Something taints the Ix. Both presumptuous and crass, it is clear they are insensible and unfocused. Such a blatant breach of etiquette deserves to be punished . . .

Outraged, Va-ákil was nonetheless intrigued, and took a moment to fine-tune her sensibilities to reach out across the quantum matrix.

And yet, their craving borders on the familiar.

The faraway mind warbled and echoed in ill-disciplined ineptitude. Even so, Va-ákil was able to savor every nuance of the feeble attempt at communication.

Infantile! Despite a contradictory sense of maturity, it emerged only recently and lacks both lucidity and any real semblance of control. Pah! Advancement toward illumination will be impossible for such a one, especially as it dares to call for aid in such a manner. As if I would deign to agree.

Va-ákil was about to dismiss the upstart when its thoughts betrayed a treasure-trove of disturbing images. Suddenly focused, she pounced on them and altered her cognizance. Her astral senses skimmed the energy lattices comprising the full extent of the vext.

What is this? They are gone? So many of my champions and subjects lost to immolation and to . . .to . . . travesty? Insects have discovered the anathema to our codex and seek to exploit us? This blasphemy cannot be permitted. Are the fools so blind as to think there won't be repercussions?

The weight of her entire race's survival rested on her shoulders. Va-ákil knew she would need to ponder her options carefully before deciding on an appropriate response.

A simple impulse created a fracture through spacetime, and the Plane of Eternal Prisms beckoned. The splintered reality within would provide her with a thousand possible solutions to her dilemma and ensure she could compare the outcome of each in minute detail. The added benefit of such deliberation was that it would also help soothe the heat of her anger before she returned to the Well.

A notion occurred to her.

Exerting her authority once more, she focused her will into an irresistible tide.

Come then, fledgling. If you would dare my presence, do so with courage.

Satisfied, Va-ákil, Magnate of all Kresh, cooled her ardor and submitted to the basest energies imaginable. Tranquility enfolded her in the welcome relief of consummate intimacy. As she succumbed to enlightenment's caress, her gaze swept the chamber in which she had chosen to hibernate.

When I have finished, perhaps I should make the effort to witness the extent of the cancer eating away at the fringes of my realm. After all, my reach is vast. Why waste such dominion on idle dreaming when it can be turned to a more constructive use?

Chapter Nine

We Will Remember Them

Mohammed found the atmosphere within the Hall of Remembrance more subdued than normal, but nobody seemed to mind: the mood fitted the occasion perfectly and created an environment fit for learning and private reflection.

Small groups clustered here and there, amid the hubbub of a multitude of different discussions bubbling away in the background. Despite this, no one appeared disturbed, for the chamber's vast scale and grand furnishings muted unwarranted distractions.

Designed to amplify sound in specific areas, the Hall always made a huge impression, especially on those visiting for the first time. Today's clique of distinguished guests was no exception. Although they knew the environs well, they were unfamiliar with its current layout, altered by the Architect in the centuries following the host nation's immersion within the Ark.

Mohammed glanced at his info-pad as he led them toward its central feature, refreshing his memory as to the names of those once the leading lights of Ardenese society.

Everyone who was anyone knew who Sariff and Calen were, as the simulacrums of both officials had been heavily involved in educating and guiding the various intakes of refugees from Earth throughout the war. And while their hybrid forms were somewhat different to their purely Ardenese representations, enough similarity remained for everyone to recognize them.

Other members of the government's ranking tier looked unfamiliar, as was the modus of their functionality.

It was common knowledge that Sariff, as First Magister, had led the Senatum. What the refugees hadn't realized were some of the more intricate specifics of Arden's parliament. The first surprise was that Calen's official title, Chancellor, identified him as chief among Arden's scientific elite.

His political counterpart's title was *Consulan*, a post currently filled by a fussy individual called Pulígio. Fiercely nationalistic and a compulsive nitpicker, Pulígio had been a constant thorn in Mohammed's side since his resurrection. Thankfully, his abrasive attitude was tempered by Sariff's deputy, the charming Shaní: a tall, strikingly handsome woman who, despite her scientific background was a natural diplomat. Everyone had taken to her, and her elegant bearing and luxuriant auburn hair drew admiring glances from both factions within the emerging community.

For some reason unknown to Mohammed she favored him, and he found it difficult to concentrate when she was around. As they strolled across the marbled floor, Mohammed noticed Shaní chatting to another senator. Despite this, her gaze bored into him and he couldn't prevent himself going hot under the collar.

To distract himself, Mohammed pretended to study something important on his pad.

Why am I acting like some stupid schoolchild?

He risked a quick glance over his shoulder.

Shit! She's still looking . . .

He coughed nervously, and Shaní countered with a flirtatious smile. Contemplating his list, Mohammed paired the images of those elders he wasn't familiar with yet—scientist and politician—with the cities they served.

Senatum disposition by zones:
Rhomane—Psi Grenushan and Gul Similan
Genoa—Psi Tacar and Gul Dal'san
Napal—Psi Davir and Gul Viranè
Elan—Psi Y'shol and Gul Olex
Locus—Psi Erin and Gul Tir'ee
Cumale—Psi Saklar and Gul Ru'bok
Floranz—Psi Do'mer and Gul Lani
Field Marshal—Sol Berek

Intrigued, Mohammed searched the following throng until he located the new military commander.

Aha! So he's *Beren's replacement? Let's hope he has his predecessor's sense of humor.* He reminisced on the memory of his friend. *Such a shame we lost him to the re-genesis protocol. It would have been nice to chat with him in person. Still, at least we have his ersatz to fall back on, unlike poor Mac—Oops! Here we are.*

They had arrived in front of a huge glowing monolith that had been constructed directly beneath an open oculus. Nearly two dozen faces turned to study the richly veined texture of its construction.

"As you know, this is the Reverence," Mohammed began, "the esoteric barometer you left in place to monitor the life energies of those transferred from Earth to Arden."

He pointed out the trapezoid atop the twenty-foot column.

"Although the construct still operates, we asked the Architect to break the link to the pyramid following the release of the bio-matrix into the atmosphere. The long war of attrition was over, and it was felt there was no real need to record every fresh death the way we used to. It served its purpose at the time, believe me. Observe for yourselves . . ."

Mohammed drew their attention to a number of breathtaking bas-reliefs cut directly into the fabric of the outer wall. Stretching from floor to ceiling, each was of a similar size and gave the impression of leaves of a gigantic book opening out onto bare rock. Thousands of names were inscribed upon the double pages of every volume, each glowing with a soft crystalline radiance.

"So many paid the ultimate price when they fell to our enemy"—he nodded toward two of his guests in particular —, "or as *you* prefer, the Kresh."

Newly revived, two of the leading members of the Horde, Buer and Caym, stood amongst the party. Slightly taller than their counterparts, they were heroically muscled, and for some strange reason that made them look much bigger than they actually were.

"Had we known at the time that our adversaries were, in fact, mutated travesties of those we had been summoned to protect," Mohammed continued, "I honestly don't know how we would have reacted."

"How many friends did you lose, personally?" Shaní enquired, moving closer.

"I'm from the Earth era of twenty-three forty-five. I was brought through the gateway seven years ago, on the seventh intake as it happens, along with Saul Cameron. We were line officers, commanding an expedition to the Pegasus Dwarf Galaxy, or as I believe you call it, the Irrolen Cluster. Our carrier, the *Regent*, was the very latest design in deep space starships, equipped with new experimental Light-Drive engines. One thousand five hundred souls set off on that journey, expecting to wake up three decades later orbiting a new home"—Mohammed snorted, and his eyes took on a faraway look——"only we ended up some place unexpected and entirely different." He sighed deeply. "Don't get me wrong, we all made it safely here. But thanks to the Horde, less than two hundred survivors remain."

He turned to survey the epitaphs arrayed around the room. "Some lost far, far more, as you can see, especially the earlier intakes. Thank goodness for the Ninth, eh?"

"Yes? Tell us about them," Shaní urged.

To Mohammed's dismay, she sidled up to him and linked her arm through his. Her skin was surprisingly warm and firm to the touch.

"Er, fo– follow me," he stuttered.

As gracefully as he could, Mohammed steered everyone across to the other side of the hall, where the largest crowd had gathered.

Visitors parted to let the distinguished guests through, and although the Senatum now possessed certain human traits, most people still stopped what they were doing to stare.

They came to a halt in front of a dais, upon which a large golden bird was displayed. Wings spread wide, adorned with scarlet and gold braiding, it topped a highly polished wooden spear. A small placard attached to the top of the pole read: *SPQR*.

Beneath the totem, a larger sign read:

SPQR
Senatus Populus Que Romanus
In the name of the Senate and the people of Rome
Serovak Pluserak Qen Rhomanax
For Security Prosperity and Rhomane

"What is that remarkable-looking creature?" Shaní breathed. "Very imposing. And the sign too. I can see some of it is written in Ardenese, but the other languages are . . . don't tell me . . ." Her face brightened. "Standard English and Latin. Yes?"

In reply to Mohammed's look of astonishment, she tapped the side of her head. "The benefits of dream-learning in stasis."

"You're quite correct," Mohammed replied, "and the creature displayed here is a bird of prey from Earth called an eagle. It's very much like the targéns you have, nesting high in the Erásan Mountains. This icon of the Ninth Legion was the banner under which the Roman armies marched. It was so important they would rather die than lose it in battle." He chuckled. "Nevertheless, we who survived are beginning to suspect it is also a symbol of a higher power at play."

"What do you mean?"

"I'm referring to the coincidences that sprang up during the concluding months of the struggle." Mohammed repositioned himself so he could face the group squarely. "Fate, it would seem, has a sense of humor. The relentless siege was an ongoing nightmare that caused a considerable drain on Rhomane's reserves. So much so that by the time the last ingathering was selected, things had become critical. The ninth batch was to be the final call for help. Imagine our surprise when we discovered it comprised a vastly different selection of candidates than usual.

"Up until then, the Architect had selected refugees from scientifically advanced timeframes. But as you yourselves discovered, technological sophistication was no guarantee of success. In fact, it worked against those early survivors who relied on photonic weapons for offense and defense. What a banquet they provided for the Horde. Unbeknown to us, the Architect must have realized this and changed tactics. In a last ditch effort, it turned instead to people from simpler times. Epochs where armaments didn't rely on energetic particles. Whether it was blind luck or no, the largest contingent of the final intake was the lost Ninth Legion of Rome. Get it? The ninth brought us the Ninth."

"*Lost* Legion?"

"Yes. Our ancient histories record the Ninth Legion as disappearing into the mists of Caledonia—that's a small island territory on Earth—never to be seen again. We thought them decimated by the highland clans inhabiting those regions. How wrong we were . . ." He gave a wry smile. "Of course, many among their erstwhile aggressors, the Iceni tribes, were also brought through with them. And what a revelation they've been, for they have proven some of the fiercest fighters we've ever seen.

"Along with that group came the Fifth Company, Second Mounted Rifles Cavalry Unit. They specialize in long range reconnaissance patrols using horses, very similar in all respects to your allorans. Of course, when they were plucked from Earth, their adversaries, the Native Americans, were also scooped up. I believe you've met the Cree?"

"You mean the Ix walkers?" Consulan Pulígio interjected.

"That's right: an incredibly spiritual people who strive to work in harmony with their environment, wherever that might be, for they believe the Creator, Napioa, seeded the entire universe with the same spark of life eons ago. In fact it was due to their shaman, Stained-With-Blood, and our very own Ayria Solram (a Cree descendant from the year thirty-three forty-three) that we were warned about the Horde's true nature."

The Senatum looked impressed by facts they hadn't known before. But Mohammed hadn't finished.

"But of course, we couldn't have put all the pieces of this esoteric jigsaw puzzle together if not for the intuition of the Special Forces commander, Lieutenant Mac McDonald, one of the most insightful people I've ever met. He made the connection between iron and its effect on the Horde's codex, and he realized some amongst the enemy were trying to communicate with us." Mohammed laughed. "Do you see why we're so suspicious? The ninth consignment brought the Ninth Legion of Rome to, of all places, Rhomane. Not only were their mundane weapons exactly what we needed, but they possessed dream walkers and visionaries who made all sorts of startling new discoveries that contributed to ending a war that had dragged on for years. Things like the Global Satcom Net, the drones, the *Arch of Winter* . . ."

"Basically, you're saying the Ninth turned the tide?" Pulígio stated.

"Yes, I suppose I am." Mohammed gestured to the eagle. "This standard has come to represent them, and the strength and dedication of everyone who came from Earth, for they willingly risked everything to ensure Arden a chance of survival. During the Battle of the Line, thousands of brave men, women, and enlightened Kresh sacrificed themselves instead of fleeing. We're thinking of asking the Architect to create a special section within the Ninth's records so their memories can be preserved forever."

"But that's wonderful." Shaní gasped and shook her head. "To include *both* peoples in your commemoration." She turned to her fellow elders. "Members, we must make this a priority once the Senatum is restored. It will do much to forge closer ties as our two peoples gradually blend."

"Yes . . . about that." Pulígio pounced: "When *exactly* does Commander Cameron intend to restore power to the properly elected forum?"

Bloody hell! Mohammed sighed. *Someone was waiting for his opening.*

"You'll have to speak with Saul about that yourself, Consulan. And your own First Magister, of course. I do know the two of them have been discussing the topic at length over the past week. But as to the specifics? Like you, I've left that to those in charge."

Shaní squeezed Mohammed's arm, and he turned to look into her eyes.

Her gaze conveyed a definite sense of humor, and a distinct impression that seemed to say "well played."

For the first time, Mohammed felt relaxed in her company.

I think I could get to like her. A lot!

*

Jayden McDonald paced to and fro along the far side of the laboratory as her colleague, Doctor Penny Frasier, completed a final series of tests. Since her proposition of more than a week previously, Jayden had been unable to rest. She was keen to know at last if her plan would work.

For the umpteenth time she glanced at the clock. *Those bloody numbers have refused to budge for the past ten minutes.*

Just when Jayden thought she might burst from impatience, Penny pushed away from the workstation and motioned for her friend to take a seat.

Jayden hurried across. "Well, what do you think? Can we bring Mac back as an avatar or not?"

Penny's face set into a mask of stone. "Honestly? I'm sorry, but I don't think it will work. I've been chatting with the Architect and a couple of experts in this field, Psi Davir from Napal and Psi Saklar of Cumale. While they agree we could construct an ersatz, it won't have the depth you're used to. Remember, Sariff and Calen's constructs had the benefit of a fully documented biometric and psidentic lattice to work with. All we have on Mac are bits and pieces. Fragments at best, based on several psyche evaluations he underwent, and images recorded from the public meetings he attended." She shrugged. "Of course, with the Architect's precognitive awareness subroutine, we could fabricate something close, but it's likely you'd always get the feeling he's not genuine enough."

Jayden struggled to hide her crushing disappointment.

"Can we at least make him part of Alan's educational program, so he has the opportunity to know his father?"

Penny's countenance fell further. "While it *is* possible, you've got to ask yourself, would that be wise? Remember, the simulator focuses thought patterns into a tangible, visible form. The boosted corporeal element you felt were the results of the holo-band's hard light emitter enhancing the strong emotions you and baby Alan experienced at the time. Your combined neural patterns generated a coherent matrix. Wouldn't it be too painful to have a construct that looked like the real thing and sounded like the real thing, yet clearly isn't? I don't know about you, but if I'd lost someone and the only way I could interact with their memory was through a simulacrum in a classroom, I'd think twice before trusting it. Putting yourself through that kind of repeated stress won't be healthy."

She knew her idea was a long shot. Nevertheless, Jayden was crestfallen.

"So there's no hope?"

"It depends what you mean by hope." Penny invited her friend closer. "Look at this; it's why I took so long running the tests."

Penny flipped a switch, and a series of DNA strands appeared on the screen.

While she was a scientist, biochemistry was not Jayden's area of expertise. "What am I looking at?"

"*That* is a sample of Mac's bio matter."

Jayden was confounded. "How . . . ? This is not my field, remember, but even I can see some of those cells look active. How can that be? Mac's dead."

"I know, but fortunately Mac died only hours before the re-genesis protocol triggered. Remember, it was so powerful the template was able to filter down through rock and soil. It interpenetrated everything but the most secure bunkers around the planet, including the mortuary where Mac's remains were kept until they were put into hyper-stasis."

"So what are you saying?"

"What I'm saying is . . ." Penny tapped the screen, "somehow, the re-genesis spores revitalized a number of the samples, including Mac's as you can see. I've got our people checking out other specimens too, just in case it happened elsewhere."

Jayden was still confused.

Penny must have realized this, for she clarified her statement. "Jayden, we can use his essence to promote the heritage of our people."

"Promote?"

"From what I see here, there's enough viable material to improve the overall genetic variation we already hold in storage. Even though we can't bring him back, Mac's DNA could contribute to boosting our existing diversification coefficient."

"So, he'll live on through others?"

"Well, yes . . . though not in the way you wanted."

A storm of emotions knotted Jayden's stomach. Renewed loss and crushed hope combined with a poignant sense of inevitability.

Then something Penny just said tweaked a nerve.

"Penny, what did you mean when you said Mac's remains *could* contribute to Arden's future?"

"You're his next of kin. In a case like this, we'd need your permission to proceed."

That simple fact struck home.

Remembering the man Mac had been, Jayden didn't have to think twice.

"Do it. Although there are no more wars to fight, I'm sure we'll all benefit from his steel in the future."

Chapter Ten

A Hard Lesson

(Se'ochan Orbit)

The teams aboard the *Chariot of Spring* had followed the same pattern for three long, laborious days. Cabin by cabin, compartment by compartment, bulkhead by bulkhead, and deck by deck.

First, a squadron of cloaked drones examined each sector using passive sensors in an effort to pinpoint the stray energy signatures that betrayed the presence of lurking danger. If none were detected, Sam and his Special Forces unit completed a walkthrough, armed with more aggressive rotating tri-d optics and the very latest soft head tactical ammunition—STA—rounds. The new bullets had been designed for use against the Horde in pressurized environments, for while they would deform, even against something as fragile as flesh, they would still prove lethal to the rarified essence of an ogre.

If the area under scrutiny passed as safe, a more thorough search would commence in slow time; undertaken by combined squads of legionnaires and Caledonians. Equipped with pistols, shotguns, and iron sulfide dispensers, they sanitized every nook and cranny under the watchful eyes of Centurion Livius Fabius of the second cohort and clan leaders Cathal MacNoimhin and Searc Calhoun, whose job it was to make sure no unpleasant "surprises" snuck by undetected.

It had taken a grueling seventy-five hours to get where they were, but after a whole day's break, the search parties were about to enter the red zone around the primary core.

As Silver Commander for the operation, Sam Pell called everyone together in the maneuvering control center and brought up an active holographic representation of the rip-drive assembly.

"The final stage of our operation will be compounded by the fact that the quantum reactor is housed within the modular platform you see before you. It's situated across two of the four main engine decks, and has access points at *these* locations." He motioned with his finger and ten glowing red dots appeared. "Each is protected by a heavily armored, dogged hatchway. Even so, if the Horde gets frisky, they won't prove much of an obstacle. So this is our plan of action.

"On my order, Coralin will trigger the release bolts on all but two of those doorways, and the drones will deploy. A synchronized pair will maneuver inside, barring the exit, while an additional unit assumes a defensive position in the corridor outside." Sam turned to face Livius, Cathal, and Searc. Addressing them in particular, he continued, "These are your rules of engagement. You have all been instructed in the use of covert radios and small arms. After the flyers go in, your men will stand-to and provide additional support out in the main passageways. Basically, you are the cover teams. Nothing comes out of engineering unless it's with one or more of my specialists. If you see anything even remotely suspicious, safety is a priority. Don't ask for clarification, kill on sight. Is that clear?"

All three men indicated they understood.

"Good. Under no circumstances are you to enter the inner bulkhead. Here's why." Sam pressed his hands together, then swept them apart. The image in front of them expanded, to zoom in on the core. "This entire construct is housed within a series of rotating gravity collars, do you see? In turn, those collars are suspended within a vacuum sheath. The energies generated in the vicinity of the spacetime rent are phenomenal, and needless to say, lethal to those not wearing protective clothing. In the unlikely event that the shit does hit the fan, the Horde might cause a release of particles that will fry you where you stand. So leave them to us and to the flyers.

"Another reason we don't want you inside is because of the setrium-4. As you know, it's a radioactive substance, and although its lethal lifespan is only five or six minutes, it'll still fuck you if you expose yourself too soon. Once you have advised me that you are in position, Coralin will saturate the interior of the rip-space compartment with an atomized version of that isotope—effectively rendering our sleeping beauties comatose—and then she'll open the remaining pair of hatches for us. Special Forces will enter in tandem from opposite sides of the ship, into *these* compartments." Two areas marked *E-D2-C3* and *E-D2-C4* changed color from red to blue. "The seals will then reengage and our targets will effectively be contained and ready for retrieval."

"Not to be negative," Livius interrupted, "but I want to make sure we're all clear on something from the start so there's no argument. If the demons manage to gain the upper hand and you perish, I take it the rest of us are to evacuate immediately?"

"Yes. The flyers have been programmed to hold the enemy at bay while Coralin initiates an emergency transport. So make sure your people check their dermal trackers before we start. They'll be your lifeline in the event of a calamity. When, and if, you get safely away, the drones will activate their micro-singularity mines and self destruct, taking out both threat and ship."

Sam smiled as the other leaders made eye contact with each other.

And the penny drops as to how serious this situation is.

"But don't worry," he added, "Even the newest members of my team have drilled scenarios like this a hundred times. We can all do it in our sleep."

The centurion and highlanders didn't look convinced, but Sam didn't have time to reassure them further. He gestured toward his own men, indicating who they were.

"As a final reminder to you, Alpha team will be myself, Stu Duggan, Sean Masters, and Bob Neville. We will breach from the starboard side into compartment C3. Bravo team is Andy Webb, Fonzy Cunningham, Eddie Roberts, and our latest addition, Joe Stark. They will enter via C4 over on the port side. You might be wondering why I've pointed my guys out to you when you already know most of them. Well, that's simple. We have standard operating procedures for such incidents and are well used to them. You are not. This is the first time we've all worked together in such a restricted and dangerous environment, and I'm keen to ensure nobody gets confused. When you're listening in on the radio, Eddie and Joe, for example, will be much easier to understand than Bravo-three and Bravo-four. Yes?"

"Aha, so you won't be using your . . . what is it you say? Call signs?" Cathal verified. "You'll be using your given names instead?"

"That's right. When things heat up and the chatter starts to fly, our voices will sound distorted because of the covert system. Using our names will make things easier for you to follow, especially if there's gunfire and goodness knows what else going on in the background. Agreed?"

The trio nodded, leaving Sam free to concentrate on final instructions. He turned to address his operators.

"Okay, guys, we are the fire team. Because of limited space inside the compartment, and the extra hassle of the protective gear we'll be wearing, I've opted for a simplified weapons inventory. We'll be sticking to the short stock version of the G40s, with P230s as backup. Both will employ enhanced trigger guards due to the bulk of the Haz-Ent gloves."

Sam paused to part his hands again and the scene within the engine core enlarged, clarifying into pristine detail. Two huge power lines could be seen emerging from a spherical module filling the chamber's center. Each was the circumference of a main sewer and ran the length of the rest of the room. As they neared the far wall, they branched off into four further conduits and disappeared through an armored structural bulkhead.

"Basically, this scene is mirrored in the compartments below, but we are fortunate that our targets appear to have congregated in this single tight cluster . . ."

"Where," Andy interjected, "I can't see the usual distortion that distinguishes their presence."

"Tell me about it," Sam agreed. "Watch this."

He manipulated the holo-medium, and a series of additional filters were added to the image, rectifying the disparity.

"Wow!" Andy gasped. "That's worrying."

The rippling distortion could now be seen but it was extremely refined, as if the ogres had gone to great lengths to ensure they would remain hidden while hibernating.

"Coralin tells me the Horde have been here for hundreds of years, ever since the great exodus in fact. If I were to hazard a guess, I'd say they discovered this rare source of almost limitless food and wanted to keep it for themselves. It's common sense, really. Why go to all the hassle of pursuing insignificant snacks through repeated skirmishes when you've got all *this* on tap? And, of course, this explains why the core is almost drained."

Sam adjusted the view so they could look down on the chamber from above. One area pulsed with a soft amber radiance.

"*That's* the point where the power lines emerge, and it corresponds to the area around the top of the rip-space fracture. The other conduits I mentioned are situated adjacent to the bottom of the tear in the compartment below. Because of the energy required to open a hole in spacetime, the AI will usually only initiate the drive system when the engines are ready to engage. To prime them, it uses an extremely volatile uritium-lydium mix. Under normal circumstances, I'm told this setup would be sufficient to power the ship for close to five hundred years. But these crafty buggers have kept the fracture open. Just a crack, mind, but enough to allow all sorts of exotic particles to bleed through in a steady stream.

"And why am I telling you this?" Sam jutted his chin toward the illuminated beacon. "The highlighted area is one of the points within the manifold where the flux acquisitors extract the fires of hell. To reach our sleeping friends, we'll have to climb on top of the very things that amplify the magno-nucleic forces before transferring them on to main distributors."

Sam fixed those gathered before him with a knowing look.

"Gentlemen, I don't need to remind you what might happen inside such an environment if anything went wrong. That's why I want equipment and weapons prep in thirty minutes. We'll be going in wearing fully integrated, hazardous environmental containment suits with null-point shielding. And check your ammunition, every single round." He glanced toward the legionnaire and Caledonians. "Ensure all of them have the distinctive blue tip of an STA round. We wouldn't want anything getting ruptured."

Satisfied, Sam collapsed the holo-image.

"I'll meet you all back here in one hour. Dismissed."

*

Sam caught his reflection in the floor-to-ceiling glass partition separating the damage control booth from the rest of the engineering deck.

Dressed from head to toe in his active-response, dalenite-titanium mix, memory alloy Haz-Ent suit, he was secure within a self-contained, highly flexible world that would provide him with a tactical edge against extreme conditions. His Kevlar battle harness and bonded thermo-flex composite facemask with merged active tri-d target imaging only added to the intimidating effect, for it made him look like a futuristic ninja from a holo-vid action game.

Hmm. The protective layer makes me look even more badass than usual. Pity it won't scare the Horde into submission. Still . . . He patted the principal weapon clipped across his chest. *I'm not here to look pretty. And the hematite compound saturating the fabric of this getup should make me taste like shit if any of them get close enough to bite.*

About him, his troop completed their final preparations and gradually moved forward to the ready line, where they waited in silence.

As the last man joined them, Sam spoke to the AI mainframe.

"Coralin, please establish a link to the *Tarion Star*."

"One moment please . . ." responded a surprisingly warm feminine voice. "Channel is now open."

"Angela," Sam called, "are you there?"

Angela Brogan, one of the best pilots Rhomane possessed, was quick to reply. "Yes, I'm here, Sam. You'll be pleased to hear the cargo hold is prepped and the restraining harnesses are ready. We'll initialize the immobilization field when we know you're on the way."

"Great to hear. Please notify command we're about to go dark. No further communication will take place until our objective has been achieved or I call *you* with an update. Understood?"

"Loud and clear."

"Good luck to you. Now get to a safe distance, we'll see you on the other side."

The line went dead and Sam addressed the AI again.

"Coralin, send the signal. I want the drones to switch to combat mode and the cover teams to take up their static points now."

"Yes, Commander Pell." There was a pause, "Hatches are unlocked and flyers are deploying. My sensors indicate each detachment is currently assuming a prime tactical position along the passageways."

"Excellent. Stand by for further instructions."

Sam signaled to his assault squad.

"Okay, switch to internals and tie in with Coralin. Set your optics to rotating frequencies. Sonic motion trackers will be our primary, with infrared and ultraviolet as secondaries. Remember, until we retrieve the ogres, stealth is of the utmost importance. Try to take them alive if you can. Stu, Fonzy? Are the gravity nets ready?"

Both specialists hoisted a pair of strange, tubelike gadgets into the air. Similar to an expandable parabolic dish array mounted on a rotating ball socket, they appeared far too flimsy to do anything helpful, let alone restrain one of the most lethal forces in twisted nature. But Sam knew better, as he'd seen them in action back in Napal. Once enmeshed within the null-field, most beasts would be rendered incapable of independent locomotion.

"Are there any further questions?"

There were none.

Right, let's get this show on the road.

"Then move out."

Andy ushered his four-man team toward the port exit, and Sam led his through the opposite door. Emerging into the starboard passageway, Sam could see a combined group of legionnaires and highlanders fifty yards farther along, arranged in an arc around the final hatch. Within seconds of stepping out, the drone hovering above the circle of men began scanning his advance.

Excellent, everyone is where they should be and on the ball.

"Coralin, will you release the gas, please? Maximum density. Let me know when the room has been sanitized."

"Understood. Dispensing setrium-4 . . . now."

Sam glanced at his watch and ran through the timetable in his head.

Less than one minute to fill the chamber. Add on a few to snare our prizes. At least fifteen, maybe twenty more to get them down to the hangar. Then we can relax. The Tarion Star*'s security protocols are second to none. So we're looking at twenty-five to thirty minutes max. Perfect, that'll . . . Huh?*

As they approached their point of ingress, Sam was surprised to see Livius Fabius lurking among the picket.

"Livius? I didn't expect to see you here."

"I couldn't resist. The bane of every commander's life is to hang back and issue orders. I decided to change that. Despite countless engagements, I've never seen a Horde ogre up close and personal, but today I will, and I'll be milking it for all it's worth in the months to come." He pulled a comical face. "Believe it or not, Cathal feels the same way. He's over on the other side with one of those . . . cameras? He's determined to snap a few selfies for the communal wall in Rhomane. For some reason, he thinks getting *this* close to a demon and surviving to tell the tale will really annoy Marcus."

Behind him, the SBS cadre burst out laughing. Every one of them appreciated Livius's blunt honesty and sense of humor. And as military men, they instantly related to his need to be in amongst the action.

"Just stay sharp," Sam cautioned, "you should know by now we can't take anything for granted around these brutes, especially as we've never encountered this particular strain before. And whatever you do, don't —"

"Engine module has been saturated," Coralin said, "isotope density now exceeds toxic levels. Seven hundred rems and climbing."

"Thank you, Coralin," Sam replied. "Prepare to release deadbolts on my signal."

He turned back to Livius. "And whatever you do, don't try to peek inside. Remember, the gas is poisonous, so stand away from the hatch until any leakage has dissipated, and then wait a further thirty seconds before you resume your position. The drone will help if you're unsure."

"It will be done," Livius assured him. "And don't worry. We know our role. Just concentrate on what *you* have to do."

Fair enough.

Sam shuffled to one side and meshed his integrated tactical channel so everyone could listen in on the Special Forces circuit.

"Okay, Alpha, Bravo, we're about to go live. Activate your stealth systems."

Sam found it eerie, watching his troop of heavily armed killers fade from sight in front of him. His tri-d imager kicked in and they reappeared, rippling in multicolored sibylline splendor as the system cycled through its program. Sam ensured his optical enhancements were operating properly and then prepared for the breach.

Stu Duggan pressed himself to Sam's shoulder. Opposite them, Sean and Bob tensed, ready to spring.

"Andy, do you copy?"

"Loud and clear, Boss. We're waiting for your signal."

"Excellent. Good hunting, everybody. Stand by, stand by."

Sam unclipped his G40 and clicked the safety catch to full automatic. Then he called to the AI: "Coralin? Free the locks in . . . five, four, three, two, one . . . *Now*!"

A muffled thud echoed along the bulkhead.

Pfffft!

The seal in front of him cracked open, venting a fine, creamy mist into the hall. Before the door stopped moving, Sam slipped his fingers behind the heavy metal plating and heaved.

"Go, go, *go*."

Sean and Bob leaped across the intervening gap. Side by side, weapons to the shoulder, they cleared the fatal funnel and disappeared inside, scanning their arcs, alert for danger. Like shadowing guardian angels, two of the drones from the corridor entered with them.

Hot on their heels, Sam and Stu stormed forward.

Sam's breath sounded harsh within the muffled confines of his respirator. Regardless, the clang of the hatch slamming shut behind them rang out like a death knell.

Jesus! Bloody idiots!

A flare of alarm jolted him from head to foot and his gaze automatically sprang to the top of the power lines. There, an opaque cloud of energized particles sparked and flared at irregular intervals, giving scant indication of the peril within.

Muzzles trained, everyone froze and waited to see what would happen.

"Who's the fuckwit?" Andy snarled from the other side of the room.

"Someone who will never work with us again, believe me," Sam snapped. "Thankfully, the noise doesn't appear to have disturbed our slumbering friends. But let's not take any chances."

"Agreed. How do you want to proceed now we have eyes-on?"

At more than six feet tall, the ribbed exterior of the main transfer conduits presented a major obstacle. Fortunately, a set of steps had been incorporated along the outer casing at two points along their length. Also, the apex of the shielding appeared flat, like the top of an aircraft hangar.

Sam assessed the situation and considered his options. He had a moment's inspiration.

"Andy, can you see rungs cut into the side of the acquisitors over there?"

"That's a yes, yes. We've got them in a couple of places, why?"

"We're going to simplify matters. From the size of the cocoon, I'd say we're looking at seven, maybe eight hostiles at most. One emitter could handle this; we've got two. We'll use both at the same time until we've got the Horde away from the core. Then, instead of splitting our catch into two groups as originally planned, we'll stick together—maintain safety in numbers. Quick as you can, get your boys on top of the mounting and remain there while Fonzy fires up his emitter. Stu will support him from over here. Once we've landed our catch, come and join us. We'll remain together and vacate, en masse, through the starboard hatch."

"Nice one, Boss. We're on our way."

Turning to Alpha team, Sam signaled they should take a knee. While they waited for their compatriots to clamber across, he seized the opportunity to study the mesmerizing distortion in front of him. A memory from the year before flashed to mind, when he had encountered the Horde in a dormant state for the first time within the confines of the underpass at Rhomane Starport.

On that occasion, hundreds of monstrous apparitions had been massed together, creating a huge rippling curtain without defined parameters. The mere fact they had been reduced to a comatose state had caused many among the colony to dream, resulting in sporadic outbursts of electrified desire which etched the outline of individual ogres in lurid, scarlet clarity.

But this was different. Regardless of the fact that the entities within the envelopment were obviously hibernating, very little evidence of their presence escaped, no more than a slight shiver in the ether roundabout. Even then, it was only because of the additional filters incorporated into the tri-d imagers that Sam could tell anything was there.

Hmm. Their barrier is extremely refined. It's almost as if

—

His train of thought stopped when heads appeared over the top of the power coupling. By the resolution of his optical array, each definitized into the spectral silhouette of a heavily armed soldier. One of them waved, and Andy's voice announced, "Hi, Boss. I'll get Fonzy right on it."

The outline atop the conduit gestured, and another wraith detached itself from the group to edge toward their sleeping prey.

"Stu," Sam called, "support him. Get your net deployed *a*-sap."

"Roger that."

Stu Duggan ran forward to take up position. As he pointed his emitter upward, the atmosphere before him erupted into a baffling fusion of intangible shadows and phosphorescent light.

The arcane shell surrounding their targets blazed in reply.

Eh? That doesn't look right.

"Coralin, what setrium readings are you seeing within this compartment?"

"Isotope levels are holding steady at seven hundred and twenty-three rems," she replied. "Twice the density sufficient to reduce the Horde to a stupor."

Sam backed away, his head to the scope of his weapon. Seeing his reaction, Sean and Bob followed suit.

A telltale reverberation thrummed in the air. The gravity well coalesced around the elusive bubble above them. The sheath thinned, and eruptions like solar flares arched out.

"Heads up, guys," Sam called out, "we've got movement in the cocoon. Someone inside doesn't like what we're doing."

"Movement?" Andy spluttered. "At this level? But that should be—"

Boom!

His outburst was lost in an explosive retort.

A shockwave pulsed across the compartment, throwing everyone to the floor. Silence followed.

Blinking his eyes clear, Sam regained his feet, amazed to see a quartet of flaming effigies leaping away from the coalescing net. Three he recognized instantly. At more than twelve feet in height, they presented an amalgamation of barely restrained power and fury condensed into a supercharged mass of hate. Crimson eyes glowered from cruel, buttresslike features, and cogent flames danced around their heads. They brandished huge fangs and talons at his men, chomping and clacking with the promise of violence to come.

Instantly lucid and focused, each monster sparked with barely suppressed rage. So virulent were the emanations that Sam could taste their malevolence splashing over him like acid.

But as terrifying as these apparitions were, the final beast to join the fray took his breath away:

Encompassed within a corona of gold and silver light, its fourteen-foot bulk was crowned by a dazzling vortex of stars, perhaps eight or nine. Their precise number was hard to tell, for they orbited faster and faster, becoming a blur which transformed into a scintillating halo. Clamorous radiance overflowed its coronet and cascaded down through the demon's aura, a sizzling infusion of might and majesty that became a permanent state of flux.

What the fuck is that*?*

"We have Horde Masters," Sam yelled. "Open fi–"

His words were drowned by an ear-splitting fusillade as hundreds of rounds per second swarmed the room. Their percussive serenade added a low-pitched counterpoint to the tympani of empty casings tinkling to the floor. The soldiers formed an arc and backed steadily away toward the door.

Sam wasn't surprised to see their assault thwarted by a well-constructed shield. Without breaking eye contact, he calmly unhooked a micro-gravity mine from his harness and flipped back the cap.

"Coralin," he yelled, "get ready to pop the hatch, and tell the *Tarion Star* to prepare for evac." Without pausing for breath, he continued: "Stu, Fonzy, kindly stop farting about and get those fuckers restrained. Quickly, before they get a chance to—"

Too late.

The largest beast jumped from the top of the coupling frame, and the entire deck shook from the weight of its landing. Flashes sparked about its aura where a thousand ricochets bounced harmlessly from its defenses. In one fluid motion, the Boss stepped forward and backhanded Stu away as if he were nothing more than a bothersome gnat.

Stu somersaulted through the air and slammed into Sam and Bob. They went down in a heap, and the incendiary was knocked from Sam's grasp.

Bugger!

"Grenade!" he bellowed. "Get out, get out, get out. Cora*liiin* . . . The door, now!"

Training kicked in. As the AI triggered the locks, the drones opened up with their heavy caliber cannons, and everyone made a break for safety.

All except one.

As Sam rolled for the exit, he caught a glimpse of Sean scrabbling toward the discarded mine.

Oh no!

The giveaway tingle of a transporter lock skittered across Sam's skin . . .

A concatenation of things happened all at once:

The deck appeared to sag as if suddenly too heavy to bear its own weight. A hidden wind sprang up from nowhere. Sean screamed and contorted into a hideously deformed shape. A dark mass appeared in the center of his body. That mass abruptly yanked the ogres off balance. Each ogre was dragged, kicking and roaring, toward the growing void hungry to engulf them. Armored wall panels tore free of their mounts as they too succumbed to an irresistible tide.

Shit! The quantum shielding is giving way.

The strength of the gale increased, and Sam witnessed a growing nimbus of light blooming to life in the middle of the mob.

Sean's heartrending complaint died as the reinforced bulkhead surrounding the magno-nucleic core ruptured. A maelstrom of conflicting energies spiraled forth, and a terrible grinding noise reverberated through the ship.

As the scene began to fade, a shockwave of searing light and heat blasted out, plucking Sam from his haven and throwing him through the air once more.

Pain exploded along his right side, and men screamed.

Sam felt himself plunging into oblivion. He braced for the impact.

It never came.

Chapter Eleven

Decisions, Decisions

To say Stained-With-Blood was perturbed was an understatement. In all his fifty-six summers, this had never happened to him before:

One moment he was standing before the full-length mirror in his bedroom, preparing for the concluding formalities of the marriage between Snow Blizzard and Inuck-Shen and the next, the room about him dissolved into a thick gray brume. He felt himself shifting through a formless void.

The odd sensation included no perception of falling or any actual movement; but instead a sense of *realization*. Only due to his prior experiences did Stained-With-Blood know what was happening.

A waking dream without the proper meditation? But how?

As much as his current predicament alarmed him, he was more concerned as to why it was happening.

Maturity won the day. Stained-With-Blood made a conscious effort to relax and allow the vision's natural flow to claim him.

Events will clarify in Napioa's own good time.

Soon, Stained-With-Blood found himself perched upon a promontory near the gaping edge of what appeared to be a huge chunk of land floating in space. A squadron of suns jostled together, bathing the panoramic vista in dappled hues of shifting radiance.

As he peered about, memories of long ago crowded to the fore.

The formation of these rocks is familiar. He spun on the spot. *As are the fir trees and the path of the tributary down there . . .*

Realization struck him.

Eagles Aerie, high on the eastern peaks of the Bitterroot Mountains back on Earth! I used to hunt them as a boy.

He took a deep breath. Gelid air filled his lungs with the tang of pine, and a surge of static energy coursed through his veins. Stained-With-Blood longed to run down the hillside and into the meadow below, where the clearing hosted game ripe for the taking. Reluctantly, he decided against it.

The Creator put me here for a reason, and here I'll stay.

He contented himself by watching the river run its course. Fast flowing and crystal clear, its surface caught the suns and refracted their light into a million blades of glittering fire.

Stained-With-Blood smiled. Not only was this creek familiar to him, but he had fished it many times in his youth. The sparkling waters held his attention. He followed the current with his eye as it flowed toward the precipice, spewing over the edge with more than natural vigor. A majestic plume of gold and silver flames tumbled into the void, adding luster to the stars above and imbuing him with an immense feeling of peace.

He glanced back to learn that he was no longer alone. An aged warrior sat cross-legged on a flat-lipped rock bordering a small pool. Even with the elder's back turned, Stained-With-Blood could see his proud posture and powerful muscling. As was customary, his long dark hair was tied back and dignified by long streaks of gray.

That was quick. Napioa must have something urgent to tell me.

Rod in hand, the Creator remained as still as stone, waiting for something to bite.

The pole bucked and strong arms flexed.

With consummate ease, Napioa flicked his catch back over his shoulder, and a fat juicy prize flopped onto the slab behind him. Only then did Stained-With-Blood realize the deity had been busy, for an assortment of brown, cutthroat, and rainbow trout lay in a heap, gasping for breath in the heat of the midday suns.

Napioa caught sight of his guest and beckoned him.

Relieved by the invitation, Stained-With-Blood skipped down the rocks. As he approached, he watched with interest as the Creator produced a blade and started gutting fish. Everything Napioa did was purposeful, and Stained-With-Blood suspected today's instruction had already commenced.

The Old Man began humming, and one of the Cree's oldest mantras reached Strained-With-Blood's ears. The melody rose and fell in time with Napioa's ministrations, and by its cadence the earthly shaman felt himself linked to the very heartbeat of the universe.

Taking care to keep the internal organs of each fish intact, Napioa removed and then strung out their entrails until hearts, kidneys, livers, and sinews were stretched into ultra-thin cords of suppressed vitality. Bringing his fingers together, the Creator wove those tissues into the fabric of the suns hovering nearby.

Completing his work, he stood back and clapped his hands twice. The cosmic web blazed brightly and expanded away from them in a mad rush. Each new strand pulled taut, heaving its own particular luminary behind it. Soon, the celestial dome was frosted with fresh light.

Napioa studied his work. He must have been satisfied for he waved, and the heavens whirled above. He signaled again, harder this time, and the expanse responded by wheeling faster.

He is demonstrating the passage of time. But to what purpose?

As if hearing the brave's thoughts, Napioa held up his fist.

The firmament froze, caught in a moment between now and then. He pointed toward a large red star. It moved closer and bathed the scene in rose-gold glory.

That must be Soleíl, Arden's sun.

The blazing behemoth continued advancing, and certain details about its composition lifted into sharper definition.

Stained-With-Blood noticed that the solar disc no longer described a perfect circle. A considerable bulge had formed in Soleíl's lower right quadrant. From it, vaporous trails of charged particles spiraled away. Condensing, these gravitated inward to become an effervescent ring of energy, a blazing blue-white corona surrounded by a pit of impenetrable darkness.

Something eats away at the sun's spirit? So small, so insignificant . . .

A coherent beam of plasma erupted from the exact center of the well. Streaming off into space, the discharge morphed into a crystallized bridge of solid ice. Soleíl shrank and dimmed, at last winking out of existence, totally consumed by the growing void.

So powerful if left unchallenged.

"Do you understand?" Napioa said. "Observe."

By now, the glittering viaduct had elongated and stretched away into the star-studded expanse. Transfixed, Stained-With-Blood could only stare open-mouthed as the ravenous maw skipped up onto the span and sped off along its length. Soon, it was lost from sight. However, he was able to track its progress, for wherever the black hole passed, the surrounding radiance of the empyrean vault dimmed.

"Do you understand?" Napioa asked once more. The Creator's eyes blazed brightly.

Before Stained-With-Blood could reply, he felt himself falling through the ethereal planes back toward a more mundane existence.

Reality solidified about him. Stained-With-Blood blinked, and found himself exactly where he'd been before this adventure began.

A threat imperils our future, one that will eat away at all life until there is nothing left. Then it will look elsewhere for sustenance. But where could—

A knock at his door interrupted his thought.

"Enter."

Snow Blizzard barged in. Resplendent in sun-bleached buckskin trousers and jacket adorned with tribal motifs, and wearing a formal headdress bedecked in elaborate feathers, he looked every inch the proud husband-to-be.

Nonetheless, Snow Blizzard looked irritated.

"Stained-With-Blood," he snapped, "ask me to endure the harshest winters, hunt a starving mountain lion with my bare hands, or stand naked in the frozen rivers of high Kalispell, and I would do so without complaint . . ."

He brandished a set of Hair Pipe ties in his hands.

"But tell me to decorate my braids with these accursed bits of sinew? I'd rather face an army of white men armed only with one blade of grass."

Despite his recent shock, Stained-With-Blood smiled.

Ah, the rigors of life for the young . . . and soon to be wed. Such urgency needs to be tempered and refocused on a more productive course.

"Come," he responded, "stand before the reflective glass and I will knot them for you. Pay attention, for someday you may perform these rites for your own sons."

Snow Blizzard's chest puffed out with pride at the mere mention of his family-to-be in years ahead. Such words, uttered by a tribal witchdoctor, constituted a good omen.

Then he caught the look on Stained-With-Blood's face. "What's wrong?"

No need to spoil the occasion with my suspicions. Not until I'm sure, at any rate.

"Nothing," Stained-With-Blood replied. "I wonder how many people from the Blackfoot would have loved to witness this day." He shrugged. "Still, life must go on. We adapt, we survive."

He lifted the Hair Pipe ties and fixed the younger man with a stern look. "As I plait your hair, I will instruct you in the duties expected of a new husband on your first night. You will be required to . . ."

*

From his position in the corridor outside, Jake Rixton could see the control center was a hive of activity. While many sat at desks, absorbed by the information displayed on their monitors, others buzzed hither and thither like worker bees. Most of the command staff, however, huddled together in small groups, deep in discussion.

Yesterday's disaster had hit everyone hard, and Jake was sure the ranking officers would be scrutinizing every facet of the operation to ensure such a debacle would never happen again.

But as much as Jake sympathized, he had worries of his own.

He caught sight of Marcus, Mohammed, and Deputy Magister Shaní together on the far side of the room near the coffee machine, and took advantage of the unexpected opportunity. Sidling inside, he skirted the outer workstations and worked his way toward his target. As he drew near, he overheard the senator enthusing about something:

". . . really is a delightful beverage, thank goodness the seeds thrive here on Arden. Our kocha is very similar, but nowhere near as flavorsome."

"I wish I could take the credit for its inclusion," Mohammed replied, "but I can't. That honor's due to the crew of the supply freighter *Fourth of July*. On the day they were snatched, they were on a resupply run to one of Earth's nearest colonies, Mars. That's a smaller planet within our solar system—"

"Yes, I've been reading about your home world and its environs," Shaní said. "But do go on. How did their mishap contribute to our good fortune?"

"They carried a large stock of what we call Robusta coffee plants, to see if they'd thrive in an alien environment. Quite a few prize specimens survived the transfer, along with the seeds, so someone thought it might be a good idea to transplant them here, in an extension of the original plan." He lifted his mug in a toast. "Robusta is twice as strong as the most common form of coffee bean of Earth, Arabica. Needless to say, we've been addicted ever since."

They all took sips.

"It somehow sets your eyeballs on fire, doesn't it?" Marcus said. "Just before it sends your head spinning."

Pleasure creased Shaní's face into a warm smile.

"Yes," she responded, "many of my fellow senators have expressed their amusement regarding the kick this drink seems to poss . . . Hello?" Shaní noticed Jake hovering nearby. "My apologies. Lieutenant Rixton isn't it? Can we assist you?"

"I appreciate everyone is busy," Jake began, "but I need to steal Marcus for a minute or so."

Mohammed glanced between the two men. When it was obvious Jake wouldn't elaborate further in present company, he nodded and clasped Marcus by the shoulder. "We'll see you back at the primary command desk. Don't be long." Then, arm in arm, he steered the Deputy Magister away.

As they left, Jake could hear the continuing conversation regarding the health benefits of Rhomane's favorite tipple.

"I'm sorry to intrude," he said. "But have you heard any updates?"

Marcus didn't immediately reply. Instead, selecting an empty beaker, he filled it with steaming-hot dark liquid from the dispenser and handed it to Jake. "There you go. You look as if you could do with a shot of kick-ass."

Raising the cup, Jake inhaled deeply. A nutty, bittersweet fragrance triggered his taste buds, and he took a little swig to avoid burning his lips. *Phew! That's hot.* As invigorating as the coffee was, he wouldn't be sidetracked. "So, Marcus, *do* you have anything for me?"

"Nothing at all, I'm afraid."

"Nothing! But there are over forty missing, and it's been more than a week now . . ." To Jake's eyes, Marcus appeared more frustrated than embarrassed. "Did you at least manage to retrace their steps?"

"Not until we thought to start a new search pattern, starting back at the clearing where the *Promulus* picked up Atticus's body five days ago."

"You had to go that far? Why?"

"Because I don't like coming up empty-handed." Marcus frowned. "I had Flavius and the drones comb the area of the Sengennon Strait until they were well past the Trident. Then they turned south, patrolled past the Caglioso massif and on to the Trechlan Gap. They got as far as the northern fringes of the Tar'e-esh before I recalled them. We needed to change tactics."

"What did you do instead?"

"I arranged for a linked squadron of nine flyers to go out under the command of one of the Architect's control sentinels. They formed a mobile grid twenty miles square and retraced Flavius's steps. We'd tweaked their emitters too, in case. Not only were they scanning for life signs, but also for unaccounted chemical and mineral concentrations—you know, anything that might betray the presence of a corpse. When we still didn't find any bodies, I ordered them to start over from the last location at which we were sure Houston and everyone else was still alive."

That caught Jake's attention. "So you think we're looking at fatalities?"

"I don't know how else to account for what we found . . . or in this case, *haven't* found." Marcus waved his hands. "Even when I had the search drones ascend to a thousand feet to extend their range, they still came up empty. We picked up birds, wildlife, game, and all manner of reptiles and lizards . . . without a hitch. But of Houston and his party? No trace. After a mile or so, their spoor simply vanishes. That's part of the reason I recalled the flight. We weren't making progress; and after the *Chariot of Spring* exploded, well, we had to divert our assets elsewhere."

Jake was about to curse when Marcus added: "By the way. You mentioned last week that you gave young Wilson an additional radio. Did he ever use it?"

Bloody hell, I'd forgotten about that!

"Yes, he did use it. And I can tell you precisely where from, too. Hang on . . ." Jake fished in his back pocket and dug out a battered notebook. After rifling through it, he located the desired page and traced his finger along the listings. "I make a point of recording all important incidents during my patrols. Aha! Here it is. Wilson contacted me at dawn, the very next day. As you can see, I noted the grid reference of his transmission. The display screen showed him calling from thirty-five uniform, seventy-six thirty-two by fifty-five forty-nine local."

Marcus's eyes narrowed. "Come with me."

He ushered Jake across to one of the nearest control stations. The young woman at the desk smiled warmly as they approached.

"Janet," Marcus asked, "would you be so kind as to show us the following location?" Jake held out his notebook and Marcus read off the numbers.

An overview of the northern zone of the Tar'e-esh Forest appeared, and they had their answer.

"Isn't that counter to their proposed route?" Marcus queried, clearly perplexed by the apparent discrepancy between Houston's stated and apparent course of action. "They're too far east."

The inevitable realization struck home. "Not unless it was all a bluff," Jake snapped.

"What?"

"Haven't you read my report? Everything changed after Houston's patrol encountered the open bunker near Quirian Hill. They were different somehow—withdrawn. Consumed by a weird compulsion that made all of them act . . . creepy. We'd come across military installations before on our patrols, but they were locked up tighter than a maiden's virtue. For whatever reason, I'm betting Houston and his cronies wanted to get their asses back there. It might explain why they haven't registered on scans. Think about it, where else are they gonna find a secure location?"

"But why would they want to evade us?"

"*That* is the million dollar question."

Marcus looked determined. "Jake, I'd like to assist you by allocating resources to scour that area, but my hands are tied. Virtually the entire drone fleet has been commandeered for low orbit patrols of Arden. They're working in tandem with the Global Sat Web and Se'ochan's extended grid in a detailed search of local space. I hope you understand: we need to make sure nothing survived the *Chariot of Spring*'s destruction. It's taking longer than anticipated, as we were forced to adjust our parameters based on the readings Coralin was able to capture in those final moments. The nature of the Horde Masters was altered in some way. They were more resilient and vigorous than previously. That's why everyone was called in. Until we have a clearer picture of what we're dealing with, we must confirm that every one of those bastards was obliterated."

As a military veteran, Jake understood Marcus's position. "So I'm stuck swatting flies for a while."

"I'm sorry, but yes."

Jake sighed.

And by then, whatever has infected the guys will probably have gotten every one of them killed, especially if Houston is cooking up some harebrained scheme to take advantage of the situation.

Mohammed's voice thundered across the din of the operations center.

"Sub-Commander Brutus, please seal the control room and ensure all nonessential personnel are escorted from the chamber. Once you've done that, get over here. I'd like your opinion on something."

Marcus waved and turned to Jake.

"Look, I've got to go. If you can think of anything that might save time when all this is over, let me know. Until then, make your own way out, and stay sharp."

Of course!

Jake caught Marcus by the arm.

"Actually, there is one last thing."

"Go on?"

"I know I haven't learned a lot of the technical stuff like you have, but has anyone thought to . . . what's the term . . . 'squawk' Wilson's radio?"

"Squawk his radio?"

"That's right. Don't they carry those little chip things inside, like a minicomputer? If the card itself wasn't destroyed and the device is still active, wouldn't we be able to broadcast an emergency code to find out where the transmitter has been discarded? And even better, if Wilson is still carrying the damned thing . . ."

"We'll find them," Marcus cut in, completing his friend's sentence. "Oh, nicely played."

Both men grinned.

Marcus enveloped Jake in a bear hug before frog-marching him through the crowd.

"You've got to repeat what you just suggested to Mohammed and Shaní. Despite the current panic, she'll love the idea. And I have a feeling he'll be keen to please her."

"So?"

In reply to Jake's puzzled expression, Marcus added, "Let's just say, you might get a dedicated flyer much sooner than I originally anticipated."

Feeling happier than he had in a long time, Jake allowed himself to be pushed across the room until he was immediately behind the Vice-Commander and Deputy Magister.

Those two were engrossed by the digital readout of a celestial chart portraying the outer regions of the Ardenese system. From what Jake could see, the graphic was divided into glowing banded zones. A bright red light blinked on and off near the edge of the screen.

"What's all the fuss about?" Marcus enquired across Jake's shoulder.

"This bugger appeared out of nowhere less than a minute ago," Mohammed replied without turning around. "It eluded every deep space sentinel and covert scanner in the region, and then, ta-dah, revealed itself in high orbit around Ladesha."

Although he was no electronics buff, Jake had a good memory.

That's the last uninhabited world in this solar system. So why would . . . ?

As he watched, a ruby sensor echo flared, and accelerated quickly away from the planet.

"Where's it heading?" Marcus asked.

"Where else?" Mohammed quipped. "The damned thing is coming straight for us."

Chapter Twelve

Just What the Doctor Ordered

With mounting exasperation, Doctor Pat Frost waded her way through the ever-growing catalog of casualties before her.

Good grief, another one has died. That makes forty-two now.

Scrutinizing the specifics of the remaining injuries darkened her mood further.

And with that degree of trauma the list of fatalities is going to increase, no doubt about it.

Pat pushed away from the monitor and leaned back to massage her temples.

Our largest single catastrophe since the war ended. And it happened on my watch. She shook her head in frustration. *Not good enough!*

"Doctor Frost, he's awake."

Pat jumped. So absorbed was she in her personal world of woe she hadn't realized Adam West, her chief nursing practitioner, had entered the office.

"I'm sorry, what?"

"He's awake, and we're having trouble keeping him restrained. You'd better come."

She knew immediately who Adam was referring to: Sam Pell.

"C'mon, let's get this sorted before he starts wrecking the place."

Snatching her ever-present info-pad from the desk, Pat followed Adam into the main wing. For the first time since the great conflict with the Horde had ended, the beds lining the walls on either side of the ward were full. A host of part-time nurses and doctors swelled the ranks of her staff. Scurrying from one patient to another, they treated injuries and symptoms Pat had hoped never to see again. Despite the circumstances, she was proud of her team.

They're certainly earning their keep. Thank goodness I insisted on extending the auxiliary medical program, otherwise we'd be swamped.

She entered a side corridor and stopped outside the door to a private room. The sound of raised voices came from within.

She turned to Adam. "Wait outside. We don't want to aggravate him further. I'll call if I need you."

"If you're sure?"

"Oh, I am. There's only one way to deal with these soldier types, and this is it . . ."

Removing a hypo-spray from one of her pockets, she entered without knocking. Covered in burns, Sam Pell was propped bolt upright in his bed. In spite of the drips and steri-bands attached to various parts of his body, he was doing a magnificent job of holding off the pair of nurses trying to change one of his dressings.

". . . give a shit what you want to give me. I need to know the condition of my men, and where they're being kept. If you people don't back off, I'm gonna start getting—"

"Enough!" Pat growled. She brandished the tranquilizer, looking Sam straight in the eye. "If you don't start behaving, *this* is the only thing you'll be getting. There's enough sedative in here to put you out for a week. Now calm down."

"I am calm," Sam replied through gritted teeth. "I'm *focused* on the fact that nobody will answer my questions."

"Then I'll be glad to help, *after* you let Sarah and Reggie change your bandages."

She held his gaze, and to reinforce the fact she wasn't kidding, waggled the hypo-spray.

"You can't blame me for doing my job." Sam moaned. "I'm responsible for them."

"And these people are responsible for your care. Relax, let them help you, and then I'll answer all your questions. Agreed?"

"Agreed." Sam flopped back onto his pillow. "Just get on with it."

Pat waited while her staff went about their business, cool yet professional. They were accustomed to difficult clients, and wouldn't take Sam's outbursts to heart.

She watched the patient himself. Although his injuries were obviously causing him discomfort, Sam put up with their ministrations in silence, staring at the ceiling throughout.

Less than five minutes later, his ordeal was over. As the nurses filed from the room, Pat motioned for Adam to leave as well, before shutting the door quietly behind him.

"I didn't mean to upset your staff," Sam said, "it's just that I have to know how the guys are. What a frigging mess. The last thing I remember is flying through the air. I felt as if a part of me was on fire . . ." he raised his arm and examined his blisters, as if seeing them for the first time, "and then everything turned into a slow-motion dance of whirling stars and blackness. What happened afterward?"

He looked up, and Pat saw horror in his eyes. She took a seat next to the bed and, although she tried to hide it, her face betrayed her emotions.

The battle-tested veteran faltered. "Ah, shit! That bad, eh?"

She decided straight talking was best. "Well, what did you expect would happen, Sam? A bloody great explosion next to the main engine core caused a containment breach. 'State of the art safety bulkheads' or no, the resultant catastrophic cascade ripped its way through the *Chariot's* entire fabric in less than ten seconds. We saw the light bloom from down here in Rhomane."

"How many?"

"We have close to ninety casualties. At last count, forty-two of those are dead. A dozen more are critical, and the rest have less threatening injuries."

"Jesus Christ! We only had a hundred and eight soldiers to begin with. Talk about a nightmare."

"It could have been worse." Pat reached out to gently squeeze Sam's uninjured hand. "Mohammed and his team have been picking through the recordings with a fine-tooth comb. There's lots of evidence, believe me. It's clear to everyone that had you not acted so promptly and issued a warning when you did, not only would everyone aboard the *Chariot of Spring* have been lost, but her demise would have taken out the *Tarion Star* as well. Considering the circumstances, you did well."

Sam scoffed.

"You might not think so at the moment, but it's true," Pat said. "My department is full of people who wouldn't be here if not for the sacrifice of your men."

As soon as she said it, Pat grimaced.

Nor was Sam shy in accepting the invitation she had unintentionally extended.

"Sacrifice, you say?" His eyes narrowed. "How *are* my guys?"

Pat remained silent, so Sam kept talking: "Don't be gentle. I watched Sean get crushed out of existence, so I know we didn't all survive. Who else got snuffed?"

"Nobody . . . yet."

"Yet?"

"The dalenite-titanium compound of your Haz-Ent suits really did its job, protecting most of you from the radiation burns and vacuum exposure that afflicted so many others. But I . . . I don't . . ."

"But you don't what?"

"I'm so sorry. Fonzy was closer to the rip-space drive frame when it ruptured than anyone else. We don't know if he'll make it."

Sam sighed deeply, and Pat could see him struggling to digest the pain of such unpleasant information. Nevertheless, he pressed grimly ahead:

"And what about the others? Those poor sods who didn't have protective armor like us? What happened to Cathal, Searc, Livius, and all their men?"

As the hardened warrior deflated in front of her, Pat felt a surge of overwhelming pity crest her defenses and fought to contain tears threatening to spill. Only with the greatest difficulty could she was respond:

"Coralin was able to pluck the survivors away seconds after your warning. However, along the outer starboard section of the ship where you were, everyone died. I haven't been told the full circumstances, but I understand the rupture blew out all the hatches on that side of the *Chariot of Spring*, turning them into lethal chunks of shrapnel. Livius was decapitated before he knew what was happening. As for the rest, they succumbed to the blaze that ensued."

"Cathal and Searc?"

"Searc is fine. He was down in the cargo area, leading the party that would have secured the Horde captives before transfer to the *Tarion Star*, he and his were protected. They were all teleported off without incident. But as for Cathal . . ."

"Just say it."

"Remember, he was on the opposite side of your compartment. While the armored doors there remained in their frames, their seals were breached. Sad to say, everyone standing outside at the time of the explosion was fried by a burst of highly energetic magno-nucleic particles."

"Oh, for fuck's sake, is there *no* end to the bad news?"

"Of course there is," Pat countered. "Many survived, and most of them are out there receiving treatment as we speak. They're sedated due to the nature of their injuries but, like you, they'll be waking up soon. When they do, go and ask *them* what they think of your efforts. If you can't wait that long, put a vidi-call through to Angela Brogan and her crew. Your warning gave her enough time to maneuver away from the *Chariot*, so she was able to save her ship. I'm sure—"

"Hang on," Sam said, "are you saying I'm the first survivor to retain full consciousness?"

"Yes, that's right. Why?"

"Pat, me and the guys are the only ones to have eyes-on testimony regarding the new Horde Masters. They're different to what we've encountered before: bigger, stronger. I dunno, I got the impression they're somehow smarter, too. You've got to get someone from command down here to go through the intel with me. Have we scoured the environs of the explosion? Have we confirmed they were all swallowed by the gravity mine? For good–"

"Citizens of Rhomane. Stand by, stand by for a safety announcement."

The Architect's voice cut Sam dead.

To Pat, it sounded as if she was listening to a recording, one she'd never heard before, for it was in pure Ardenese. Thanks to the nano-flecks saturating her system, however, she fully understood the booming voice:

"Citizens of Rhomane, a possible threat to public safety has been detected on long-range scanners. Please do not panic. The city will enter lockdown mode in T minus ten minutes. I say again, the city will enter lockdown mode in T minus ten minutes. Power reserves are at full capacity, and you shall suffer no loss of services. Primary shields and defense systems will be activated shortly thereafter. All command officers and members of the Senatum, go to your designated posts. Emergency response personnel, report to your departments immediately. Citizens are advised to return to their homes if possible. Any family members outside the city's environs are being advised of the threat via their sub-dermal chips. Do not be overly concerned. Drones are being dispatched to assist those who need transport."

Concealed backlight strips along the outer walls illuminated, burnishing everything with a warm amber radiance.

Doctor and patient stared at each other, too surprised to speak or move.

The message repeated: "Citizens of Rhomane, a possible threat to public safety has been detected. Please do not panic. The city will go into lockdown mode in T minus nine minutes . . ."

"Were you aware of this system?" Sam snorted, unnerved in his vulnerable situation. "Because I wasn't. And as the black ops commander, I should know everything pertinent to our security."

Pat shook her head. "I didn't have a clue. Look, I'd better get back to my office and see what's happening. I'll bet you a steak dinner this new alarm is connected to the emergence of our friends from stasis. It makes me wonder what other protocols they have up their sleeves that they haven't told us about yet."

She headed for the door.

"Don't forget my intel," Sam shouted, "whatever the bloody hell else is happening, Saul and Mohammed still need to know what we saw."

"You can tell them yourself," Pat called back. "I'll have Adam bring you an info-pad. Once you've logged in, your clearance should grant you access to the mainframe despite all the hoo-ha."

With that, Pat bustled from the room and disappeared into the main ward. As she rushed toward her office, she saw a series of lydium panels rolling silently down from the ceiling. Surprised, she stopped to watch.

Another little gem we didn't know about? Not that I mind; in a few minutes the entire hospital wing will be inside an impregnable shield. I couldn't have prescribed a better remedy myself.

*

Battered and bruised, Wilson Smith forced his way into the interior of a thorn-laden thicket and collapsed, exhausted by his exertions. He seized this rare moment to ease the pounding in his chest and take stock of his situation.

Seven days he'd been on the run. Seven long and arduous days, during which he'd hardly stopped except to doze or snatch a quick bite from his dwindling rations. For the first seventy-two hours he'd easily kept ahead of his pursuers; he was young, fit and fueled with adrenaline-fueled panic.

Since then, growing fatigue, dehydration, and gnawing hunger had slowly taken their toll, leaving Wilson beset by nagging desperation.

He'd saved himself by fleeing south, deeper into the heart of the Tar'e-esh, instead of heading north as his pursuers would expect. But after a week of cat-and-mouse evasion, he suspected his enemy had probably grasped his strategy.

Ha! We'll see about that. They thought I'd be a pushover just because I'm young. Well, screw them all! As soon as I find a river or other water to refill my canteen, I'll be striking out west for the highway. I'll get to the abandoned mining colony easier that way; and once I find a new radio, I'll be outta here and spreading the word about what's really *going on.*

As quietly and deliberately as he could, Wilson pressed deeper into the undergrowth, edging his service revolver from its holster. Soaked with sweat, his clothing stuck to him like a second skin, making movement difficult. Worse, the multitude of welts crisscrossing his exposed flesh throbbed mercilessly, irritating him more than the swarming insects besieging him in endless, buzzing enquiries.

With infinite caution, Wilson clicked through the weapon's chambers.

Only four bullets left. Three for them, one for me.

A cold determination set in.

It'll have to be enough. They won't take me alive. I'll never let myself. . .

He shivered and let the notion fade. *No! Don't think like that, Wilson. You're gonna survive, you're gonna escape, and when you lead the posse back here, you're gonna kick some ass.*

His spirits bolstered, Wilson got as comfortable as possible and rested the gun in his lap. He decided there'd be no harm in relaxing awhile.

Yeah, I'll just catch my breath for a minute or two, and then get back on the trail.

Heavy lids fluttered together. A mistake, for the rustle of leaves overhead, the moan of wind through branches, and the competing birdsongs aloft soon serenaded him to sleep.

Jolting awake, Wilson snatched at his revolver.

What the hell? I must have dropped off.

The woodlands seemed too quiet. From the angle of the sunbeams piercing the canopy, a couple of hours must have passed since he'd stopped to rest. Eyes wide, Wilson stared deep into the sea of green, alert for signs of trouble.

He found none and sharply exhaled.

Phew! Idiot, you could have—eh?

He cocked his head to listen. A faint but merry chuckling sound teased at the edge of his hearing.

Is that a waterfall?

Uncapping his canteen, Wilson confirmed it was empty.

What a stroke of luck. I was wondering where I'd be able to top up. Once I've had my fill, I'll go on until nightfall. Then I'll try to work out exactly where I am.

He eased himself out from the brambles. Finding nobody around, he crept toward the sound of salvation.

A pool came into sight. Situated at the bottom of a small gorge, it was fed by miniature rapids cascading their way down through the higher rocks like mellifluous serpents.

Must be a tributary of the Esteban. At last, things are going right.

He scanned the opposite shore. Displaying the maturity of someone far older, Wilson picked up several stones and cast them in different directions.

Then he waited.

Nothing moved.

Well, I guess I'll have to take the plunge.

Pistol at the ready, Wilson inched out into the open and knelt by the water's edge. Without taking his gaze from the tree line, he unscrewed the lid of his canteen and submerged the entire flask beneath the icy, fast-flowing current. In moments, it filled to the brim.

Now it's my turn.

He leant forward. Dipping briefly into the chill water, Wilson brought his hand to his lips and swallowed.

A shadow from behind him cut across the rocks.

He began to turn, but lightning blurred his vision. The bolt brought with it a terrible radiating pain that intensified with every second.

The world receded. Wilson pitched forward. A numbing embrace enveloped him, and then the lights went out.

*

"What do you mean, it disappeared?" In spite of the distinguished company, Saul Cameron was incensed. "I thought you said we were monitoring it?"

"We were," Mohammed replied calmly. "And then it vanished."

"How? I thought the defense grid was up to speed now that—"

"Hang on a second," Mohammed said firmly. "This bloody thing—whatever it is—eluded every deep space scanner and covert watchman throughout the quadrant. We only saw it in orbit around Ladesha because it chose to reveal itself. When it took off, we managed to track it until it reached Vesta, but there it faded from our screens again."

"Heading?"

"Same course, same speed. It's coming straight at us."

Saul noted how the Deputy Magister squeezed his first officer's arm. Something about the look in her eye roused his suspicions. Seldom wrong when he got such a hunch, he decided to follow his intuition to see where it led: "And we haven't been able to tag it since?"

"Nooo, but . . ."

You're on to something, aren't you?

"What is it, Mohammed?"

The automated warning began cycling again, and everyone paused to listen.

"Citizens of Rhomane, a possible threat to public safety has been detected by our long-range scanners. Please do not panic. The city will go into lockdown mode in T minus five minutes. I say again . . ."

Mohammed cocked a thumb toward the speakers. "How come the Architect knows to issue a statement? Don't get me wrong, I know it's linked into our systems, but why not do it when the *Chariot of Spring* blew up? All that metal flying around up there. All that potential for mayhem. I mean, how much would it take to knock an orbiting platform or satellite out of position?"

As his friend spoke, Saul glanced repeatedly between the two people in front of him. Up until now, Shaní had been remarkably supportive of his first officer, especially if he offered insightful comments on difficult situations. However, instead of enthusing at his latest deduction, the Deputy Magister maintained an expressionless mien.

The discrepancy was so odd, Saul couldn't help but notice.

I've seen blank faces before.

He decided to test the water: "The city is reacting in a way we've never previously witnessed. But this isn't the first time it's done so, lately. I'm betting we've activated a hidden subroutine, or something else built into the network protocol stack that responds only to Ardenese DNA."

Saul glimpsed the slightest tightening of Shaní's mouth. That subtle reflex told him all he needed to know.

A thrill surged through him. *Gotcha!*

He raised his voice slightly. "Strange, that. Regardless of the fact we've been looking after the future of their entire race, maybe we *human*-based hybrids don't pass the latest requirements in some newly-resurrected security policy . . ."

A gaggle of nine senators swept into the chamber, Calen and Sariff among them. Directing his words their way, Saul concluded, "But I've got the damnedest feeling that things are about to change."

Pulígio, leading the new arrivals, heard Saul's remark and sneered. Nevertheless, he managed to refrain from any further reaction as the hustling group approached and came to a halt in front of the city's leader.

Saul greeted them formally.

"First Magister, Chancellor, Consulan, Sol Berek, Senators. Perhaps one of you would like to turn off this false alarm?"

Calen grinned. Sariff inclined his head toward his colleagues and with a satisfied air announced, "You see? I told you he's a worthy candidate. As are his entire command staff. You forget, my avatar became closely involved in their struggle over the years, as did Calen and Beren's . . . Pherôn rest his soul. While the rest of you were lost to oblivion, their ingenuity kept Arden alive. We need their insight and fortitude, now more than ever."

Everyone seemed to agree except Pulígio, whose lips pursed as if the taste of something distinctly unpleasant had caught in his mouth.

The recorded message began again, this time announcing the four minute marker.

"Ladies and gentlemen." Saul stood to one side and gestured toward the primary computer console. "Would you be so kind? I think the time for charades is over, don't you?"

"Thank you, Saul," Calen muttered, "but that won't be necessary." The Chancellor glanced down.

Intrigued, Saul scanned the area between them to discover what Calen was staring at, but he could see only the strange hexagonal tiles paving the floor of the command center from one side to the other.

Berek, Sariff, and Calen huddled closer together, their hands held out in front of them at waist height. Each spoke in turn:

"Recognize Psi Calen, Chancellor."

"Recognize Gul Sariff, First Magister."

"Recognize Sol Berek, Field Marshal."

A beam from one of the overhead emitters bathed their forms in ethereal emerald light. When this blinked off, a gray metallic cylinder shot up from the floor, faster than the eye could follow. Once in position, the top of the block slid back to reveal a psycho-dermal interlink.

"Triune sequence recognized," the Architect replied. "Security core accessed. How may I assist?"

"Assess current threat level and identify source," Sariff commanded, "and mute the damned alarm until I say otherwise."

"As you wish." The droning automaton cut off. "Stand by for further information . . ."

A few seconds later, the Architect continued: "Incoming vessel confirmed as the Avenger class dreadnaught, *Shadow of Autumn*. Mission parameters, classified. Intent, yet to be evaluated. Records indicate the *Autumn* was designated part of the Trojan Program. In my opinion, therefore, she will be operating on isolated protocols."

Sariff glared at Calen and Berek.

Calen shrugged. "Don't look at me! As far as I knew, she was still in space dock at the Exordium starship yards when the outbreak occurred. We thought her lost along with the *Star of Summer* during the initial attack." He turned to Berek. "You know what this means, don't you? The final download must have been completed in time to initiate her escape and evasion procedures."

Berek's eyes flared. "So the advanced RTB system works?"

"It appears so," Calen replied. "But I wouldn't like to find out for sure until we've interrogated her system."

"Excuse me," Saul interjected. "RTB system? And did the Architect say she's a dreadnaught? I thought the Avenger class family was all cruisers?"

"We'll explain everything shortly," Sariff temporized. "For now, we'd better make sure she still responds to our authority and stands down."

Fuck me! They don't know if it'll obey them yet?

Saul glanced at Mohammed. His first officer was edging toward the manual override module on the city's orbital defense console.

Sariff gestured for his comrades to step even closer. As they crowded around the hexagonal column, the First Magister said, "Architect, connect us to the *Shadow of Autumn*'s AI."

The green light again washed across them. A resonant voice boomed out from the speakers:

"This is Seraphim. State your identity."

Although graced with a feminine tone, her inflection indicated that Seraphim was not to be trifled with.

The trio held out their hands and repeated the procedure they'd employed minutes earlier to access the security core. This time they submitted to the additional invasion of the psycho-dermal interlink. A series of ultrafine fibers sprouted from the top of the module. These wavered in the air like anemones dancing in an ocean current before piercing the flesh of each officer along one arm, neck, and head.

Saul winced in sympathy, but none of those concerned appeared to mind.

"Recognize Psi Calen, Chancellor."

"Recognize Gul Sariff, First Magister."

"Recognize Sol Berek, Field Marshal."

"Triune sequence acknowledged," Seraphim replied, "wait . . ."

The line went quiet while the entity scrutinized the information presented to it. Seconds later, it was back:

"Identities confirmed. Authenticate."

One by one, each senator responded.

"Authenticate Psi Calen. Requiem, service, five, five, castle, three, unity, child, zero."

"Authenticate Gul Sariff. Moon, flower, rhobexi, one, nine, zero, war, pen, nine."

"Authenticate Sol Berek. Water, life, four, stars, rizet, mannequin, sand, two, peace."

Unexpectedly, the Architect added its own sequence.

"Recognize the Archive, Rhomane home world central command. Authenticate: tree, ark, three, Soleíl, three, Arden, sheath, web, zero, Se'ochan, wind, skin . . . confirm?"

The room fell silent.

Everyone held their breath while the deadly AI construct assessed the answers it had received.

At last, it responded.

"Rhomane central, this is Seraphim. Security access protocols verified. Please stand by for the transfer of command codes on my mark . . . Mark."

The main view screen flared to life, and a host of additional hexagonal interface ports sprang into position.

Well, would you look at that? Why am I not surprised?

Saul chuckled.

People cheered, but Seraphim's announcement silenced everyone:

"*Shadow of Autumn* reporting, what are your instructions?"

Sariff glanced at Saul, an expectant look on his face. "Commander?"

"What? You're asking *me*?"

"Seraphim has adopted Rhomane's operating parameters, expanded to include your staff. You now have access at the highest level, and she will obey your orders without question."

Although Saul's face remained impassive, the military man inside him crowed in delight. He coughed and swallowed repeatedly before he could speak. "Seraphim, this is Commander Saul Cameron. Please decloak and park in high north polar orbit. Once there, initiate a full security sweep of ship's environs to ensure you are free of infestation. When that's completed, mesh with the Architect and initiate a full memory and archives download. Further updates will be forthcoming shortly. Understood?"

"Understood, Commander Cameron."

The picture on the main screen blinked. When it resumed, all saw the spectacular view above Arden. Then the idyllic scene shivered.

Three miles of lethal tactical divinity—personified by bristling guns and metal—manifested before them.

Jaws dropped in surprise.

Jesus Christ, she was already here, only we never knew it.
Then he had a comforting thought:
And now she's on our side.

Chapter Thirteen

There's No Place Like Home

As the great doors closed and people in the auditorium settled down, Shaní gazed about this place she hadn't set foot in for centuries: the great arc of the Senate. Built to seat nearly five hundred people, its perfect acoustics would propagate a speechmaker's words to all corners of the tiered chamber without voices being raised. Hidden speakers built into the fabric of the walls and supporting pillars were ancillary to the anechoic chamber's flawless function.

She looked up at her old seat, midway along the Senatum Balcony. . .or, as their benefactors deemed it, the command level. . .and wondered how much of a fight would be necessary for her to reclaim it.

The thought of controversy made her smile, for she had won many encounters here, in wars of words that decided the fate of billions.

She snorted.

I lost a few too, if truth be told.

Shaní eyed her greatest adversary of old, Consulan Pulígio, strutting like a bantam rooster in front of the human delegation on the far side of the hall.

Crafty old hornet, up to his tricks again. People are already using that phrase he coined. 'Human Halflings' *indeed*! *If we don't watch him, he'll foment division among the populace during this transitory phase that'll be difficult to expunge in the long run.* She narrowed her eyes. *Hmm, I think I'll make that issue my personal business from now on. After all, thanks to the Architect's wisdom it'll be difficult to tell us apart within a few generations, and we'll need to stand united before the changes which are coming.*

Beyond Pulígio, another matter of personal business caught her eye. Even at this distance, Shaní could tell Mohammed found Pulígio's posturing boring, if somewhat amusing. His expression told all. And her skill at reading faces made her a lethal contender on the floor.

Their gazes met, and Mohammed flashed his eyebrows in an "O God . . . kill me now" plea for help. Her heart skipped at the mere sight of him.

Oh, for Pherôn's sake. Why have I fallen for him?

She was about to cover her embarrassment by going to his aid when Sariff strode out to the speaker's dais and called the meeting to order:

"Fellow leaders of Rhomane, if you would kindly find a place around the bottom level, near the platform, we'll get underway. Do forgive the setting. I know we're all accustomed to sitting in the balcony, but until we've extended its seating, there simply isn't room." Sariff pointed to a buffet laid out to one side. "On the plus side, we have an assortment of snacks to devour. And best of all, an entire urn of Robusta to drain . . ."

A chorus of rousing cheers met his announcement, and he scowled in dismay as Gul Lani, one of the newer representatives from Floranz, led an immediate charge of younger delegates toward the coffee machine.

Ignoring them, Sariff continued: "Let's get down to business. Today's forum is being conducted in the Ardenese tradition. Commander Cameron suggested we take turns chairing the meetings so that both factions, for want of a better term, have the opportunity to see how the other operates in matters of statecraft. A splendid idea, for when the time comes, we'll be better able to choose the most suitable aspects of government for the new unified Senatum. So without further ado . . ." He checked the itinerary, then waved his pad in the air. "You've had the memorandum for a week and been given ample opportunity to respond. Today should be a formality. We'll run over the current state of play here in the city, discuss the proposals regarding political change, iron out any last minute hiccups, and then formulate how best to proceed in light of recent developments. . .especially as it's been confirmed the *Shadow of Autumn* is free of contagion and ready for service."

The First Magister scanned the crowd to allow for last-minute motions. When no comments were forthcoming, he turned to face Shaní, smiled, and extended his hand.

Here we go . . .

She got to her feet and walked toward the platform.

Sariff explained: "For those of you who haven't met her yet, this is Shaní, the Deputy Magister. Her position involves acting as the main speaker during sessions. Bad news for her, since she'll have to run through the details with you; but great news for me, as it means I can relax and grab a mug of Robusta before it's all gone."

Sariff scurried toward the refreshments while Shaní struggled to maintain composure.

He's been around our friends for far too long. If he gets any more laid back he'll be in danger of grazing his head on the floor.

As she assumed her position, the filters around the exterior edge of the dais turned blue, amplifying her voice to compensate for background chatter.

"Commanders, Senators." Shaní made a point of smiling warmly at her audience, and began: "As Sariff indicated, we'll get the boring but essential stuff out of the way first, and then concentrate on more important things. Unfortunately, this means we start with politics. May I refer you to that section in your agendas?

"As you can see, we think a coalition government will be the best way to proceed initially, so people have ample opportunity to adjust to the differences among us. Doing so now will alleviate problems later and, despite what the die-hards might say,". . .she delivered a withering glance in Pulígio's direction. . ."the populace *will* agree. However, while most are aware they simply wouldn't be here were it not for human intervention, too many keep drawing attention to our dissimilarities. Therefore, the prospectus outlines a means by which the current command structure will be amalgamated into the Senatum. You will note the steps are structured and sensible. They recognize that while we are of diverse origins, our future isn't. This is *our* home now. A place for *all* of us. And while the merger will take place gradually, we, as Arden's leaders, must set the example by living a united lifestyle *now*."

Shaní glimpsed Pulígio's tight-lipped frown. She took a moment to memorize the faces of those grouped around him, especially the colonial representatives without current seats of office.

He's already building his new little cabal. I'll have to watch him carefully.

"Can you summarize the breakdown again?" Saul Cameron requested, "so everyone here is clear on the matter."

"Good idea." Shaní transferred the image within her notebook onto the main view finder.

It read:

Senatum disposition by zones: Arden
Rhomane. . .Psi Grenushan and Gul Similan
Genoas. . .Psi Tacar and Gul Dal'san
Napal. . .Psi Davir and Gul Viranè
Elan. . .Psi Y'shol and Gul Olex
Locus. . .Psi Erin and Gul Tir'ee
Cumale. . .Psi Saklar and Gul Ru'bok
Floranz. . .Psi Do'mer and Gul Lani
Field Marshal. . .Sol Berek

After giving everyone a moment to skim its contents, Shaní resumed her explanation, addressing Saul in particular:

"For the past twenty years or so, the transferees were forced to adopt a rigidly disciplined way of life. That's no longer the case; politicians must now resume the oversight of government." She gestured to the screen. "This is a register of the current officers of the Senatum in respect to home world. As our community grows, we will expand our hierarchy to include those with political acumen, as opposed to purely militaristic expertise. These must settle on the various continents of Arden as follows . . ."

She amended the overview to show the agreed upon allocation of manpower.

"People will be spread thin at first, but that's to be expected until each city is repopulated. We also took other factors into account. As you recently discovered, each of the sectors around Arden was accountable for a specific aspect of our economic and social stability. For example, Napal was responsible for scientific research; Locus, agriculture; Cumale, industry; Floranz, medicine, and so forth. This arrangement will be reestablished as soon as possible, especially as its infrastructure is already in place. Perhaps now you understand the distribution a little better, for we married the expertise of your staff with the needs of each province."

Shaní was relieved when most of her audience responded in favor.

"Ah, I'd thought as much," Saul replied. "But if you don't mind my asking, certain names are missing?"

"That's because they'll be staying here, as in the case of Mohammed and yourself. Your roles in leading refugees have been similar to that of a First Magister, Consulan, and Sol all rolled into one. We need you among the highest level of government, and have been discussing suitable positions for you both. Due to the range of your talents, we created new positions of Advisor and Deputy Advisor—"

"Do you think that truly wise?" Pulígio interjected. "Might not our people react adversely to aliens forming part of our government?"

The small faction surrounding the Consulan muttered agreement.

"What?" someone called out from the back. "Surely you're not referring to the *aliens* who sacrificed themselves by the thousands to keep our hope alive?"

A louder rumble of approval came from voices around the auditorium:

"Bravo!"

"Hear, hear!"

"Well said."

"Have you *ever* considered keeping such ill-advised opinions to yourself, Pulígio?" someone else piped up. "You ought to try it. Contrary to what you might think, it won't make you look more stupid than we already think you are."

Waves of laughter rippled back and forth among the throng, and the Consulan's supporters suddenly evaporated. Some even leaned away from him in a visible demonstration of rejection.

Would you look at that? Shaní was delighted. *A clear majority of my people are in favor of this merger . . . as they should be.*

A hand rose from among the press.

"The floor recognizes Gul Similan of Rhomane."

One of the eldest representatives, Similan was a well-respected official whose word carried influence. As he rose from his seat, everyone fell quiet, intrigued by what he might say.

The senator took his time. After he had tidied his robes and gathered himself to his full height, he announced, "My apologies for the interruption. But I wish to add a point we would all do well to consider: The Consulan has expressed his concern as to how our citizens might react to having, as he terms them, *aliens* on the Senatum." He gestured to the front tier where Buer, Caym, and Zagam were seated. "And yet not once has he raised a single objection to the presence of those who were former Lega'trexii of the Kresh. Beings who, although of Ardenese origin, were so mutated, so warped, that they sought the extinction of our kind." He paused for effect, concluding, "Don't you think that odd?"

Unable to contain his frustration, Pulígio snapped, "So what are you alleging . . . exactly?"

"Why, my dear man, I thought it was obvious," Similan countered. "You appear to have a stick up your ass about our saviors from Earth. . .a situation quite unbefitting for one holding high office. It is my suggestion that we would all be better served if you sought the assistance of the worthy Doctor Frost. Perhaps she knows of a procedure to extract the source of your irritation?"

The room exploded in unbridled hilarity. Similan himself merely sat back down as if nothing untoward had happened.

Oh, well played.

As much as Shaní longed to join in, she knew she daren't. She must steer the meeting back on course.

"Attention please!" she barked.

Unaware she could project her voice in such a manner, most of the humans jumped. Several among the Senatum must have forgotten, for they too were startled into silence. Their reaction was sufficient to restore a modicum of order.

"Thank you," Shaní crooned. "Now where were we? Ah yes, we were expressing how happy we all are that Saul and Mohammed will be adding their wisdom to the Senatum over the coming months." She ignored the exaggerated "Hrmmph" issuing from the vicinity of the Consulan and his supporters, and breezed on: "As I mentioned, both commanders will be remaining here, exercising their function . . . akin to that of civilian police commandants. Anything impacting law, order, public safety and so forth will come under their jurisdiction. So start planning ahead now, and let them have your recommendations regarding the best way to proceed."

Shaní gazed around the room, making brief eye contact with trusted individuals among the throng. "Shannon, Marcus, Searc, Sam. While Sol Berek will retain overall command of the military, that entity is still embryonic. Only ten thousand soldiers remain to us, and most of those are yet in stasis. Your fighting style is vastly different to ours, but it's what won the war, so we need to incorporate aspects of your training into our own."

She addressed each officer in turn.

"Shannon. You will be Sul, Berek's second, with oversight of the covert Watchman system. I understand you've already familiarized yourself with the role? That's great news, given our heightened state of alert.

"Marcus, you will be Director of military training. Searc will be your second. We're relying on you to choose the right warriors to whip our forces into shape in double quick time. We are not the civilization we once were, and after the current threat has been addressed, we'll need you to improve our defensive capabilities drastically.

"Sam. Nice to see you out of hospital by the way; welcome back to the land of the living. You'll be surprised to know we don't have anyone like you or your team. That needs to change. You will be Commander of our new Ranger Initiative, a rapid reaction force of specialists trained to handle a whole host of hazardous and difficult situations. Recent losses have devastated your numbers. When the current threat is over, we'll want you to scour the ranks of our existing military. . .and whoever else you think might prove useful. . .and begin training them for tactical operations. A point for you to note is that you will exist outside the usual chain of command. You'll answer to Sol Berek and the upper echelon of the Senatum, understood?"

"Loud and clear," Sam replied. "But only as long as you keep *that* idiot off my back." He pointed at Pulígio, who bridled at the insult. "Not to put too fine a point on it, but you should know by now that when it comes to what we do, *we're* the experts, not some prickly old fart with an overinflated opinion of his own self-importance. *We* know if something is achievable or not, and I won't have my team endangered by his brand of bullshit . . ." Spontaneous applause met the lieutenant's remark, which grew louder as he added, "It wouldn't be healthy."

Pulígio huffed and turned his back, and Shaní was forced to cough to mask her laughter. Then she caught herself, for the Consulan's reaction reminded her of something important.

Shaní motioned for quiet and searched the crowd for the small cluster of Native Americans she had spotted earlier. She located them over to one side, partially hidden behind a pillar.

"Stained-With-Blood," she called, "are your people still intent on declining positions within the new governing body?"

"We are," he replied, "for such things do not concern us now there is so much land to settle. We will be content to learn its secrets awhile, and become one with its rhythms and its people, until the generations pass and the Cree are no more."

"Very well, we accede to your wishes. But know that a seat will always remain open, and all the more so for one who walks the Ix."

The brave stared impassively back, ignoring the invitation.

Clearly, his mind was made up. Nonetheless, Shaní couldn't resist a last-ditch attempt to win them over.

"A pity," she sighed, "for the Kresh are also with us now, and were keen to serve with one who has walked their halls."

Stained-With-Blood inclined his head. "Should they be in need of counsel, the Kresh need only seek me out amid the dreams Napioa sends to guide my way, or at my home. There, they are always welcome."

At the front of the hall, Buer, Caym, and Zagam turned in their seats and nodded toward the shaman with obvious respect.

Stained-With-Blood and his fellow elders returned the gesture, and everyone fell quiet once more.

Ah well, I did my best. Must keep things rolling.

"That's reassuring to know," Shaní acknowledged. "I suppose I'd better conclude this part of our conference by reminding everyone: our draft proposed that all public servants keep their current titles until the New Year, whereupon the latest Senatum format will take effect. Elections will be held every four years as per the old arrangement. Any dissenters?"

There were none.

"Good, our unity will ensure the proper foundations are in place for subsequent revivals, especially as it is our intention to include the remaining senators from the outer colonies within the next phase. An essential step, as I'm sure you'll appreciate, to ensure our constituency continues to benefit."

Shaní cleared the screens and consulted her info-pad. *At last we get down to the nitty-gritty.* "Okay, it's time to concentrate on the aftermath of the *Chariot of Spring* disaster. Pat, how are things down in the medical wing?"

Doctor Pat Frost leaned forward in her seat.

"Remarkably well," she replied, "particularly since Psi Grenushan and his team joined us. I'm so relieved you had a few doctors in the first batch of resurrections. Talk about providence. Thanks to their expertise, we've been able to save two of the casualties we'd earmarked as terminal."

"What are the latest figures?"

"Forty-eight dead, forty injured, and twelve walking wounded. However, six remain on the critical list. They absorbed too much radiation, I'm afraid. So we're keeping them heavily sedated and as comfortable as possible until they fade away."

"I see. And what about their families?"

"Fortunately they were all soldiers from the ninth intake. Only a few of them had formed new relationships, so we have no next of kin to notify. Apart from Corporal Cunningham, of course. But there's not much we can do in his case, as technically he was already dead."

Although only recently restored herself, Shaní had made it her business to learn as much about the people she would be living with as possible. The poignancy of Pat's remark wasn't lost on her.

Of course! Fonzy was married, but essentially lost his wife when he was brought here to save us. Damn, but fate can be cruel. She'll never know . . .

"Any other problems or difficulties?"

"Not really. We're more than equipped to deal with the rest of the symptoms you get from an incident of this nature. High intensity burns, toxic poisoning, internal trauma from vacuum exposure, crush injuries and the like. It'll be a matter of managing everyone on an individual basis, and getting them on the appropriate course of remedial therapy."

"Thank you, Pat," Shaní replied sadly. "Please continue to do all you can to extend the lives of our fallen heroes. And if there's anything you need, I'm sure no one here would dare deny your request."

"More doctors and nurses would be lovely," Pat declared, "and trainers too, if you have them tucked away anywhere? Seriously. Not to put too fine a point on it, the sooner you revitalize people like that, the sooner my staff could become qualified using some of your more sophisticated equipment." She tapped the side of her head. "Sometimes, the nanobots aren't quite enough."

Nice point . . . and of course, we all benefit in the long term.

"Architect?" Shaní called. "Please implement Doctor Frost's suggestion during the next selection period. Target physicians, clinicians, nursing practitioners and medical technicians as a priority. Public officials can tag along later. The sooner we make *all* our healthcare staff aware of what's available, the better."

"Yes, Deputy Magister," the AI responded. "Appropriate amendments will be made."

"Outstanding." Shaní took a quick peek at her computer. "Next item is the debris field resulting from the explosion. Shannon, seeing as you've only just been appointed I'm sorry for coming at you so soon, but do you have any updates?"

"None to worry about," Shannon replied. "Thankfully, I didn't have a lot to do personally. Berek and I linked the Ardenese and Se'ochan Satcom Nets together, reconfigured their targeting emitters, and took anything and everything remotely dangerous out of the sky. As a precaution, I've also had the sentinel grid scouring the system ever since, looking for any residue energy signatures that might be suspicious."

"And how far have you deemed it prudent to check?" Consulan Pulígio enquired, his voice laced with sarcasm.

Oh, for goodness sake. Shaní was about to interject, but she caught a glint of steel flashing within the new Sul's eyes. *Hang on, this should be interesting.*

Shannon twisted on her bench, and turned to face the fastidious senator squarely. Without saying a word, she stared at him until his face flushed red and he took refuge among his shrinking clique of friends. Only then did she speak:

"Knowing the Horde as we do (and don't forget, *we* do, seeing as we beat them), I've extended the search as far as the next planets out in either direction. Danobe, close to the asteroid field, and Issander on the sunny side. No hits so far, but I'd suggest maintaining the sweeps until month's end, to be sure." Shannon inclined her head. "Is that good enough for you, Pudgy? Piggy? What *is* your name again?"

Beside Shannon, Sam Pell's shoulders were shaking with ill-concealed mirth, as were virtually everyone else's. He reached out to take her hand, and began patting it affectionately.

Shaní smiled. *Oh yes, I think I'm going to like our new girl . . . a lot!*

"Thank you, Shannon. That's a relief to hear."

Only then did Shaní realize how intimate the innocent gesture between the couple was. *Hello . . . ?* They realized she was staring at them. To cover herself, Shaní asked a question.

"Sam, I understand you recently gained intelligence potentially useful to our endeavors? Now that it's been vetted, would you like to share what you've discovered with the entire Senatum?"

"I certainly would; it'll have a direct impact on how we proceed."

Sam tapped away on his notebook for a second before the main viewer sprang back to life, showing the images captured by his helmet-cam whilst on board the *Chariot of Spring*.

"If you don't mind, I'll remain seated," Sam said. "My leg's still heavily strapped, and standing is uncomfortable."

"No problem, please explain your concerns."

Sam allowed the entire incident to play through, from the point where he entered the engine core until the moment of the explosion. Once the clip had finished, he reset the recording to the moment everything started to go wrong.

"Although you've only recently returned," he began, "I know you've all been thoroughly apprised of events occurring ever since human refugees began coming to Arden. Much of that information has to do with the Horde and the mutated results wrought upon your own DNA, stemming from a side effect of the rip-space theorem. Those files included detailed reports of our dealings with the enemy, which are now much more comprehensive thanks to the insights of Caym and his friends. I'm glad I won't have to elaborate on the basics, because I need to concentrate on the Horde Masters."

He superimposed several separate diagrams over the screen. "These pictures represent those who fight their way back to a measure of lucidity. They come in three varieties, dependent upon the degree to which they can influence the physical and esoteric planes around them. The varieties are: Praefacti, Tribuni, and Lega'trexii. The weakest of this group are the Praefacti. Newly enlightened, they possess only two flames in their distinguishing coronets. That changes as they gain strength. Tribuni have four, and the most powerful entities we ever encountered. . .like Angule, their Battlemaster. . .have crowns adorned with six blazing stars. Another indicator of potency is their size and aura. Angule, for example, stood over twelve feet in height and could surround himself with a blistering force-field resistant to every weapon in our arsenal. You might wonder why I'm emphasizing this? Well, we thought we'd learned everything there was to know about the Horde. But we were wrong. Please observe . . ."

Sam removed the overlay and the main recording rolled forward, frame by frame, treating the audience to an ultrafine, slow-motion replay of the moment the shimmering cocoon of energy next to the hyper-drive ruptured, and the Horde Masters came spilling out.

Shaní was mesmerized by the sight of their ancient enemy. She'd been asleep for hundreds of years, but the horror of those final days came flooding back instantly. The creatures before her defied explanation. She found them fascinating, yet repulsive. And as shocking as three of those beasts were, they paled into insignificance in the company of the fourteen-foot brute whose presence dominated the view field.

Wreathed within a gold and silver skein of dazzling light, terrifying to behold, its imposing bulk was enhanced by a crown that radiated with immense power. Hungry flames hovering above its head flared, and then blazed to life. They orbited so quickly it looked as if an angel of death had appeared to reap a fresh batch of souls.

Without realizing, she'd stopped listening to Sam's account, and had to force herself to pay attention:

". . . it's only now that we've had the opportunity to study the recording in detail that we can confirm *this* particular specimen could generate ten . . . I believe the correct term is Jînnereth stars? Yes, you heard right, ten! Now, don't forget, Angule represented the pinnacle of Horde authority living on Arden. Even Imperator Vetis didn't turn out to be as powerful as he was. But for all his strength, Angule only possessed six flames. *This* bugger had nearly twice that amount. This explains why it was so big, *and* why it was capable of doing this . . ."

The recording jumped to the point where the Controller leaped from the coupling frame and landed on the floor in front of Sam and his men. Its shield sparkled under the assault of thousands of bullets, none of which caused it the slightest concern. One brave soldier attempted to intervene, only to be swatted away like an insect. The image froze.

Picking up where he left off, Sam explained: "What worries me is that the Master didn't even flinch. Our Haz-Ent suits contain an active-response, dalenite-titanium mix. They're capable of stopping small rockets. And while they can't prevent the transference of kinetic energy, they are laced with enough hematite to repel all but the strongest ogres. Let me clarify what I mean. If an ogre grunt tried to do what that boss just did, it would explode instantly. And while their leaders are a different kettle of fish, our uniforms have been designed to withstand their assault and deliver a shock sufficient to stun them. Even if the worthy Angule himself tried to grab us while we were wearing one of these suits, he'd be disorientated sufficiently for us to bag him with a gravity net." Sam replayed the scene, cocking a thumb at the Master. "But as you can see, though it cuffed Stu senseless, our friend here didn't even cringe. This particular entity is faster, stronger, and more resilient than anything we've faced previously, so we'll need to adjust our strategy before we even think of starting round two."

Shaní was unnerved to think anyone would be willing to face off against such an adversary.

And yet, both he and his men have done so over and over again. Then a sudden thought plagued her: *But where is the value in this information?*

As if Sam had read her mind, he deactivated the screen, stood upright, and turned to face the Senatum.

"Now to the crux of the matter: Have you ever wondered *why* the Architect waited so long before bringing the first humans through?"

Everyone in the room fell silent.

"Consider this logically. You were under siege, you needed help, and you had the technology to summon assistance at the drop of a hat. But your AI construct chose not to use it. Instead, it waited until you'd taken the drastic measure of submitting your collective essences into a vast ark. Even so, centuries passed before the Architect deemed it necessary to activate the gateway. Why? Well, I wasn't sure myself until I'd had a chance to ponder the question, so let me tell you what I think. Basically, it all comes down to *food*."

Backs stiffened and eyebrows furrowed, but before anyone could question what Sam meant, he blustered on:

"Again, let's take this step by step and consider matters rationally. The infection which broke out on Exordium spread like a plague through Latinus Prime and Illumina before anyone realized what was happening. Easy meat, for each of those planets was clustered in a region of space set aside for top-secret research and hemmed in by the Verianda Nebula. Almost everyone died. Those few who did get away unwittingly spread the contagion, for the Horde hid away on fleeing ships and took advantage of the ensuing panic. Many of you here are from the outer colonies and no doubt remember what that experience was like."

Shaní watched as some stared off into space, their minds captured by the memories Sam had invoked.

"In the ensuing panic, you fail to realize that not all the Horde followed. You're fighting a losing battle; in only fifteen months, your enemy strips you of all you've built over thousands of years. So, there they stay, and nobody gives them a second thought. Time goes by. The vast majority of the monsters follow you all the way back here, where you end up being packed together like sardines. . .er, sarthela. . .in one little city. Now, let's look at the specifics."

People shifted from foot to foot, crossed arms over chests, but Sam's words had them mesmerized:

"Endless waves of demons come beating on your doors. Their food supply is dwindling, so they're frantic, fighting for survival. Survival of the fittest. Those who grow too weak are devoured by their larger, stronger cousins. This explains why you saw so few Masters in those early days, for those you *did* see were all on restricted diets. They could only develop so far, especially after you yourselves were faced with a similar predicament, and submitted yourselves to the Ark.

"That was a turning point for the Architect, and a big clue to our puzzle. Why? Well let's reason on it: At that point, your protector knew the future was safeguarded, but only so long as the Horde didn't get inside. The lydium barrier was doing its job, so the AI was faced with a dilemma. Should it risk calling for aid immediately, knowing the beasts would detect fresh life force and risk all in their frenzy to get at it, or would it be better to wait for most of them to turn on each other as they slowly starved to death?"

By now, everyone in the hall had recovered from their shock, but no one dared interrupt.

"Personally, I think the Architect made the right choice. Its only mistake was failing to appreciate just how sensitive the

Horde are to proximate energy. After all the people were gone, your enemy clung to the hope of reaching the rip-space core and backup generators they could sense, still at work inside. Of course, when the city's power reserves started waning, the Architect was forced to enact the Gateway Protocol anyway, and *we* started coming through. Needless to say, our presence acted like a red rag to a tarig, and the war of attrition began again. . .lasting for twenty, long drawn-out years.

"While all this was going on, we'd forgotten about the colonies. I mention them now because probes sent out since the release of the re-genesis matrix confirm there's very little evidence of infestation on planets surveyed so far. This fits our hypothesis that most of the Horde pursued the fleeing exiles here, while a minority remained behind to feed on whatever they could scavenge. But I didn't want to base my presentation on pure assumption, so I did some digging. Guess what? Those worlds devoted to agriculture are either completely free of Horde presence, or harbor only random and dwindling pockets of them. However, in territories where science and engineering dominated, Horde concentration is much higher and grouped around centers of industry. Do you see? *It all comes down to food.* The ogres in a position to secure sustained sustenance grew strong enough to develop into Masters; once enlightened, these each gained the capability to spin a cocoon and enter the hibernat, a state in which they can suspend bodily function. That's the only way they could have survived this long . . . if barely. And this realization presents us with a quandary, for while the surveys indicate the survivors are weak and few in numbers, the same can't be said for the Horde still on Exordium, Latinus Prime, and Illumina. Places where, in your own words, you delved into highly classified projects that bent the laws of nature and physics, and wielded energies which could shatter worlds, destroy suns, and transmute the very essence of life."

Shaní could feel the entire audience hanging on Sam's every poignant word.

"Is it any wonder that specimens originating from those planets are superior? I'm betting the examples aboard the *Chariot of Spring* are only a taste of what's to come. Remember, *that* alpha Controller feasted upon the engine core of an Avenger class starship. Who knows what the ones on Exordium have been feeding on? Whatever they're eating is advancing them far beyond anything we've ever—"

"Then why not just wash our hands of the accursed place and let them rot?" Pulígio's challenge cut through the stillness like nails down a chalkboard. "They're obviously too powerful for us to vanquish. The most prudent form of action would be to quarantine the entire sector. They're stuck in the middle of a black hole cluster anyway, so leave them well alone there."

Sam turned to face his accuser: "Unlike you, I'm sure the Senatum aren't suffering from a death wish. The schedule provided for today's meeting contains a précis of the latest warning we've received from Stained-With-Blood. While I appreciate that some of you might scoff at such portents, we of the human community don't. His insights have proved unerringly accurate in the past. Not once have—"

"Surely you don't believe in such foolish fantasies?" Pulígio spluttered. "Especially when the future of our race is at stake?"

Sam limped slowly across the floor until he stood directly before the opinionated senator. Despite his injuries, or because of them, Sam's stance was openly menacing.

Unaccustomed to being challenged so directly, the Consulan leaned away, unnerved by the soldier's proximity.

Shaní smiled to herself.

Yes, shut the hell up, you idiot. I think Sam's about to make an important point and we don't need you confusing the matter.

"Foolish, you say?" Sam spoke low, yet his words rang around the auditorium with bell-like clarity. "The thing is . . . people like you love the sound of your own voices. You put your mouths in gear while the brain is still in neutral. You never consider that others might be in a better position to make an informed decision. Well, guess what? *I am*. Part of the reason you're here today spouting bullshit is because of the guidance provided by people like Stained-With-Blood. And Ayria Solram too, come to that. Dream walkers. People, I might add, very much like your own kin: Caym, Buer, and Zagam. Because of their mutations, their perceptions became refined. Heightened, so they can dream walk, or as the Kresh term it, traverse the Ix. . .the boundary between realities your scientists manipulate when they teleport or initiate a pathway through rip-space. You see, just because insignificant specimens like *you* can't grasp its existence doesn't mean dream walking isn't real. It is. We've amassed too much proof to believe otherwise. *That's* why we can't bury our heads in the sand and wait for the Horde to come crashing through our doors. If they do, we've been warned: they'll consume all life here *and* elsewhere too. And do you know why I'm so certain?"

Pulígio's jaw flapped as if detached. Sam didn't wait for him to fix it.

"I didn't think you were paying attention. Instead of listening, you've ignored the point I'm making and tried to find any contrarian position which might increase your own standing. Don't you feel your race. . .hell, *our* race. . .is worth protecting?"

"What *is* your point?" Pulígio scoffed, in an obvious attempt to save face.

"Just this . . ." Sam stepped back to address the group once more. "Some of you present today met Angule, the most puissant Kresh ever to exist on Arden. You who didn't have the privilege have no doubt read about him. Without fear of contradiction, I can say that Angule was no beast. He was one of the deepest, wisest, and most self-aware creatures I've ever come across. Not only was he highly intelligent, but his tactical and strategic acumen were without peer . . . as evidenced by the six Jînnereth stars within his crown." Sam pressed a button on his info-pad to restore the image of the Controller aboard the *Chariot of Spring*. "Our friend here had ten. My *point* relates to a misgiving I've harbored awhile now. You see, I've a suspicion that those ten stars meant our friend was not only stronger than Angule, but sharper too. And that worries me, because if there are vastly more intelligent entities back on Exordium, what the hell might they be doing with your latest technological advancements? One way or another, we've got to go find out. To do otherwise would be suicide."

An unexpected shock coursed through Shaní. From the reaction of the audience, she could see she wasn't the only one stunned.

Oh my goodness! How did we miss it?

Without another word, Sam returned to his bench and sat down. Shannon squeezed his good leg and then took hold of his hand and stoked it.

Despite her startlement, Shaní was enthralled.

Hello? There it is again. I was right!

Shaní had no time to bask in the glory of her discovery, for another realization suddenly struck her:

Oh no! And we've only just gotten used to being home again.

Chapter Fourteen

A Sense of Anticipation

Wilson stirred. The deep, penetrating ache radiating through his shoulders and arms reminded him he was still tethered to the ceiling by chains. Sure enough, when he focused on them he could feel the telltale throb in his hands getting worse by the second.

A recurring problem, since he'd been bound so that his feet only just reached the flagstones. When exhaustion claimed him, his knees folded and his full weight pulled on his limbs, cutting off his circulation. Within minutes, the growing pain would tug him back to the misery of consciousness.

Although dry and free of decay, the cell stank of feces and urine. He opened his eyes to see a rare glimmer filtering through a small barred grill high in the door opposite him and illuminating the rest of the chamber. By its scant light Wilson could see Harper and Stark were still absent. Their manacles hung open, mocking him, foreboding.

His skull pounded as if a stage coach had been driven across his head. He took a few deep breaths, trying to clear his mind.

Screams from farther along the corridor outside dragged his sluggish consciousness back to his predicament. He straightened his legs and pain radiated through his joints, reminding him how badly his muscles had cramped. Before he could stop himself, he moaned aloud.

Goddamit!

Wilson bit his lip, trying to stifle the noise, but blood rushed to fill the capillaries of his fingers and caused him to groan even louder.

Shit! If they heard that they'll know I'm awake and . . .

Too late.

A buzz issued from beyond the doorway. Ponderously heavy, the hatch cracked open. A wedge of light intruded, bathing him in light and making him squint.

Two forms flew through the air to land in a heap nearby. Wilson was horrified. His fellow prisoners had been only slightly older than he, yet the skeletal hands of decrepit old men now protruded limply from their ragged sleeves. Hollow eyes peered at him from blackened sockets. He glanced between them, their faces pleading for release with heartrending desperation. Moments later, both men gasped and flopped down onto the cold hard floor, where they lay still.

Harper! Stark! My God, what have they done to—?

An indistinct figure entered the cell, and Wilson cringed in horror. Roughly humanoid in shape, its pale sweating skin billowed and warped as if a ghost caged within was struggling to get free. When it undulated closer, Wilson was shocked to recognize this surging apparition was Joseph Mitchell, Second Company's sergeant, and Houston's ever-present minion. Or had been, once: whatever menaced Wilson wasn't entirely human.

"Joe? What the hell happened to you?"

The scar on Mitchell's cheek gave him a demonic air as he closed the gap between them.

Wilson could see that Mitchell's eyes were black and wild; his hands opened and clenched repeatedly; he gasped to catch every breath.

"Are you all right, Joe?" Wilson was frantic to connect with anything that might still resemble camaraderie within the stricken soldier. "Is there anything I can do for you?"

"As a matter of fact, Lieutenant, there is."

No!

Mitchell's hand snaked out and grabbed Wilson by the hair, yanking him forward and lifting him clean off the floor, tearing open the scab from the wound on the back of his head in the process. Wilson whimpered in distress.

Jesus Christ! What is this freak going to do to me?

The next thing Wilson knew, something slammed against his ribs and fire erupted in his chest. He howled, long and hard.

"Stop now or die!"

The command was barely more than a rasping exhalation. Nonetheless, it had the desired effect, for Mitchell released his hold. Relief flooded Wilson's system, only to be replaced by agony as the chains pulled taut, twisting his arms cruelly behind his back.

"I've told you before," the voice continued, "*he* is off limits. How can we hope to fulfill our objective if we waste the advantage so recently gained?"

The former sergeant backed away and hissed in defiance.

"Don't be stupid," the unknown entity warned, "you're nowhere near strong enough to challenge me. If I were you, I'd go help the others prepare for our departure. We have a narrow window of opportunity, and I can't waste time in ill-disciplined charades."

The mutated trooper moved toward the exit.

"But understand this. Ignore my orders again and you will be . . . *removed.* Now get out before I change my mind."

Mitchell snarled in suppressed rage before fleeing the cell in a tumbling mass of shadows.

Wilson stared wide-eyed toward the doorway where his savior hovered.

It appeared to be studying him closely and chuckled quietly, a forced sound, devoid of warmth or humor. Darkness congealed around it in concentric waves, and Wilson was fascinated by the way its extremities flared and faded from sight in a confusing contest of refracted light and dense obscurity.

"How are you managing, my boy," it crooned? "I do hope this current arrangement isn't too restrictive?"

My boy?

Recognition coursed along Wilson's spine. "Uncle James? Is that you?"

"It is. Or at least, it was. Now, I do believe I'm on my way to becoming someone else entirely; someone *better,* in fact."

"What are you talking about?" Wilson was puzzled. "Anyone can see you're ill, contaminated by something." Rising panic clutched at his bowels, and he glanced toward his fallen comrades on the other side of the cell. "Are you going to try to infect me, like them and all the rest?"

"Oh no, no, no, dear boy. You're far more valuable to me alive, healthy and intact." Houston edged closer, a dreadful manifestation no longer a man. "Once you've served your purpose, however, I can't honestly say *what* will happen to you, as I don't think that will be up to me anymore."

He's finally lost it.

Wilson twisted in his shackles, scouring the room, desperate for any means of escape.

I've got to get away from here before it's too late.

"But it already *is* too late," Houston chided."For you, at any rate. And after a week as our guest, do you *really* think you'll ever manage to break out of this place?"

Before Wilson realized what was happening, the phantasm that once had been his uncle swooped forward and clamped both hands around his head.

Wilson shrieked and descended into darkness.

*

Ephraim Miller sat uncomfortably in the rear passenger seat of the main flight deck, trying to calm his nerves. Beside him, Calen appeared totally unconcerned that a former centurion of the Roman Ninth Legion was assisting in their take off today, and was busy congratulating Marcus on his progress as a pilot.

"That's very kind of you to say," Marcus murmured in reply to the latest compliment, "but I can't take all the credit." He gestured to the woman in the captain's chair. "Angela's efforts have been amazing, and of course, the neural linkup makes things seem so much easier than they actually are."

"Don't listen to him," Angela interjected, "his manual and mental dexterity is just fine. As I keep reminding him, you can't gain one without understanding the other. Marcus needs to progress, and today will be as good an opportunity as any. The warehouse guys loaded the *Promulus* prior to our arrival, so it's only us." Angela caught the look on Ephraim's face. "Don't worry, Professor. Just admire the view to take your mind off things. I'm here, and I won't let anything happen to your old bones."

"Old indeed!" Ephraim huffed. "Calen's got nearly a hundred years on me, but I don't hear anyone reminding *him* he's an old-timer."

"What can I say?" Calen quipped. "You're either blessed with the right genes or you aren't."

Ephraim couldn't resist taking the bait.

"That's just it. We *all* have the bloody genes now, so why am I not looking any younger?"

"Perhaps it's because you're an ancient soul," Marcus chipped in. "The re-genesis matrix recognized the maturity you so evidently possess and . . . Oh, hang on a tic . . ."

A gentle whine filtered through the cabin as Marcus fired up the rho-field generators. Qualified to fly himself, Ephraim watched the legionnaire like a hawk and admitted that he performed the procedure flawlessly.

Marcus and Angela went through the preflight checklists. Although they were supposed to be completed via telepathic interface, the soldier's inexperience allowed Ephraim to listen as Marcus kept lapsing into vocalizations.

Sounds proficient too. Maybe I'll get a chance to relax after all?

The hum rose in pitch; the great bank of ready-lights flashed. Ephraim detected a slight tremble in the ether, a sure sign Marcus was feeding power into the exo-net that would isolate the craft from the effects of gravity.

A deeper background thrum trembled along the deck.

Here we go, any second now.

"Environmental systems green," Marcus announced. "Cross checks complete. Rhomane City, this is the *Promulus*; we are ready and standing by. Can you confirm the sky is free of traffic?"

"*Promulus*, this is Rhomane City, you are cleared for takeoff. Rise to one thousand feet and select vector alpha, one, three, delta, until grid upsilon fourteen. I say again, rise to one thousand feet and select vector alpha, one, three, delta, until grid upsilon fourteen. Once in position, you are to proceed to high orbit along a twenty degree geo-methric trajectory. Confirm?"

"Roger that. Rise to one thousand feet and select vector alpha, one, three, delta. Upon arrival at grid upsilon fourteen, proceed into high orbit along a twenty degree geo-methric trajectory. Wilco, over and out."

The tone outside the windows blushed lilac as the *Promulus* ascended like an elevator to the predetermined height. Looking relaxed, Marcus eased the vessel away from the busier lanes nearer the city until a soft background *ping* indicated he had reached the correct coordinates.

"Under normal circumstances, we'd boost straight into the thermosphere". . .Angela's voice sounded smooth and in total control. . ."but as this is your first launch, I'd advise you to take it a bit slower. At least until you get used to the velocities we can achieve."

Marcus nodded.

Down below, Rhomane gleamed, a construct of silver spires and crystal archways amid a sea of purple-green grasslands. A sight that always reminded Ephraim of the opening scene of a fairy-tale adventure. He leaned forward to gaze in wonder at early morning sunrays glazing the topaz waters of the Asterlan Lake and the burnished coals of the Garnet Mountains, far to the northwest.

He'd just found the ruby crest of those distant peaks when they streaked into a blur. Arden retreated beneath them. Rose-gold hues gave way to olivine and turquoise splendor. His perception changed, as if they'd been lifted free of the world's disc and balanced on the cusp of a glittering champagne corona. . .a boundary signifying the transition from life into death.

Thanks to the gravo-magnetic sheath surrounding their craft, Ephraim hadn't felt the slightest movement.

He'd also forgotten to breathe.

Incredible.

Relaxing into his seat, Ephraim studied his pilot's back, watching as the legionnaire's fingers flew across the controls.

And even more incredible to think that one such as he *from so very long ago has been extended the privilege of witnessing such a sight.*

But the time for sights wasn't over. The *Promulus* banked and swept in toward the northern pole of Arden. From their perspective, Soleíl rose again; her warming rays tinged a sea of cotton-candy clouds with pearlescent-cream and auroral outlines.

Even with the filters engaged, the sun was blindingly bright until its glare was suddenly eclipsed by something much closer.

"Is that . . . ?"

"Yes. That's it, Ephraim," Calen replied. "The *Shadow of Autumn* has been in refit for more than five weeks now. I must admit, I was somewhat taken aback to learn you'd not been up here to see her for yourself."

"It's not been for want of trying," Ephraim complained. "Believe me. But Saul, Caym, and Sariff have me buried on a project that must be completed before departure." He seized his opportunity. "By the way, since I have you alone and free from the ever-present pack of wolves, when *do* you think she'll be ready to leave?"

"Eight days, maybe nine." Calen shrugged. "We were fortunate that Brent and Asa had been working for so long to refit the *Arch of Winter* with the new Slingshot system. While the cruiser's specifications aren't a perfect match for this dreadnaught, the modular design of the Avenger class allowed us to swap out and replace what we needed pretty quickly. We just can't rush. The jury-rigged coupling nodules we initially threw together are what triggered the cross-systems blowout a fortnight ago. Since then, we've taken our time, had the Architect manufacture an entire set of upgraded master gel-packs, and we'll start fitting them today."

"So we're that close?"

"Yes. We'll run final tests over the remainder of the week and see how the disparity affects stealth and main operations. Then it should be full steam ahead. In a way, it's fortunate we'll need to use only a fraction of the ship's facilities. Restricted crew and limited active compartments will allow Seraphim to maintain a close watch over power reserves and security issues. She's designed to run on fully automated tactical systems, so this should be a piece of cake."

"And what of the Slipstream capabilities of the Slingshot Drive?"

"From what we've assessed so far, it'll run with between eighty-seven to ninety-five percent efficiency. More than adequate for what we need the engines to do. Once it's all over, we'll get her back here for a major refit, and install a mission-specific drive platform."

"Heads up, gentlemen," Marcus said, "I'm about to take her over the top. Ephraim, you'll want to see this."

As they crested the spine of the ship, Marcus swung the *Promulus* around so its bow continued facing toward the imposing clarity of the *Shadow of Autumn.*

Ephraim caught his breath.

Oh my . . . how can we possibly fail?

Chapter Fifteen

Good Hunting

The Plane of Eternal Prisms faded from sight as Va-ákil, Queen of all Kresh, descended toward the realms of normalcy once more. Her aura appeared more subdued than before she'd entered. In fact, had others observed her exit they might have dared to suggest that what she'd witnessed within the fractured reality of the multiverse had affected her more deeply than she'd care to admit. Fortunately, no one was awake to make such an error, for she was Magnate and such allegations could only end in a show of strength and inevitable death.

Still, what she had experienced could not easily be dismissed.

It is clear I have several options. But how to proceed? All involve great cost.

Her senses skimmed the anagogic nodes saturating the places in-between, where echoes of reminders still dwelt, if only in fading memory.

And we have paid such a price already.

She glanced across to where her legion commanders rested in harmony, content to sup upon the marrow of the cosmos until creation itself ran dry.

Her mate, Prime Catalyct Altás, slumbered to one side together with his generals, Prátors Xophan, Tadãhk, wise Ilion, and the twins, Romũle and Remíle. Of all those who had served her during the Great Release, these were her most loyal advocates. Around them, forming a circle of protection, lay her tried and trusted Lega'trexii: I'ban, Señal, Na'vil, Gortan, Dex, and Ul of the silver thoughts, along with Báchor, Morka, Tagrim, Orock, and Athul. On the fringe, the only remaining Tribuni left to her, Thale, Vorg, Rau, Tisél, and Sion, formed an outer perimeter.

There had been more, of course, but many of those left behind after the teeming hordes had joined the star hunt had soon grown restless. Ill disciplined and uncouth, few demonstrated enough focus to ascend toward illumination. These had been sacrificed to the greater good. Of those achieving the Duarium, most proved too tempting an opportunity to resist. The entire ranks of the Praefacti had been decimated in that way, but their loss had provided sweet solace and reminded the survivors of their true nature.

Regardless, sufficient potency remains. Should I need to engender a fresh spawning, the ranks of our battle fodder will seethe to the call of ultimate release once again.

A note of caution intruded.

However, the realization that lesser beings can threaten the sovereignty of our codex is cause for concern. A closer look at our adversaries may prove insightful?

Va-ákil cleared her mind and compressed her will. In moments, she had become a concentrated needle of awareness within the universe about her, a tiny but majestic construct, as awesome in her complexity and purpose as she was unfathomable.

She floated free and relaxed, a pinpoint lost amid a rippling sea of perpetuity where a trillion luminaries swarmed in silent homage.

How easy it would be to let the tide sweep me where it will. Alas, the Ix beckons, as does our destiny; and I must be away.

A brief intake of breath refined her acuity even further. A network of energy sprang forth, ablaze with spectral patterns never witnessed before. From Va-ákil's viewpoint, it was as if she were viewing the contents of a quasi-ethereal intergalactic brain; a flickering accumulation of Jovian thoughts and ice-cold impulses that flared to life before skittering away like frightened prey. But she knew better, for while this medium appeared frangible, it would remain long after the most enduring suns had frizzled out of existence.

Seizing one of these discharges, she altered the substance of her spirit and blended to its essence. Plasmic chills coursed through her complexus, and Va-ákil found herself wheeling through the heavens like a wraith, speeding toward her goal.

She cast her awareness toward the nearer worlds, where her kin had been marooned following the war. Two were nearby, encompassed within the same localized web of contradictory gravity as the prime colony.

Though isolated, other hives had clearly exploited the abundant power sources scattered across the face of those planets and flourished. Va-ákil's heart trembled in sympathetic approval.

Those nests farther out, however, painted a different picture.

Their hold on life was tenuous at best, nonexistent at worst. In the few places where they had managed to gather in numbers, the principals were shadows of their former might, clinging to survival with a desperation that stoked the embers of her rage.

Fools. Without hope, they lost themselves to lust and paid the ultimate price for their folly. Such lack of judgment has desecrated the sanctity of our purity and only hardens my resolve to see this ended.

A glacial tenor frosted her psyche until it tarnished to deepest midnight. Va-ákil squeezed, constricting her potential into the geodesic ley line itself. Thus augmented, her thoughts were boosted to the periphery of dissolution. Lightning flashed across the landscape of her mind, and suddenly, she was there.

Crushing brilliance assailed her from every angle, overwhelming her senses in an amethyst and emerald assault that all but blinded her. Taken aback, Va-ákil recoiled and sheathed her soul within a cocoon of baffling obscurity.

Thus armored, she dialed down her sensitivity and peered out once more. Only then did she realize she was not under attack. Her alarm had been triggered because she had materialized within the magnetosphere of the celestial body below, and her refined consciousness had been shocked into a hyper-allergenic response.

She sounded the environs of both moon and planet.

Although not teeming with life, what is there is both vigorous and redolent with vague recollections of . . . of . . . how strange. Have I been here before?

Even though it should have been impossible, multiple signals washed across and through the rarified form of her essence, registering *something* was there. Va-ákil felt those energies coalesce about her. Distracted, she was forced to relinquish her grasp on the esoteric foothold anchoring her in place. Geophasic tension came into play, and the Magnate was immediately yanked backward by the weird rubber band effect created whenever the vext was warped in this manner.

Va-ákil went willingly, for she had gained valuable intelligence.

Such a confusing contradiction. Such a baffling amalgam of discipline and ineptitude. The fledging was there, chattering away like a demented automaton on its uniquely discordant wavelength. But so were others. Quieter, these possessed a refinement and discipline that can only come from centuries of application and fidelity. It was as if I . . . it was so similar to . . . She needed to digest the implications, and shook her great head in an effort to kick-start her reasoning process. *How could such a thing occur?*

Her momentum was declining. Projecting ahead, Va-ákil confirmed she would soon be back within her corporeal shell. Scant seconds remained. She hoped these would be enough to quell the turmoil building within her.

And the bane-metal? Is that *how they seek to intrude within our sacrosanct halls? But to what end? And why did that world remind me . . . remind me of a time before time when everything was so . . . different, so bland and inconsequential?*

A compression wave bloomed in the distance.

I am approaching the arch.

Uninvited sentiments unearthed ancient recollections buried within the darkest roots of her core. She braced herself, and voices welled up from the blackness, only to fragment and rebound away, resounding and refracting through the vaults of her immense intellect, carrying whispers she'd rather not hear.

Longing . . .

Nostalgia . . .

Va-ákil alighted from the void with the grace and poise expected from one of her station. Nonetheless, alien concepts continued worming their way into the deepest vestibules of her doubts. Once there, they prodded and poked until an alarming evocation forced itself across the outer layer of her mentality.

Something called Home?

The queen was outraged.

Such notions are abhorrent. Pathetic. Fragile. Weak. They will not be tolerated.

She thundered, and sublime expression ignited the extremities of her threshold in purple and argent glory. Her Jînnereth crown blazed, and telestic energies cascaded onto the floor and walls. The discharge intensified, snapping and stabbing about the chamber until the aural backlash generated became so intense the air itself threatened to combust. Encompassed in spiraling bands of scarlet and indigo plasma, Va-ákil slammed her paws together and released a shockwave of immense proportions.

The cavern rocked, and her cabal of leaders surged from the platform in a roiling maelstrom of ardor and murderous intent.

My Queen. Altás was foremost among the Prátors. *Do we fight and feast?*

Behind him, spurs stomped and fangs gnashed, slavering in anticipation.

Soon, Prime Catalyct, soon. She paused to transfer her findings directly into their minds. *First, we prepare. Take Xophan, Tadãhk, Romũle, Remíle, and dear Ilion into the wastelands above. Distribute your Lega'trexii wisely. Gather as many children of the Duarium and Triarium as can be found. Bring them into the halls above this installation. We spawn. And to do that, we require nourishment of the rawest stripe.*

And if too few are found?

Va-ákil glanced toward the dais where the remaining Tribuni huddled in innocence.

Then bring me our young leonads. Their strength and vitality should be sufficient that we might only require two, maybe three to lay down their lives. Of course, we won't tell them that . . . it would spoil our sport.

Dark humor radiated among the group.

And then we hunt? Altás pressed.

Then we wait!

The generals ground their tusks in frustration.

Have no fear, my valiant few, Va-ákil reassured them, *you will revel in the confrontation you so justly crave. But you have seen our foe through my mind's eye. They possess bane-metal that robs us of our dignity, and they are cunning. So we must exercise guile to an even greater degree. Though stronger, we lack numbers. Nonetheless, we possess something they do not . . .* A shiver of delight caused Altás's aura to flash white. *The Citadel of Tainted Dreams. Only the most dominant of the Praeturium Tier may enter the realms of those thrown down in combat, for that strand of the Ix is beset by snares and peril. Fortunately, the privilege extended to those of us maintaining a superior form means we can not only resist the temptations within the sanctuary but retain sufficient puissance to emerge alive. While you prepare our army, I will take it upon myself to walk amongst the phantoms of our kin and learn from their mistakes.*

Va-ákil bathed her confidants in strengthening light.

Little does our enemy appreciate the danger we Kresh represent, for even in death we may cause their undoing.

And then *we will feast upon their souls?* Altás's avidity was relentless.

A ridiculous refrain surfaced in the back of Va-ákil's mind, something the twittering fledgling had been humming as he went about his narrow little schemes. The import of its meaning suddenly registered, and Va-ákil couldn't help but express her mirth. The sound was similar to the squeal of a pneumatic drill in the moments before it snapped.

My Queen?

Oh, we will feast, Altás, most certainly. Though not in the way you might think, for we will also adopt a different strategy to those we have used before. Believe me when I say brute force won't work on this occasion. What I *have planned will.*

And that is?

I will tell you upon your return, for it is essential we begin our task immediately.

Knowing better than to question his Magnate in front of the others, Altás bowed formally and led the other masters from the cavern, leaving Va-ákil alone with nothing but the background hum of machinery for company.

The fledgling's ditty kept weaving its way through her feelings, and the more she thought about them, the more the sentiments behind the words struck her as appropriate.

She began humming, and discovered the equivalent esoteric tones soothing and conducive to her preparations.

Well, who would have guessed? Now, where was I?

"Will you walk into my parlor, said the spider to the . . ."

*

Saul Cameron turned into the corridor leading to his private administrative suite and quickened his pace. After several weeks of bickering and wrangling, he at last held the final draft in his hands; the template for the mission briefing that would seal the fate of Arden.

And everything else, if Stained-With-Blood is right.

He knew the others awaited him inside. Calen and Sariff, long-term stalwarts who had supported the human colony through thick and thin from the very beginning; Mohammed, whom he'd known longer and trusted more than anyone else; Consulan Pulígio, as obstructive to Saul's every move as the day was long; Shaní, whose soothing temperament always kept things from boiling over; Sol Berek and his new Sul, Shannon De Lacey, who appeared to be getting along famously. And Sam, in his role as head of Special Operations would be there too, along with Marcus and Searc, two individuals whom Saul wished he could clone and turn into an army.

And not all of them are going to like what I have to say.

He stopped just beyond the entrance, steeling himself for the ordeal ahead.

Make or break, we create our own destiny today. And for once Pulígio isn't going to be the only fly in the ointment.

Saul grinned and stepped forward to trigger the external sensor. When the doors slid silently into wall recesses, he wasn't surprised to find the main office empty. Sure enough, everyone had crowded into the convention room where he kept an antique-style coffee percolator purloined from one of the Husker-Trent crowd.

Typical.

The gathering noticed his arrival and waved cheerily. Even Pulígio seemed unnaturally chirpy, which immediately put Saul on edge.

"I do hope you've left some for me, Marcus?" Saul shouldered his way through the old-fashioned glass door. "I've worked up enough of a headache sorting this nightmare out to last a month of Sundays. I need something to take the edge off."

"The third pot is just about ready," Marcus replied. He held the jug aloft and swished its contents. "I knew you wouldn't mind, so I took the liberty."

"Third pot?" Saul was aghast. He looked around the oval-shaped conference table and couldn't fail to notice how everyone's mugs appeared suspiciously full. "You're supposed to drink the bloody stuff, not inhale it."

"What can I say? With a dozen of us crowded in here, and your tiny goblets . . . Are you sure you didn't get them mixed up with eggcups?"

Several people laughed and raised their drinks in salute.

Ignoring them, Saul shuffled toward his position. Once there, he sat and immediately activated a small box embedded within the arm of his seat. A barely discernible whine thrummed out, rising in pitch until it soared beyond hearing.

Discerning his mood, everyone settled down.

"Someone's keen to be getting on with it then." Marcus handed Saul his coffee. "Unless the force field is there to prevent anyone else from getting their hands on your personal stash of Robusta?"

Despite it being piping hot, Saul took a long, deep pull of the rich, aromatic beverage and smacked his lips in satisfaction. In reply to the looks of astonishment on several faces, he explained: "Asbestos tongue. A skill acquired after long years in the military when the shit could hit the fan at the most inopportune moments . . . and often did." Saul's clarification acted as an icebreaker. "My apologies," he continued. "While I appreciate the courtesy the Senatum extended in allowing *me* to make the final choice, it's put me under a great deal of pressure. A hell of a lot is riding on what takes place over the next several months, so I've done my best to weigh the needs of our people against what resources we have available." He paused to press his info-pad into the table slot before him. "If you would kindly place your own notebooks into the link, I'll transfer the verdict to you. Understand, while I'll be happy to listen to any concerns you have, what you read in this report isn't open to debate. I've made my choice. Here's a breakdown of the main points."

A directory appeared on each screen. Saul allowed his audience a few minutes to skim the bullet points, then took control. He projected a larger version of the contents onto the holo-field suspended above the table, and manipulated the controls.

"Okay, ladies and gentlemen, let's get to it. As you know, we've had to employ a three-tiered strategy. While that will severely reduce manpower here on home world, particularly in respect of the revitalization of the outer districts, it's an evil we'll have to tolerate. We simply don't have the luxury of waiting until the restoration schedules boost our numbers sufficiently to make things comfortable, so this is an overview of the way it's got to be.

"The *Shadow of Autumn* will head directly to the Ularan Spur where she will use her stealth capabilities to enter the Verianda Nebula undetected. Once inside, her operating procedures will be directed along two main avenues of investigation. Assessment of the circumstances on each of the three planets—Latinus Prime, Illumina, and Exordium—and then, dependent upon what is discovered, the execution of specific micro tasks; for example, the retrieval of mutated expatriates and salvage or destruction of technology.

"While the *Autumn* is thus engaged, the colonies expedition led by the frigates *Paladin* and *Dark Falcon* will be hard at work throughout the rest of the protectorate. Their particular remit will be to follow up on the latest scan results. On those worlds where no Horde presence was detected, they will verify those findings before reseeding the atmosphere with the re-genesis matrix. Life will be allowed to return, and outposts will be reestablished as our own numbers increase. The same can be said of those settlements where we confirmed the continued presence of our friends, except that it'll obviously take a little longer. To maximize safety, setrium-4 will be dispersed as needed. Once resistance has been neutralized, teams will round up pockets of ogres that remain and secure them within null-point compounds along with a suitable power source to sustain them while they undergo metamorphosis. The planet itself will be quarantined during this phase, and placed under the supervision of one of our primary sat-link modules. The command platform will carry a full complement of drones to undertake repairs of each colony's satellite system and monitor developments on the ground. Now, each—"

"You're making this sound very nice and easy." Pulígio smirked. "But how have you managed to find the people to undertake all these mercy missions—and who, specifically, is going to Exordium?"

Without bothering to look at the thorn in his flesh, Saul altered the readout within the info-cloud. A register of citizens appeared, divided into specific categories. By far the largest group was comprised of Roman soldiers.

"Thank you for asking," Saul responded. "The lists speak for themselves, but I'll tell you anyway . . ."

To make a point, however, Saul took his time drinking the rest of his coffee, and only then resumed: "Notwithstanding the huge losses suffered during the Battle of the Line, the Ninth Legion still represents the major physical element of our armed forces. Obviously, Marcus had to redeploy his units following that encounter, and created three oversized cohorts comprised of a minimum of five hundred and twenty men. They are the foundation we turn to when things need doing. The revival program for our outlying cities, for example, was only possible because of their help. They're as industrious as they are resourceful." Saul looked directly at Pulígio and held his gaze. "*That's* where I got the manpower. I intend to leave Arden in the capable hands of Lucius Claudius Tacitus and the Second Cohort. The colonies expedition will get the Third, under Sextus Vergilius Martilas. While troop disposition will be down to him, I have no doubt he'll divide his numbers between both ships, and put his Optio, Marcus Aurelian, in command of one company. This leaves the cream of the Legion available for the main event. It's my opinion we'll need the very best fighters to contend with whatever we might find."

"Five hundred and twenty men?" The Consulan held his gaze. "For an enterprise of this magnitude? Is that all?"

"Of course it isn't *all*," Saul snapped, "and if you took your head out of your ass long enough to actually study the plan, you'll see each contingent has ample backup."

Pulígio went to open his mouth again. A robust squeeze to the shoulder, delivered by none other than the Deputy Magister, stalled him.

Saul glanced her way and winked.

Good girl, Shaní. Pity I'm going to have to tear your world down as a thank you.

He decided it best to forge ahead before anyone else could interrupt.

"Right, to the second part of the Consulan's question." Saul adjusted the readout again, focusing on one list of names. "*This* is who will be going to Exordium. I'll clarify part of my thinking process as I go through it, but don't use that as an excuse to start arguing. Understood?"

Miraculously, everyone nodded.

Yeah, we'll see.

"Because of the significance of this undertaking, we need someone in charge who can be trusted to act prudently, who's been tried and tested in the heat of battle; someone we can rely on not to crack under pressure. This commander must also be a person that men and women will respect. Mohammed, that person is *you*."

Mohammed's expression showed surprise, and then went flat. Reading his countenance, Saul was heartened to see a slight smile remain at the corner of his friend's lips.

I thought so. He's gonna enjoy himself.

All those good feelings disappeared, however, when he glanced toward the Deputy Magister. Her initial shock at the announcement was passing, and ill-disguised pain came hot on its heels.

And so it begins

"You're going to need an outstanding second," Saul continued, "a warrior who is not only held in high esteem by the legion and Senatum alike, but an ambassador who has applied himself to a deeper understanding of Arden's culture and her technical sophistication. Marcus? You'll be going along as well."

The former general didn't move a muscle.

Addressing him in particular, Saul explained: "As you know, Flavius Velerianus has a strong character and can be rather . . . opinionated. With such a large number of his men forming the bulk of the fighting force, I'm thinking ahead to avoid any possible hiccups. The smooth progression of good order is paramount with a task like this."

Comprehension dawned on Marcus's face. "That, I can understand, my friend. Thank you for the vote of confidence."

Beside him, Searc Calhoun crowed with delight and slapped Marcus hard on the back. "Ha. We'll rouse hell together, brother. You'll see, just you and—"

"Hang on," Saul said, "I didn't mention anything about your highlanders. The Second Cohort are good, Searc, but with the loss of so many defenders to other projects, they'll need support from those we can rely on. From what I've seen over this past year, that's you and your men. I'm sorry, but I have to ensure Rhomane is left in strong hands, so *you'll* be staying here."

A terrible passion gathered behind Searc's eyes, and Saul wondered if it might spill over into violent expression. The whole group felt the tension. People fidgeted. Marcus reached out and placed his hand over that of his comrade. Gradually, the fire faded, and Saul saw everyone relax.

"My lads will be disappointed we've not been invited to your wee shindig," Searc grumbled, "but when I explain that we're needed to babyshite the ladies o' the Second Cohort and carry their skirts for them, I think I just might win them over with only a fraction o' blood being spilt."

"Thank you for your patience," Saul replied, "I won't forget this. There'll be plenty of trips out in the future, particularly to clear up the colonies as the quarantines are lifted. I promise you, we'll do all we can to ensure you and yours get first dibs on those missions."

Fellow council members showed their support by offering murmurs of agreement, and Saul extended his hand in the time-honored fashion. "Deal?"

Searc hawked back the contents of his nose and spat into his own palm before accepting the shake.

Bugger! I'd forgotten they do that.

Not knowing what else to do, Saul cleared his throat and prepared to carry on. He did, however, ensure to keep his arm as still as possible while deciding where he could rid himself of the congealed phlegm without causing offence.

Oh great, it's already starting to trickle.

"Er, anyway . . . it's not *all* doom and gloom for the Caledonians. Since Ullas Ferguson and his clan were decimated during the Battle of the Line, Angus McGregor has picked up the reins admirably. He's taken the Damnonii back to their mounted hit and run traditions—traditions, I might add, which will prove very useful to the overall mission objectives. As we now have a surplus of horses, I've had Angus drilling with Jake Rixton and his detachment over the past month to see how well they work together on long range reconnaissance patrols. You'll be pleased to know the Damnonii show a great deal of panache for that kind of thing, both in and out of the saddle, so I've included them in the list. They'll team up with Jake and boost his platoon back to company strength. We've promoted Jake, to make it clear who's in overall command, but adding Angus will provide a lot of additional on the ground cover which will leave Sam and his guys free to do what they do best. Talking of which . . ."

Saul leaned forward so he could concentrate solely on the black ops leader.

"Sam? I looked over your proposals and have agreed to them. This is how I've decided to distribute your squads. You will note it reflects the new ranks, to denote your expanded responsibilities, both effective immediately and when you get back."

He tapped a brief sequence into the screen, and a small chart, divided into four subdivisions appeared. Saul directed everyone's attention to them.

"As you know, since Sam inherited the Special Forces team a year ago, he's been working hard to rebuild their strength. An operative's life involves a high degree of mental fortitude to handle the nature of the work and the mortality rate that goes with it. Realizing this, he initiated a program by which he's been able to handpick a small nucleus of candidates who appear to have what it takes. Initially, newer entrants will serve in a reserve capacity, but if they do well in the field, there's a proviso to make each position permanent. This will be especially important once the Ranger Initiative commences, as it will give us a pool of experience to draw on.

"The new breakdown is as follows, and is comprised of the permanent members of One Troop, together with the reservists of Two Troop."

"Saul, I see you've kept Angela Brogan and Danny Ricci together and have paired them opposite two of the new revivals, Revan Caspar and Ferell Hernias. Have you thought about getting them up to the ship to liaise with Seraphim? Remember, much of the actual flying will be undertaken by mental interface. They'll need time to engage with the *Autumn*'s neural interlink and get used to Seraphim's distinct personality matrix."

"Already taken care of. They departed first thing this morning, as did the other department heads. I know they've only got a few days, but I want them familiarized with their new surroundings prior to departure . . ." *Oh, that reminds me.* "My apologies, Mohammed, I've been quite remiss."

Saul cleared the screen and replaced the image with a live-time feed from orbit. From what he could ascertain, the cambot must have been on the leeward side of the great vessel, for everyone was treated to an abrupt close-up of what looked like multiple tiers of glittering diamonds, burning fiercely within framed metal encasements.

"Allow me to introduce you to your new commission. You'll find her shipshape and ready to go."

From this angle, the myriad twinkling lights made the *Shadow of Autumn* look like a planet-sized mainframe that had been left running to solve a monster computation. As the relay drone maneuvered onto the sunny side, however, they discovered this would-be CPU was like no other, for it was nearly three miles long and studded with spars, struts, astral navigation clusters, an awe-inspiring variety of cannon emplacements, and a whole host of gun and torpedo ports.

Sleek, black, and heavily armored, she looked every inch the predator she was designed to be.

The room went quiet, and Saul noted with satisfaction the look of hunger in Mohammed's eyes.

Good. He'll need that fire in the days ahead.

"As some of you are already aware, this little lady has been refitted and equipped with mission specific offensive and defensive platforms. The Menta accelerators, for example, are now loaded with iron-tipped shells possessing a one-in-ten explosive hematite ratio. Her Phoenix ballistic missiles have been swapped out too, and replaced with the new Jaguar tactical strike warheads. Basically, we're arming her to the back teeth with anything that will neutralize the Horde, be it on a small or large scale. Vortex generators, singularity compressors, setrium mortars. And if things go tits-up, we have a dozen of Ephraim's latest babies, Leviathan planet-crushers . . ."

"Are you sure that will be necessary?" Pulígio remarked, clearly shocked by the calculated statement he had just heard. "This isn't the first time you've talked of large-scale destruction. I thought we were going to all this bother to save our people, not wipe them out willy-nilly?"

"One way or another, the nightmare ends," Saul replied. "We hold all the cards now, and from what I've seen of the RTB—the Reactive Tactical Battle system—we also hold an ace up our sleeve. Even if a disaster occurred and there was a catastrophic loss of life, Seraphim would be capable of completing the mission."

"Which is?" the Consulan pressed.

"In those circumstances? The complete sterilization of the Verianda system. My priority is the survival of Arden, with or without your mutated cousins. And if they dare threaten our existence, they won't survive to enjoy any temporary success they might achieve."

A deeper hush descended.

It's probably best I wrap this up before too many spanners get thrown into the works.

"Look, we've got a big day ahead of us tomorrow, and a lot to take on board. I suggest you take a copy of my decision home with you, so you have time to digest its implications. If anyone manages to think of a valid reason for an amendment, *and I do mean valid*, then by all means, my door is always open. But don't delay. Final mission prep starts at dawn. Thank you."

Saul made his way through into the main office and stood in front of the panoramic windows. Here the air was much cooler away from the press of people, so he seized the opportunity to open a vent and snatch a few deep, invigorating breaths as he admired the view. He sighed and massaged his temples. The headache was still there, niggling away in the background. He had a sneaking suspicion it would remain that way until everyone had departed safely on their respective journeys.

Quiet footfalls approached from behind, and Saul detected a sweet fragrance with citrus undertones.

Shaní.

"Well done, Commander," she said warmly, "a difficult task, handled deftly and with precisely the right amount of firmness."

"Thank you, Deputy Magister. I've had to become quite the ambassador since we arrived here, so it'll be nice to share the load once things begin to change." He pinched the bridge of his nose. "And *that* can't come a day too soon."

"I appreciate how you feel," Shaní cooed, "for power carries burdens everyday folk cannot begin to imagine. And *you* have carried them longer than most." She moved to face him. "Forgive me, but I noticed you were out of sorts during the meeting, so I thought it prudent to approach you swiftly, especially while your final comments are still fresh in the mind."

Here it comes. She's going to ask me to take Mohammed off the mission.

"Go on?"

"Your appointment of Mohammed as mission leader was a wise move. He is much loved and respected . . ."

"Buuut?"

She smiled, and the gesture put Saul on edge as much as it relaxed him.

Why do I feel like I'm being circled?

"You are most perceptive, Commander, so surely you can see? Even with only a brief glance at your directive, I discerned at least fifty-three Ardenese names on the list. Not a great number, true, but my people will be fulfilling essential roles nonetheless. Would it not be a course of prudence to include a member of the political wing of the Senatum within the command ranks? Not to interfere, of course, but to demonstrate their contribution is recognized, and to provide a vital link to home that will remind them of what they are fighting for. After all, the Ninth have their eagle."

Caught unawares, Saul didn't know how to respond.

Is she trying to palm Pulígio off on them? He had to admit, the notion had a sense of karma to it. *And he* is *fiercely nationalistic.*

Shaní fixed him with the look she usually reserved for troublesome customers, and gently took his hand in hers.

"At such short notice, I fear I may have presented you with something of a quandary. But fear not. To ease your turmoil, I volunteer *my* services, and will explain my decision to the other senators tonight. I am sure they will be most gratified by the wisdom of including one of our number on such a vital endeavor."

Saul was stunned. Maneuvered into a corner, he could only stare in mute wonder at the skilled dexterity of the politician before him.

Shaní took his silence as a sign of agreement. "Then it's settled."

Before Saul had a chance to respond, she patted his hand, spun on her heels and breezed from the office. Only then did he burst out laughing.

"What was all that about?" Mohammed queried as he entered the room.

"*That*, my friend, was a lesson in getting what you want without your opponent even realizing they've been duped."

Saul embraced his friend of eleven years and in a conspiratorial tone, whispered, "For the love of God, never, *ever*, teach that woman how to play poker. She'd have the shirts off our backs before we'd even realized what hit us."

From the look on his face, Mohammed clearly found that thought intriguing.

I rest my case. You're hooked, and you don't even know it.

PART II

"... where the foe's haughty host
in dread silence reposes"

— *Star Spangled Banner,* Francis Scott Key

Chapter Sixteen

Lost in the Right Direction

Caym stalked the bowels of the *Shadow of Autumn* like a metronome. Totally alone, he allowed his cadenced steps to fill the empty holds and slipped his mind into neutral, a waking meditation to help him while away the dullness of his existence.

They'd been in deep space over a month now and, although the dreadnaught was huge, the boredom daily reflected from the same old faces, the dreariness of eating the same food, and the tedium of staring at the same walls—whether in the mess hall, recreation deck, or his duty station—grated on his nerves.

The foray onto the surface of Illumina the previous week banished the monotony of a schedule dictated by military routine, but the excitement quickly faded away. All too soon he felt cooped up again, like a leonad waiting to pounce.

Acting on impulse, Caym had obtained permission from Mission Commander Amine to scour all cordoned-off areas of the *Autumn* on the pretext of completing additional security sweeps. One part of the ship was much like any other, but patrolling an extended range eased the frustrations building inside him.

As Caym patrolled, he had time to reflect on the changes this past year had wrought:

Strange, that freedom should bring such a degree of willing confinement. I was part of something primal, something grandiose and quixotic . . . And now? He gazed at yet another sterile passageway enwrapping him like a womb. *Now I'm not only restrained by the limitations of a physical body, but also by restrictions I've imposed upon myself by joining this vessel.*

Caym had never fully recovered the memories of his life before he became Kresh; those little details could have helped him remember who or what he'd once been. Snippets came from time to time, fleeting and far between. Regardless, he wondered how anyone in their right mind would consent to spending protracted periods away from home aboard a floating prison.

This is what animals must have felt like in those antiquated centers the history clips reveal we used to have in bygone days. What did they call them again? Oh yes, zoos. But those animals weren't willing; they were captives.

He broke his stride near the main hub dividing the aft and center bulkheads. Several compartments at one end of the mile-long hangar bay below his position had been converted into a quarantine area. There lay the recovered Kresh, sleeping, secured within gravity nets and cocooned within a neural and biometric field of healing energies. Invented by Dr. Penny Frasier, a xenobiologist specializing on his kind for many years, these would protect both crew and subjects while the ogres underwent metamorphosis.

A transformation I myself completed only a short time ago.

On a whim, Caym decided to see what all the fuss was about, choosing stairs instead of the elevators or transporter pad. He mused on the inclusion of such an outdated feature on an ultra hi-tech starship.

Who would have thought that, for all its sophistication, the Shadow of Autumn *would need a stairwell? Mind you: should all else fail, we can always rely on our own two feet.*

Round and round Caym went, down and down, his footsteps echoing along deserted hallways. This emptiness was standard operating procedure for the vessel isolated any compartments not in permanent use. Caym traversed decks where the only illumination was the emergency lighting system. Strung out in pairs like eyes and spaced wide apart, the eerie red strobes glowed balefully, creating yawning chasms of darkness where hatchways should be. For some reason, the strobes made him uneasy. He chuckled.

Who would have imagined a former bogeyman could be afraid?

The sensation intensified unexpectedly, only to subside as abruptly as it began. Still coming to terms with his new fleshly existence, Caym halted and stood stock-still: *Hmmph! One of the pitfalls of being limited within this condition? I have no control over certain automatic reflexes, and they're an unpredictable distraction. Perhaps I'll ask Penny for some advice while I'm here.*

Resolutely, he resumed his walk, soon finding himself in the arterial passage leading toward the flight deck. The closer he got, the more signs of life intruded. From what he could see, most people were wearing either hospital scrubs or adapted Haz-Ent suits.

He approached the final intersection. A crimson beam lanced out and washed across his body. Two drones appeared out of a concealed hatchway, energetic and ballistic countermeasures already deployed and trained on his position.

"Remain still," the cold, hard voice of Seraphim intoned. "State your name and purpose."

"Caym, of the Senatum Kresh, as you can plainly see. I'm here to speak with Doctor Frasier, as I hope to offer assistance with her special patients."

A delay ensued while the AI determined the veracity of his request. Fortunately, he didn't have to wait long.

"Thank you for your patience, Caym." Seraphim's tone had warmed considerably. "Your biochip has now been added to the list of approved crewmembers allowed limited access to this site. Please ensure not to cross into any area bordered by a red line unless escorted."

"I wouldn't dream of it."

The doors swished open as the sentinels melted away. Left to his own devices, Caym entered and found himself immediately attracted to activities on the other side of a huge reinforced window. When he got close enough to peer down, he saw that the landing bay for executive shuttles had been cordoned off and transformed into a makeshift hospital ward. Therein, row upon row of cots stretched into the distance. Shaped much like circular bathtubs, each contained a shimmering gelatinous blob of ectoplasm which oozed and bubbled as if being gently heated from below.

Having undergone the process himself, Caym knew the esoteric characteristics of his kinsfolk were slowly being coaxed back toward their original corporeal template.

"Incredible, isn't it?"

"Eh?" Taken by surprise, Caym started, and turned to find Penny Frasier standing beside him.

"Incredible, isn't it, to think we can undo hundreds of years of damage in a matter of months?" She frowned. "Or perhaps it would be more accurate to say we *start* to unravel the damage with science, and then let your bodies do the rest."

Caym could appreciate the doctor's reservations. "I'd like to say I know what you mean, Doctor, but that would be inaccurate. Don't get me wrong, a small portion of my mind knew changes were taking place. But for the most part, I was stuck inside a daydream, and I didn't want to wake up." He jutted his chin toward the simmering mass. "So what is it you're actually doing?"

Penny pursed her lips before answering: "Let's simply say we're trying to reassemble a puzzle. I take it you've seen the jigsaws lying around the various restrooms back in Rhomane and here on the ship?"

"Yes, I have. I can see why you humans love them; they're quite relaxing."

"Well, this process is similar. When your original form mutated, it warped away from its natural pattern: the rip-space field picked up your 'box' and shook its contents so hard everything became scrambled at a cellular level. So, what we're doing here is jogging residual memories. We're reminding *their* bodies of the picture on the lid." Penny indicated the complex around them. "Once a subject is subdued, we immerse them in a biophysical stew containing all the ingredients their mutated DNA needs to return to its normal state. Using a bioformatic algorithm I designed, we pinpoint specific nucleotides within their matrix and reactivate them. When that's achieved, we bond them to a mutagenic agent; in this case, a fabricated compound of the cryptogen. That done, we zap the host with an energetic stimulus such as X-rays, gamma rays, or alpha particles. Then we add the final reactive agent: the re-genesis matrix, which elicits a corrected nucleotide explosion at the molecular level. This in turn kick-starts the proper functioning of their DNA." Penny gestured toward the ranked cots. "As you can see, all we need do is keep our subjects in an induced coma while the magic does its work."

Caym grunted appreciatively. "Gradually, all the pieces are shuffled back into place, so it ends up like the original picture on the lid?"

Penny smiled. "Almost. There's the hybrid factor to take into account and, of course—the weird interrelation between self-awareness and memory. Each plays an important role in the restoration of full cognitive functioning."

Caym noticed how the doctor's comment spurred her to become more focused.

Without a shred of embarrassment, she studied him closely. "How much of your former life do you recollect?"

"Not much. Every now and then a memory comes, but when I try to latch onto it, it's like trying to recall an event I never witnessed. You might describe it as a strong déjà vu, or as feeling lost while knowing you're traveling in the right direction." Caym sighed. "Most exasperating."

"And yet you automatically remembered how to drive a skimmer. Fly a shuttle. Carry out complex functions on a computer, and all sorts of other things that would take considerable time to learn."

"Your point?"

"Give it time, Caym. You're going through a period of adjustment, much more so than your pureblood cousins. Relax. Be yourself. We suspect most things will come back to you eventually. But you can't rush it, I'm afraid . . ."

Penny's voice trailed away; her head cocked to one side.

Caym noticed how the doctor's interest in him intensified the longer she watched him.

She narrowed her eyes. "What did you actually want here, Caym?"

"I came to ask your advice. It's been more than two months since I awoke, but it's obvious my hormones haven't settled. My emotions keep running away with me. One minute I feel I'm in danger of snapping someone's head off; the next, the slightest thing gives me the jitters. I can't have that. I'm here to offer my support to crewmates when they face danger, or to any Kresh that might wish to communicate instead of attack. How can I be of use to anyone if I can't maintain self-control?"

Penny's gaze flicked from side to side. Caym could almost visualize the neurons flaring inside her brain as she tried to find a solution to his predicament . . .

"Of course!" She snapped her fingers. "Despite what happened to you physically, we must recall the psychological and physiological changes wrought upon you as well. If I was forced to use one term to describe a Horde ogre, it would be . . . anger, or fury, or pure unadulterated rage. What about concentrated ardor, or vehemence? Intense fervor, perhaps?" She waved an apology. "Sorry, I know that's a good half dozen expressions, but it highlights my point. The transformation didn't mutate only your body. It warped your feelings too, in a way that's affected your instincts, sentiments, and intuition. Everything about you was supercharged. What it all boils down to is the fact you've been overdosing for centuries. It'll take a while for your system to wean itself down from a constant state of hyper-frenzied anxiety."

Caym was crestfallen:

"Is there anything I can do to speed the process?"

"I can only tell you what *I* would do in your situation. Whatever sets you off, face it until you master it. It won't be easy, but it'll be the quickest way to establish exactly *which* situation produces *what* reaction. Once we know the triggers, we can determine the next stage of attack."

"So you'll help me?"

"Of course." Penny patted him on the arm. "I've studied the Horde for most of my life on Arden. What use would I be if I didn't put what I've learned into practice when somebody actually needs it?"

"Thank you, doctor, that's good to know. I'll get right on it."

"Good to hear." Penny glanced at her watch and grimaced. "I have to go. My rounds are overdue and I can't let things slide, especially with the number of patients I have under my care." She turned, and called back over her shoulder. "Listen, I'm due a rest day tomorrow. If you stop by my cabin after the lunch schedule is over, we can discuss things in detail and devise a more structured plan. Sound good?"

"Thank you. Yes, I'll be there." Caym watched her depart.

So, what winds me up?

Several things sprang to mind.

Those damned council meetings. I could understand holding them on a daily basis if we'd encountered problems, but just for the sake of it? There's being thorough, and there's being anal. And listening in on petty arguments, too. I know soldiers whine to let off steam, but the mess hall is supposed to be a place of relaxation, not constant bickering.

A sudden realization struck home.

The trouble is, if I start there I might hurt someone. No, I need somewhere secluded. Somewhere away from . . . oh!

A perfect solution presented itself.

That chill I got on the way here. It's bothered me ever since; and really, where else am I going to get an opportunity to practice away from prying eyes?

*

An age had passed since Va-ákil last ventured to the surface, but that was understandable, for circumstances rarely warranted it. The fleshly infestation had been harvested many cycles previously and, once eradicated, left behind many contrivances profuse with nourishment. However, none were more abundant than those within the cave system where she subsequently entrenched herself.

Moving there had been a shrewd gambit: although adolescent, she had sensed something special about the raw power so artfully concealed. Revenant in nature, it provided the catalyst for tremendous growth and maturation. And as time passed she'd not only had unrestricted access to its blessing, but she'd chosen her champions wisely.

Just as well, for once the unworthy dross of her kind had been flensed from existence, those with a far stronger claim had come, demanding their share of sweet and unlimited solace. In a determined manifestation of strength, she'd denied those challengers and cast them out, demonstrating her fitness to lead both the spawning and her race.

Va-ákil had become Magnate that day, and set the precedent by which the three principal hives would be governed. She'd attempted to extend her influence, of course, but those Kresh occupying planets farther out refused to listen, being consumed instead by the urge to strip their worlds bare and live under their own governance.

So, while other nests flourished briefly before perishing, the triumvirate thrived and endured, spawning ever greater subjects, the potential of whom were without peer among their kind.

And for what? She thought again of recent events. The effort only darkened her mood and left a bitter aftertaste across the peripheral folds of her receptors, for while her strategy had worked perfectly, there had been a price.

In taking the bait, the enemy revealed much about their motivation and resilience. Nevertheless, I don't feel the circumstances warrant celebration, for it was a costly victory, and I now must ensure that the forfeiture of an entire colony was not in vain.

Va-ákil stared out across the basin.

In centuries past, majestic forests and sweeping grasslands surrounded the city positioned at the center of the plain before her in a sea of emerald-green and lilac vibrancy. Now its gleaming spires lay abandoned, its ruins themselves obscured behind a permanent veil of dust whipped by hurricane winds.

A fitting tribute to the desolation we unleashed.

She sighed.

I stand at the fulcrum with a sky as tall as forever before me. But the farther I look, the more the horizon stretches away into uncertainty . . .

And the price! Thousands lost to perversion.

Breakers of pain crashed against her resolve, resonant with whispers of her future's end. As they receded, each raked shrieking scores along the spine of her soul, mocking her for failing to devise a less drastic solution.

It was not *a failure.* Her determination to succeed solidified. *I did what needed to be done, and must capitalize on what I have learned—or their sacrifice will have been for naught.*

A glacial overtone crystallized the timbre of her will. Va-ákil extended her senses and reached out toward those she had known since the birthing vats.

I can still feel them . . .barely. But they are fading from my perception and their intimacy will soon be lost amid the static wash of lower life forms.

Caution vied with boldness for mastery of her codex, and once again Va-ákil found herself wavering.

Our paths present an ugly truth to face, for each is stained with guilt upon an ebbing tide of remorse. No matter what I do, what we are now is lost.

This fact pained her more than she ever could have imagined.

Cursing, Va-ákil opened her mind, peering through the fabric of spacetime to witness the consequences of courage.

As foreseen, perpetuity at rest awaited. Abundance had led to stagnation and decay, a spiraling chaos where eventual extinction would cause them to fade like mist from the annals of history.

Yes, that result lies far into the future, but it is inevitable nonetheless.

The other choice was just as destructive, requiring a willing obliteration of identity, an act that would transform their very nature into something different, something alien, and repulsive.

With the instant upon her, Va-ákil recoiled from both.

That is not progress.

But a third option waited. It glowed dimly before her, provocative, teasing her. She bathed in the scope of its cadence and dared to hope: despite great peril, the tenets of their faith could remain pure.

A verse from an ancient hymn came to mind, which newly awakened Kresh sang on their elevation from ignorance to enlightenment.

Inaugurated,
I do not seek absolution for the actions that led me here,
For my origins were benighted and bereft of reason.
Like musk that scents my presence,
I cloak myself in dominion and sovereignty

And dream of loss as eloquence.
Now baptized in a catalyst of infinite malice,
I take what I want, and when,
And begin the ascent to mastery.

As the song faded, fresh intent manifested in the ether about her.

Do I still have the courage to risk losing it all to gain everything?

The scales of doubt fell from her eyes, and Va-ákil made her decision.

Chapter Seventeen

On The Crest of a Wave

Waiting for his guest to arrive, Mohammed flicked through the report of the previous week's mission. He couldn't suppress a twinge of regret.

The Architect's intrusion into his life had resulted in an eight-year hiatus from journeys into deep space. Was it truly more than a decade since Mohammed had last been in combat in a vacuum environment? Yes, that long. Regardless, the first major engagement of this operation had yielded a resounding victory. So much so that the soldier in him was secretly disappointed when the entire event turned anticlimactic.

With intelligence on the latest genus of Horde ogres as yet incomplete, command was unsure how good the new strain might be at detecting energy emissions. In view of this, Mohammed chose to adopt an evasive approach, hoping to improve the odds of a successful outcome. He was assisted by the inherent dynamics of the Verianda Nebula, which were extremely volatile. Surveys confirmed that thirty-two percent of the singularities within the cluster were rotational.

Armed with those particulars, Mohammed directed the *Shadow of Autumn* to cloak, and under cover of its stealth technology deployed the ship to a location where the concentration of conflicting gravity fields was weakest. After plotting an appropriate course, he ordered the engines shut down entirely; this allowed the dreadnaught to drift inside. Having entered, the crew utilized the spinning ergospheres of the first three black holes they encountered to gradually adjust their trajectory and gain speed. Finally, they exploited the magnitude of a lone neutron star to slingshot them toward their objective: Illumina.

Mohammed smiled at the memories those maneuvers conjured.

Many years before, he'd attended an art exhibition held in Paris by Morgan Zayin, one of the world's top photographers. Several of Zayin's pictures had been taken on slow exposure, capturing the split-second when a series of strobe lights exploded inside an abandoned warehouse. The images produced symptoms very similar to retina burns in everyone witnessing them, and Mohammed had never forgotten how surreal the experience was.

Threading their way through the endless well of darkness, interspersed as it was with isolated clusters of blinding intensity, made Mohammed feel as if he were navigating that same canvas from long ago, for the visual effect was almost identical:

A photonegative extravaganza that was utterly mesmerizing.

Even better, his strategy proved faultless, for it allowed the *Shadow of Autumn* to fall upon its prey without mercy.

Within seconds of the starship's arrival, scans confirmed the presence of more than two thousand Horde scattered throughout three major research facilities. While some fiends detected the intrusion and roused to immediate action, it did them little good, for vast clouds of atomized setrium-4 rained down upon their positions.

Thus surprised, most brutes simply fell into a stupor, while those remaining alert or offering marginal resistance were obliterated from orbit by precision bombing.

Once the gravity fluctuations subsided, the *Shadow of Autumn* seeded the target atmosphere with the re-genesis template. Mohammed needed only to wait a few days for the matrix to take effect before deploying groundside retrieval teams. These recovered the eight hundred and seventy-four subjects deemed suitable for relocation. They then quarantined the planet itself, leaving it in the care of a command sat-module and its squadron of drones. Programmed to remain undetected for protracted periods, the drones would only activate fully once the entire system was clear of all opposition.

It's a different type of warfare than I'm used to, that's for sure.

He reminisced about people he'd known whilst serving in Earth Fleet, and missions undertaken during a twenty-year career that had seen him advance from a young flight officer during the Mars Colonial Rebellion of 2322 to full Commander under Saul Cameron during the Breach of Pintus 12, in 2340.

Those were heady times of battles won and comrades lost, where life expectancy could be counted in months or even weeks for those who couldn't focus on the job at hand.

He glanced at the pale scar running from elbow to wrist along the back of his left arm.

And sometimes, it didn't matter how good you were. Survival was down to blind luck.

In 2342, when the war ended, Mohammed and Saul parted company. While Saul stayed in the military, Mohammed accepted a position on the faculty of the Hawking-Tesla Institute of Science & Technology, one of the most prestigious cosmological universities in the world, based in Geneva.

And if I'd had my head screwed on, that's *where I'd have stayed. But oh no, the pull of the cosmos was too strong. All it needed was for Saul to call me out of the blue several years later, and I had to go and throw everything away. But how could I resist? The XO's position for the Pegasus Dwarf Galaxy expedition was a dream come true. All the more so as we were the ones chosen to test the* Regent*'s experimental Light-Drive propulsion unit.* He snorted. *Experimental deathtrap, more like.*

He thought the irony of the situation rather poetic.

And here I am, tinkering around in a floating three-mile-long city whose sophistication makes the Regent *look like a brick in comparison . . . and they* still *haven't fathomed how to make engines work properly.*

A gentle chime alerted him to someone at his door. The com-link revealed it was none other than Psi Calen.

Perfect timing!

"Hi, Calen," he activated the lock. "I've been expecting you. Please come in."

Arden's preeminent scientist entered and took a seat in front of the captain's desk while Mohammed launched straight into what was bothering him:

"I'm worried about maneuverability. I know we couldn't expect miracles, especially when you consider how quickly we got the *Shadow of Autumn* mission ready, but what's the problem with our FTL drive? I feel like I have to play nursemaid all the time, instead of the all conquering hero. The Verianda Nebula is several light years across, and I need to jump around to our targeted incursion points at the drop of a hat . . . if this undertaking is to stand any chance of success."

"I appreciate your concerns," Calen replied, "but there's nothing I can do at this juncture. Remember, we rushed to retrofit this vessel using engines that employ different operating parameters than she was originally designed for. Her volume and density are considerably larger. Even with the interlock upgrades we've installed, we're bound to experience a lag between command initiation and actual execution . . . At least until we've ironed out the glitches and improved the correlation between drag and displacement."

"So why has this started happening now, do you think?" Mohammed was keen to understand anything that might enhance or detract from his ability to fulfill the mission directives. "Where on earth could the surges be coming from?"

"I don't know," Calen admitted, "since we're faced with something of a contradiction. With the old power core still in place, I'd say the answer would be easy to find, because rip-space travel requires a colossal amount of power to bridge the gap between two distant points simultaneously. But we're not doing that with the new Slingshot Drive engines. All *they* do is engender an artificial event horizon so we can harness the accelerative potential created by gravity. I've been wracking my brains, and I can't find anything about the catapult process to account for the discrepancies we've seen—especially as Slipstreaming is slower, but far more energy efficient."

Mohammed tapped his index and forefinger against his lower lip. "Are there any outside influences you can consider? The oscillations didn't manifest strongly until we entered the rarified dust cloud surrounding the Verianda Nebula itself. Might the nacelle intakes have picked something up? An exotic particle? Or might there be a correlation between the proximity

The holo-field enlarged, and everyone spent a moment examining the expanded roster. It read:

One Troop Disposition:

Alpha Team:

Samuel Pell (CPT)—Robert Neville (Cpl)—Joseph Stark (SPC)—Edward Roberts (SPC)

Bravo Team:

Andrew Webb (1LT)—Stuart Duggan (Sgt)—Tosh Wanabe (SPC)—Katy Wilson (SPC)

Technical Specialist—Severin Robins

Two Troop Disposition:

Charlie Team:

Jeremy Kane (2LTr)—Ellen Anderson (SPCr)—Raheem Steed (SPCr)—Gary Collins (SPCr)

Delta Team:

John Hodgson (CPLr)—Hamilton Bristow (SPCr)—Mark Levi (SPCr)—Gregory Sanderson (SPCr)

Technical Specialist—Emily Thorne

"Needless to say, One Troop will be joining the crew of the *Shadow of Autumn* in their entirety. Two Troop will divide themselves between the *Paladin* and *Dark Falcon*."

Saul then brought up a final roll of names.

"This is a rundown of the various departments. Admin, engineering, medical, CIC, and so forth. I've tried to spread knowledge and skill sets as best I can. As you will note, I've kept those with an understanding of special operation procedures grouped together, as their know-how will prove invaluable to you . . . As will those former members of the Kresh who are willing to support this venture."

Mohammed indicated he wished to speak.

"Yes, my friend?"

of so many rogue black holes and our micro-singularity generator?"

Calen looked baffled. "Not so far as I'm aware, but after you mentioned the problem to me several days ago, I took the liberty of asking Seraphim to monitor the situation. Since then, she hasn't broached the subject but she may have detected something . . . or at least some place to start."

Good point.

"Seraphim, would you join us please?" Mohammed called out, "full visual representation."

"Certainly, Captain," a feminine voice responded, "one moment . . ."

A subliminal thrum reverberated around the room, and a prickling sensation fluttered across Mohammed's skin. Then Seraphim appeared.

Never before had Mohammed witnessed a full manifestation, and it took him by surprise. He'd expected the simulacrum to look like a senator or other city official. Instead, the AI had chosen the guise of a middle-aged military officer. With its athletic build, bobbed hair, and form-fitting coverall, Seraphim cut an imposing figure.

"Captain Amine, Chancellor Calen." Seraphim inclined her head. "How may I assist you?"

"You've no doubt been monitoring our conversation." Mohammed wouldn't mince words with a simulacrum, no matter how fetching. "Have you any idea why we've been suffering from spasmodic energy spikes?"

"No, not a one. Following Chancellor Calen's request, I have completed several cross-system diagnostic assessments; you will be pleased to know that, although temporary, the power core is operating within foreseen limitations. The Slingshot system produces the equivalent of one hundred and forty-four trillion zephyr-joules of power. While I would prefer a quotient in excess of two hundred trillion, this amount is acceptable for current demands from a craft of this size. We are not engaged in a series of running battles. Therefore more than sixty percent of the bulkheads have been sealed and life support discontinued to those areas. Under these circumstances, maintenance of essential services produces no significant drain on resources; and I have plenty held in reserve should the situation change."

"So why are we suffering the pulsations?"

Mohammed was surprised to see the ersatz express itself with one of the most human gestures in existence: It shrugged.

"I have no definitive answer at this time. The Hieram ram-scoop intakes remain free of obstruction, the matter-antimatter fractionators and plasma injectors are untainted by impurities, and the flux acquisitors are managing the magno-nucleic amplification stream well within acceptable parameters. And yet, the kinematic potential experiences spasmodic flux." Seraphim's head kinked to one side. "In my opinion, the lull might come from stresses caused by the difference in size between the *Arch of Winter* and *Shadow of Autumn*—or, more likely, the proximity of so many black holes in such a concentrated area of space. Such anomalies present a contradiction within spacetime. Even the Ardenese do not understand them fully. We could be experiencing an undetectable gravitational wash. Think of it as an overlapping network of conflicting fluctuations which interrupt or interfere with the transfer of subatomic plasma particles. Thankfully, the disparity does not appear to affect overall performance capability, so we really can't complain."

"Oh, I'm not," Mohammed responded, "I'm merely concerned that the surges might create a weakness, an Achilles' heel if you like, and give us away. Tell me, when these cascades occur, can you determine if we're emitting anything tangible the Horde might pick up on?"

Seraphim ruminated for an entire blink before replying: "No. The *Shadow of Autumn* is meant to run silent. She is insulated against the possibility of such leaks. And once the covert protocols are activated, she will remain invisible to outside scrutiny because those systems run on completely autonomous circuits. Yes, they derive their power from the core, but once charged they function independently. From what I have been able to ascertain, the irregularity appears isolated to the free flow of latent potential within the vector drive assembly. I must confess, this presents a paradox I am unable to fathom."

"So nobody's been down there tinkering?"

"Captain, apart from a single service corridor I've kept open for maintenance purposes, that entire area is without air or heat and is guarded by a paired set of armed drones."

"And our defensive and offensive capabilities are in no way compromised?"

"Certainly not. Chameleon and null-shields are at maximum capacity. The armory stores a full complement of Excalibur torpedoes, Viceroy vortex generators, Jaguar tactical strike missiles, Sparrowhawk interceptors—including Stinger and Hornet variants—and, of course, the Leviathan planet crushers. The only armaments used thus far are a dozen Octopod singularity compressors and forty thousand liters of setriun-4. My reactive tactical battle system employs a multilayered invasive firewall sheath that keeps each magazine operating independently. Each one is protected by a rotational cloud matrix, so that it is impossible to anticipate where the command protocols are operating from. As I mentioned, so far the glitch remains confined to the power transfer conduits. If it suddenly becomes nomadic or goes anywhere near the caches, it would arouse my suspicions and trigger an automatic level ten lockdown."

That's me told, then. "Thank you, Seraphim, I suppose that will be all."

The AI faded, leaving the two men to ponder the problem in silence.

Eventually, Calen asked, "So, what are you going to do?"

"What *can* I do except go with the flow? The fluctuations are more a niggling pain in the ass than an actual threat. And they're confined to the Slingshot core. No big deal when you consider it's the thrusters and aqua drive we rely upon in battle. No, I'm inclined to monitor the situation for now and see how it goes."

"And if the problem persists?"

"We're due to rendezvous with the *Helexia* the day after tomorrow. If the hitch continues after we've handed off our current batch of Horde, I'll just have to adapt my strategy. It's either that or think of a way to obliterate the entire nebula."

"What? You'd really consider that option?"

"Calen, you've seen what those monsters can do. What other choice would I have?"

Chapter Eighteen

You Know the Drill

A cascade of sizzling stars descended from the huge bay's upper reaches toward the combatants waiting on the deck below. Packed tightly together, their shimmering shields created a dappled effect, as if the surface of a pond had somehow been encapsulated where a convex plane of metal should be.

As each missile struck, a distinctive crackling sound lifted above the bark of command and counter-command, and lurid bursts etched the air in pyrotechnic blooms of red, yellow and golden light.

Somebody howled. A soldier fell to the deck, clutching his foot and writhing in agony. His compatriots moved to close the gap, laughing cruelly. But not for long . . .

"How many times do I have to tell you?" Marcus bellowed. "Keep your shins covered. This isn't the Empire anymore! Our foes are not human. You're supposed to be members of the First

Cohort, for Pluto's sake, not a bunch of raw recruits learning which way to piss on a windy day."

Exasperated, he threw his helmet to the deck.

"Right, gather round and I'll run you through it . . . *again*."

He signaled to the section of sagittaria positioned farther along the flight deck to fall-in on him as well.

"That looked painful."

Absorbed by the antics of the defenders, Marcus hadn't realized someone was behind him. He turned to discover the Deputy Magister studying him closely.

"Shaní," he snapped by way of greeting, "forgive me but I don't have time to stop and exchange pleasantries. These new patterns have to be drilled into them before the Latinus Prime objective. We might not be so lucky next time around, and until they learn to respond automatically, any ground engagement will prove extremely risky. A difficult task, as you just witnessed, for they are expert in habitual tactics and keep reverting to those when under pressure."

"Excuse me," she replied pleasantly. "I was merely remarking the difference in fighting styles between the various units practicing down here. I find it fascinating to watch how closely your men are bonded. If I keep out of the way, may I listen and observe?"

"Certainly, but bear in mind the air will shortly turn blue. I'll have to tear these idiots off a strip to drive my point home."

"Don't let me distract you." Shaní smiled, and Marcus caught a sparkling warmth in the depths of her eyes as she backed away. "Who knows, I might even learn something new? A word here and there, perhaps a phrase or two?"

He snorted.

Nothing she's not heard before, I'm sure.

Walking swiftly to a white board, Marcus waited before it, hands on hips and a scowl on his face as the first centuria congregated about him. He let them stew until they started to fidget. Only then did he begin: “Look, none of you have to carry much equipment, so this should be easy.”

He picked up a flexible X-frame device and activated it. The casing expanded and the distinctive mirrorlike sheen of a null-barrier sprang into existence.

Marcus waved the shield about.

“See how light it is? This adaptation of the scutum was designed especially for us. We’re foot soldiers and proud of it. We fight the enemy up close and personal, face to face, and *this*,” he brandished the screen, “should make our job a lot easier. So, when we form testudo—the tortoise pattern—we don’t have anywhere near the weight on our arms or strain on our backs as previously. Thus, keeping formation should be simpler, since the null-field allows monitoring of enemy movements while preventing them from seeing yours . . .”

The injured veteran hobbled across to join his comrades.

Marcus didn’t miss a beat: “Felix, glad you could join us. Please tell the rest of the centuria what you did wrong.”

“I raised my shield, sir, the old-fashioned way.”

“And what have I been telling you to do henceforth?”

“We ground it and keep our feet covered.”

“What do we do, people?” Marcus projected his voice so he could be heard at the other end of the hangar.

“We ground it,” they sang back in unison.

“I can’t hear you,” he boomed.

“We ground it, sir,” shouted the ranks, much louder this time.

Marcus moved closer to them.

“Yes, you’ve all served in one capacity or another for over a dozen years and are perfectly trained—to do things the old-fashioned way. The Legion way. But then you weren’t fighting soul-sucking monsters. Now you are. Any exposed flesh will afford the Horde an opportunity to fuck you, and through your absence, fuck your comrades as well. So, thanks to Felix, we're all totally fucked and will be running circuits for thirty minutes before the end of our training session today."

Muffled complaints echoed through the lines.

Marcus ignored their protests and turned his back, drawing a series of dots, rectangles, and miniature diagrams across the white board. Once he'd finished, he faced them again and chose a fraternal tone:

"Brothers, I could understand if this was all new. But it isn't. The configurations are almost identical to what we employed in Gaul and Cantabria. You're the cream of what's left of the glorious Ninth. I recommended you for this phase of the mission because Captain Amine needs the best, and that's what you are. Fighting together for well over a decade we built up a lot of habits, *good* habits I might add, that kept everyone alive. But it should also mean you're experienced enough to adopt new tactics quickly. And gentlemen, these tactics have been designed to save your life."

He gestured toward their uniforms.

"The new coveralls, for example, are lightweight, breathable, and fire resistant. They keep you warm when it's cold; they're laced with a hematite compound to stop our ever-hungry friends from feasting on you. The helmets are modern, incorporate a tri-D rotating visual enhancer and headphones for radio contact; they'll protect your skull from the crush injuries the brutes inflict when roused to a frenzy."

Marcus indicated a selection of medieval-looking and hybrid ballistic weapons arranged on stands either side of the whiteboard.

"Now, our armaments present a larger hurdle, for we come from simpler times than most. And yet, all of you are proficient in small arms use and the intricacies presented by the heavier machine guns, otherwise you wouldn't be here. You needn't be concerned, for although I'll discuss tactics with you another time, we won't be overly reliant on these futuristic weapons either.

"Why not? I'll tell you. We are here to discourage resistance among the Horde. Our objective is to recover as many subjects as we can for re-genesis processing. Not an easy task: our only guarantee is that our enemy will fall over themselves to get within killing range of us *until* we have motivated them to listen. To inspire cooperation, each of you will carry a fully automatic submachine gun and pistol. Some will be issued with grenades and mortars. You've trained with them, so you're well aware how much lighter they are than the kit we once carried: our resultant increase in stamina and power will be a deciding factor in any encounter. Once we've expended our ammunition into the initial Horde charge, we'll revert to time-tested implements, but with a twist. For example . . ." He paused to heft a twenty-five-foot long pike. "*This* is what I thought might pose the greatest challenge."

He lowered the pole so everyone could see its details more clearly, and noticed how even Shaní moved closer to gain a better view.

"Now, I know this looks like the sarissas of old, but thanks to the ministrations of Professor Miller and his team, it isn't. Allow me to demonstrate." Marcus peered along the ranks of his men, as if searching for someone in particular. "I need a volunteer . . . Felix!"

A burst of laughter met this announcement, and several nearby soldiers shoved the *volunteer* forward to a chorus of whistles and catcalls.

"Thank you, Felix," Marcus continued. "If you'd be so kind as to stand over there, just out of reach?"

As the legionnaire limped across to take his place in front of everyone, Marcus pointed out the features of the spear.

"For those of you forming the principes ranks, this will be your main defensive weapon once your bullets are spent. Get used to them. Each live sarissa will be tipped with a miniature gravity mine to fell several ogres at once. Obviously, the detonation will take the end of the shaft, too, but look here . . ."

Marcus lunged forward, delivering a stunning blow to Felix's torso. Winded, the unfortunate soldier doubled over and crumpled to the floor. Nobody sneered or offered other ridicule, for they were fascinated by the fact that a six-foot long section at the tip of the sarissa had simply shredded away in a fog of orange and white mist. As the dust dissipated, a mean-looking, double-edged blade was revealed.

"That powder you've just seen represents a cloud of microscopic iron filings. The concentrate will be sufficient to disrupt a Horde Master's matrix, as will the sarissa's cutting edge. On the real thing, the skewer itself will be made from a lydium-steel composite resilient enough to withstand the force created by each brute's immolation. Speaking of which . . ." Hand over hand, Marcus fed the handle back through his grasp until he reached a gleaming bevel approximately nine to ten feet from the tip. Tapping it with his finger, he continued: "This little beauty is an energy diffuser. Basically, it absorbs the potential generated by an ogre's destruction and dissipates it before it can become a feedback charge. Arranged as you will be in overlapping manipular formation, you'll present a formidable obstacle to the enemy's advance."

Raising the butt of the sarissa high, he slammed its heel into the deck with a resounding *clang*.

"You might be wondering why I've chosen this latest weapon, out of everything in our armory. The reason is simple: I anticipated a few hurdles for us to overcome as we adopt new procedures and adapt to modified tactics. And with something like *this*, I could understand that, for mastering its use will entail a departure from the drills we exercise and employ so well . . ."

Marcus let go of the handle, allowing the pole to clatter to the floor. As it came to rest, he snatched up his scutum again and held it high.

"However, I didn't imagine for one minute that men with your know-how would still be having problems with shield drills. The old ones weighed in at over twenty pounds. These babies are only five pounds, about the same weight as your dicks. And I know how much you like to play with them . . ."

A smattering of laughter rippled through the crowd.

"What's more, they afford enhanced protection. They're five feet tall and thirty inches wide. And as you've noticed by now, once deployed, their magnetic lock bonds them together until *you* decide to activate the release. Their operation is simple. So why are you having so much difficulty grasping the fact that it is *essential* to keep them on the floor? The Horde will do everything in their power to take you down; if they spot any exposed flesh, they'll be on you faster than a whore in heat . . ."

He threw the contraption toward Felix. As the unfortunate warrior caught it, the active plane of the null-field came into contact with his skin. There came a sizzling retort, and he folded to the deck for the third time that day.

"This will put them off, because (as you've just seen), the threshold delivers an esoteric shock that stuns organic life, and absolutely fries anything possessing an arcane matrix."

Marcus pointed toward the largest diagrams on one side of the board.

"You all know the maneuvers and formations for deployment like the back of your hands. They're a simple adaptation of what we used against the Gauls—with a few minor differences to account for our modified armaments—so there's no excuse to forget them. The cohort will be split into four centuriae. Each centuria will be divided into three lines: The hastati, who will initiate the engagement and soften the enemy's advance; the principes, who will provide tactical cover and aggressive response with our new sarissas; and the skirmishers on either side who will ensure the Horde don't get too frisky along the flanks. This is nothing new. I will leave these basic maneuvers up on the board so you can commit them to your obviously flaky memories, for I have a feeling you will need to rely on them sooner than you think. Weigh them off, people. Remember to keep the shield grounded. Practice these drills over and over until you think Felix won't make another mistake and drop us all in it."

A gentle hubbub percolated among the men before him.

Time to wind this up and reinforce the lesson. "Right, we're going to start the exercise all over again. Before we do, let's enjoy that little jaunt around the flight deck I promised."

A low-key muttering broke forth. The centuria grouped together and stripped for their punishment.

Marcus turned to the centurion leading the First Cohort.

"Tiberius? I want the names of the last ten men in, along with anyone else stupid enough to get hit by a flare when training resumes. Anyone on that list will complete an additional two laps of the entire hangar at the end of the day: that's another five miles."

A collective groan arose from the troops. But Marcus noticed with satisfaction how their preparations suddenly picked up. Several legionnaires were already sprinting away.

Ha! That's more like it.

"Won't that make them too tired to carry on?" Shaní enquired. "Especially poor Felix, who must be feeling rather the worse for wear?"

"On the contrary, it'll keep them fit and their minds focused. Remember, if they screw up here, they get up and do it all over again. Out there, they won't be so fortunate. They'll thank me in the long run . . . excuse the pun."

Shaní giggled, and Marcus started divesting himself of his clothing.

"What are you doing?" she enquired. "Surely you're not retiring for the day while your men are still training?"

"On the contrary, I must set an example in all things. If they get to complete a punishment, so do I. That's what makes us such an efficient team." He grinned. "You see, you *did* learn something new today."

Marcus was just about to set off when he noticed the Deputy Magister staring at his loincloth.

By all that is holy?

"Can I help you?" he asked, bemused by the obvious fascination his crotch held for the most powerful woman on Arden.

Shaní dropped her voice and her eyes.

"I do apologize for being forward, but as you know, Mohammed and I are becoming closer, something I am keen to encourage. Indeed, Mohammed himself also appears pleased by this arrangement and conducts himself as a true gentleman."

The worldly-wise politician appeared troubled.

Intrigued, Marcus pressed for clarification, "*Buuut* . . . ?"

"I'm still learning about the differences between our two races, and sometimes . . . how can I put this . . . ? Mohammed can be a stick-in-the-mud. It's difficult to get him talking about certain . . . subjects—which is rather annoying." She glanced about and sidled closer. "So I was intrigued by something you said a few minutes back. Tell me, are all human males so well endowed? *Five* pounds in weight?"

Marcus felt his eyes pop, and fought to keep his amusement from showing.

Seeing his reaction, Shaní appeared mortified. "Oh, I've offended you. I'm so sorry. I really should—"

"No, no, no; not at all." Marcus gestured toward his men, by now nearly two hundred yards away. "It's only . . . I really must go. Otherwise I'll eat my own words and incur that extra punishment I mentioned."

He gave her a brief hug before retreating as deftly as he could. "But as I'm sure you'll agree, this is a subject you should broach with Mohammed himself. I tell you what: when you're enjoying your meal together tonight, mention—in passing—what you heard here. Use it to begin a deeper, more meaningful discussion. You'll see; he'll really appreciate it."

Especially if I can get to an intercom first to warn him. Prude or not, he's a military man and knows the drill.

"Thank you, Marcus." Shaní giggled. "Your candor is much appreciated."

"My pleasure . . . Now if you'll excuse me, Deputy Magister, I really must fly."

Marcus turned on his heel and made haste to catch up with the trailing runners.

As he went, one thought spun round and round in his mind:

Gods, Mohammed will owe me for months with the mileage he'll get from this one.

*

Swallowing his anxiety, Caym closed his eyes, relaxed his muscles, leaned back against the cold bulkhead, and adopted the simple cadence Penny Frasier told him to try in this situation.

In through the nose. Out through the mouth. In through the nose, out through the mouth . . .

With each exhalation, Caym visualized his chest and deliberately willed his heartbeat and respiration to slow.

As his acuity blended with the ambiance saturating the atmosphere, hesitancy gave way to incredulity. The solidity of the walls around him and the deck beneath his feet faded, and he fell into a more tranquil frame of mind.

Well, would you look at that? How the devil did she know it would work on someone with my physiology?

Somehow, the lurking sense of menace that had made his hackles rise on the way down to this level had transmuted, changing into an overwhelming sense of freedom and release.

In through the nose, out through the mouth . . .

Both hypnotic and exciting, the impression of his breathing became colored by a pleasing timbre which created an enigma of mutated sounds and augmented feelings. Equally atonal and melodic, these enfolded him in an envelope of sensations as elegant as they were primal.

It's almost as if two distinct personalities within a vast consciousness are battling for dominance.

Whatever the influence was, it boosted the theta waves trickling through Caym's brain into a rousing flood of shimmering, sympathetic urgency. His perceptions rippled as if someone had thrown a stone into the translucent substance of his thoughts, and before he was aware of it, his consciousness expanded outward in concentric waves.

Whispers teased him from the shadows, inviting him to partake of the basest desires, reminding him of what he once was and should be again. His heart beat wildly in response, protesting at the strictures of its enforced confinement within a mortal coil.

This is a test, a contest of will between the various facets of my own psyche. The id wishes to take control again and lead me astray along a flight pattern of migrating thoughts and receding intelligence.

Once-buried memories of his first awakening in the crèche pits, where only the most savage beast stood a chance of survival, resurfaced with a vengeance. Brutally frank, they assaulted his nerves in a chaotic display of wanton ferocity: a supreme expression of selfish desire made manifest.

I *want.* I *need.* I *take.*

The instinctual drive to crave was as potent as it was hard to resist.

No! That dark side of my character is now inaccessible, sealed away behind a wall of impeachable guilt. I know what I was. What I did. Once enlightened, my actions elevated beyond the consideration of others or the need for reproach. Now descended, my superego seeks to hold me accountable for crimes I cannot retract . . .

Caym seized the swell of emotions raging against the crag of his identity and tried to make sense of what to do.

What did Penny say?

"Human children are much like Kresh in many ways, full of inbred drives and sentiments that require immediate expression or gratification. And what's more, they are entirely without embarrassment regarding those demands. But as they gain awareness of the world around them, they begin to appreciate their place in it and how others perceive them. Therefore, their id is modified by external stimuli, which in turn molds cognitive function and common sense. It tempers their passions and helps channel them into a more constructive outlet. Do the same."

But of course . . .

Caym felt a surge of hope within him.

I know the value of right and wrong, of good and evil. But for the most part, as one of the Kresh, I didn't . . . At least, not until the end when I realized the need for change and joined Angule's rebellion. So why should I feel shame and try to suppress what I had no control over? Kresh are not iniquitous, they are merely beings without morality who think only of themselves. I am what I am . . .

I am me.

He felt as if a weight had been lifted from his shoulders.

Because of what I was, my senses have been heightened, elevated beyond the hopes and aspirations of those shackled to a mundane form. This is also true of my emotions. I should not be afraid to express them. They are an essential part of who I am and what I will become

"Be yourself. . ." Penny had urged.

The wash of contradictory enchantments receded.

Caym hovered between worlds, suspended in the overlap between the real and the imaginary. Then it was over. A metal bolt protruding from the wall frame behind him felt like a knife in his spine, and brought with it a chill that somehow leached through his clothing and into his bones.

Alerted to his surroundings once more, his lids fluttered open. He looked both ways along the yawning chasm of the darkened corridor.

Pernicious ruddy eyes regarded him unblinking, creating a flashback filled with scorching gazes and steaming fangs. But these were no monsters waiting to pounce from concealment.

Ah, they're just the emergency strobes stretching off into the distance.

By their scant illumination, Caym could see his breath fogging the air in front of him.

The temperature has dropped. Is life support still on?

He glanced at his wrist pad. The schematics showed his present location as E—D32—0—C-A—T12, exactly where he should be. A bar-graph beside the display revealed how quickly oxygen levels were dropping. Beneath it, the time read: 20:44.

Caym thought his mind was playing tricks, so he increased the glow of the backlight.

How? I've been here for over an hour. They must have thought I'd moved on and reduced life-support.

Confused, Caym started to make his way along the hall, back toward the main stairwell.

But why did they not pick up my signal, or think to check?

He verified his position again and glanced about him.

This is the deck below, and three frames along from where I first got the creeps.

He paused to cast his senses into the ether about him, and confirmed his readings for a third time. On this occasion, a subtle thrum tickled his ears, its resonance playing along the hairs of his exposed flesh. At the threshold of hearing, it hinted at hidden potency.

Hello?

He placed his palm against the bulkhead and the sensation grew stronger, as did the impression of power.

Of course! He worked his way down the passage, trailing fingers along the cool metal. *There are flux acquisitor relays located behind the walls. These particular ones commence their journey at the core, four or five levels above me, and stretch off toward the main distributor junction at the exhaust ports over a mile away.*

He stared back into the murky depths behind him.

The concentrated presence of so much magno-nucleic force in one area must be creating a dampening field. And an obvious security risk. So . . . ?

Comprehension dawned.

Aha! So it's not trepidation then. It's apprehension of another kind. My refined senses are picking up on what others, or perhaps even instruments, can't detect. The presence of hidden energy . . .

"Be yourself . . ." Penny's voice echoed in his memory.

And because of my origins, I perceived it as a threat.

Two sentinels appeared at an intersection fifty yards in front of him. Their visible sensors swept the corridor in scarlet and emerald contrasts that only made the gangway look more ominous.

And as if on cue, here they are . . .

One of the wandering beams washed across Caym, snapped back, locked on, and intensified.

If I've been down here for an hour without being missed, it's something we need to tighten up on.

Both guards accelerated, bearing down on him at great speed.

Before they could reach him, Caym held up his wristband for inspection, along with his other arm containing the biochip.

"Before you ask the obvious, I am Caym, of the Senatum Kresh, and if I may inquire, where in the seven hells have you been? I was escorted down here by two auto-sentries more than an hour ago to conduct visual security checks. Why has nobody thought to ensure my welfare since?"

A pregnant pause ensued as the flyers verified his presence, and Caym was intrigued when one of them started examining the confines of the corridor. Focused rays of light lanced out from various points along its circumference. The drone obviously detected something, for its initial probes became a chorus of rapid beeps and polemic burps that passed back and forth between the pair at a pitch Caym found hard to follow.

"My apologies," Seraphim eventually announced, "but radiation levels in this vicinity evidently mask the presence of organic life. An oversight on my part which prevented your absence from being noticed."

"An error I hope you will rectify? Although we're in deep space, we *are* nevertheless on a war footing. Breaches like this need to be ironed out. From now on, I want all isolated passages locked down and permanently patrolled—from within—by paired sentinels. Life support suspended. Please notify Captain Amine of my recommendations."

"It will be done."

"Good. Although I checked this area myself, I suggest you both scout it and confirm every hatchway is bolted and sealed. You know the drill."

Satisfied, even triumphant, Caym made his way back toward the aft hub, reflecting on his real concerns.

Thank goodness it was merely my over-sensitive awareness and not a true case of the heebie-jeebies. I'd be no use to anyone if I were afraid of my own shadow.

Chapter Nineteen

Onto a Winner

The moment the turbo-lift doors opened, Shaní knew she was in the right place: the unmistakable smell of allorans assailed her nostrils, triggering memories of a childhood spent among the rolling hills of Selán, close to Genoas, where her parents owned and managed a large stock-farming enterprise.

Although the business had involved the selective breeding of both commercial and farm animals, the allorans were by far her favorite; she'd spent many hours in the saddle as a young girl, riding the woods and sweeping grasslands which surrounded their estate, savoring sights and sounds too many of her classmates living in the municipality rarely got to enjoy.

As she grew up and moved into politics, Shaní had been forced to spend less and less time doing what she loved best. Nonetheless, she'd visited home as often as her hectic lifestyle would permit, for she found riding the only real way to unwind from the stresses inflicted by the hustle and bustle of city life.

Thus, it was with a keen sense of anticipation that Shaní exited the elevator, for Jake Rixton had promised her the opportunity to exercise some of the platoon's horses.

I can't wait. This setting might be sterile and strange, but at least I'll ride. And from what I've seen, these . . . horses *are almost identical to allorans. Strange, how many similarities there are between our two worlds and the countless species that—oh my!*

The past month had been one long rollercoaster rush of activity. From initial boarding and loading procedures and the launch itself, through subsequent familiarization with the new systems in a space-borne environment, the exhaustive preparations for and the consequent execution of their first assault on Illumina, to the ensuing treatment of those ogres captured in the aftermath. And there'd been no rest since then, as training continued apace for the next phase of the operation, Latinus Prime, which would soon be upon them.

Demanding work. And it was because of that pace Shaní hadn't been able to visit the stable blocks until now. What she saw delighted and amazed her.

Considering the setting and the circumstances, I'm impressed with what they've achieved.

A series of prefabricated shelters had been erected adjacent to the central hangar bay, directly opposite the freight lifts. Measuring some one hundred and fifty feet long by fifty wide, they looked sturdy and warm, bright and airy.

Carryall in hand, she strolled forward and peeped inside the rear doors of the first barn. It contained a dozen stalls. Down at the far end, a large open tack room led out to adjacent wash and prep bays by the entrance. Like any enclosure she'd expect to see back home, the loft was filled with hegh, and the central aisle lined with small sacks of sitrá, vroim, and the Earth equivalents: grain and oats. Grooming equipment and personalized saddles hung from wall brackets outside each box, and despite the area's busy appearance, everything was neat and tidy and where it should be.

Shaní couldn't help but laugh.

It looks so ordinary. How did they manage to erect these so quickly?

Once again, she marveled at the ingenuity displayed by the mainly human contingent.

What they lacked in technological sophistication before coming to Arden, they've more than made up for in positive thinking and application. The Architect did well.

A small knot of troopers and highlanders were gathered around a stallion, tending to a small cut on his left foreleg. Shaní noted the care and attention they lavished on their mounts, indicating the character of the men themselves.

She approached the group.

"Excuse me, can you tell me where Captain Rixton might be?"

One of the troopers glanced up.

"Ma'am," he replied, straightening tall when he recognized her, "I think you'll find him between the last two barns. We discovered some extra passengers earlier this morning, and Angus and the boss are trying to work out what to do with them."

"Passengers?"

"Yes, ma'am. You'll see what I mean when you get there."

The soldier obviously thought his duty done, for he tipped his hat and rejoined his companions around the horse's feet.

Shaní picked up the pace.

Is he referring to stowaways? Perhaps he's found Lieutenant Smith and some of the missing men? But . . .

As she neared the penultimate hangar, she heard raised voices inside. From the sounds, at least two people were having a heated discussion.

". . . we going to get up there, man? It's almost as if the wee little buggers know what we're about and seek to bait us. I'll have their eyes for—"

"We've no choice. If we allow them to get established, they'll spread like wildfire and be into everything before we know it."

She recognized the second speaker as Jake.

Then the other must be Angus McGregor.

"So? Ye have a gun. Just shoot them."

"If I do that, it'll probably damage something and only scare the rest off."

The Deputy Magister rounded the corner and found both leaders staring up into the barn's eaves. Small dark shapes flitted round and round in the shadows, ducking and darting about in an aerial display of stunning finesse.

Ropillos!

Shaní knew ropillos of old. A small rodent with leathery wings, these had a macabre taste for carrion, blood, and animal manure. An unsavory combination that meant their bite often spread infection through the herds and flocks they plagued. Originally forest dwellers, the flying pests had long ago infested the warm, cozy shelters the Ardenese had constructed to house their animals, migrating into new habitats.

Not content to feast upon livestock, they were destructive varmints who would chew through almost anything to get at materials suitable for nest-building.

She immediately realized what had happened.

Fooled by the aseptic environment of the *Shadow of Autumn*, someone had been sloppy when checking visiting supply ships. In ones and twos, the critters must have stolen aboard over a period of weeks, hiding out of sight until the sheds were built. Presented with a nesting ground that reminded them of *Home Sweet Home*, they'd moved right in and claimed squatters' rights.

"Acrobatic little so-and-so's, aren't they?" she announced gaily.

Both men jumped; clearly taken unawares.

"Yes, they are," Jake replied, "and a pain in the ass."

"I told ye, just shoot them," Angus insisted. "The little bastards might look cute and friendly, but when our horses start falling foul to colic or the screaming shits, we'll have only ourselves to blame."

"Actually, there'll be no need for that," Shaní replied. "I have just the thing."

She placed her carryall on the floor and unzipped the top flap.

As she rummaged around inside, she explained: "I grew up around animals in a rural setting, so as you can imagine, we were plagued by ropillos all the time. The darn things would hide in trees and bushes and all sorts of places too hard to reach. We discovered killing them only attracted others, for the newcomers feasted on corpses of the old. No, it wasn't anywhere near as effective as instilling the fear of god in their ravenous little minds."

"Fear of god?" Jake mumbled. "How?"

Finding what she was looking for, Shaní stood and unraveled a long sinuous loop of flexible, copper-colored metal.

"This is a mastig," she declared, "and it delivers a nasty electric shock through the stingers on the end. Observe . . ."

She flicked her wrist and the tool uncoiled on the floor before them. No sooner had it come to rest than Shaní raised her arm high and glanced upward to assess her targets. Her hand flashed forward and from side to side.

Once, twice, three times in quick succession:

Crack! Crack! Crack!

Sparks snapped through the air, and a corresponding number of small furry bodies fluttered to the floor, stunned. The rest of the colony followed them down and cavorted above their fallen comrades before fleeing for the safety of the rafters.

"I gotta get me one of those whips," Jake gasped.

"Me too," Angus chipped in, "I don't suppose ye have one going spare?"

"I'm sorry, a what?" Shaní had never heard the term "whip" before.

"It's what we call them on Earth," Jake replied. "We carry small ones from time to time, but nothing like the size of yours. This could come in very handy." He held out his hands. "May I take a closer look?"

Shaní handed it over, and noticed Jake's faraway look. She received the impression he was thinking deeply about something.

I'd better explain its features. "The grip is twelve inches long, and is fashioned from the heartwood of the toran tree, making it strong, resilient and flexible. It's also coated in an adevix solution. This provides an additional barrier against any lingering charge that might build up from its use." She traced her fingers along and past the handle. "The lash is made of an elasticized coridian-selanite compound, which on my mastig is threaded into and around the stem. They all differ in length, according to the user's height and preferences, but because I often had to use mine from alloranback, I opted for a longer one." She tapped the pommel. "*This* one is nearly thirty feet long."

Shaní pointed out a dull red band about halfway along its shaft.

"That's the insulation washer which prevents static flashover. Particularly important when you consider the final twenty inches of this thing are made of a highly conductive hyperflex alloy that we call the stinger."

Jake was captivated: "Does it have to be charged or will it run on batteries?"

"When it's in regular use, I need to charge it once a week."

"And can the capacity manifested be altered, say, into something much more potent?"

"Yes, it can," Shaní replied. "Why, what do you have in mind?"

Jake handed the mastig back, and ushered Angus away a few steps. "Let's give the lady some room," he whispered, "and let her show us how it's done."

To Shaní, Jake added, "Once you've cleared the nests out for us, I'd love it if you'd consent to come and see Calen with me. Angus and I have been wracking our brains regarding one of the new strafing exercises we've been asked to consider. To no avail; you might have shown us the answer. The whole maneuver is designed to support the legion guys on the ground, cavalry included, so I didn't want to reject it out of hand. But up until now it looked like we might get screwed, as it entails getting up close and personal with the enemy without killing them. Crazy, eh? Man on man, I wouldn't mind so much. But against the Horde? With some of the Super Masters we've encountered, that's the *last* place I want to take a horse, new protective shields and harnesses or no. It's just too easy for them to get spooked and throw a rider, or become targets themselves.

"However, if Calen thinks he could adapt a consignment of these beauties to wield an iron and steel compound cracker, or something even nastier by the time we arrive at Latinus Prime, I think we may be onto a winner."

"I like the way you're thinking," Angus chipped in. "We'll be able to maintain a full gallop and cut the buggers down to size from a distance without endangering our lads or the mounts." He slapped Jake on the back. "I think I'm going to like this development . . . especially if I can get one to demonstrate to the rest of my rabble."

Shaní was somewhat surprised by the turn of events. "Can I at least get a ride first? It's been centuries, and you *did* promise."

"Deputy Magister," Jake grinned, "if you can help us get what we need, I'll make sure a horse is put aside for your personal use for the rest of the entire trip."

How can I refuse?

Flexing the mastig to its full length, Shaní looked up into the eaves to seek her prey.

"It looks like everyone's going to be happy then," she said as she caught sight of her first target, "although I don't think the ropillos will agree."

*

Head thrown back, Wilson Smith reveled at the summer's kiss on his brow and the caress of a cool wind across his cheek. Through lids shut tight, the world was a sea of phosphorous white and burnt umber splotches. He opened his eyes and urged his horse forward, clucking to establish a speed of descent, his attention on the rolling gait of his mount as it picked its way down a small embankment toward the babbling brook below.

The horse halted, grabbed its bit and tugged. Wilson slackened his reins and his mount bent its neck to the stream.

Dazzled by the play of sunlight on water, Wilson felt suddenly thirsty. He shifted to one side and reached for his canteen, startling his mount, who shied rightward explosively.

Overbalanced, he lost his seat in the saddle and shot sideways toward the waiting rocks.

The ground rushed up to embrace him and agony exploded behind his eyes, filling his vision with blistering fireflies that left lurid trails across his fractured vision.

Everything went dark; sensation faded. Except for the pain. That merely tightened its grip on the fragile kernel representing his entire existence, squeezing until he was forced to bite his lip to prevent himself crying out.

Misery drenched the atmosphere about him, and only with the greatest effort could he raise his head. The strain made him feel nauseous. He gagged and brought up bile.

Where . . . ?

His skin still prickled, as if a chill breeze were plucking hairs, one by one, from his flesh. The sound of running water had become the wash of other liquids, rushing from one place to another behind insulated pipes and conduits. Had circumstances been different, Wilson might have found the muted flow relaxing; but as things stood, the melody did little to ease the pinions burrowing their way into his skull or the bands squeezing the breath from his lungs.

He retched again and felt himself slip closer toward ultimate darkness.

Of course, why would things start getting any better now?

He peered about the strange chamber of his prison cell. Dim red lights in the corner did little to lift the gloom. However, because he'd been here for an eternity, he made out an ominous darkishness nearby and two shapes closer to him on the floor.

Harper and Stark.

Or whatever's left of them. Why the hell they're going to all this trouble to keep us alive, I don't know.

A shadow detached from obscurity immediately in front of him.

“Why?” it hissed. “Becausse you will sstill be of sservice before the end.”

Wilson recoiled in horror and tried to kick himself away, across the room—a useless effort, for his muscles had atrophied and the air was too thin to breathe properly. He fell back, limp, waiting for the inevitable.

“Is that how you get your sport now,” he raged impotently, “watching us suffer? Just end it, why don’t you?”

“Patiencce, patiencce,” the rasping voice crooned. “Your time will come ssoon enough. But until then, we can’t have you exxpiring and wassting our besst laid planss now, can we? Allow meee . . .”

The outline of a barely humanoid arm flared into existence. Illuminated from within by a tracery of blue and red veins and pulsing golden light, its translucent skin belonged in a different world entirely.

The terrible hand descended and pressed against Wilson’s chest.

Flames tore their way along his spine, exploding in chrysanthemum bursts behind his eyes.

Somewhere in the distance a wretched soul screamed.

Wilson never believed for one moment he was the source of such a cry. He was too busy dying.

*

Arranged like an amphitheatre, the main briefing room adjoining the operations center aboard the *Shadow of Autumn* reminded Mohammed of a combination between the Senatum back on Rhomane, and an old-style movie theatre from the twenty-second century.

Semicircular in shape, seats in tiers arose from a position immediately in front of the captain’s podium, itself offset to one side of the platform. This arrangement afforded the audience a clear and unobstructed view of a twenty-foot-wide cinematic viewer, while allowing Mohammed direct line of sight with his staffers.

As the last command-level officer entered, Mohammed activated the desk pads and the primary monitor. A military-looking emblem appeared on each screen, spinning slowly on its axis.

"Thank you all for coming," he began. "You'll be glad to know that the *Helexia* is safely away with her eight hundred and sixty-three survivors; she should be back at Arden within three days. By then, we'll be nearly ready to mount the next phase of our operation. So, if you refer to your terminals, you'll each see a précis of the details included in Marcus's final mission prep for—"

"Hang on a second," Shaní said, "'eight hundred and sixty-three'? I thought we recovered more than that?"

"We did, but eleven didn't make it. While we expected fatalities among some more seriously injured individuals, we were shocked when three of the Controllers died. Penny's still looking into it, which is why she isn't here, but every one of those deceased Masters appeared to be stronger than Lega'trexii class. We're beginning to wonder whether there is something different about their codex that reacts adversely to the re-genesis process."

"So what *are* they, exactly?"

"We still don't know." Mohammed glanced across to the opposite side of the room where several former Horde members huddled together in a small group.

Why do they still insist on keeping themselves separate?

"Caym, before we start, can you briefly shed any light on the matter?"

A former Lega'trix, Caym shook his great head.

"No idea. As I've mentioned previously, to us, Angule was the very epitome of Kresh magnificence. You saw for yourselves how impressive he was. It's hard to imagine anyone stronger, and yet . . ."

"Do you suspect this reaction to be a characteristic of the new strain?"

Caym gestured toward his friends.

"We've talked about this among ourselves and are still undecided. Our faction was unusual because we desired peace and yearned for change. As we underwent re-genesis we submitted to the process: we cooperated with the neural balm introduced to amplify the program. Nonetheless, Zagam, Urium, and Roth are amongst the most powerful of those who were representative of the other faction, and Zagam was Lega'trexii. While he wasn't happy to surrender his authority initially, he could do nothing to prevent the metamorphosis once the template became established."

"So you're saying the re-genesis matrix might not be potent enough to induce the change among those who are . . . what, *Grand* Masters? Could there be something about *them* that makes them powerful enough to resist it?"

"A distinct possibility. Fortunately we are blessed that Zagam is the most scientifically astute of us all. He's down in medical now, helping Penny investigate the circumstances surrounding each death, and those of your 'Grand Masters' in particular."

I can't risk it. I'll need to adjust our strategy.

Mohammed caught the Deputy Magister's attention: "Shaní, we have to crack on with the briefing, but I was wondering if you'd liaise with Caym, Zagam and Penny once this meeting ends? We've only a few days before our next objective. Any intelligence we can glean from this recent tragedy might make a big difference to those who'll go in on the ground."

"Certainly, I'll be glad to help."

"Excellent." Mohammed turned to address the room. "In fact, I want you all to appreciate that every snippet of intel will be valuable, since our next undertaking may entail a drastic revision of the tactics we employed previously. For example, look at the environment we'll be playing with . . ."

He pressed a button and a glaring disparity replaced the revolving logo on everybody's screens. Referring to it, Mohammed continued: "This is an overview of the Latinus Prime system. You can't see it from this distance, as it's situated within a cluster of ten—yes, I said *ten*—black holes. What you're looking at are the accretion discs created by each quantum event, so you can only imagine the degree of instability saturating this entire sector."

The picture changed and zoomed slowly inward, treating everyone to a simulated "fly-by" of the strangest cluster they had ever laid eyes upon. As the camera got closer, Mohammed referred to each feature in turn.

"Note the huge debris field, an obvious consequence of conflicting gravity on former planets. Latinus Prime is the only solid body to survive. We think that's due to Arabis, the sun she orbits. Arabis is a neutron star, which as you know are stellar remnants composed mostly of electron degenerate matter—that's fermions, to the non-scientific amongst you—the building blocks of what our Ardenese friends used to create their lydium barriers. It's incredibly dense, so (due to the Pauli Exclusion Principle which prevents fermions from occupying the same quantum state), something unknown occurred during the formation of this system to prevent both the star and Latinus from being crushed.

"Regardless of the process, this area is beset with tidal shearing, and thanks to the fact that Arabis is also a pulsar, awash with intense gamma bursts and electromagnetic radiation."

"So basically, the Horde will be hyped-up on the cosmic equivalent of amphetamines," Sam cut in, "and leaping about like Mexican jumping beans?"

"Precisely. It's a nightmare scenario, and one we must get past before we can go on to our final objective."

"I take it *that's* what you were referring to when you mentioned we'd have to revise our tactics?" Sam continued. "That whole region looks like one big shit-storm of warped physics and 'fuck off, you're not welcome here' . . . excuse the expression. I'm no egghead, but even I can see we can't rely on the sneaky approach we used last time."

"No need to apologize, your description is spot on. Sadly, that's not all there is to it. Remember, Illumina was a scientific research facility. Latinus Prime is at the opposite end of the scale: she was a military testing ground and represents a whole different world of dark delights . . . as you can see."

Mohammed clicked a hand-held control and an overlay complicated the onscreen image. Two glowing streamers appeared. Approaching the planet from opposite directions, both trails meandered their way through the huge asteroid belt dominating the system. Along each path, a number of glowing beacons signaled the presence of the danger Mohammed referred to.

"While we've been away, I asked Rhomane to remotely initiate a cascade diagnostic. I wanted independent verification of the results provided by Seraphim. Ladies and gentlemen, what you see here are the only two corridors by which this maze can be navigated. You will notice a number of sensor relays and defensive positions scattered along both routes. And these"—he pressed the button again, and a further series of flashing dots materialized, scattered in a haphazard fashion throughout the debris field—"are a network of covert seek-and-destroy drones, a kill zone's welcoming committee for any stupid enough to try sneaking up uninvited."

Mohammed paused to let the news sink in, and was gratified to see each and every one of his officers studying the charts closely, making notes as they went.

Sharp as ever, Sam expressed the first opinion: "From what you're saying, the system is obviously active, yes?"

"I'm afraid so," Mohammed replied. "Calen and Shaní informed me on the way here that this might be the case. Now we know for certain. This entire arrangement was designed to operate independently during a crisis; it's equipped with specially adapted generators which absorb electromagnetic radiation. Expanding on your earlier metaphors, think of it as an astral power grid running on solar steroids. We expect that our approach will be monitored, and some form of signal sent back to Latinus Prime."

"So basically, we have to walk up the garden path, knock on the door and politely wipe our feet before we go in?"

"Yes. If the ship was running at a hundred percent I'd risk trying to thread my way through the minefield. After all, the *Shadow of Autumn* is built for covert operations, and this should be right up her street. And if it came to a head-on fight, so what? There's no other ship as heavily armored as she. But I can't take the risk of compromising our overall objective."

"*Do* they know were coming?" Marcus asked bluntly. "My legion will be forming the bulk of your fighting force. I need to adequately prepare my men for a war of attrition if we're facing an all-out battle."

"While there is that risk, it's highly doubtful," Mohammed responded. "Let me remind you why. You've all been briefed about the effects of gravitational time dilation. Briefly put, the closer you get to an object possessing significant gravitational mass, the more time slows down. So, just imagine the effect the Verianda Nebula is having on us at this very moment. The whole cloud is beset by multiple conflicting fluctuations, nowhere more so than around Latinus Prime. Because of this, the entire sector had to be seeded by temporal compensators to keep everything in sync with the universe outside. Under normal circumstances, that would be bad news for us. However, *we* have the Chancellor and Deputy Magister with us, who possess the command codes to disable the compensator grid as we pass through. So, even if the Horde can actually monitor any of the sophisticated equipment emplaced on the planet's surface, it won't do them any good. By the time anything registers, we'll be on top of them. And even better, if they try any form of SOS beacon to summon help or to alert others to the presence of intruders, we'll be well away before anyone on Exordium can receive that message." He shrugged. "Of course, with the advent of the Grand Masters, we have the *telepathic hail* factor to consider, but I'm afraid there's nothing I can do about that."

"There is now," Caym interjected.

All eyes turned toward the Horde contingent. For some reason, under their scrutiny the former ogres were acting in a peculiarly introverted fashion.

They've been keeping a surprise from us and didn't want their raw emotions to give the game away before it was time. A tingle surged across the surface of Mohammed's skin, and the reason for the Horde's apparent reticence became clear.

"Would you mind explaining your behavior?" he said.

Caym glanced toward Calen, as if asking for permission to speak. Mohammed noticed the scientist respond with the slightest nod.

Hello? It looks like someone else is in on the surprise.

With the utmost care, Caym lifted something out of a sealed box at his feet, and held it up to the viewfinder on his desk. The main screen flickered, refocusing upon a small metallic device that looked like a thumb-sized mechanical spider with six instead of eight legs.

Caym cleared his throat.

"For want of a better term, this is a psyche-bug. Following our transmogrification, my brothers and sisters noticed that although we had returned to a modified fleshly form, we each retained an echo of our former abilities as full-blown Kresh. Not only are we stronger and more robust than our pureblood brethren, but we possess superior speed, stamina, and reflexes. And while our emotions are known to be up and down at the moment and something of a pain in the ass, this has a plus side: we've retained an aspect of the telepathic link enjoyed amongst the collective."

Mohammed couldn't contain his excitement.

"When you say an 'aspect' of the telepathic link, what do you mean?"

Caym looked thoughtful. "We are not as powerful as we once were, let me make that clear. Nevertheless, something about our mutation allows the areas of the brain responsible for hyper-cognitive awareness to remain energized. We think that's the reason why we're having problems with our emotions. Contrary to outdated opinion, psi functionality isn't affected by concentration. It's determined by emotional response. It stimulates the primitive limbic system of the brain, not the intellectual. That's why you see these gifts displayed amongst the half-crazed children of the Triarium Tier. They have no control over what they're doing, yet instinctively send and receive thoughts and impressions. Of course, as enlightenment develops, so too does the finesse and range of those faculties involved."

Mohammed could see looks of astonishment etched across every face.

"So, what in particular can you do, and how will these bugs assist us?"

"Since things are settling down and we're regaining a degree of control, we've noticed our intuitive perceptions returning. Besides our ability to walk the Ix, we're talking about telepathy, astral projection, and in certain circumstances, precognition; although that gift is rather difficult to control even for Masters of the Unium Tier."

"Are you serious?" Mohammed could barely believe what he was hearing.

"I'm deadly serious," Caym replied. "But as I mentioned, we'll be nowhere near as influential as we once were. That's why I spoke with Penny and Calen. We realized you might make use of these abilities, and wanted to see if they could do anything to help boost the right areas of our brains." He held the chip in the air. "*This* should do the trick."

"Hang on, *should* do the trick? Don't you know if it works properly?"

"Oh it works, but this is only a prototype. If we get your blessing, Calen will produce one for each one of us. We're lucky that we already know each other's minds intimately. So, once we've had a bit of practice, we should be able to run interference. With some tweaking along the way, we'll be strong enough to block any telepathic messages from getting through. Even from one of their Grand Masters."

Bloody hell! We're on a definite winner here, and . . . hang on . . .

One thing Caym said gave Mohammed pause for concern: "Don't you employ your dream-walking capacity in the same way?"

"No, we don't. Spanning the Ix, or 'dream-walking' as you call it, is entirely different—esoteric in nature and intertwined with all sorts of cryptic factors triggered when the subconscious picks up on telestic vibrations in the ether: once activated, it takes you where it will. Telepathy operates entirely through conscious thought. *We* choose the when and the where and the how. If we refine these units properly, you might find they work on other subjects as well."

Bloody hell, I hadn't thought of that.

"Thank you, Caym. Needless to say, I want this development looked into and exploited a-sap." Mohammed glanced across to Calen and Shaní. "Senators? Would you both add this to your list of priorities? If we can get this initiative up and running, we'll have a major tactical advantage. Please include Marcus in the loop, too. He's responsible for forming our attack strategy against Latinus Prime, so he needs to be kept up to date with anything that might influence his planning."

Caym grunted in satisfaction.

"Okay, people, listen up. Within the hour I'll be plotting a course for reentry into the Verianda Nebula. You know our target. Pre-mission briefing will take place at noon tomorrow. Ensure anything that needs to be addressed is brought up then, because once we start the next phase, things may get mighty sticky, mighty fast."

Chapter Twenty

And So It Begins

As was his custom, Sam Pell lingered off to one side and ran through a mental checklist. It was a habit he'd developed over many years and countless battles, and the only surefire way he knew to relax and set his squad a good example.

He studied them as they waited, geared up and ready to go; hi-tech ninjas huddled around the emergency transporter pad, situated to the rear of the ancillary CIC compartment.

The rest of Alpha team was comprised of Bob Neville, who had come along in leaps and bounds over the past eighteen months; Eddie Roberts, a man so quiet and unassuming it was difficult to appreciate what he now did for a living; and Joe Stark, their latest addition, cold as an iceberg under pressure. Opposite them stood Bravo team, made up of Andy Webb, freshly promoted to lieutenant; Stu Duggan, looking as bored and detached from the tension around him as always; Tosh Wanabe, a former native of New Tokyo and one of the most dependable guys Sam had ever met; and Katy "Lady P" Wilson, hard as nails and no-nonsense as the day was long, despite painting the death's-head logo on her helmet a hot pink, instead of squad silver like everybody else.

Beyond her stood their new technical specialist, Severin Robins, whose job it was to stay on board the *Shadow of Autumn* and provide the live-time covert link that could mean the difference between life and death when things became hairy.

Tried and tested, all. Although this was the first time they would actually work as a unified troop, Sam was confident they would be forged anew as they were baptized in fire, and gel into a team Mac would have been proud of.

As warriors, theirs was, perhaps, the hardest chore of all, as they would be required to wait patiently within the confines of the bridge while planet-side units under Marcus Brutus tried to subdue the enemy sufficiently for retrieval protocols to be initiated. A difficult task, for no one needed to be reminded that the Horde would rampage to the last in their frenzy to destroy or be destroyed.

The Legion must also look out for positions of strategic or military importance, and places from which the Grand Masters might marshal their army. Only then would Sam and his specialists be unleashed. While everyone else was mobilizing with the aim of saving life if they could, Sam and his team were there for one purpose only: To kill.

And from what I can see, everyone just wants to get on with it now, and do what we're trained for. I know . . .

Sam strolled across to Severin and bent to his ear.

"Sevvy, I see we've got a number of spare terminals down at the far end. Link through to Seraphim and ask her to fire up half a dozen of them, would you? Don't worry about causing a distraction. Her servers are compartmentalized, so you can make the enquiry through the R&R channel. Request a variety of computer war games. I want to keep everyone relaxed but mentally alert for when we get the order to go."

"Will do, boss; right on it."

Sam turned away, motioned to Andy Webb, and opened a feed on the troop's internal comlink:

"Andy? I've organized a spot of entertainment to keep everyone frosty. Tell the guys they can dump their kit on the ready line, but keep it in deployment formation so everyone knows what's where." Sam pointed to the rearmost set of workstations. "Use those positions, they're out of the way and close enough to the pad that we can respond in seconds. Sevvy should have them up and running in a moment. I'm just going forward to see what the state of play is. I'll leave this frequency open."

"Nice one, boss. I'll start organizing a pool."

Satisfied his team was catered for, Sam made his way into the main CIC section.

He found a hive of chaotic order and discipline. Those not employed at command posts were gathered around the central island with the captain, Chancellor, and Deputy Magister, watching the latest developments unfurl within the main holo-cloud.

Sam sidled up behind Mohammed and listened in.

"Two minutes until terminus," Seraphim announced. "Captain, please commence final systems checks."

"You heard the lady," Mohammed snapped. "We're nearing the end of our approach vector. Calen, what's the condition of the temporal grid?"

"We're in the clear," Calen replied. "As we exit the corridor, Shaní will initiate a cascade failure. Hopefully it will overcome all existing firewalls and expand the shut-down sequence into their orbital defenses."

"That's music to my ears." Mohammed adjusted focus and looked up, "Section heads, report."

A stickler for efficiency, Sam was impressed by the way each department sounded-off in turn without further prompting.

"Life support switching to EMS mode. Backup generators activated. Emergency bulkheads primed and sealed. Escape pods armed."

"Sickbay and triage response stations alerted and standing by."

"Defensive countermeasures prepped and ready to deploy. Shields and cloak at maximum strength."

"Offensive protocols, online. Menta-accelerator and mechanical sequencers initiated. Bow, midsection, and aft magazines loaded. Energetic weapons charged. Primary silos and tubes are hot and ready for launch. Cyber-link is live."

"Reactive Tactical Battle System is now at your disposal."

Sam couldn't help but notice how everyone's attention remained riveted on their respective screens as the process rolled through to completion. The sight filled him with a sense of pleasure.

We're in good hands. I tend to forget, sometimes, I'm not the only specialist here. Everyone's an expert in their own field.

"Excellent news, people," Mohammed declared. Although there was no need, he raised his voice. "Away teams, your status please?"

The response was immediate and methodical.

"*Minas*, cross-locked and standing by."

"*Abeille* here, cross-locked. Awaiting your signal."

"*Ballarat*, standing by. Cross-locked and holding."

"*Eurus* is cross-locked. We're ready to go."

"*Orison* reporting. Cross-locked and standing by."

"Gold command, this is Silver." The voice of Marcus Brutus rang through loud and clear. "All drop ships have signaled personnel and equipment as loaded in combat formation. Prelaunch auto cycles are engaged and primary couplers are in synchronous mesh. Internals show green lights across the board. Cross-lock and drop station sequences initiated. Awaiting your command for final release."

"Thank you, Marcus," Mohammed responded. "God's speed to you all. Opening outer doors . . . *Now*."

"Approaching threshold," Seraphim cut across the chatter. "Twenty seconds."

A shimmer in the air to one side caught Sam's eye as Seraphim herself appeared, a six-foot tall simulacrum of focused attitude, replete with stylish bob and military-grade space coveralls. No sooner had she materialized than the backlighting turned scarlet.

"RTB avatar activated," she intoned, as if anyone needed to be reminded of what her presence signaled. "Red alert status established."

Time to be getting back.

As Sam reentered the rear compartment, he heard Mohammed call out, "All departments: stand by, stand by." And after a brief pause: "Main batteries, prepare to open fire. Seraphim, initiate drop ship release countdown and deploy full tactical countermeasures on my mark . . .

"Five, four, three, two, one . . . *Mark*!"

*

So great was the leviathan's speed and so huge its bulk that when it suddenly stopped, appearing as if from nowhere, a vacuity formed in the substance of reality that sent shockwaves propagating throughout the entire system.

Va-ákil and her generals—Prátors Altás, Xophan, Tadãhk, Ilion, Romũle, and Remíle—looked on impassively. Safe within the Ix, the ripples made little impression on them.

See how quickly they react? Altás remarked, his thoughts laced by seeds of grudging respect. *No sooner have they arrived than their shock troops deploy en masse, seeking to obliterate all trace of resistance. And note too, the tenor of their aggression. None of the energetic weapons dare kiss the surface where our kin lie in wait. Someone aboard that craft is astute.*

The heretical tinge to Altás's feelings didn't go unnoticed by his queen, but she forgave him without hesitation: his was the soul of a Prime Catalyst, and the call of battle was interwoven into his very nature.

Good! she told herself. *Although he tries to conceal it, he respects our enemy. This ensures he will not mistake their tenacity for chaos when the time comes.*

But what of our brethren? Romũle queried. *See how destruction rains down upon them in different forms, with explosive and implosive accompaniment? Will not untold tragedy be wrought upon those exposed to such blasphemy?*

The harvest will be bitter indeed, Va-ákil replied, *but necessary. Preparations have been made. Imperator Erubus is Praeturium, as are Verid and Sinnalé. Their strength will prevail.*

Even against the bane-metal? Can you not feel the astringency of its presence through the vext? We are millans from their location, and yet the anathema of our existence still manages to insult us, as does the nature of the gas they distribute. You saw how it reduced even the most vigorous Kresh to bleating provats. Oh, the shame. To be led to the slaughter in such a way. It . . . it—

Be at peace, Altás urged, his mood teetering dangerously close to sublime expression. *We are well aware of the invasive nature of the weapons these vermin employ. Your Magnate has spoken. Erubus has been counseled as to the appropriate strategy, and he will utilize it, while those willing to sacrifice themselves will act as the ultimate distraction. Exercise patience; once the true nature of his response becomes apparent, you will taste the resonance of his peoples' feasting even though we observe from our sanctuary here.*

But surely you—Romũle's protestations were cut short as the inky backdrop became laced with coherent beams of crisscrossing light. Unseen compressions throbbed through the heavens.

A smug overlay added a rosy tint to Va-ákil's aura.

You see? she crooned. *We are mighty. Of that there is no doubt, but we are also wise. Why waste ourselves in valiant release, only to fall to insects who can unravel our codex? Note how a simple exercise of the intellect can redeploy their own weapons against them. Do you appre*—She faltered as the arcane vista before them clouded. *My apologies, the conflicting gravity within that system must be interfering with my ability to maintain clarity. One moment please, while I rectify the situation.*

Va-ákil isolated the requisite segment of her mind within a theurgic cocoon and reached out across the span of intervening leagues.

Among their kind, only Prátors were strong enough to bend the orphic causality nodes of the Ix to their will; and as Magnate, she was preeminently skilled at such a task.

Nonetheless, Va-ákil's astral sight refused to focus.

She looked toward the tiny flickering star at the center of the system. Rotating at more than seven hundred times per senand, its electromagnetic emissions stabbed out with mesmerizing exuberance.

She slavered at the sight of so much raw and unadulterated nutrition.

Its mass is immense, yet that is not—?

Something both alien and familiar brushed against the obsidian sheen of her psyche. Choral yet hesitant, its spectral nature possessed a character that simply shouldn't have existed.

What? Acting on reflex, Va-ákil attempted to latch on to the elusive identity, but it evaded her grasp. *That cannot be right?*

Va-ákil refined her acuity even further and set off in pursuit.

The others sensed the delicious texture of her urgency and bristled. Aggression exploded through every pore, every facet of their being, and a terrible malevolence coalesced about them.

Are we under attack? Altás queried, his desperation to vent his rage evident from the electrostatic skein crackling across the threshold of his visible nimbus. His autonomous response spread like wildfire among the rest of the assembled ogres.

They began to howl.

Silence! Va-ákil roared. *Someone dares interfere, attempting to block my farsight. I must concentrate and . . .*

Her memory flicked back to the moment she'd sought out the source of the infestation and discovered the planet upon which they thrived in growing numbers.

A world where I have never been, yet it is a place that taunts my recollections.

She called on the vast intricacies of her reserves and relived the moment again in luminescent clarity.

. . . Such a contradiction. Such a baffling amalgam of discipline and ineptitude. The fledging was present, that's for certain, chattering away like a demented automaton on its

uniquely discordant wavelength. But so were others. Quieter, these possessed a refinement and discipline which comes only from centuries of application and fidelity. It was like I . . . it was so similar to . . .

Realization crashed down upon her.

They were once Kresh!

Chapter Twenty-One

By the Numbers

"All drop ships are in the pipe, five by five," Seraphim announced, "vectored approach, tactical spread. Instruments show their hull plating as charged and shields deployed at maximum strength."

"Thank you," Mohammed replied. "While you complete your analysis of the surface, I want you to target every single thing in sight up here. If it's in our way, remove it. Employ the blitzkrieg protocol. Establish a bubble around this vessel, free of hazards, and open up a tunnel through that crap for our people. Understood?"

"Roger that." Seraphim froze, and her eyes glowed blue. A diffuse halo of the same color encompassed her head. "Blitzkrieg protocol in . . . three, two, one . . . *now*."

A barely discernible vibration thrummed through the deck beneath Mohammed's feet as the holo-cloud expanded into a full exterior view of the environs surrounding both the *Autumn* and Latinus Prime.

Death scourged the area in a wash of supercharged particles and metal, and Mohammed was ashamed of the thrill surging through him as they unleashed Armageddon upon their foe.

Yet the psychedelic display was as perplexing as it was mesmerizing. “Seraphim, what are we actually seeing?”

“Our initial assault is proving effective. Pinpoint lasers are disabling the satellite network, while the plasma guns are neutralizing every covert sentinel squadron exposed by the Deputy Magister. A dozen of the larger platforms and relay stations in high orbit are currently under fire from our photonic cannons. Setrium-4 canisters are already seeding the atmosphere, and midship Menta accelerators have cut a clear path down to the landing zones. Fore and aft batteries are strafing the ground in those vicinities to counteract resistance. Jaguar tactical strike missiles with hematite warheads and Octopod singularity compressors are already en route, programmed to impact the surface thirty seconds prior to the arrival of our assault teams. That should create sufficient dead zones to allow troops to erect shield walls and establish a beachhead before the Horde can respond.

“For your information, Sparrowhawk interceptors and Excalibur ship-to-ship torpedoes are also locked and loaded, ready for use when the rest of the defensive grid is exposed. I estimate removal of the current threat in less than three minutes from now.”

Mohammed breathed a sigh of relief. *I think we have the element of surprise.* He had a sudden thought. “Seraphim, please verify that we’re allowing nothing energetic to reach the surface?”

"I confirm that all particle beams are limited to the solar environment. However, to counter the risk of a near miss, their matrices have been programmed to dissipate while still in the troposphere."

"And your scans of the redundant and surface-based installations, what are they showing?"

The AI didn't reply, so Mohammed assumed she hadn't heard.

"Seraphim?"

Mohammed turned to see a frown creasing the avatar's usually phlegmatic face. His spine tingled again with an entirely different chill from the last.

Then the heavens blazed incandescent.

*

Hold! Caym's telepathic voice boomed into the ether. *Hold it together. Don't panic, we're still all right. All they know is that someone's watching.*

Are you sure? El'chan, youngest amongst them, protested. *One has seen us. I can feel its presence getting closer.*

Yes, I know. But I can cut the link any time I want, so stop panicking. There's no way I'll allow it to ride the primary node all the way back here. Caym raised his hand. *Give me a moment, I need to concentrate and ascertain what it's actually doing.*

Caym compartmentalized his persona with ease and split his consciousness into two distinct facets. One part maintained a close watch on the approaching menace, while the other seized the opportunity to give his companions a much needed once-over.

Beside him, Zagam radiated an aura of calm. Like Caym, he was a past Lega'trix of the Unium Tier and well versed in the nuances of arcane manipulation.

The rest of the quintet was less resilient.

As former Tribuni, Roth and Urium were holding their own, controlling their fear remarkably well. El'chan was a different matter: newly raised to Praefactor at the time of the re-genesis awakening, she had scant prior experience of enigmatic conflict.

Still, with the rest of our kin back on Arden, this is the best I can hope for. They'll have to do.

Caym checked the integrity of their telestic concert. A construct of syntagmatic design, it sequentially molded the minds of individuals together to become a unified cohesive whole, a harmonically linked consciousness whose mutual latency exceeded the sum of its parts.

Due to the vagaries of the mutations wrought within them, their potential summed less now than previously. Nevertheless, Caym was delighted by what he saw, for they had achieved a resonance that produced a remarkable amplification dynamic.

It will do . . . for now.

As pleased as he was, Caym didn't let their initial success distract him from his objective.

Our adversary won't be expecting this . . . so, let's see what I can glean about them as I project an offer to parley.

A momentary touch was all it required.

With a mighty flex of his will, Caym severed the link and abruptly ended the union.

"What?" Zagam demanded, blinking away his surprise at the maneuver. "What did you see?"

"They are led by someone, female in nature. She—whoever *she* is—has immense power. I've never witnessed such strength. Even without augmentation, her aptitude is colossal. What's more, they're clearly not interested in making friends."

"So what are they doing up here when everyone else is down on the planet?"

"That's just it, brother. They *aren't* here. In the instant we made contact, I learned that we are dealing with an astral projection from light years away . . . *through* the Ix."

"The Ix?" Zagam gasped. "But how is that possible?"

His shock was reflected by the others.

"I haven't a clue. Regardless as to *how* she does it, she *can* do it. She presents an obvious danger. We must inform Mohammed at once. If we're in range of her thoughts at this distance, goodness knows what mischief she can inflict."

Or any *of her supercharged minions, come to that.*

*

A loud *clunk* reverberated throughout compartment.

The *Abeille* fell away from the belly hatch and Marcus's stomach lurched, flooding his system with adrenaline. A brief surge forward was followed by a moment's weightlessness before all sense of momentum ceased.

Ah, the ship must have entered the vacuum of space.

The mood within the hold changed, and several of his legionnaires began their pre-battle rituals.

Good. Now we're underway, the men will be able to focus on the job at hand.

Staring through the viewport, Marcus saw the protective barrage begin. A miniature shooting star flew past, blazing a fiery trail through the sky. He blinked as this was followed by another. Then another. Then a dozen more. Within a heartbeat, the small flotilla was encompassed by a veil of scalding plasma and white-hot metal, a shimmering conduit along which they could gain safe passage to the planet's surface.

He pressed his face to the glass, spellbound by the silent play of light on dark.

"Twenty seconds until atmosphere," their pilot announced, "expect some turbulence. If you're not already strapped in, I suggest you do so now."

Yanked from his reverie, Marcus scanned the line to glimpse a few stragglers leaning forward, fiddling with their equipment.

He snapped his fingers to draw their attention: "Buckle up and stop fussing. You've already checked everything a thousand times."

As his men settled back, Marcus occupied himself by running through the opening stages of the operation.

Okay. Ten minutes until we land. The Minas *will drop Flavius and his hundred and thirty men into the precinct right outside the command faculty. The* Ballarat *will land east of them with Seneca's centuria, while Tiberius will deploy from the* Eurus *to the west. We'll be right behind to provide a fortified stronghold in the event our assault stalls and we need to regroup. The* Orison *will offer fire cover from the air until shield-walls are erected, whereupon she'll land, allowing Jake and Angus to prepare their snatch-squads and position the cavalry where they're needed most. So . . .*

His gaze was drawn back to the hypnotic show outside.

So, once we have our beachhead . . . ten, maybe fifteen—

A light strobed through the ether, and a blinding flash caused Marcus to jerk away from the window.

Pluto's beard!

Morbid curiosity got the better of him. Peeping out, he saw an expanding debris field not two hundred yards from their position. In its center, a strange billowing cloud folded in upon itself, as if an invisible mouth were inhaling the contents of this new glittering pall.

"What in Hades' name was that?" he called over the radio.

"*That* was the *Minas*," yelled the pilot, "stand by . . ."

Flavius? No!

A fusillade of metal from the ruined craft pattered against their shields, followed moments later by flotsam and jetsam of another kind. Marcus's heart went out to them, for some were still kicking and writhing against the frozen vacuum leaching life from their lungs. And there was nothing he could do.

Close-by, another glaring ribbon crackled past.

What the hell?

"Pilot," he bellowed. "Where are those beams coming from?"

"We are under fire from the planet's surface . . . wait . . ." Two sizzling bolts of lightning glanced off the hull, causing the plating to shriek like a banshee. The ship lurched to one side. "Correction, we are being targeted by the surface *and* platforms in orbit. Taking evasive action. Hang on."

"Helmets closed!" Marcus's voice thundered through the cabin. "Visors down. Ensure your emergency packs are primed and ready to deploy. Remember, if this craft is breached, activate your emergency beacons and try to relax. Conserve your oxygen while you wait for rescue."

The *Abeille* bucked again.

"But what do we do in the meantime, sir?" someone called out.

"Do? We fight. Emergency crews, you've practiced this drill enough. Get your asses over to the ancillary guns and see what you can do to help. The rest of you, check your gear is stowed and pressure valves are sealed. In the meantime, I'll contact the *Shadow of Autumn* to see what the devil they're going to do to stop us getting plucked like figs from a tree."

*

"Captain," Seraphim called, "I'm registering anomalous power spikes in multiple locations throughout the orbital network. Whatever they are, they were artfully hidden and appear to be arranged in clusters."

Mohammed, otherwise engaged with an incoming message, didn't catch the avatar's words: ". . . appreciate that. Thank you for bringing this information to me, Caym, I'll notify everyone as soon as I can." He ended the call and spun back toward the command post. "Say again?"

"I said we're getting additional . . . belay that, they're decloaking and joining the fray. Captain, most appear to be concentrating their fire solely on the drop ships."

"What are they, more covert seek and destroy drones? I thought we were supposed to be taking care of them?"

"We are taking care of *them*," Seraphim countered. "These are different. Sensors confirm the existence of a number of geostationary modules, dormant up until now."

"So who's operating them and, more to the point, how?"

"Accessing primary schematics . . ." Seraphim's aura flared white, then paled back to blue. "Ah, I have it." She manipulated part of the holo-screen, and the image of an intricate, many-faceted transgenic construct materialized within the field. Structured as a set of concentric arcs and polyhedrons arranged on gimbals around a central sphere, its outer lattices were multidirectional and studded with weapon ports.

Bloody hell, that reminds me of one of Kepler's cosmological models.

"They're smart platforms," Seraphim continued, "part of a major overhaul and upgrade Arden central instituted during the last set of refits three months before the Horde outbreak. From what I can determine, they function on a totally isolated system. They're equipped with a form of chameleon shielding I've never seen before. Quite ingenious, since they're also hybridized with a doppelganger-shift emitter."

"A what?" Mohammed couldn't believe his ears.

"A brand new form of stealth technology, still experimental when I was under construction. From what blueprints indicate, the master modules are designed to remain hidden while emitting mirror readings at multiple points simultaneously to confuse enemy sensors."

The bridge shook as the dreadnaught absorbed a number of direct hits.

They don't seem to mind showing us where they are now.

"So what are you doing about it?"

"I have already increased the protective barrage and initiated countermeasures."

"Explain."

"I directed Fore and aft Menta accelerators to first destroy those threats in closest proximity. Once completed, I will expand the kill field and include energetic weapons."

"Won't that leave the landing zone vulnerable?"

"A tactical necessity. By the time our assault teams arrive, the Jaguar missiles and Octopod compressors will have sterilized the area." Seraphim jutted her chin toward the image of the smart platform. "We have more pressing problems. Their onboard control systems have been switched from automatic. No matter how I initiate contact, they're refusing to recognize my override command. Destroying them will take considerable time: I am now registering more than a thousand units."

"A thousand?" Mohammed gasped. He staggered as a further torrent of strikes peppered the shields.

Several heads turned toward him, concern etched across their faces.

"Can we fight through all this?" he asked, more for their benefit than his.

"It will prove expensive in resources and exterior damage, but the *Shadow of Autumn* was designed to absorb punishment without losing functionality. In any event, most of the enemy's firepower is currently focused upon the drop ships, so we can . . . damn. We have just lost the *Minas*."

"Fuck!"

Get a grip, Mohammed. Prioritize before all this runs away from you.

A possible short-term solution presented itself.

"Revan, Ferell?" He shouted at the duty helmsmen. "Take the *Shadow of Autumn* into a lower orbit. Put her bulk between our people and those satellites. Seraphim? Augment our barriers to compensate, and once we're there, hit those positions with everything we've got. Clear a space for emergency rescue teams to work unhindered. Calen, Shaní? *Please* do what you can to countermand the override block. We need those additional assets out of the way." He took a deep breath. "It looks like we're about to witness just how sturdy the *Autumn* really is . . ."

From his position at the command console, Mohammed glanced forward and could see the two pilots engaged in an animated discussion.

Are they arguing? "Why are you not taking us down?"

Revan turned in his seat and shrugged.

"Captain Amine, the ship is unresponsive to our instruction. We are sending the appropriate commands, but something is interfering with the process—"

"Ground batteries have opened up," Seraphim interjected, "and the satellite pods are receiving fresh instruction from the ground . . . Interesting."

Caym's message of only a few minutes before sprang to mind: *The mental interface!*

"Seraphim," Mohammed barked, "I think we might have a security problem, especially with those systems operating by means of telepathic command. I'll explain later." He raised his voice. "Everyone, listen. Disengage from your workstations now. Seraphim, recall our people immediately and fully deploy your Reactive Tactical Battle System. Take over. I'll relay my orders through you."

Seraphim stepped back from her position and stood at attention. The air thrummed with energy; the encompassing nimbus about her head deepened from blue to red to match the alert status. The piping along the shoulders of her uniform also adopted the same ruby highlights. Once transformed, she resumed her place and stared at Mohammed:

"Orders?"

"It is clear our intelligence on the Horde is inadequate. The Grand Masters possess a capacity we don't fully understand. I strongly believe they have the ability to influence any system operated by means of mental interlink," Mohammed gestured toward the holo-cloud, "as demonstrated by their surprisingly well-structured resistance and the navigational problems we are experiencing. Seraphim, once you've signaled our ships, initiate the Omega Protocol."

"Understood."

Calen and Shaní were shocked.

"You're not serious?" Shaní queried.

"Completely." Mohammed leaned toward the Deputy Magister across the console. "I made it perfectly clear what would happen if we ever started to lose control. And as you have been at pains to express on many occasions, Latinus Prime is a military research center. Weapons here are even more sophisticated than on the *Shadow of Autumn*. If the Horde can reach out and take that potential to the stars, they present a greater danger than we ever imagined. One we cannot allow to exist."

He turned to face Seraphim. "How long do you need to initiate sanitization?"

"I can launch the Leviathan planet crushers within twenty-three seconds."

"And have you recalled our people?"

"All remaining ships are en route, Both the *Abeille* and *Orison* have sustained such damage that they're maneuvering in on thrusters. Fear not. I have adjusted defensive and offensive procedures to compensate."

"Time factor?"

"Several minutes."

"And you're confident we can survive this?"

Mohammed was surprised to see the AI construct actually smile.

"If you don't mind me expending the magazines? Certainly. While this will entail a resupply stop before we move on to Exordium, it is the most prudent strategy to adopt . . . one I would unquestionably take if functioning alone."

Praise indeed. Mohammed considered his options, and the seeds of a terrible but necessary course of action took root. *Not only will it solve our problems once and for all, but it will send a clear message.*

"Okay, everyone gather round. This is what we're going to do."

*

Feverish determination spurred Va-ákil to greater efforts.

The telepathic query had been feather-light and competently aimed. Even so, she had detected it immediately.

However, her ethereal snooper was no slouch either, for no sooner had she sought out its identity than it perceived her scrutiny and took flight.

Cold fury clawed its way through her complexus as she tried to reconnect the severed psychic node.

Where is *the abomination that dared to approach me in such manner . . . ?*

The thought pattern had been bizarrely intoxicating: provocative; laced with regret for aspirations lost and dreams unrealized. Moreover, it resonated with a sincere and profound hope.

Why? What could it hope to achieve by such a pointless exercise?

Va-ákil, irritated, closely observed the vext about her. For some reason, the continuum's essence had blossomed at the touch of the exotic psyche. Although the entity had now fled, the subatomic particles saturating the fabric of spacetime continued to chime through darkening hues as its echo faded.

She found the experience most distracting.

Other, lesser minds intruded. Not deliberately, for the great vessel before them incorporated a provision for higher mental function as part of its operational procedures. Nevertheless, as she latched onto and sorted through each one, the original signature became ever more distant.

Eventually, she admitted defeat.

Magnate? probed wise Ilion. *Are you all right?*

Projecting strength and reassurance, Va-ákil turned to her generals and opened her mind so they could witness what had happened.

Addressing her Prime Catalyct privately, she added, *Notify Erubus to initiate the next phase. Stress that he reveal to our guests the consequences of crossing us.* Va-ákil meshed briefly to his complexus. *But Altás,* also *advise him to proceed with caution. Now they are closer; I sense some amongst these insects who were once . . . they were . . .*

Jumbled misgivings spilled over into the ether.

Was it the fledgling you talked of? Altás was insistent, hostile.

It is *there with its minions,* she replied aloud so the others could hear, *but thankfully it is silent for once and in hiding. No, this was different: our intruder was once Kresh. And not only does it appear to be allied with the vermin, but it seeks to champion a peaceful resolution.*

Stunned, her advisors were quick to express their suspicions:

Peace? Are you sure?

A ruse to distract us, perhaps?

Or make us lower our guard?

And call off the attack?

Have they learned of your existence, and now seek to capture a prize?

Have you considered . . .

While Va-ákil allowed their concerns to wash over her, a perplexing echo from her time within the Plane of Eternal Prisms returned to taunt her from shadows. Precognitive in nature, it chilled the outer nimbus of her codex and caused a crystallized rind to manifest across her receptors. No matter how hard she tried, Va-ákil couldn't shake free of an impending sense of inevitability. Or its cost.

Is this truly the path to salvation? Suppressing a snarl, she strangled her doubts. *One way or another, I'll find out soon enough.*

With a thought, Va-ákil steered their collective perspective to a safer distance.

We will observe the outcome from here. Regardless of how well you might feel the battle is going, watch closely, for I fear a hammer blow might fall—and from the most unlikely of places.

While they waited, Va-ákil allowed her mind to wander, and a passage from a familiar song repeating itself in her mind.

And dream of loss as eloquence . . .

And dream of loss as eloquence . . .

And dream of loss . . .

Chapter Twenty-Two

At the Gates of Darkness

As the final seconds ticked away, Mohammed studied multiple representations within the expanded holo-cloud, pondering for the umpteenth time whether he had made the right decision.

The ravaging host infesting the planet below; the myriad weapons those *supposed* beasts had artfully arranged and cunningly employed against them; and the conflicting celestial forces that would tear the ship apart if they strayed too far off course: contemplating these helped settle his conscience.

I have no other reasonable choice. The mere fact that this place exists represents an unacceptable threat to life, a threat cosmic in scale. And they can now manipulate physical objects against us as well.

He skimmed the partial inventory they'd been able to recover and gritted his teeth.

If only we could have taken this place intact. The upgraded tech would have meant we'd never need fear anything again.

He sighed and cast his eyes heavenward as another potent blast struck the *Shadow of Autumn* head-on. *I rest my case. Still, I suppose that's a sign I need to get this show on the road.*

"Seraphim, start moving us away. Sublights, slow ahead, evasive course" — he stared at her — "as we discussed. Augment shields and reserve forward magazines for Leviathan deployment. Prime all other offensive and defensive assets. Prepare to open fire."

Now that the time had finally arrived to enact the order, a subdued atmosphere settled across everyone present: Calen; Shaní; the rest of the bridge crew; and, of course, Sam and his team, who had chosen to stick around to watch how the end-game played out.

Mohammed had hoped Marcus would be able to join them, but the legionnaire chose to remain with his men and those few survivors of the *Minas* who'd been plucked from vacuum before their air ran out.

"What's the safe minimum distance for what we have in mind?" he mused aloud.

"To create a rotational, low grade singularity?" Seraphim responded. "Prudence dictates a safety margin of at least seven million miles."

"Rotational?" Calen exclaimed. "How on earth are you going to manage that? Although she's denser, Latinus Prime is slightly smaller than your own home world. One or two Leviathans will certainly crush her out of existence, I'll grant you, but to create sufficient energy for directional mass? Mohammed, we basically don't have the watts."

Mohammed fixed Calen with a direct look. Somehow, he managed to keep his face expressionless.

If only you knew.

Aloud, he replied, "Oh, I've got a trick or two hidden away up my sleeve . . . you'll see."

Without explaining further, Mohammed leaned over the command console and began typing. He paused to steady himself as the ship's defensive measures absorbed another flurry of well-aimed shots before continuing with an air of urgency.

Let's finish this.

"Seraphim, target *these* specific coordinates for sterilization. Hit everything else with a multidirectional helix. Commence salvos, all batteries, in three, two, one . . . *Mark*."

The firmament blazed with fiery comets and nova flares. Despite her size, the dreadnaught shuddered.

Mohammed had no time to relish the feeling of being responsible for all that firepower, for he had more to do. Much more. He depressed a button and watched as more than seventy billion zephyr-joules of power thundered with pinpoint accuracy into an area of the planet's surface measuring a mere fifty yards wide.

Earth and rock liquefied, turning instantly to glass; the ground beneath caved in as if the underlying strata had simply vanished. The process accelerated. Within seconds, the encroaching beam had bored through the crust like a hot knife through butter, causing steam to belch forth and the crater to widen. Volatile in nature, those gases were closely followed by great gouts of magma.

"We are now more than two miles in," Seraphim announced. "As anticipated, the Horde have sensed the energies involved and are swarming toward it."

Well, there goes discipline in the ranks.

"Thank you, Seraphim," Mohammed replied. "Wait until we breach the mantle and then increase power. Deploy the Menta accelerators now, and add a few tactical missiles. Make it look as if we're putting up a bit of resistance . . ." The *Shadow of Autumn* bucked as a particularly vicious concussion taxed the shields. "And set up an exclusion zone around us. These bloody potshots are trying my nerves. Use the vortex generators and Octopod compressors. Suppressive spread, six volleys, ten second intervals. The additional gravitational eddies they create should screw their targeting systems long enough for us to pass the point of no return."

"Aye aye, sir; deploying countermeasures . . . *Now*."

Mohammed didn't wait for the results. He lifted a chain from around his neck and held it up before him. A small green gem hung from the end. Shaped like a six-inch long hexagonal rod, it reminded Mohammed of an old-style pencil artists from Old Earth liked to use in bygone days for sketching and other creative works.

Except this device wasn't designed to create anything.

He moved into position opposite Calen. "If you'd be so kind, Chancellor?"

The Chancellor removed a similar launch key from around his own neck and took his place at an identical station directly across the module.

Mohammed announced, "Seraphim, compartmentalize RTB for Sterilization Protocol. Confirm?"

"Confirmed."

The air shivered and a carbon copy of the AI construct appeared within the holo-cloud. It glanced at both men. "Proceed."

Mohammed placed his hand against a glass screen and lowered his head toward a retinal scanner.

"Recognize Mohammed Amine. Captain."

Opposite him, Calen shadowed his movements.

"Recognize Psi Calen, Chancellor."

"Identities confirmed. Please Authenticate."

Mohammed placed his crystal within a tiny indentation in the exact center of the panel. He pressed gently, until it had sunk down half its length.

Click.

"Authenticate Mohammed Amine. Shakespeare, zero, zero, one, Tempus, origin, nine, nine, Sophia."

For a second time, the Chancellor mimicked Mohammed's actions.

"Authenticate Psi Calen. Requiem, service, five, five, castle, three, unity, child, zero."

"Thank you, gentlemen," Seraphim continued. "Authentication confirmed. You may now proceed."

Mohammed nodded toward his friend, and they simultaneously depressed their respective keys the remainder of the way.

"Sterilization protocol established." A chime sounded, and as the holograph faded from sight, Seraphim intoned, "You may now continue."

Right, time to see if this plan of mine works.

"Seraphim, how are we doing?" Mohammed returned to his station and divided the display into two opposing vistas; one of the planet's surface, the other depicting an exterior view of the ship, facing toward Arabis.

"Photon incursion is approaching the mantle boundary and about to infringe on the outer core." She glanced toward a different monitor. "I estimate we have fifty, perhaps sixty seconds remaining before the enemy can reestablish a viable target lock."

Excellent.

"Initiate firing sequence, Amine revenant one. When missiles are away, divert backup power to shields and accelerate to half-speed ahead."

"Firing sequence, Amine revenant one. Commencing program."

A drone echoed throughout the CIC and illumination dimmed abruptly. By themselves, the remaining red-alert backlights created an ominous, ruddy glow.

Hmm. Talk about setting the scene perfectly.

Mohammed leaned forward, eyes fixed on the screen.

A scintillating succession of plasma balls appeared. Stretched out like a string of pearls, they sped toward the planet on a one-way voyage to oblivion. Mohammed thought their luster one of the purest, most beautiful sights he had ever seen. Nevertheless, their brilliance did little to hide their purpose.

They triggered an instant response from the enemy. Each jewel became the target of a punishing onslaught.

"Twelve!" Shaní spluttered. "I thought you only needed one or two Leviathans to destroy a planet? There'll be nothing . . . it'll be . . ."

"What makes you think they're all planet crushers?" Mohammed countered. He winked, raised his hand, paused, and then clenched his fist. "Seraphim . . . *Now*."

A vortex materialized four hundred yards off the port bow.

"Is that . . . ?"

The Deputy Magister gaped at the sight of a further ten gleaming projectiles. In close formation, they floated gracefully toward the gateway under a sizzling deluge of covering fire.

"Mohammed?" Calen inquired.

No sooner had the torpedoes crossed the threshold than the portal winked out of existence.

Behind him, someone chuckled. Mohammed heard that person approach, and a hand clasped him by the shoulder. "Well played," Sam whispered in his ear. "*Very* well played. This is gonna be fun."

Sam spun on his heel and called to his team, "Quickly guys, on me. We'll watch the show out back. I have a feeling we'll want to be strapped in for the finale."

Within the main holo-screen, perspective changed as filters were added to show Arabis in all its glory. It may have been only seven miles in diameter, but its flickering blue-white radiance created a spectacular presence.

Mohammed turned to face Calen. "You asked me a few minutes ago how I was going to create a rotating black hole?" He pointed to the image before them. "There's your answer. That thing is spinning at more than seven hundred times per second. If we've got our figures right — and by *we*, I of course mean Seraphim and I — then once the collapse is triggered we should have all the momentum we need to permanently end this threat, here, now, and forever."

Calen looked confused.

"But what about neutron degeneracy? Arabis only possesses three, maybe four solar masses. She's plainly not dense enough."

"Taken care of. We primed the Leviathans with more than a pound of pure lydium. When those babies go, it'll trigger a chain reaction that will increase her density a hundredfold. Remember, she's a neutron star: she's already halfway to becoming what we need." Calen was obviously flabbergasted, so Mohammed continued. "Why do you think I had Seraphim jump the torpedoes? They're far too heavy to fly there themselves . . . speaking of which . . ." He addressed the AI: "About *now* might be good, it should coincide nicely with the demise of Latinus."

"Very astute, Captain," Seraphim replied. "The two events will occur remarkably close together."

Like an unfolding flower, a second gateway bloomed to life beyond the sun's corona. Seraphim added another filter so everyone could clearly see the string of Leviathans dip toward the dazzling penumbra.

"What happens now?" Shaní mumbled. "And how quickly?"

"To be honest, I have absolutely no idea," Mohammed admitted. "This has never been tried before. From what Seraphim can calculate, once it starts, things will progress very quickly."

They waited.

It wasn't until Mohammed felt a pain in his chest that he realized he was holding his breath.

C'mon already.

He needn't have worried. Irrespective of its audience, the soul of the little pulsar was irrevocably changed. The immeasurable force of gravity increased, overcoming the outward pressure exerted by her natural processes and compressing her toward a point of infinite density.

But Arabis fought back.

A blinding conflagration erupted, blanching the vault of the heavens and scalding the interior of the bridge in a wash of light so bright that onlookers cried out in pain and covered their faces.

Bloody hell! What would that have been like without protection in place?

Mohammed studied the scene closely: a nearby band of asteroids had begun to shudder. While smaller members of the group immediately broke orbit and commenced skittering busily toward the sun, larger fragments tarried, tumbling over and over before joining their smaller comrades on their final journey.

"Add another UV layer to the screens," Mohammed called out. "And zoom us in closer."

Seraphim did as instructed, and their vista transposed. Mohammed now felt sure he was looking into the eye of a god whose retina was comprised of hypersonic jets of plasma and supercharged ribbons of light.

A scene empyrean in scope and splendor.

Then the entire corona flexed, and neon tendrils lashed out into space. A futile gesture, for the magnitude of the developing maw beneath forced each streamer to curl back and fall to its doom.

The pupil rippled in an agitated sea of static and then contracted, as if the deity had stepped out into bright daylight. Actuality distorted and became viscous, forcing each passing second to labor for its next breath.

Transposing toward a darker shade of blue, the surface plane of Arabis flushed indigo, violet, and then red. It continued to contract and darken, then blushed through crimson, scarlet, garnet, and mahogany.

The orbiting debris field reached full flood. Blazing streamers saturated Arabis's atmosphere, whirling inward from all compass points in a celestial merry-go-round of high energy release and photonic discharges.

Time froze. For an instant, everything locked in place relative to its own position, as if the galaxy were paying homage to the moment when everything would change forever.

When time resumed, Mohammed discovered reality had deformed, for only the leading edge of each asteroid had changed position. Elongated beyond reason, their surface parameters stretched off toward the darkening orb like strands of melted gray cheese.

Then the lights went out.

The *Shadow of Autumn* rocked as an influx of irresistible gravity attempted to pluck her from space. Safely nestled within her cocoon of protective physics-warping energies, she remained free of the fatal currents now ripping the rest of the system apart.

"Swap view to Latinus Prime," Mohammed ordered, "and maintain current heading. Once you assess the way as clear, accelerate to full sublight speed ahead."

"Roger that," Seraphim replied, "maintain current heading, full ahead when clear."

The screen flickered.

Although he had expected a scene of utter carnage, Mohammed was still shocked at what he saw: Latinus Prime was no more. In its place, great hunks of rock and a sea of other detritus orbited a glowing nucleus from which great gouts of flame erupted at irregular intervals. Some pieces were pulled toward the siren's call of Arabis, while those closer to the fulguration snapped, shattered, and folded back on themselves as they succumbed to the jaws of the nearer micro-singularity at the planet's former core.

Amid the devastation, tranquility could still be found: a swathe of dust particles orbited the central mass, gracing it with a ring of violet hue. Alas, its splendor was short-lived, and soon it too was swallowed by the irresistible hunger of its progenitor.

Mohammed found it difficult to tear his gaze from the expanding void.

"We did it. We actually did it," Calen gasped.

"Yes, we did," Mohammed mumbled, "but at what cost?"

Despite their victory, Mohammed didn't feel celebratory and found himself recalling a quotation from the fabled Friedrich Nietzsche, a nineteenth century philosopher and cultural critic.

"Battle not with monsters, lest ye become a monster, and if you gaze into the abyss, the abyss gazes also into you."

Under the circumstances, he felt the passage rather apt.

Chapter Twenty-Three

A Walk on the Wild Side

Stained-With-Blood accepted his lot with an overwhelming sense of déjà-vu. He knew better than to question Napioa's judgment, but lately he wished the Creator would at least give him a little more warning before demanding his attention.

His current predicament was a prime example. One moment Stained-With-Blood was sitting in Saul Cameron's private office, discussing the proposals for the resettlement of his people with the commander himself and a small group of Magisters, and the next, his spirit had been transposed here, to the familiar slopes of Eagles Aerie, high on the eastern peaks of the Bitterroot Mountains.

The Old Man obviously has something urgent to discuss. He shrugged away the inconvenience and made himself comfortable. *The sooner I relax and let things unfurl, the sooner I can get back to my body.*

It didn't take much effort, for this place always made Stained-With-Blood feel he could reach up to touch the sky. And what a sky it was. Azure, vibrant, and endless, it possessed a grandeur that always reminded him how insignificant humans really were.

And how weighty our responsibility as caretakers.

He looked out over the plain before him. This too was vast, stretching off as far as the eye could see like a rolling brown and yellow comber. And yet, for all its majesty, Stained-With-Blood immediately realized something here was amiss.

Not only was the atmosphere much drier than normal, but the waving grasslands below appeared parched, as if no water had fallen for months. Signs of neglect were evident. Right at the base of the prominence upon which he sat, Stained-With-Blood spied a large circular area of trampled grass, with a fire set at its center.

Whoever was responsible had been careless, failing to ensure that the blaze was properly damped and extinguished before leaving. Even at this distance, he could see embers within the hearth being fanned back to life by a stiffening wind.

He sat forward, watching as sparks began to fly. They spat and sizzled, blackening nearby blades and stalks at the slightest touch. Soon a budding number of glowing cinders rode high into the air on an invisible vortex. Up and up they went, cavorting and dancing like a rabble of pyrotechnic butterflies, drunk on the elixir of life.

As the embers reached his plateau, they were snatched away on a gale and blown toward a distant escarpment, smudging the horizon with the promise of perils to come.

Stained-With-Blood waited.

The sun set and the moon usurped its place. A pulse rode the ether, and each celestial body began negotiating the heavens at breathtaking speed. Accustomed to such events, Stained-

With-Blood adjusted his position, settled in, and mentally prepared himself for a lengthy sojourn. However, not a score of celestial turns elapsed before the cycle slowed to a halt and daylight returned.

Dawn brought a perplexing sight:

Beneath him, the scorched vegetation had withered and died. Weeds and brambles sprouted where lush grass had once graced the savanna in a crown of swaying hues. The far side of the expanse fared no better, for smoke blackened the horizon with the pall of a funeral pyre.

Higher and higher it climbed, a thickening blanket which blotted out the sun and carried the stench of carrion and decay.

Experience came to the fore, and Stained-With-Blood's intuition kicked into gear:

The end of our existence approaches . . . He glanced toward the base of the cliff. *And though this blight germinated elsewhere, it was seeded close to home.*

Focused by the nature of his dream quest, he studied the details of the all-enveloping brume as it boiled toward him. Storms raged and lightning flashed within its depths. And yet, not a single raindrop fell upon the desiccated soil. The malevolence approaching Stained-With-Blood refused to shed a single tear of sympathy for the havoc it inflicted on the world below.

Green things shriveled, blackened, and expired. Rivers boiled and ran dry. Anything in which the breath of life resided charred to the bone and was consumed.

A bitter harvest indeed, for our enemy now seeks to establish a new foothold from where they will ravage afresh.

Stained-With-Blood's attention jerked once more to the seat of the original fire.

Does this mean our absent friends have gained success? Or have they succeeded only in chasing away the evil? Perhaps something has happened to the great craft in which they cruise the celestial hunting grounds?

"You begin to understand then?" an unexpected voice announced. "That is well, for prompt action is required."

Stained-With-Blood turned to find a tribal chieftain right behind him. Ripened by many summers, the warrior's gray-streaked raven hair made a decorative braid for a crown of eagle's feathers. Powerful arms enfolded a broad chest, and argent orbs gleamed out from beneath ancient brows.

Napioa.

"Yes, I understand only too well. If left to flourish, the danger will encroach upon pastures new. From there, it will spread and blight all life once more."

Although the when and the how still eludes me.

As if reading Stained-With-Blood's thoughts, Napioa sighed. "Ah, then it would appear you must yet find the wisdom to know what must be done. The spirit realm is transforming, my son, and great changes lie ahead. Be a rock for your peoples."

Peoples?

The Creator faded from sight, his silver eyes the last to dissipate. As they winked away, Stained-With-Blood jolted awake.

"Stained-With-Blood?" Saul's voice was laced with concern. "Are you all right?"

"You need not fear, Saul Cameron," Stained-With-Blood replied, "at least, not for me. Our compatriots who journey into the heart of enemy territory, however, might be another matter."

In reply to Cameron's confusion, Stained-With-Blood offered, "Let me explain . . ."

*

Frustrated beyond reason by the wanton slaughter of her kinsfolk, Va-ákil vented her fury in a manifestation of sublime authority, an expression as inevitable as it was dreadful. More than a hundred innocent children of the Triarium Tier became sacrifices to her wrath; and although her actions drew the approval of her generals, this could not appease the gremlins gnawing at her mind like scavengers on carrion.

Standing apart from the others on the edge of a rocky outcrop, her gaze wandered the wilderness before her as she berated herself privately, safe in the knowledge her thoughts would not be overheard.

Fool! We are Kresh, above the mundane creatures that threaten our existence. Although I need to set the example in all things, I must act with greater wisdom. In truth, all I have done is commit a similar atrocity to the vermin infecting that craft . . . albeit on a smaller scale. What's more, I've denied us a useful wave of cannon fodder for the coming conflict.

Va-ákil paused to savor the sweet nectar of the freshly ingested life force now saturating her codex.

And as glorious as this feels, such contradictions must cease if we are to survive.

She tried to lighten her mood by thinking ahead to the clash that would surely come.

The dish of vengeance will soon be served upon those who have dared such atrocity. And when it is, they will provide a source of greater satisfaction . . . in quantity, if not quality.

Attracted by the resonance of her brooding, Altás moved to approach.

Prime Catalyct? she called. *Do you want something?*

My Queen, although you conceal it, I can sense your rising ardor. Do you have a plan to counteract the outrage we witnessed?

You know me too well. Va-ákil turned and ushered her Battlemaster to one side. *The parasites are overeager to reclaim us for their diabolical ministrations. Whilst repellant, we must encourage their belief in such attitudes, for I'll not allow what happened to Erubus and his ilk to befall us here. However, while helping them realize their ambitions, it is essential we inflict a price upon them, grievous in nature.*

You talk of submission?

Only figuratively. Va-ákil moved closer and lowered the tone of her thoughts. *Fear not. Let me share an interesting facet I learned from the mind of one of the minions aboard their craft.*

She displayed an image in the ether between them.

What is *that,* Altás rumbled, *and how can such an innocuous thing assist in our victory?*

On their world, they call this device an onion. Something I believe they ingest. However, it isn't its lack of nutritional value that attracted me to its usefulness, but its symbolism to the strategy we will adopt. Here, let me explain . . .

*

James Houston—or the entity that had once been James Houston—was deeply concerned. Despite the changes he had willingly invited, he knew the path ahead was still beset by obstacles and fraught with danger.

He thought back to the day he'd found the military outpost deep in the heart of the Tar'e-esh Forest. He hadn't known it at the time, but the facility contained a rip-space splinter, a binate of the main fracture back in Rhomane and its abstruse cousin, the gateway portal. Both devices in such close proximity acted as esoteric lodestones, and the fresh anomaly had manifested without artifice or manipulation of any kind. Once discovered, however, residual memories still lingering from the now-absent mind of Permian Hasanem furnished Houston with an inkling of what he might achieve.

His life changed that day.

Houston's first contact with the rupture infused him with a sense of euphoria and a heightened state of awareness which was instantly addictive. It was savage, wild and unpredictable. Something about the nature of the exotic medium appealed to his basest desires, those inherent in every human psyche and usually buried away. Nevertheless, longer exposure brought with it the consequences of immersing organic tissue within the quasi-orphic environment of hyperspace without the additional safety feature of a temporal sheath. Mutation.

Even so, he reasoned obstinately, *it was definitely worth it. I've never felt so alive, so completely in touch with the pulse of every living thing around me*.

He assessed what had become of his human flesh.

Of course there's the change itself and the hunger to contend with, but that's a small price to pay for expanded dominion and near immortality . . .

Nevertheless, a major hurdle still plagued him.

Now all I have to do is prevent her *from killing me.*

He reflected on the all too brief episodes when they had made contact.

I know she looks on me as an abomination—something to be squashed at the first opportunity—but if I continue to show my worth, I might just pull this off.

Ever the pragmatist, especially where his own self-preservation was concerned, Houston tried to think of the simplest solution.

Of course, if I could just find some leverage, something that meant the world to her, it would make this a whole lot easier.

Chapter Twenty-Four

Windows of Opportunity

Fussing like a mother hen, Shaní added the finishing touches to her center display and decided to reposition one of the forks a millimeter leftward. Satisfied at last, she lit the tapers and stood back to admire her handiwork.

Perfect.

Although far from Spartan, facilities for entertaining aboard ship were meager. The officers' mess boasted silverware, crystal glasses, and high quality table settings, yet the little embellishments which would turn a simple meal into something more intimate were sorely lacking.

The candles, for example, had been a nightmare to procure; only due to the benevolence of some among the Ninth Legion had a major detail of Shaní's plans not been ruined.

Many soldiers still observed the ritual of Saturnalia, an event on their home world paying homage to a deity called Saturn. Rushlights were used for such worship and, ever industrious, the legionnaires had continued making their own since arriving on Arden by dipping the dried pith of rush plants in tallow extracted from cattle and provats.

Even then, fortune continued to smile on Shaní. Those original tapers were foul creations that spat only a little less than they stank. But most of the men added extract of tasmin or jale to the mix along with other herbs and spices, so their candles not only looked beautiful but smelled wonderful too . . . much to her relief.

She glanced around the cabin and decided the cushions on the couch needed a final plumping to bring them up to standard. Then the scene was set.

Just in time, for the chime sounded.

Her eyes flew to the clock.

Five minutes early? She grinned. *Yet another arrow to add to his quiver.*

Shaní had made no secret of the fact that she found Mohammed's company stimulating. She deemed him kind, intelligent, thoughtful, and witty. And even though she'd always thought him tall, dark and handsome, she found his profound respect for the customs and beliefs of others even more attractive.

They'd spent many hours together discussing their disparate cultures and the histories of their peoples. And somehow, despite the fact they'd never displayed overt affection, they'd managed to fall for each other.

Of course, Mohammed's feelings had been hard to detect, as his natural reserve meant he played his cards very close to his chest.

But I *held all the aces, and in the end, I got my man.*

The destruction of Latinus Prime the previous day was a turning point, for the fact he'd been forced to destroy an entire planetary system had disturbed Mohammed deeply.

He'd wanted to unburden himself, and Shaní was delighted to discover *she* was the one he naturally sought on such an occasion. They'd talked long into the night, and she seized the opportunity to end the evening with a promise of dinner and a simple kiss.

The kiss. Shaní's heart skipped at the recollection.

Men! That Earth saying I learned from Jake the other week is most appropriate. You can lead a horse to water, but if its name's Mohammed, you have to hold its head under to ensure it drinks.

The intercom pealed again.

I suppose I'd better let him in then. Her gaze fell upon the cushions once more. *But not before . . .*

One quick pummeling later, she made her way to the entrance, dimmed the lights, and welcomed her guest:

"Mohammed." She smiled warmly. "What a surprise, I was expecting someone else."

He looked over her shoulder and took in the scene. One eyebrow arched, and the answering smile which graced his features made Shaní's stomach flutter.

"So I see." He raised two sealed carafes of wine. "I suppose I'd better cry myself all the way back to my cabin and drink these in solitude?"

"Two? Are you trying to lower my inhibitions in order to seduce me?"

Mohammed's jaw dropped and started flapping. "I . . . I, er, I wouldn't." He coughed. "I wouldn't dream of—"

"Well, you're not coming in then," Shaní retorted. "I thought we were past all this awkwardness."

Mohammed caught himself and his eyes narrowed. "I have a feeling your sense of humor will plague me for years to come."

"That's what I'm hoping." Shaní leaned in to kiss Mohammed's cheek, then stood aside to let him enter. "Help yourself to the goblets on the table. Chef has told me the food should arrive in about thirty minutes, so we've a chance to resume our 'conversation' from last night."

Shaní realized a pivotal moment of truth had arrived.

"So tell me," she breathed, "was that the pressure of life talking, or did you mean what you said before you left?"

Mohammed poured two glasses of wine and handed her one. When he looked long and hard into her eyes, Shaní's heart beat so wildly she found it hard to breathe.

"Of course I meant it," he replied, "just because I'm reserved and won't rush things doesn't mean our relationship isn't important to me. It is. I look on it as something very special, something enduring, and . . ."

Just what I wanted to hear.

Shaní squeaked and threw her arms around him. Hugging him tightly, she whispered, "Now you've had the balls to admit what's been on your mind, I expect you to show it a little more, especially around the others. They all know we have a thing anyway, so if you lighten up, I promise to stop teasing you in front of them so much." She stepped back. "Deal?"

"Deal."

Mohammed extended his hand. Shaní brushed it aside, pulled him close, and planted the most passionate kiss she could muster square on his lips.

For once, she felt him relax immediately and was just about to suggest they take their drinks through into the adjoining bedroom when someone rang the bell.

That can't be the food already?

With the greatest reluctance, Shaní disengaged herself from Mohammed's embrace, cursed the chef for being so damned professional, and headed toward the door.

Over her shoulder, she warned, "Whatever you were thinking at that moment, keep thinking it. If this is our meal, I'll get rid of the steward in a few seconds, and we can reheat it later."

She almost punched the switch in her struggled to compose herself.

The door swept to one side, and Shaní was so surprised to find Calen standing outside that she stepped back a few feet—and froze.

Taking her gesture as an invitation to enter, Calen strode into the cabin, waving his info-tablet in the air like a fan.

What the . . . ?

"Mohammed, Shaní, so glad I found you," Calen gushed. "You're not going to believe what I have here . . ."

Shaní glared at him, but Calen didn't notice. He rushed across the room toward Mohammed without pausing for breath.

"A few of us have been going over the rest of the intelligence package we managed to download before Latinus Prime was destroyed. With Seraphim's help, we've decrypted quite a bit of data." He held out the pad. "Look at this."

Shaní could tell Mohammed was annoyed, but Calen was too excited to realize he'd interrupted a special moment. Mohammed's ever-present sense of duty won the day. Snatching the tablet from Calen's hand, he read the contents of the first page.

His brows furrowed and his head craned forward.

Oh no, what now? I had it all planned . . .

"It says here they were prepping a focusing array for an artificial wormhole," Mohammed spluttered. Then his eyes popped wide. "For a military-grade precision translocation project? I thought Rhomane was the only place possessing a gateway of that magnitude?"

"So did I," Calen replied, "but you know these military types. As we're still within the Verianda Nebula, I haven't been able to check to see what Berek knows about it. All I can say is that we'd been at peace for more than two thousand years before the Horde stirred things up. Nevertheless, the upkeep of a military deterrent was one of our top priorities. Space is vast. As our territory expanded, we had to stay prepared for whatever we might find. This is obviously part of an ongoing agenda."

Mohammed was still confused. "But I thought *you* invented the gateway?"

"I based my theorem on the work of a brilliant young astrophysicist, Katiél Feran. She initially toyed with the concept several years before I did, but was never able to solve the degradation that arises when you transfer a quantum package over vast distances. I used her calculations as a starting point, and thankfully managed to push the project through to completion."

"Just as well we destroyed the damned thing, then. Can you imagine what the Horde could do if they ever managed to get their ha– What?"

Calen's face was etched in concern. He glanced at Shaní, then back at Mohammed. "That's just the point." He balled one fist in emphasis. "Latinus Prime was only developing the focusing array. From what the report highlights near the end, there might be a working generator on Exordium."

Shaní realized her chances of making this a pleasurable evening were evaporating rapidly. She studied Mohammed's face and saw him becoming more absorbed in the dilemma with each passing second.

Oh, he'll remember the evening all right. But for all the wrong reasons. She sighed and increased the interior illumination back to normal. *I'd better call the mess and make that three meals. We might be here for some time.*

*

Having been in Arden for close to eighteen months, Sam sometimes forgot that many of his compatriots came from much simpler times than his. Nevertheless, occasions like this reminded him that warriors were always warriors, no matter how many centuries divided them.

Following the destruction of the *Minas* and the death of almost everyone on board, Marcus had taken the lead in a memorial ceremony commemorating the passing of their brethren into the afterlife. Along with Marcus's legion, every fellow soldier aboard the *Shadow of Autumn* had been invited to attend the event, and Sam had ensured his squad was among those present.

The ceremony was a moving affair.

The men had erected an altar on the main hangar deck, upon which personal mementos were affixed or arranged. Then, one by one, officers stepped forward to place Charon's obol—a coin to pay for each soldier's safe passage into the world of the dead—within a specially crafted urn. Normally, the tithe would have been placed in the deceased person's mouth or over the eyes prior to cremation. But since so few bodies had been retrieved, Marcus decreed an adaptation of the manner in which the ferryman's payment would be rendered.

Following the service a ritual meal was eaten, during which each man toasted those now absent and cast lots for the honor of firing the urn out into the depths of space. Marcus told them it would serve as an eternal testimony to the bravery of those lost in battle. A noble and fitting gesture, yet the mere thought filled Sam with a sense of loss and frustration which prompted him to consider a more appropriate response.

The longer the celebration continued, the more Sam gave the matter serious consideration. He couldn't be sure if their beliefs might prohibit what he had in mind, but Sam had a gut feeling the legionnaires would jump at a chance for their fallen comrades to have a final say, for it possessed a sense of karma that would appeal strongly to any fighter.

He determined to approach Marcus once the event concluded and run the proposal past him.

Easier said than done, for at the closure of the memorial Marcus made an extraordinary announcement.

He offered, upon their return to Arden, to lead a team of artisans in the construction of a special mausoleum that would display the names and service details of Flavius Velerianus and his men.

The declaration prompted a great deal of foot stamping, whistling, and cheering. Then Marcus's men flooded forward to surround and congratulate him.

As Sam watched the mob congregate about their leader, he recalled again how wide was the skill set of these "simple folk."

We tend to forget men like this were not only responsible for the construction of most of the roads throughout their empire, but for the majority of Rome's prized monuments as well.

Eventually, Marcus spotted Sam waiting at the edge of the crowd and made his way through the press.

"Well met," he said, clasping Sam warmly by the forearm. "What did you think of our service?"

"Potent," Sam replied, "and moving. No wonder your boys are such a tight knit bunch. The sense of camaraderie invoked was powerful. Hell, I'm not even in the Ninth, yet it made *me* feel like I belonged to something extraordinary, something bigger than myself."

Marcus smiled.

"Thank you, I like to do what I can to lead by example and show the men we're part of a very special family. One day, especially now the resurrections have started, we'll all have a chance of settling down, starting families, and growing fat. But until that day comes, we'll always have each other."

Sam seized his opening: "And are you really happy that the remains of those who were ambushed are going to float around in space forever?"

"No, not really. None of us are. But what other opportunity do we have of honoring them?"

"Come with me for a moment." Sam embraced his friend and led him to one side. "I don't wish to cause offense, so I thought I'd broach the subject in private first and get your initial reaction."

"About what?"

"Payback. This is what I was thinking . . ."

*

In silence, Zagam, Roth, Urium, and El'chan followed Caym down multiple flights of stairs until they arrived before the huge bulkhead doors marking the juncture of the aft and midship sections of the *Shadow of Autumn*. Two heavily armed patrol drones stood guard before the entrance, a scenario repeated on all eight engineering decks.

No sooner had Caym's party started its approach than the leading unit scanned them from head to toe, while its counterpart deployed weapons and swooped down to assume a covering position.

Oh, for pity's sake.

"Good morning, Seraphim," Caym remarked dryly. "As thoroughly repetitive as ever, I see. Look, you know why we're here, so cut the theatrics: Let us in."

The sentinel made no reply, its strobelike scarlet beams continuing to play across the group until they focused on the forearms of each in turn.

"All representatives of the Senatum Kresh have been recognized," Seraphim announced. "Good morning, Senator Caym, are you here for the security rounds?"

Why does she let these things act like they don't know what's going on? "Yes, that's right. My colleagues were looking for something to occupy their free time, so I suggested they get some exercise walking the corridors. Their help should cut the patrol by over an hour. I take it oxygen has been restored?"

"That is correct. Be advised, radiation levels exceed safety limits for organics around compartments E-fourteen through twenty-two."

Seraphim's voice always sounded blunt and somewhat robotic when it issued from one of the sentries.

Part of the intimidation factor to deter unwanted guests, I suppose.

Aloud, he responded, "Thank you for that. Fortunately, our heritage allows us to withstand a higher dosage over a longer period than most of our shipmates. But"—he tapped a badge pinned to his chest—"we have our personalized dosimeters, and we'll make our way out if they indicate we've stayed too long."

"Very well. I have notified all automated patrols and stationary checkpoints within the engineering section, so you should be able to proceed unhindered."

A loud *clunk* reverberated through the floor and along the walls, and the great doors cracked open. As they inched apart, cold stale air exuded into the stairwell.

Seraphim continued: "Do you wish for additional illumination and warmth?"

"No, that won't be necessary either. We are more robust than our natural cousins and see well enough in the dark that the emergency beacons will be quite sufficient."

"Noted. Please proceed."

Without a further word, Caym ushered the company inside.

Although the gloomiest recesses of the drive section no longer fascinated him, it remained one of the most deserted areas of the ship and perfect for speaking privately, away from prying ears.

The party descended until they reached the arterial deck, whereupon Caym gathered them together.

"So, what do you think?" His voice echoed along the central shaft and adjoining passageways.

"The resonance is bloody awesome," Urium remarked. "I can see why you want to come here all the time." He cupped his hands to his lips. "Hello . . ."

"Hello—hello—hello—hello," warbled a fading reply.

Since his revival, Urium's sense of humor had come along in leaps and bounds. While most of the crew—and the more inexperienced members of the Kresh contingent—seemed to relate to that, Caym found Urium's behavior inappropriate at best and annoying at worst.

Caym hid his irritation: "For those of you suffering a sharp drop in IQ," he stressed. "I am, of course, referring to Mohammed's request. Any comments? Or should I say, any *pertinent* comments?"

The younger members of the group sobered instantly.

Beside him, Zagam took a deep breath and shook his head.

"If you're asking for an opinion," he offered, "then I'd say we have no choice. Our task will be difficult, certainly.

Dangerous, too. Sadly, it is also necessary. And as *we* are the only ones with a chance of piercing the veil around Exordium, that duty falls to us. Can you tell us anything else about the mission?"

"At this stage, not a great deal. Mohammed learned only last night that our lost brethren might have access to an automated, working gateway. As we speak, his team of specialists interrogates the system, hunting anything to help confirm or deny his suspicions. Until then, we must act as if the information is true. Fortunately Exordium possesses only one continent, Origen. It is highly unlikely they would have placed such a contrivance on one of her many archipelagos, so I think it's safe to assume we can begin our search there. Our best bet would be to start near Barsoonet, the capital, and then work our way—"

"What if the damned thing is underground?" Roth interjected.

"I beg your pardon?"

"If they have a portal, wouldn't they position it underground? We're clearly not talking about teleport pads like we have aboard ship or for site-to-site transfers about Rhomane. If this thing is like the gateway beneath the ark room back home, capable of spanning the vast light years of the galaxy in an instant, its power requirements will be huge. Logic dictates they would have located it below the surface in a geologically stable area."

He's right! "So we concentrate on those areas possessing the greatest tectonic stability first," Caym continued Roth's line of reasoning, "and if they've stationed it near a city or main installation, even better."

"Don't forget the energy spikes," Urium chipped in. "If this thing has been left activated all these years on a remote sequence, it'll be firing at all times of the day and night. As

Roth indicated, without focus, its energy requirements will be substantial, and—" The young prankster slapped his hand against his forehead. "Food!"

"Food?" everyone echoed at the same time.

Urium's eyes were wide with sudden comprehension. He looked toward Zagam first, then back to Caym. "Don't you see? Although I never reached the level of maturity required to employ the Ix as you two did, I had enough skill to manipulate the vext. Yes, my initial attempts proved shoddy. Lacking accuracy, I wasted precious energy. But we can all attest to the fact that experience brings both refinement and precision. We fine-tuned our abilities over time, so teleporting became an elegant, natural and simple means of travel. Something we did without conscious thought or effort. And why? Because we learned through trial and error to puncture the superficies of the spacetime continuum as opposed to simply smashing our way through. Now, although we're talking about a mechanically generated portal, it still must obey the laws of quantum mechanics. Without the focusing array, it'll be—"

Of course . . .

"Wild and uncontrolled." It was Caym's turn to interrupt. "And in our previous forms, such a source would prove irresistible."

"Like I said . . . food." Urium shrugged. "If this queen has established a stronghold, I'm betting it'll be atop the gateway. Where else can she find an unlimited source of high-quality nutrition?"

Caym regarded the youngster in a new light.

Keep it up, he sent telepathically. That's *what I want to see more of. Well done.*

Aloud, he announced, "Right. So we have an unexpected window of opportunity. I suggest we begin refining our telestic concert. We have the watts to cover the range, but we need to increase our augmentation co-efficiency if we hope to achieve maximum resonance. If we spot the queen while she's relaxed, we'll need to follow her peripheral broadcasts to their source without alerting her to our snooping."

"It didn't seem to work last time," El'chan complained. "She was on us so quickly you barely had time to sever the connection."

"There was that," Caym conceded. "But we were in the middle of a battle, and she was already super-energized within the Ix medium. If you're ever strong enough to achieve that state of awareness, you'll discover everything about you will be hyper-sensitized. Your perceptions, reactions, cognitive functioning . . . the lot. What's more, it was our first time working as a cohesive unit during a crisis, and we were taken by surprise. That won't happen again. Calen's tweaked the psyche-bugs to improve efficiency; all signs of the discordant sub-harmonic that distracted us have been removed. Basically, if we manage to catch her with her guard down, we'll have the edge we seek. Remember, we'll only confirm the existence of the gateway. We'll be in and out before she knows it."

Zagam wasn't convinced: "Regardless, I ask you to employ a multi-tiered level of protection, Caym. Like you, I was of the Unium Tier, but never before have I witnessed majesty such as hers. Not even the great Angule could stand against her. Her crown possessed twelve—*twelve*—Jînnereth stars. I never thought such puissance possible. Even her aides, although beneath her in power, enjoy a mastery beyond ours. I sensed the purity of their malevolence in the background, as did you. No, brother, before we seize this opportunity, we must do all we can to ensure it doesn't come back to bite us, for if that happens, I doubt we'll survive."

He has a point, Caym admitted to himself, *but we still have to try . . . and soon.*

Chapter Twenty-Five

Knocking on the Door

"On approach to southern terminus," Seraphim announced. "We will exit the Verianda Nebula in T-minus thirty seconds."

"Thank you, Seraphim," Mohammed replied. "As soon as we're free, reset clocks to Galactic-Rhomane-Standard. With the temporal mitigators out of action, goodness knows how far off we are. Once we're synchronized, send an all-clear signal to Arden to let them know we're okay. Then move us into an elliptical pattern, a thousand miles out should do. As we go, deploy defensive buoys, standard formation, and back them up with sentry drones. You can maneuver *them* into closer orbits of the ship to make an exterior assessment of the hull. Send repair teams out there too, with escorts. Not only do I want eyeball checks of each zone where you registered damage, but special attention paid to any areas where 'unwanted passengers' might stow away."

"Roger that. Threshold cleared, scanning for beacons. Located. Synchronizing onboard networks now. Welfare signal, away."

"Excellent. While you have the opportunity, complete a full system by system diagnostic. Level ten. I want everything shipshape before we begin our run on Exordium. Until that's complete, maintain yellow alert status, but stand down emergency watches."

"Understood. I will—Captain, short-range sensors are picking up another vessel, two hundred thousand megs out, approaching off the starboard bow. Its weapons appear to be charged."

"Raise shields, bring the defensive grid online and identify."

Who the hell would that be? It's too soon for—

"Instruments indicate it is a Corvette class starship, the *Helexia*. They're hailing us."

The Helexia*?*

"Open a channel."

The frosted veil of the holo-cloud coalesced within the focusing array to reveal a stunning image of a woman:

With long silver hair, porcelain sharp oriental features, and jade green eyes, Sandi Chang made most people look twice. Since she looked half her forty-two years, she seemed like a child sitting in the captain's chair while the grownups were away.

"Sandi," Mohammed's voice was laced with concern, "this is unexpected. Is everything all right?"

"Strange," she replied, "I was going to ask you the same thing."

"I'm sorry? We've only this second sent the all-clear. The Latinus Prime mission was a complete fubar. We had to expend considerable ordinance to get out of there. We sent an update, what? . . . forty-eight hours ago? Didn't you receive it?"

"Mohammed, our last contact from *you* was ten days back. The *Paladin* and *Dark Falcon* have also been redirected here."

Ten days? But we've . . . bugger! Destroying the mitigator field must have messed things up more than we realized. "So you were sent to look for us?"

"Not really. We knew the severe gravity fluctuations within the nebula might create a discrepancy, temporal compensators or not . . . No, Saul Cameron dispatched us. Stained-With-Blood has had one of his visions. Said you needed help. So here we are, all nice and shiny."

"Please tell me you've brought supplies?"

"But of course. This poor lady's bursting at the seams. I don't know the specifics of what Stained-With-Blood saw, but the inference was that you'll have one hell of a fight on your hands. So we came prepared."

Humph! Tell me about it. "Pity dream-walking doesn't take chronological variances into account. We've already had the mother of all battles, and to us it was only . . ." A chill ran down his spine. *Or have we?* Aloud, Mohammed continued, "Sandi, once you've started transferring everything across, would you be so kind as to teleport over to the *Shadow of Autumn* with your senior officers? I'll be waiting for you in the briefing room."

"Why, got some war stories to exaggerate?"

"Let's just say there's more to this new strain of Horde than we realized . . ." As he spoke, one of the tactics their enemy employed during the last firefight suddenly came to mind. "Hang on. You say you've been sent to assist? Were you given a timeframe?"

"As long as it takes, why?"

Mohammed almost jumped for joy.

"The Horde tried to screw us with a sneaky trick that's given me an idea. If you don't mind helping out, I've a way you can act as a distraction while we sneak in the back door."

"Sounds intriguing. I'll see you soon."

*

Back to back, two sentinels whirled slowly round and round in midair, maintaining an ever-vigilant watch over the five individuals in their care.

Below them, safely ensconced within a protective barrier of infrared, thermal, and photonic properties, Caym, Zagam, Roth, Urium, and El'chan appeared to be relaxing, sitting as they were in a circle, holding hands.

In reality, while their bodies rested within the cool interior of the *Shadow of Autumn*'s main engineering deck, their minds were far away. Light years away, in fact. And at this very moment, the nucleus of their conjoined psyches was descending upon the broad expanse of a gray and ochre colored world, bathed in wan light from a brown-dwarf sun.

As executive of the concert, Caym lightly sounded the biosphere.

Fibril echoes lingered, teasing him with spectral reminders of the teeming diversity which once graced this planet with vibrant life. Today only a desolate husk remained, where dust storms ravaged brittle, wind-scoured deserts.

An impressive chain of islands still stretched more than halfway across its globe, splitting a vast ocean and connecting both sides of an immense, world-spanning continent in a lopsided grin like a string of broken teeth.

The mélange of flora and fauna here must have been breathtaking, Caym remarked, *can you sense it?*

A chorus of affirmations rang back, along with bitter resentment at wonders lost and potential wasted.

Good, use the resonance of its memory to strengthen your resolve. This *must not be allowed to happen again, anywhere. Now prepare: we approach the treacherous part of our mission.*

Though powerful beyond compare, the anagogic enchantment they'd employed to span the vast celestial distance was also delicate in the extreme. Any distraction, the slightest discordant thought, and the intricacies woven into its making could be undone.

Lend me your strength, Caym instructed. *I need to compress my spirit into a needle of intent capable of piercing the veil that clouds our sight.*

They did so willingly, and a silent scream reverberated through their concert. Agony piled on agony as each bent their will to the task. They refused to let go, refused to be daunted by the scope of their endeavors. Yet such was the intimacy of their link that Caym was forced to share his own suffering while experiencing his comrades pain as if it was his own.

Hold, he cried. *Hold fast*!

A gyre of anguish stretched their awareness along a rack of misery.

On and on went the agony as the pressure mounted. And still they denied the chaos that could tear their sanity asunder.

Then, just when their torment threatened to claim them forever, the wave crested and the sudden release brought a flood of endorphins to render all memory of distress obsolete.

Concordance! Quickly, Caym urged. *Erect sheaths about your minds to keep relief from giving away our position.*

He needn't have worried. Even Zagam was too exhausted to express the slightest thought or feeling.

Caym was momentarily shocked:

My, how far we have fallen. Once, we could have achieved this with but a moment's notice. And now, even augmented, we are reduced to brittle leaves underfoot.

Spurred on by that alarming realization, Caym chose not to linger. Leaving his compatriots to recover their senses, he lightly probed the planet below.

Deserted!

He tried again.

It's almost as if they knew we were . . .

A pulse of aggressive magnitude issued from a confined area on the surface. Though invisible, the shockwave resonated toward the stars with an urgency that tugged at appetites within him he'd hoped were long dead.

Curiosity overcame him.

Ignoring the distraction of an intervening sandstorm, Caym zeroed in on a modest facility crowning a plateau above an enormous plain. Even at this distance, he could see the strata about the complex palpitate, as if the ground itself suffered a seizure.

He commenced his descent.

Another blast of wild and unrestrained theurgy stung his receptors. This time, it seemed that the ground had liquefied, for a rippling wave radiated away from the source of the eruption at startling speed.

Oh, this is the place all right. But I must tread carefully, for until I confirm the actual presence of a gateway, the slightest misstep may cause our undoing.

Featherlight, he allowed his scrutiny to blend with the grains of dirt and grit forming the dust storm. Thus he swirled down onto his target and into the shattered remains of what looked like a sophisticated operations center.

He extended his range and discovered the place was deserted. However, the emanations from below ground confirmed his suspicions.

They've just finished feeding? I'd recognize that timbre anywhere.

Old hunger pangs intruded. To divert himself, Caym studied the rocks beneath his metaphysical feet. Some were porous.

This region must have been saturated in ages past. Perfect.

Like a wraith, he percolated down through the strata, layer by overlapping layer, vein by divaricating vein.

His existence dissolved into a confusing mass of light and shadow. Huge wedges leaned every which way at once. Some were dark; others shimmered with suppressed radiance. Still others displayed a bubble-wrap texture that looked like they might collapse at any moment. While much was easy to traverse, some lodes were so dense and opaque even his astral sight couldn't penetrate them.

Fortunately, the effusion of pleasure swelling in potential beneath him kept Caym on course, and soon he emerged at one end of a vaulted dome filled with sleeping monsters, fat on the pith of creation.

And let's hope they stay that way.

Hovering near the roof, he reduced his presence to a tiny spark of insignificance and took his time examining the darkened surrounds of this new and exciting environment.

Hmm, the cavern looks natural, and judging from its structure was formed by running water over thousands of years.

Corridors now led into and away from the feature, along with a number of more canny additions, included to assist the functioning of mysterious and unknown technologies arranged in tiers along the chamber's outer circumference. A host of twinkling lights indicated these were still active.

It makes sense. This place is more than a mile underground, and each seam helps to form a layered defense against the energies pooling at—

An undulant resonance blistered the atmosphere. Expertly hidden, but to Caym's sensitivities the subterfuge itself indicated a heightened state of awareness.

Someone isn't asleep.

Intent on discovering the source of that distortion, Caym drifted toward the center of the gallery. He spotted a raised platform there. Above it, two U-shaped cuffs hung in midair, each reaching toward the other as if vying to be the first to grasp the twirling helix hovering between them. Reality's prism bent in its proximity, as if the void represented a zone of irresistible mass. Sure enough, Caym sensed fresher air being drawn down through labyrinthine passages in response to the siren song of a vacuum.

A tear in spacetime! And from the look of the darn thing, it's permanently open at this end. That means the terminus must be wandering, uncoupled and—

An icy rind crackled throughout his nexus.

Gods, if they knew what they had here, they would . . . it would . . . Such calamity. I must get safely away and notify Mohammed.

Caym was about to relax his hold on the fey program anchoring his will in position when a sigh in the ether on his left caught his attention. He altered his perceptions, and a silver-gray hemisphere appeared.

It's the same anomaly I noticed upon my arrival. What's more, it's arrayed slightly out of pitch with the normal resonance of this plane. Very clever.

On impulse, Caym formed a gossamer probe and allowed the invading currents of air to waft it gently toward his target.

Someone is *awake and what's more, they're protected within a construct of stunning finesse.*

He glanced throughout the massed ranks sleeping below him. Creatures that represented the equal of what he once was—and beyond—slumbered all around.

Yet of their queen, he saw no sign.

It has to be her. I wonder . . . ?

With utmost caution, Caym threaded his way through the intervening shroud toward the silver hemisphere. At first, the interior of the cocoon remained an inchoate blur. But the more he wove, the more his senses clarified.

Unfortunately, his success proved his undoing:

No sooner had he penetrated the cocoon's final layer than the larger of the two entities within blazed its response. A dozen shafts of blinding light flared, and a steely cord of awareness snapped toward him.

The queen's psychic grip burned with violet and gold overtones. Although formed in an instant, the neural assault issuing from her mind was superlatively focused. It closed about Caym like a bear trap for the briefest instant, and then swatted him away like a bothersome insect.

Amazing. She released me? But . . . why?

Not waiting for answers that might be deadly, he fled.

As his spirit forded a static wash of conflicting emotions and relief, a powerful voice echoed through the ether after him:

I know you now, Lega'trix. Caym of the Unium Tier no more. Though lost, you might yet be saved. Do not forsake what you once were and what your heart yearns to be again . . .

*

Safe within the insulation afforded by their shield, Altás was able to express his feelings without fear of reaction from the massed host reclining in slumber about them. Just as well, for his outrage threatened to ignite the air: *Does this vermin seriously seek to curry favor?*

Of course it does, Va-ákil responded, *for it wishes to stay alive.*

But it is an abomination.

In its current state, yes, it is. However, its tenacity for survival intrigues me and presents us with possibilities I'd be a fool to ignore.

And is the intelligence it proffers accurate? Reliable? In all honesty could you ever trust this . . . this thing*?*

It wants to live, Altás, as I said. And it is well aware that its current situation is unlikely to facilitate that longing. Make no mistake. Its thoughts were laced with desperation and the seeds of a deep-seated desire to manipulate others. Nevertheless, it is naïve in the ways of higher mind function and could not hide the truth of what it overheard. A most fortunate state of affairs. Especially for us, don't you agree?

The penny dropped.

So, you seek to exploit it?

The veneer of Va-ákil's mind softened. *Its desire for self preservation is extreme. I would have that ingenuity working for us . . . for now, at any rate.*

And you would permit its close proximity? Although mollified, Altás remained agitated. *But its mere presence would defile your station. What would the others think? Your purity would—*

— survive the scandal intact. Va-ákil finished her mate's sentence for him, although not as he had intended. She exuded an air of firm resolve. *Extreme times call for extreme measures, my Battlemaster. You have seen what those fleshly insects can do, and how readily they resort to extermination.*

Altás brooded quietly for a moment. Then he raised a query. *So, how will you manage to get it to us here?*

The Houston? We need only cause a distraction. Regardless of the way its thought patterns disgust me, it already possesses sufficient strength to manipulate the vext. But it is unskilled. Unfocused. It must learn discipline with all haste.

Altás radiated alarm. *Surely you're not proposing . . . ?*

Oh, no, no, no, certainly not, and especially when there are those among us who are keen to regain my favor. Rest assured, Houston's education will be furnished by those who will do anything to avoid my wrath.

She bonded to his mind and extended the range of their sight, up into the planet's exosphere.

For example, the floating citadel above us presents opportunities we may utilize. If they act in union, it is within range of our lesser kin, and will allow us a closer look at our would-be new addit–

Something alien fluttered at the extremities of Va-ákil's perceptions:

An intruder?

Elusive as a wraith, it nevertheless possessed an aching familiarity that triggered her immediate response. Twelve concentrations of purple-white light flared into existence about the crown of Va-ákil's head. Her aura blazed, and her mind lashed out instinctively to pluck the sprite from its perch.

She expected resistance, or at the very least, a cry of anguish. Yet not once did her prey writhe in agony or beg for mercy. *Its probe is refined and exquisitely tempered. This creature is obviously skilled in the ways of . . .*

. . . I know *you?*

In an instant, she skimmed the history of the entity who dared intrude; she could sense its regret at the loss of something it had once treasured beyond life itself.

True to its nature it still hungers. And more? Much more . . .

On a whim, she extended an unprecedented invitation and released it.

It fled, and she followed it toward a well-constructed nucleus of other minds. Though insensible, all were joined in harmonic sympathy.

Well, well, well.

As the essence of the watcher spirited both itself and its companions away, she called out: *I know you now, Lega'trix. Caym of the Unium Tier no more. Though lost, you might yet be saved. Do not forsake what you once were and what your heart yearns to be again . . .*

She watched him go, and then turned to face her Prime Catalyct.

Gather your Lega'trexii and Praetors. Have them select those who are expendable and bring them to me. It appears that fate is keen to force events.

Chapter Twenty-Six

Step Up the Pace

As the command teams from both ships filed from the briefing room, Sandi Chang lingered behind. Even at a distance Mohammed could see she was troubled, for she studied her info-pad closely and chewed her bottom lip.

"Sandi," he called, "stay a moment, would you?"

She turned and strolled back through the crowd toward his seat, situated next to the main podium.

Mohammed waited for the last person to leave before sealing the door so they wouldn't be disturbed.

"I'd like to apologize for the speed with which events are occurring," he began, "but we're on the clock now, so that can't be helped. And while I know everyone will obey my commands without hesitation, I don't expect them to do so blindly . . . especially not a fellow captain." He sat back. "So go on. Spit it out."

She grinned. "Am I that obvious?"

"I'm good with faces." He shrugged. "And too long in the tooth to ignore the opinion of others . . . even if it's obvious they disagree. So tell me, what's bothering you?"

She waved her tablet in the air. "Are you sure this is the way you want things to pan out? Because I can't help feeling we shouldn't divide our forces against an overwhelming foe."

"I can appreciate why you might think that way, but the Exordium system presents us with a golden opportunity we'd be stupid to ignore. Let me explain a few things I didn't have time to touch on in the briefing."

Mohammed activated his terminal and brought up a computer recreation of their target on the main viewer.

"Unlike our previous objectives, Exordium has—or should I say, *had*—two sisters, Vilén and Liberty, which occupied orbits farther from their sun. As you can see, both were shattered millennia ago when the three rogue singularities that plague the vicinity were first attracted there. However, because Vilén and Liberty were situated just beyond each black hole's active zone, galactic shearing was only sufficient to rupture their integrity, not consume them."

He altered the picture to zoom in on the debris field that was once Liberty, then divided the screen to show the same view of Vilén.

"Notice how each of the masses revolves around the proximity of its former core? That's because mutual gravity between the shattered pieces is sufficient to prevent further dispersion. In effect, they're now planetesimals. If not for the presence of the black holes, they'd reform."

"How do you know this, and why does that support your plan?"

"Well, for a start, although the data we recovered from the Latinus Prime archives is fragmented, what we have is quite extensive—a wealth of information we'd never realized would prove useful. For example, they have orbital records of all the star systems within the Verianda Nebula dating back over a thousand years. Watch this . . ."

Mohammed manipulated the controls, and the display flickered back to an overview. Each simulation accelerated forward in its orbit, and froze.

"Bearing in mind that we need more than a day and a half to get into position, *this* is where Vilén and Liberty will be at twenty-three hundred hours, Galactic Rhomane Standard Time, the day after tomorrow."

Mohammed paused to let his fellow captain take in the details, and then depressed a final button. A bright red line traced forward from the edge of the nebula until it reached the vicinity of Vilén.

"Notice how the planetesimals mask your approach? Remember, you won't be able to cloak, as you'll be trailing a number of navigational buoys to make *Helexia*'s spectral signature appear much larger than it actually is. What's more, several of the buoys will have one or two of our Phoenix tactical strike missiles strapped to them with warheads exposed. What a shame, because it'll make it look like you're trailing ionized gas." Mohammed smirked. "So far as the Horde are aware, we took a thorough beating to destroy Latinus Prime. It would be reasonable to assume they'd expect the *Shadow of Autumn* to be damaged. Who's to say we wouldn't go after them on Exordium before we'd had time to complete proper repairs?"

Sandi's eyes sparkled in comprehension, and Mohammed's expression stretched into a smile as he continued:

"We know the Horde are far from the mindless animals we once thought, and this new strain have proven extremely intelligent, perceptive, and astute. Not only are they skilled tacticians, but they can manipulate any system that incorporates a mental network. If our friends are watching—and I'm betting they will be—they'll be expecting us to attack soon. And if we were forced to do that nursing battle damage, they'd anticipate a sneak attack, or as sneaky as you can be with a whacking great leak in the side of your ship."

"So *that's* why we're skipping about and coming in from the opposite direction." She exhaled deeply. "We're not merely dividing their attention and resources. You're hoping our presence will distract them sufficiently to allow the *Shadow of Autumn* to park right on top of them."

"Ta-*dah*!" Mohammed threw his arms wide. Sobering, he added, "Of course, much will depend on the accuracy of other intelligence we gleaned before Latinus Prime was destroyed. A portion of that data alluded to the protective grids of all three planets, including details of automated upgrades, refits, and the encoded protocols for both overt and covert defensive clouds.

"We'll be approaching under the cover of our null-shields at just under light speed. As soon as we're in range, we'll send the lullaby signal. If we see the system start to deactivate, we'll punch it to full FTL and decloak in close orbit. Before they know it, the atmosphere will be seeded and the bombardment underway. Once the grid is down, *that's* when you can make your final approach and assist in picking off any orbital assets we miss. Then, depending on how it goes, I'll make the decision as to whether we try to retrieve likely subjects or simply cut our losses and eradicate the entire system."

Although I sincerely hope it's the former.

Mohammed watched as the full implications of his plan registered on his counterpart's face.

"I like it," Sandi allowed. "How soon before we can get underway?"

"Conservative estimate? A couple of hours yet." Mohammed leaned across to deactivate the monitor. "I'd prefer to have everything fully locked, loaded and squared away before we part company. That way, all we need do is concentrate on getting to the final staging areas by the specified time, because once everything kicks off, I don't think we'll have time to catch our breath."

*

One of two indistinct shapes on the floor whimpered.

They're still alive?

"Harper? Stark?" Wilson hissed as loudly as he dared. "Are you all right?"

Stupid question . . . idiot!

Wilson inhaled deeply, trying to control the severity of his own nausea and adjusted his position to ease the pain radiating through his shoulder joints.

Of course they're not all right. The radiation should have killed us long ago. I dread to think why they're keeping us alive.

He grimaced as his circulation restored a heightened sense of feeling along his arms.

Still, while we are, there's always hope.

Only the previous day, or possibly two—it was hard to tell when hours stretched into an eternity of anguish—someone had walked along the corridor outside. The things keeping him captive had obviously anticipated he might try to call out for aid and feasted on him to the point of oblivion.

Sneaky bastards.

The memory of the indignity and helplessness of his situation filled him with impotent rage. His heart palpitated wildly. Before he realized what was happening, Wilson retched, tasted bile, and vomited so violently he soiled himself and almost passed out.

He didn't care. He was past caring, praying fervently for his misery to end.

Something clucked its disapproval.

Wilson caught his breath.

A skein of light flickered brightly in one corner of the compartment, to be quickly swallowed by the gloom and boiling shadows distending lazily toward him.

They're here.

Despite the perspiration drenching his body from head to foot, Wilson's blood ran cold. He knew it was useless to resist what was coming and tried to conserve what little strength he had.

"Ffear not, young nephew," Houston crooned. "It iss only I and ssome friendsss."

The miasma dissipated into three distinct clouds, two of which hovered above the prone figures on the floor. Sparks flared, and the men groaned.

"What are you doing?" Wilson demanded. "Leave them alone."

Houston ignored the plea.

With scant regard for their welfare, Harper and Stark were dragged from the cubicle by invisible hands. In spite of his own discomfort, Wilson winced as their heads bumped and bounced across the raised sill of the hatchway.

"Where are you taking them?"

"You'll ssee ssoon enough," Houston warbled. "It'll be your turn very ssoon now."

"Why, what's going on? What's happening?"

The phantasm approached until it undulated in the air right before him.

"Let's jusst ssay, thiss place isn't conducive to your health. It's only because of my loving concernss that you've been kept alive thiss long. And now we're on a tight sschedule, I thought it besst to move you before you become too ill for . . . what we have in mind."

Tight schedule? He's taking me outside?

It was as if Houston could read his mind.

"Oh, and even though there'ss nobody out there to hear your pathetic plea, I ssimply can't take the rissk you might ruin thingsss . . ."

Wilson felt the hairs across his body stand on end. His skin prickled, and then the terrible, piercing ache of the drain began all over again.

He passed out to the serenade of a chilling assurance.

"Don't worry, little pet, you won't have to endure thiss much longer. Oncce we have you ssafely sstashed away, it'll be . . ."

*

The combined crowd of Damnonii warriors, cavalry soldiers, and the odd deckhand attracted by the buzz, gathered round for the demonstration. The excitement was understandable, for while the intricacies of the whip were old hat to many in the throng—especially the troopers—most among the highland band were seeing its finesse for the first time.

Shaní stepped into the makeshift arena hastily arranged within the confines of cargo bay four, and strolled to the exact center. Around her, wooden blocks formed a ring atop of a series of drums, saddles, and crates of varying heights.

"Remember, because of the maneuvers you will shortly undertake, you won't have to be as accurate as I am," Shaní advised. "So don't worry about finesse. However, try to cram in all the practice you can, because using one of these from horseback isn't as easy as it looks."

She unraveled the device in her hands and held the hilt in front of her.

Compared to her mastig, this particular item felt heavy and cumbersome, but that was to be expected, for her own whip, made from toran heartwood and an elasticized coridian-selanite compound, was designed to stun ropillos (small batlike creatures, that had proved the bane of rural farmers for years); an elegant tool, it was swift to deploy and easy to wield.

But this *is for creatures of a much more resilient nature.*

"For those who might not have experienced one of these up close, the entire weapon is constructed from a custom blend of sprung steel and an amalgam of selanite and kovex. As you can see, the pommel is quite short and weighted to counter the length of its business end. It has been fashioned with deep grooves along the inner surface, and coated with an adevix solution to help it stick to your skin, even in humid conditions. Adevix is what we call a charge-dampening coagulate, so it prevents excess energy from traveling back along the lash to stun you. Added safety features include the twin cup hilts at either end of the handle. They aren't just for show: they contain insulation compounds to prevent static flashover. Basically, once you grip this tightly, it isn't going anywhere."

Shaní fed the whip through her hands until she came to the lash.

"Now, *this* is a thing of beauty. The blend of polymers creates a strong, resilient, and flexible deterrent. The iron content is more than five times that required to disrupt the integrity of a Kresh Master, and has been combined with the hyperflex alloy incorporated into the dart at the tip—or as we call it, the stinger. Everything from the handle forward can be used to kill Kresh. That's twenty-eight feet of fun . . . let's see how well it all comes together, shall we?"

In one fluid movement, Shaní grasped the new weapon firmly in her right hand.

Hmm, it's much livelier than it looks.

The barb began to rise and fall, obedient to each flick of her wrist.

She stepped forward, raised her arm, and whirled the handle around her head. A deep thrum announced the moment the whip snapped toward its first targets.

Crack! Crack!

Two wooden bricks disappeared from their perches.

Crack! Crack! Crack! Crack!

Four more went tumbling in quick succession.

As if by invitation, her audience moved nearer, whooping and whistling in delight. On the spur of the moment, one of the highlanders tossed a block back into play.

Thwack!

The whip snatched the block from midair in the blink of an eye and sent it spinning across the deck. A chorus of cheering and boisterous foot stamping followed.

In short order, Shaní dispensed with her remaining targets and gathered the elongated thong into her arms.

She then motioned for quiet, and pointed toward a number of human-sized mockups.

"Okay, now listen in. Those are your practice targets. I procured them for you so you can drill on something much smaller than the bulk of a Kresh ogre. If you can zero in on these, you won't have much problem hitting the real thing from horseback. Those of you familiar with whips, or as I call them, mastigs, team up with someone who's never used one before and help them."

She then pointed to two long crates on the opposite side of the arena.

"Your playthings are over there. There are only twenty to go round so far, but Calen tells me the next batch should be ready by late afternoon. So don't worry. There'll be more than enough for those of you who are proficient."

No sooner had she finished speaking than a mob materialized as the men crowded round, eager to be among the first to test their new toy.

Shaní stepped back and let them get on with it. She was joined by Jake and Angus.

"Thanks for that," Jake said. "So how do you think my scheme turned out?"

"Pretty good," she replied. "Although bulkier than my mastig, and shorter in the handle, it's surprisingly robust and effective. You might have noticed I had Calen remove the strap you'd originally suggested? Even with the popper release system, the strap's too risky. Can't have someone dragged from the saddle because of getting snagged or caught by . . ."

She paused midsentence, cocking her ear as a stream of colorful language punctuated the din.

Someone mistimed their stroke. And what was that . . . ?

"There's a word or two I've never heard before." Shaní turned to Angus. "What is a windae-licking paukit?"

The Damnonii clan leader became very sheepish, keen to look anywhere except in Shaní's direction.

I see.

"Until another time then, Angus. But rest assured, I will find out."

The noise became even louder.

As did the cursing.

"Gentlemen," she advised the officers, "You'd best take charge of your men before someone gets hurt. Give them an hour or so. Then call me over, and I'll demonstrate how it's done from horseback to anyone still standing. I know it's pushing things, but we really don't have a choice. Remember, by this time tomorrow, it'll be nearly over."

Chapter Twenty-Seven

An Untimely Diversion

"Captain to the bridge . . ."

The automated message from Seraphim snapped Mohammed from his daydream. In it, Shaní was taking him to meet her aged parents for the very first time, and he had been wondering what to say to put their minds at rest and assure them he'd take care of her for the rest of her life.

I must have dozed off. He shivered. *Saved from a fate worse than death . . . the dreaded in-laws.*

"I say again, Captain Amine to the bridge."

Mohammed jumped to his feet and made for the door.

It swished open, and he noticed everyone else at their posts, including Shaní and Calen. Her eyes narrowed the moment she saw him, and he realized his face might be giving away certain feelings of relief.

Composing himself, Mohammed assumed his position at the command console.

"Report."

"We're coming up on the outer marker," Seraphim replied.

"Status?"

"Main battle systems and emergency redundancies have been activated. Emergency bulkheads are primed and sealed. FTL drive is spinning up. Defensive and offensive protocols are charged. All cyber-links have been encrypted behind a hydra-class firewall and are now live. The Kresh will be unable to infect our systems as they did last time."

"That's good to hear. And our away teams?"

"Marcus reports the *Abeille*, *Ballarat*, *Eurus*, and *Orison* are in the chutes, cross-locked and ready to deploy. Sam's special operations team is in the ancillary CIC compartment, prepped and ready to go."

"Excellent. What about the *Helexia*?"

The AI avatar paused and responded: "Covert scans show her on course and on schedule. She is currently approaching the blind side of the Vilén planetesimal field. ETA until exposure, just under four minutes."

Mohammed ran through the proposed timetable in his head.

Perfect. "Thank you, Seraphim, prepare to transmit malware program. On my signal, please, in three, two, one . . . *Now*."

"Transmitting. Stand by."

Mohammed turned to Calen.

"You're confident this virus will work?"

Calen nodded. "From the simulations we ran, most certainly. We decided on a gentler approach to avoid an aggressive response. When you think about it, a simple update of the 'friend or foe' algorithms is by far the easiest solution. If their automated defenses don't view us as a threat, we shouldn't have anything to worry about."

"That premise appears sound," Seraphim announced. "Long range monitoring stations are already acknowledging our presence and, and—wait . . ." The avatar's eyes blazed brightly as she completed thousands of computations within a few seconds. "Yes, I can verify our status has been authenticated and is being shared throughout the network. The entire grid should update within sixty seconds."

Bloody hell! It's working.

Mohammed tried to think of anything they might have missed. "Does that include the covert platforms and the seek and destroy interceptors?"

"We can't be entirely certain, but from what the haze cloud is indicating, that's an affirmative. We will shortly be in the clear."

"Time and distance to target?"

Seraphim glanced into the top portion of the holo-screen where a long string of glowing numbers rapidly scrolled by. She gestured and they froze and enlarged, showing; *34:530:972-003.*

"Thirty-four and a half million megs. If we go to FTL now, that gives us a flight time of just over three minutes."

"Initiate Slingshot Drive and issue final announcements on my command." *Here we go.* "Okay, punch it."

Mohammed felt his extremities stretch the moment the imperfectly blended hybrid system kicked in. It was accompanied by a surge and a change in pitch to the vibrations thrumming through the deck.

Seraphim raised her voice and opened a ship-wide channel: "All departments stand by. Our ETA to target is now three minutes and five seconds. Prelaunch cycles are engaged and locked on auto-hold. Battle stations, battle stations."

"By the way," Mohammed waved to catch Seraphim's attention. "The moment we arrive, take out any remaining orbital assets. Virus or not, I want the sky clear for our—"

"Captain, you won't believe this but I'm picking up an SOS."

Seraphim's sudden announcement shocked Mohammed quiet and seemed to catch everyone else by surprise. Ignoring the worried chatter in the background, he gasped, "Is it the *Helexia*? Is she in trouble?"

"No, the broadcast appears to originate from the Kalina Star Base. She's in high geostationary orbit above Exordium's northern magnetic pole."

"I thought that place was dead?"

"To all intents and purpose it is." The holo-cloud trembled, and Seraphim brought up a computer simulation of an impressive construct. A central globe, measuring more than a quarter of a mile in diameter appeared, connected to a five-tiered external halo by eight support struts. The outer circumference of the ring was studded with airlocks and locking collars of all shapes and sizes. "Kalina was one of two mid-altitude stations serving Exordium. At their height, each facility managed hundreds of shipments every day. Records indicate Tsa'reth, her sister station situated in the southern hemisphere, had been totally destroyed during the initial Kresh outbreak."

"And Kalina?"

The image wavered, and the pristine edifice was replaced by one of utter devastation.

The bottom half of the sphere and the entire western sector of the encompassing loop were gone. In its place, a large cloud of debris circled an unseen center of gravity. Here and there, the mass was punctuated by hanging strips of hull plating and jagged pieces of metal. Only three walkways remained.

"Her reactor blew apart," Seraphim explained. "As you can see, the disaster took out the entire engineering, environmental control, and recycling sections, along with most of the support struts. From what it says here, explosive decompression ripped its way through what remained, leaving very few compartments intact."

"So the beacon is automated?"

"On the contrary. Although there's interference, I'm getting a live-time feed; and what's more, there's another transmission coming in. Audio only."

"Well, let's hear it."

Seraphim did as requested, and a loud hiss issued from the speakers. It intensified, crackled, and then clarified into words:

"Hhhhelp-help me-me! For-or God's sake help me-e. Is anyone there-ere?"

Wilson Smith?

"Why is it jumping?"

"I cannot say for certain," Seraphim replied, "but the loop appears to be the result of a time lag."

"Gravitational dilation from the black holes, perhaps?"

"While that is possible, I'd have thought it unlikely since we've not yet disabled the temporal compensators."

"Hhhhelp-help me-me," the plea repeated. "For-or the love-ve of God, you've gotta get me-e outta here-e."

Mohammed couldn't contain himself. "Wilson, is that you?"

He held his breath . . . and waited.

"Mmmohammed?" The young man's voice was clearly relieved. "Thhank the stars-rs. Please, you gotta do—do something, don't let-et them—" His petition cut off abruptly.

"Syntax and modulation patterns recognized," Seraphim announced. "There is a ninety-eight percent probability that was Lieutenant Wilson Smith."

Maybe so. But what the hell is he doing all the way out here? "Get that signal back. And see what you can do to clean it up."

"I can't," Seraphim replied, a look of puzzlement etched across her features. "It's been severed at source."

At source?

"Oh really? Scan that station. Use whatever frequencies you must without triggering an aggressive response."

"One moment . . ." Seraphim's photonic nimbus flared as she reached across millions of miles in an effort to solve the enigma. "I have it. Life sign, no . . . make that life *signs* detected." She shook her head. "Now I have only a single reading. Residual radiation is making a precise lock extremely difficult. However, I am receiving thermal, spectral, and harmonic indicators of a human-Ardenese entity within that structure. I suspect the energy fluctuations may be interfering with my sensors."

That's convenient. Alarm bells rang in the back of Mohammed's mind. *There's no way this is a coincidence.*

He reached out toward his workstation and depressed a button: "Captain Pell? I need to speak with you now, face to face, on the double."

The sound of heavy boots approaching resonated along the deck. A space-age knight, complete with armor plating and tactical battle harness stomped in and stopped before Mohammed. The visor snapped up, and Mohammed found himself staring into the cold eyes of a killer prepared for combat. Mohammed knew that look. It signified a caged beast stood before him.

Sam Pell smiled, and the beast was gone.

"My apologies for dragging you through here," Mohammed said, "but your people are the only ones trained to manage untimely diversions, and I have a feeling we'll be needing your particular skill set in the very near future."

"What have you got?"

Mohammed gestured, and Seraphim replayed the entire recording and visual overlay of the Kalina Star Base.

"Seraphim's managed to authenticate the call as a near-perfect match. Despite what you might think, *that's* the voice of our missing cavalry officer, Wilson Smith. And what's more, it's coming from the orbiting station you see in the holo-cloud."

Sam's eyes narrowed and his chin dropped. Mohammed could almost see the beast hurling itself against the bars of its cage within his colleague's head.

"That may be so," Sam replied quietly, "but you *do* know this is a trap, right?"

"The thought had crossed my mind."

Sam hefted his modified Heckler Koch G420A with specialized quad-column magazine.

"Fortunately, springing traps is our specialty." He tapped his weapon, turned to face Seraphim, and continued: "Download a full spec sheet of that place to my wristpad, and send a copy to our Technical Specialist, Severin. Once that's done, work with him to establish a traffic light system . . . do you understand that term?"

"I do," Seraphim replied. "I made it a point to study your standard operating parameters after I had been activated."

"Good. Anywhere that is missing, destroyed, blown away, toxic or otherwise contains insurmountable obstacles is to be designated as a red zone. Select an amber area as our infiltration point and means of approach. Look for anything where hull integrity is intact or sufficient for partial pressurization."

"No greens?" Mohammed chided. "I thought they were supposed to be good for you?"

"Not on the diet I have in mind." Sam patted his weapon once more. "And when you think about it, they shouldn't really exist. It's too obvious. I'll be avoiding like the plague anywhere that's ripe for human habitation . . . *on the way in*, anyway."

Hmm. Mohammed chuckled. *Good thinking.*

"I take it that means we might persuade you to look at such a route on the way out?"

"We may have no choice, Mohammed. If that *is* Wilson, and he is managing to hang on by his fingernails as the scan suggests, then the teleport process might finish him. No, we'll evac him the old-fashioned way and get him to an airlock. That reminds me: Reserve a route from the location of his bio-sign back to the nearest serviceable docking port, but ensure our insertion point is well away from it. I don't want things fucked up by any subsequent firefight along the way."

"Will do."

"And in preparation for such an event, what ships do we have going spare that might be able to assist us?"

"Several." Mohammed shrugged an apology. "But we're lacking pilots to fly them. That's why we were able to clear so much hangar space and share them out with the other cruisers."

"What about my standalone EMT shuttle?" Seraphim interjected. "She's fully equipped and operational, and programmed to function with an RTB avatar and medi-crew. It might present the perfect solution."

Sam's eyes widened. "Add a squadron of attack drones to protect us and when this is all over, I'll dance along the hangar deck in a tutu and army boots."

Seraphim's face clouded for a moment and her aura flickered, a sure sign she was interrogating her archives for cross references to Sam's terminology.

A broad grin split her face. "Done. But only if I can record it for the annals of history."

"Looks like we have a deal."

Sam and the avatar high-fived, and the soldier stomped from the control room. Even before he reached his team he was shouting orders.

Mohammed stared at the AI interface in amazement.

Bloody hell. I never realized she'd been programmed with a sense of humor.

Seraphim caught his expression.

"In an effort to better interact with those I serve, I made it a priority to study your customs. It seems Earth warriors appreciate comedy, even in times of stress, so I –" Her expression became abruptly serious. "Captain, I'm detecting energy spikes groundside. They originate in the vicinity of Barsoonet. Several emissions appear to be directed toward Kalina Star Base."

Shit! They're going to attack the station.

"Time to target?"

"We will arrive in just over one minute. The *Helexia* will sail free of Vilén's Oort cloud in fifty-five seconds."

A whirlwind of options spun in Mohammed's mind. His gut instinct indicated the only viable choice.

"Signal the *Helexia*. Tell her to increase to half light-speed. As soon as she appears, the Horde's scanners will be on her like a rash. Hopefully the presence of a more aggressive target will divide their attention . . . at least until they realize she's a diversion. By then, it'll be too late."

"Roger that."

Mohammed had another idea. "Where did you say Kalina was situated?"

"In geostationary orbit above Exordium's north pole."

"What's the distance between the station and our target?"

"As the crow flies, two thousand six hundred and sixty-three miles."

"And what Horde sign are you getting?"

Once again, the band surrounding Seraphim's eyes gleamed bright.

"Negligible. While there are sporadic pockets at various settlements throughout Origen, it is my tactical opinion that they are gathered in greater numbers within protective bunkers, behind shielded areas, or perhaps subterranean cave systems."

Okay. While the setrium-4 isotope is only effective to a depth of two miles, the re-genesis matrix can interpenetrate the crust until it reaches the planetary core. So . . .

"Seraphim? Has the base come under fire yet?"

"No, although the magnitude of the energy fluctuations are increasing exponentially."

So, what if Kalina isn't a target? What if they're gonna use that power to . . .?

Mohammed was blessed with a moment's inspiration.

The re-genesis matrix. They seek to avoid it.

He came to an instant decision:

"Seraphim, coincide our arrival as near as you can to the moment the Horde begin scanning the *Helexia*, and take us out of FTL right on top of Kalina. Do not engage stabilizing thrusters. Instead, employ a sublight teleport program to get Sam and his team across to the infiltration point. As you do that, initiate an automated friction-launch of the EMS shuttle and its drones. Allow our momentum to bruise the atmosphere and then commence a combined salvo of Octopod singularity compressors and Hornet ground-busters to soften them up. Blitzkrieg protocol, two second intervals, ten salvos. Send out the setrium-4 and re-genesis pods midway through the cycle.

"Once that's done, take us back up to launch altitude and destroy all orbital assets in our vicinity. When everything is clear, start the attack and pound anything that moves until our troops are on the ground. Understood?"

"Loud and clear."

Mohammed glanced at the mission clock and opened a ship-wide channel.

"All departments, this is the CIC. Prepare for hard deceleration in . . . Five, four, three, two, one . . ."

*

Aboard the *Abeille*, Marcus Brutus brooded in silence. He could see his men were nervous, but he was glad of that, for only a fool would deny his fear under such circumstances. Having lived and fought with them for decades, he knew this was the anxiety experienced by combatants in those final moments before conflict when the blood, sweat, and tears of training came together in the adrenaline-fuelled anticipation of battle.

And truth be told I can't blame them for being edgy, especially after what happened to the Minas. *That lack of control over your own destiny is enough to drive any warrior to distraction.*

Marcus studied the veterans ranked before him.

Well, I've done what I can.

Along with their new weapons, each legionnaire was now suited in thermoflex coveralls and kovex helmets, clothing specially designed for pliability, while affording a high degree of protection against temperature extremes or exposure to a vacuum.

They want . . . No, they need *to be getting on with things instead of just sitting here. All this waiting around isn't good.*

He grinned. *I know . . .*

Leaning across from his seat, Marcus activated the ship-to-ship comms unit.

"Soldiers of the Ninth Legion. Brothers. This is your commander speaking. You know who I am and what we've faced together. Gods, we've fought side by side for more years than I care to remember. Spilt an ocean of blood, and shed a fair bit of our own in the process. Although this foe is new to us, we know them well. In all truth, they cannot say the same, for they have not yet faced us. The Ninth held their kin at the Line in Rhomane, and we'll hold them again, here, today. And why . . . ?"

He paused to let the weight of his words sink in, then raised his voice.

"Because today we remember Flavius, our friend. Today we remember our glorious dead, those comrades unjustly slain by cowards from afar. Yes, today we return the compliment . . ." Marcus was forced to take a breath as expressions of agreement barked up and down the hold, ". . . and in the best traditions of the legion, when we do, *we* won't hide behind walls or cower in caves while others do our dirty work for us—"

The shouting became strident, and Marcus could hear similar sentiments being expressed by his fellow warriors on the other ships.

"Today, we fight," he roared, "hand to hand, face to face." He pumped his fist into the air. "For Flavius . . ."

"For Flavius," came the resounding reply.

"For our brothers . . ."

"Our brothers."

"For the Ninth."

"The Ninth."

Each response grew louder and louder until Marcus thought his eardrums might burst.

As the cheering died away, a cool, calm voice cut through the revelry.

"All departments, this is the CIC. Prepare for hard deceleration in . . . Five, four, three, two, one…"

Perfect timing.

Chapter Twenty-Eight

Taking the Bait

Ice needles pierced his flesh and the world blanched gray.

For a heartbeat, Captain Sam Pell became dislocated from reality, as if his soul had departed his body and drifted in a sea of infinite solitude. Encompassed within an instant, eternity stretched before him, only to dump him unceremoniously back into the here-and-now before he'd had a chance to enjoy it. Insects invaded the confines of his suit and crawled across his skin.

A world of blackness solidified around him.

Momentary weightlessness registered before the micro-g compensator adjusted to its new environment. As Sam descended to the floor, a perceptible whine issued from his optical display unit. The interior passageway, with its profusion of floating slow-motion wreckage, clarified into pristine detail.

Around him, his assault squad moved to secure their position. No words needed. Working in pairs, they fanned out until every avenue of approach, every potential threat or hazard had been considered and judged negligible. Only then did a chorus of affirmations ring in his earpiece.

Less than ten seconds from arrival. Not bad.

"Okay, guys," he breathed, "set motion and energy trackers to rotating hybrid cross-frequencies. Three-second primary cycle, with an extended pulse every six seconds. Hold this location until I confirm our position and route."

Sam opened a secure channel to the *Shadow of Autumn*:

"Sevvy, are you copying our telematics and audio?"

"All helmet-cams and microphones coming through loud and clear, Captain Pell."

"Just Sam, please. Update us with a tactical overview."

"Transferring data . . . *Now*."

A 3-D image appeared on Sam's wrist monitor that reminded him of a portion of a broken wheel having only three spokes. Each spoke led across to the central hub. The outer rim showed subdivisions comprised of amber, green, and then a final amber segment.

Glancing ahead, Sam could see a sealed pressure barrier in the distance. Its position corresponded to the change of color on his readout.

Hmm. So there's air behind that hatchway? Somebody's gone to a lot of trouble to bait the front door.

A blinking red dot indicated that his team had been deposited in the first amber area on the eastern side of the station. As agreed, they were only yards from an arterial corridor connecting the outer disc to Kalina's central sphere. Every now and then, the sliding door leading inside swished open and shut as a piece of wreckage floated by.

Interesting. Not only do we have power, but the safety protocols appear to be malfunctioning. There's no way that entrance should be operating. Unless somebody's anticipated our tactics?

Sam transferred the details to everyone's HUDs.

"Okay, Sevvy, we've got that," he announced. "Verify route and objective."

"Your target is located within the main infirmary, here . . ." A blue dot appeared, very close to the heart of the facility. "To get there, proceed along the connecting passage in front of you until you reach the primary module. Once there, turn right and look for an emergency service stairwell along the inner wall to your left after about twenty-five yards. Descend one flight, and make your way down the eastern arterial corridor toward the central elevator shaft. The medi-bay will be the large unit on your left."

"I take it this area has life support like our welcoming mat?"

"You assume correctly. Seraphim's scans indicate no sign of the Horde, but the area is awash with radiation, which they may be using to feed and mask their presence."

"Talking of radiation, how is our missing man?"

"The signal has not moved since Seraphim first detected it. If Wilson Smith is there, I doubt he'll live much longer."

As if he stood a chance anyway. "Okay, we're about to move out. I'll leave this channel open so you can listen, but do not allow the CIC to engage us in conversation unless they speak through you first, or in the event of an emergency. Understood?"

"Understood. You have been transferred to main bridge speakers."

Sam considered the specifics of the route ahead and beckoned the lieutenant to his side.

"Andy, Bravo can take the lead. Leave your chameleon shields active. I don't want us registering until we absolutely must." He peered toward their first hurdle. "If that's an airlock-style double portal as the plans suggest, use something from the debris field to activate it so we can check to make sure both sets are synchronized before we move off."

"Roger that."

Andy tapped Tosh Wanabe on the shoulder. Together, they walked across and took up positions opposite the entrance, weapons raised. Andy nodded, and Stu Duggan and Lady P shuffled forward. They waited a moment before Andy scooped the nearest piece of wreckage out of the air and tossed it toward the sensor. The hatch opened. After checking the interior, the entire group peeled inside, whereupon the door closed silently behind them.

It was Sam's turn to steer his men into place.

On his signal, Bob Neville and Eddie Roberts crept forward until they were stationed at either side of the entrance. Once they were settled, Sam directed Joe Stark to follow him to a position on the opposite side of the gallery.

As they waited, Sam surveyed their surrounds for any sign of danger. Details began to stand out. A shredded floor grate marked the point where shrapnel must have pierced the deck's armor plating. He assessed the shape and angle of the grooves and followed the missiles' likely trajectory. Sure enough, several slivers of metal remained, sticking out of the wall a bit further along. Two holes confirmed where some of those splinters had punctured the membrane and continued their journey out into the void of space.

Something else caught his eye. A trail of dark splotches led away from the damage toward the adjoining corridor.

Some poor soul must have got injured in the blast and tried to escape. I wonder if they made it?

He didn't have time to dwell on the images that scenario conjured. The doors opened again, and Lady P called them forward.

"Boss, the channel ahead is clear. We have evidence of explosive decompression and three bodies inside—looks like they might have been trapped during the original calamity. But apart from that, it's safe: no Horde or sign of booby traps. LT is working on the seal down at the far end."

"Thank you," Sam replied. "Let's get this show on the road."

They filed forward and entered the reinforced strut.

As Lady P had indicated, several large tears in the fabric walls indicated where projectiles had torn their way through the passage. These examples, much larger than those Sam had originally seen, had obviously caught the people inside unprepared.

He couldn't resist the urge to examine an actual Ardenese in the flesh, even one freeze-dried and bloated by the bacteria that had once saturated his guts.

The first subject was a young man, a scientist from his clothing, close to seven feet in height. Sam noted how the purebloods stood taller than their hybrid counterparts, and had longer limbs with lighter musculature. He also remembered their eyes were supposed to be topaz, but this fellow's were white and frozen solid like the rest of his corpse. From what Sam could see, there wasn't a single mark on him.

One of the young scientist hands was clenched in a death grip around the sleeve of a fellow worker. This other person looked older, a woman with flowing hair that fanned out in a honey-blonde nimbus around her head. Her white-and-gold coat showed rosy-black stains around the abdomen, and several large icicles of a similar color orbited in close proximity.

Sam put two and two together:

She must have been the one injured in the outer ring. It looks like this poor sod was trying to help her; they probably got caught here as the air and pressure bled out.

He stared up and down their tomb.

Damned lonely place for a hero to die.

The final casualty was a much older man, a member of the Senatum from the cut of his robes. Impaled through the neck, he was pinned against the far bulkhead by a long shard of metal which obviously had killed him.

Poor bugger.

"Boss?"

Sam was tugged back to the present by a call from his second-in-command: "What have you got, Andy?"

"My instruments confirm we have atmosphere on the other side of this door. Pressure also appears close to normal. Still no gravity."

"Got that. Stand by, everyone." Sam stared up at the ceiling. "Sevvy, did you copy, and can you add anything we need to know?"

"Yes, I did," the tech-head replied, "and I should emphasize that you are about to enter the only area on Kalina forming a green zone. If the Horde have prepared an ambush, this will be the most dangerous part of the station. However, I am unable to verify as nearby high-intensity emissions are preventing my sensors from penetrating the main hull. In my opinion, this is too much of a coincidence to ignore."

"Agreed. Can I have an update on our support?"

"As arranged, they launched the moment you beamed across, with orders to stand clear until you've made an assessment. The EMT shuttle has no stealth capabilities, so she has been tasked to the leeward side of an orbital command platform just over a mile from your position. She is powered down, so her signature should remain blended with the satellite.

A dozen sentinels are deployed in tactical formation about the area. Eight of them are cloaked."

Sam assessed his options.

"Andy, ask Seraphim to instruct four of the covert models to break formation and come across to the Kalina. Two will complete an exterior scan of the base itself. When everything kicks off groundside, they can monitor for additional damage or signs of danger. The other pair will shadow our movements from outside. If they spot anything untoward, notify me immediately."

"Yes, Capt– Sam. Seraphim's monitoring and said it will be done."

Sam gathered everyone together.

"We're obviously going into a hot zone. However, secrecy remains our priority. If you encounter the enemy, rely on your chameleon shields to avoid them if possible. Only engage when you have no other option. One of the reasons I've asked for the drones is that if everything goes pear shaped, they'll provide cover from outside the station and create one hell of a diversion while we get our casualty out. Of course, if he's already dead, simply activate your signal enhancers and Seraphim will teleport us off. Understood?"

Everyone answered in the affirmative.

"So, how do you propose we get through *this* without raising suspicion?" Andy asked, cocking his thumb toward the exit: "Those sensors are active."

Sam was struck by a moment's inspiration. *How thoughtful.*

"Since they've gone to all the bother of switching things on for us, we'd better show our gratitude . . . but not in the way they'd probably expect. Tosh? Nip back to the outer ring and bring us a few of the larger pieces of rubbish, would you? Three or four chunks will do. Pick anything that'll make a noise as it bounces off other stuff." Sam glanced back along the umbilical. "We'll also use what's on hand in here. If the Horde has infiltrated the station, they'll already know that bits of dross can float about everywhere, some of which will activate the odd door here and there. I'm hoping that's about as much physics as they can remember, otherwise it'll make what I have in mind that much harder to pull off."

"Which is?" Andy probed.

Sam held up a finger and strolled back toward the young hero and the woman he had tried to help. Using one hand, Sam gently maneuvered them in the direction of his waiting squad. As he approached, he explained: "Let's just say these two are going to serve Arden one last time. It'll be nice to think they were involved in a spot of payback."

Tosh returned, carrying several insulating strips and a fire extinguisher.

Perfect.

"Okay. Andy, you and Bravo team go through first. Use the stuff Tosh grabbed to help you. Once inside, secure the area around our point of ingress. We'll follow using the bodies. As we enter, we'll leapfrog you and provide cover around the emergency stairwell leading down to sickbay. When we're done, I'll issue further instructions."

Sam ushered his men away a few yards so Andy could prepare his group. In moments, Bravo were ready to go. Weapons to the shoulder, they triggered the hatch and disappeared through the gate.

Less than thirty seconds later, Sam heard Andy calling:

"Area checked. It's safe to move."

This is where we find out how switched-on our esoteric friends are.

As slowly and gently as he could, Sam guided the cadavers toward the interior section of the base. He took his time, mimicking the movements bodies might make when subjected to microgravity and inertia. All progressed smoothly. Once inside the inner passage, Sam paused to assess their new situation.

Immediately to his left, another emergency bulkhead barred their way. On the right, the hallway followed the curve of the main sphere and out of sight. He spotted the entrance obviously prepared for them fifty yards farther along the corridor, illuminated by a gleaming spotlight.

After patting the cadavers in the direction he wanted to go, Sam took Alpha team along the passage until they reached the stairwell. The automatic doors stood open, and the control panel had been destroyed.

It's like following the clues on a treasure map.

He stared at the other access points lining the inner circle.

Hmmmh...

"Bob, Eddie? I'll cover the entrance with Joe. I want you two to leave a surprise at every single doorway leading off this section. They might hide unwanted guests who'll come out to play once we've committed ourselves to the rescue. Let's make sure our hosts are dissuaded from pursuing us."

"Micro mines," Bob enquired, "or the gravity compressors?"

"A combination of both. And ring this doorframe too, once we've gone. If they try sneaking up on us, I want people to hear the explosions down on Exordium."

His men moved off, and Sam signaled for Bravo team to move up. "Andy, you'll note the locks here have been disabled. You'll probably find the same down below. Divide into pairs and check a couple of decks to either side of where we want to go. Leave the same deterrents as Bob and Eddie at each threshold. When you've done that, wait for us at the entrance to the medical level. And by the way, if you discover doors wedged open like this one here, depress your mic button three times in a row and we'll all switch to full tactical."

"Roger that. What about you?"

"Joe and I will maneuver our new best friends downstairs. God knows how the Horde might be trying to monitor us, but if we give them something to concentrate on, it could act as a distraction when the shit eventually hits the fan."

"Good idea."

The two leaders regarded each other for a moment longer, then everybody set-to, intent upon their own tasks.

Sam and Joe began edging their *friends* down the first flight. They had just reached the intermediary landing when the entire base rocked. Strong vibrations radiated back and forth through the substructure, and Sam was alarmed to hear a loud groan resonate through the air. A fresh cloud of dust billowed from a large overhead vent. To his surprise, the pressure caused the grill to fall away. Then an arm dropped into view.

What the hell . . . ? They must have been desperate to try hiding up there. "Sevvy? Is there anything we should know?"

"Nothing to concern yourself with." the specialist's voice sounded calm. "Your mission has gone undetected thus far. We are merely experiencing the overspill from a broadside initiated by Barsoonet's defensive batteries. Most of the flak was aimed at the drop ships. All the same, some volleys went astray and were neutralized in your vicinity."

"Are we likely to get any more?"

"Hard to say. I will task Seraphim to make a greater effort in future."

Mind you, it could prove quite useful. Sam had another brainstorm:

"Sevvy, how are Lieutenant Smith's vitals?"

"Fading rapidly. If you don't get there soon, I doubt there'll be much anyone can do. Remember, like everybody else, his body is still in a state of gradual flux as the re-genesis matrix reworks his DNA toward its permanent hybrid form. If too many cells mutate, even the triamphetemopiate ampoules I issued before you departed won't help him. His molecules will start to unravel."

Shit! We'd better stir things up a bit.

"We're going as fast as the environment permits. If you want us to accelerate the timetable, you'll need to afford more of a distraction than the drones can provide. Tell you what. Could you get Seraphim to detonate something below Kalina's main sphere in about a minute, perhaps a minute and a half? It would prove most helpful."

Phhht—Phhht—Phhht.

There's the signal.

"I can certainly manage that, Cap – Sam. Unless I contact you in the meantime, expect a further shockwave or two, ninety seconds from . . . *Now.*"

I'd better get a move on then.

"Assault squad, this is Alpha one. Switch to full tactical measures and activate your null-shield generators. Chivvy things along." He glanced down and saw Andy waiting for him at the next landing. "What have you got?"

The lieutenant pointed toward a control panel on the wall. "As you can see, the circuits are completely fried. Now come and take a closer look . . ."

Sam did as he was asked, and Andy continued: "Whoever did this was an amateur. Note the grooves and deeper gouges caused by talons? It severed the wires before they melted. This tells me we're dealing with an energy-based entity. And now"—he gestured again—"if I could draw your attention to the prime killing zone in front of us?"

A long single thoroughfare stretched away from them. At more than one hundred and fifty yards in length, it certainly appeared spacious, but Sam knew it wouldn't give them room to maneuver if the Horde did what they usually did, and simply swarmed them.

To the left, a series of large, triple-glazed reinforced windows provided tantalizing glimpses of a darkened medi-bay interior, illuminated from within by the twinkling lights of an assortment of machines and treatment bays. On the opposite side of the passage, the wall was punctuated by four floor-to-ceiling, double-leaved pressure gates. Closed tight, Sam didn't have to guess too hard what might lie behind them. Down at the far end of the passage, the open jaws of the central turbolift shaft yawned wide.

Prime killing ground indeed.

By now, everyone had returned from their assigned tasks. Sam indicated they should gather round:

"Okay, guys, we've got no choice but to walk into the lion's den. In my opinion the Horde are concealed within the compartments to our right. Whatever their signal to attack may be, I don't foresee it coming until we've reached Lieutenant Smith's location. So from here on in, I want everyone on tiptoes. Although it's obvious they'll try to overwhelm us with numbers, we won't make it easy for them. In less than a minute from now Seraphim will provide a timely distraction—one I anticipate will be an excuse for even *more* rubbish floating around down here. When she does . . . Tosh? Throw whatever items you can find at the first couple of gateways. Hopefully, anyone inside will get spooked enough to jump the gun and settle the issue once and for all.

"However, if they maintain discipline stay quiet, Joe and I will send our Ardenese friends on their way to see which doorways are functional. Andy? We'll probably find those on your side sealed from within. If that's the case, your team will travel along the corridor, using whatever micro mines and gravity compressors you have remaining to ensure our hosts meet with a lethal deterrent. When they do decide to play, I want their numbers drastically reduced from the word go. We'll cover you while you do that. Once we're back together, we can initi–"

The entire installation shuddered and the stairwell shook from side to side.

"There's our cue. Go, go, *go*."

Tosh stepped out, took aim, and let fly.

Thud. Thud. Thud.

With a final heave, he sent a heavy metal bar on its way.

Clang!

Sam instinctively winced and ducked. Then he grinned. *Idiot! I knew it was coming and it still made me jump.*

They waited.

I've never known the Horde to exercise such restraint. Perhaps they're not—

A much stronger, secondary detonation throbbed throughout the hull. Despite the microgravity saturating the environs, most of Sam's group was forced to brace themselves against the wall.

"For fuck's sake, Severin," Sam growled, "tell Seraphim I said a *distraction*, not a holocaust with us painted as the bull's-eye."

Fighting down the palpitations of his wildly beating heart, Sam yanked the cadavers into the walkway and signaled Joe to help him wrench them apart.

A sickening *crunch* marked the moment the young scientist's fingers finally released their grip.

Sam didn't have time for sentimentalities. "Watch the exits," he barked, "and list each one that still operates. Alpha will look right; Bravo, left."

Parted for the first time in centuries, each corpse went spinning along opposite sides of the corridor. Sam paid close attention, alert for anything that might provide evidence as to the Horde's tactics. Two minutes later, he had his answer:

Not a single gate had triggered.

"Andy, what have you got for me?"

"Boss, only three opened up. The third, fourth, and eighth doorways along."

"Okay, deploy your team. My boys will cover."

As everyone fanned out along the walls, Sam seized the opportunity to peer in through the fourth window. Even with his advanced optics, the interior remained a mystery: The entire medical facility was divided into numerous separate sections, arranged in tiers around a variety of treatment platforms, private suites, and operating centers.

He compared what he saw to the diagram on his wrist pad. *Ah, I see. There are two distinct wings, mirroring each other. They obviously operated from one side while keeping the other in reserve. A sound strategy. Everything would be in place and on hand in the event of a crisis. Hmm, it seems to check out. And according to this, Smith should be in that cubicle block . . .* he traced his finger along the glass, *there. Right near the back.*

He sighed.

Of course, where else?

A faint blue pulse indicated someone in that rear room remained alive. Barely. Then the atmosphere sizzled, and the beacon split into two readings before reverting back to normal.

I see what Seraphim meant by the radiation down here.

Something niggled in the back of his mind.

But if so, why are the pulses coming from across the corridor instead of down below where the main reactor was? And why hasn't this level of toxicity killed Smith yet?

Sam adjusted the resonance of his optical scanner. *There are lots of obstacles between us and our target. Maybe we can use that to our advantage.*

He glanced up and down the passageway again. With his people busy completing their tasks, his own attention fixed on the gaping chasm of the central turbo shaft.

I wonder what the hell happened to blow it out entirely? Sam coaxed his readout to show an enlarged overlay of Kalina. *Jesus, it runs straight through the entire base.*

A shock of realization coursed along his spine. *So why have we got atmosphere? Unless someone deliberately erected a force-field to create an environment that would draw us in.*

Any doubt that the Horde were here now evaporated. As soon as his squad finished their ministrations, Sam ushered them together in a protective arc:

"How many were you able to booby trap?"

"All of them," Andy replied. "And then some."

Sam could hear the humor in his friend's voice. "What do you mean?"

"Stu thought it might be worthwhile trying the plaxi-acid we use to melt through chain link fences, to see if we could fuse the doors in some way."

"And?"

"We smeared a thin film of it around the seals at floor level, and it worked like a charm. I think it's bonded the actual panels to the deck. Probably won't hold for long: we *are* talking about bulkhead gates, after all. But every second counts, eh?"

"Nice one. Do you have anything left over?"

"No acid, I'm afraid, we used it all up. Apart from that, we still have one gravity compressor and four micro mines."

Now that's handy.

Sam glanced back into the medi-bay and checked the schematics again. In particular, he studied the specific arrangement of the workstations along each aisle.

Making a decision, he transferred the internal layout onto everyone's HUDs:

"In a moment, we will enter via the door behind us and proceed to the third circle of reception desks, *here*." One ring of equipment glowed green. "We'll hold at that site while Eddie and Lady P create two specific kill zones."

He motioned for Eddie and Lady P to step forward.

"As you can see, when those gates opposite the sickbay open, the Horde will be naturally inclined to charge at this door and the next one along. I doubt any will even bother with the entrance up near the elevator shaft." He turned to point at the gangway inside. "Look how the equipment and primary walkway act as a natural channel. We'll use that against them. Place the compressor and mines in such a way that the majority are persuaded to run toward our defensive position along that main route. Got it?"

"Yes, sir," they said in unison.

"Okay. Set motion and energy trackers to covert pulse. Half-second cycles. In we go."

Well accustomed to working with one another, the squad formed into natural pairs and began a slow tactical advance toward their first objective.

Sam concentrated on his own arcs and adopted the expanded state of awareness which all operatives assume in high stress, closed environments.

Voices sounded-off around him.

"Oxi-bed and auxiliary stations checked."

"Watch that corner, LT. The lockers form a blind spot."

"Already on it . . . it's safe."

"First-tier assessment modules . . . clear."

"Cover me, Stu, choke point ahead."

"Will do. Wait . . . Got you, proceed to . . ."

"Dead area ahead, Bob. Flank and converge."

"Copy that."

"Secondary modules...clear."

Although Sam let the chatter flow through his mind without distracting him, it warmed his heart to note how the newest members of his squad blended so well with his tried and trusted companions of old.

"Door three now rigged," Eddie's unruffled tones announced. "Lady P?"

"Just setting the pressure gauge on number four . . . All done. Meet you at the first main junction."

Sam arrived at the designated nursing post and trained his gun along the counter. Joe stepped forward and peered over the top, weapon at the ready. On Sam's signal, Stu and Tosh fanned out and peeled one way, Bob and Andy the other. The first pair looped in behind to check the rear of the desks, while Bob and Andy continued on toward the consultation booths.

Sam joined them and took stock: *So far we haven't triggered anything, but I'm sure that's about to change.*

He checked Wilson Smith's position on his HUD. Once again, the signal flared into two distinct signatures before fading back to a single pulse.

If this is right, he should be in one of the rooms behind these stalls.

A half-formed thought nagged him, but he couldn't quite put his finger on it.

As usual when he had a moment or two to catch his breath, Sam checked the area around him for faint but telltale signs that might explain what had happened. There weren't any. The medi-bay looked pristine.

Too pristine.

This is a star-base hospital, for goodness sake. A place this size should have some indicators appropriate for the main infirmary. But there aren't any. It's as if it's been sterilized of all evidence that humans ever existed.

His gaze came to rest on the huge gateways out in the eastern corridor.

The Horde aren't the mindless savages we once thought. Nevertheless, we've all witnessed how willing they are to spend themselves to achieve their goals. How could they be so sure we'd *be willing to risk this many people for one man? That concept would be totally alien to them. Unless . . . ?*

Sam felt he was on the verge of understanding something important, something crucial that would help solve the mystery, but once again circumstances overtook him:

"Everything's ready, boss," Lady P called. "Kill zones are primed, and Eddie's laying out the last of the grenades."

"Okay then," Sam replied, "this is it. Bob? I want you to pair up with Lady P and start working your way out from the treatment hub toward door number eight. Prepare an extraction route that will give us a clear run. Eddie, when you've finished over there, you're with me. As our best medic, I want your opinion on Smith's health, particularly if anything about his condition seems fishy. Have your triamphetemopiate ampoules to hand.

"The rest of you, get ready and stay sharp. You know the drill. When they come, they'll come fast and hard. We're carrying twice the amount of ammo we're usually issued with. Even so, conserve it; let the traps do their job. As the Horde converge on you, make a point of retreating behind the treatment cubicles before making a run for the exit. They'll mask what you're doing for the first twenty yards or so. When the grenades go off, we'll have a nice big hole in the floor between them and us. Eddie and I should already be running with our casualty by then, so cover our backs when the ogres start jumping across the gap . . ."

"And if he's not there, boss?" Stu asked.

"Then it's easy: We kill as many slavering bastards as we can before activating our pattern boosters. There'll be no need for stealth anymore, so Seraphim will be able to substantiate a lock on our signals and we're outta here. Once we've resupplied, it'll be a quick turnaround down to Exordium. Either way, we're in for a fire-fest today."

"Good hunting then," Andy murmured.

"Good hunting," Sam echoed.

Sam waited for Eddie to complete his previous task, and then together they moved toward the private suites.

A simple standing partition barred the way. Mindful of any last minute traps, Sam went left, Eddie right. Converging on the other side, they stopped to get a better sense of their new environment.

A short hallway led away from them. Hanging curtains, limp in the negligible gravity, indicated a total of four rooms in this section, two on each side. Life signs issued from the last one on the right.

Sam suspected they were being baited, for he could see a gentle pearlescent glow spilling out into the corridor through that doorway.

Talk about dangling the worm.

Using hand signals, he indicated they must clear the empty suites first.

They zigzagged their way along the line, only to discover the drapes were purely ornamental, a feature affording a degree of privacy to those being treated inside. Behind each curtain, a see-through door and large window allowed a clear and unobstructed view of the interior.

Because of this, they quickly ascertained all of the other suites were empty. Finally, Sam prepared to confirm the reason for this entire mission.

Using the end of an equipment frame, Eddie stood close behind Sam and pushed the intervening blind aside.

Sam peered in through the entrance. He knew the CIC aboard the *Shadow of Autumn* was monitoring their progress. Nonetheless, he began a commentary explaining what he was seeing.

“I’ve got a casualty,” he hissed. “Prone, on a treatment platform in the center of the room. Union cavalry uniform. Wait for details . . .”

As Sam peered around the rest of the compartment, Sevvy interjected:

“Sam? Despite the barrage, Seraphim has ordered the EMT shuttle to close. ETA, three min – *Shit*!”

“What’s happening?”

“Apparently we have a malfunction aboard the transporter. One of the escape pods just launched.”

“I thought there wasn’t anybody on board the medi-craft?”

“There isn’t. It’s being flown remotely, by Seraphim. Hang on . . . Seraphim’s just advised me that if the pods take damage, they’re designed to jettison in order to prevent subsequent catastrophic failure. And—”

“Cut the chatter unless it affects us directly,” Sam said. “Are we in danger?”

There was a slight pause.

“No, you’re in the clear, Mohammed and Seraphim said they’ll sort it.”

“Roger that. Then ignore what’s going on outside and concentrate solely on what I have to say.” Sam resumed his report: “Apart from the target before us, we have an equipment locker at the foot of the bed, an instrument panel in a recess down the far end, what looks like a mobile treatment trolley in one corner, and a huge fan on the ceiling with a central glowing light. Do you copy?"

"Yes, yes. Proceed."

"Good. For your information, we are about to move inside."

His heart racing, Sam gave the signal.

Sliding silently into the room, Eddie scooted over to the far wall. Sam waited for him to get into position before he himself advanced. As he did so, he discerned a faint, oscillating warble break the silence.

"Stand by . . ." he snapped. "Eddie, where's that sound coming from?"

Each scanned the room as they continued edging forward.

"The cabinet," Eddie whispered. "Be careful. Whatever's in there is emitting some kind of blue light."

"I'll see what it is," Sam replied. "You check on our man."

Weapon poised, Sam triggered the catch. The rack snapped up, and he found himself staring at one of the strangest devices he had ever seen:

A golden ocular, slightly larger than a man's head, crowned the contraption in a sea of liquid hues. Every second, the collar emitted a different tone and a streaming ribbon bloomed forth. Celeste, cyan, turquoise, and sapphire. Each shade was encapsulated within a sizzling tendril of plasma, shimmering and shrinking as it went, creating ever-decreasing circles that caught the eye and caused a lightheaded effect.

Sam found it instantly mesmerizing.

Umbilical arms fitted with an assortment of attachments sprouted from a riblike cage below the optical array. Sam's attention was drawn to several nodes blazing like miniature suns. He'd only ever seen that effect once before.

It's like the psi-tutor. But that was a hyper-advanced bit of kit, even for the likes of the Ardenese. If this—

He heard a gasp behind him.

"Jesus Christ! There are *two* of them."

Two?

Sam turned and ran to the far side of the bed. Sure enough, another trooper lay motionless, face down on the floor. He knelt, turned the second soldier over, and recoiled in horror. "What the hell? It's an old man. He must be over a hundred years—"

"Captain Pell?"

"He looks emaciated, as if . . . Eddie, does your guy look like this?"

"Captain Pell?" The voice in his earpiece became more insistent.

"Yes, sir," Eddie replied. "I can't believe what I'm seeing, but this is *not* radiation poisoning. It something else entir – Shit! It's Harper."

"What?"

"Zebedee Harper. One of the guys from Fifth Company. Who have you got?"

As tenderly as he could, Sam lifted the poor man's head.

Hooded eyes fluttered open and widened in shock. "Thank God," the man mumbled weakly, "the nightmare is over at . . . at . . . lasss –"

Sam looked on helplessly as the wretch's pupils suddenly dilated. Only then did he recognize the ravaged face he held in his hands.

Stark. He was—

"Captain Pell, this is important. Can you hear me? Captain Pell . . . I said, can you hear me?"

At last the avatar's repetitive badgering registered:

"I hear you, Seraphim," answered Sam. "What do you want?"

"Fast as you can, Captain Pell. I need you to step back to the cabinet and focus your helmet-cam on the various features of that apparatus."

The urgency in Seraphim's words spurred Sam to action.

"Certainly, why?"

"It resembles a blueprint I recovered from Latinus Prime, relating to a sophisticated piece of medical equipment, a prototype capable of measuring and duplicating a person's psidentic and biodentic patterns."

"It does *what*?"

"Simply put, it was designed to replicate the esometric and biometric templates of those severely injured in teleport accidents. The principle behind it works on the premise of implanting recorded data of the subject onto stored DNA. Think of it as replacement tissue, as opposed to cloning. Quite ingenious really, but sadly, open to a host of *weaponized* adaptations . . ."

As stunned as Sam was, he was nevertheless struck by a sudden notion:

"Hang on a second. We've got Harper and Stark. Where the hell is Smith?"

"That's what I'm trying to emphasize," Seraphim said. "From what I can ascertain, this device can be operated remotely through mental interface. If someone capable of telepathic functioning could project an accurate enough image, this machine would pick it up and generate a bio-field that could be mistaken for an actual person. It might explain why I have detected humanoid life signs within the faulty escape pod."

Suddenly, all the pieces of the jigsaw came together.

Smith? Bugger! This was just a ruse to get us here.

"Are you telling me—?"

"Boss, Harper's body is rigged! Look out . . ."

Eddie's sudden warning dominated Sam's entire world and he reacted on instinct. By the time he heard the next word, Sam was already diving through the curtain.

"*Bomb*!"

Sam felt rather than heard the detonation. Rolling with the shockwave, he came to his feet and aimed his weapon's muzzle back toward the cubicle, aware that further danger might be pursuing them.

Beside him, Eddie had adopted the same maneuver, albeit from a kneeling position.

They needn't have bothered. The trap was sprung.

The concussion blew Harper's remains upward and outward. Bloody entrails and all manner of viscera covered the partitions and ceiling in a crimson, gray, and green wash. Some of the larger particles continued bouncing back and forth off the walls and tiles in a spellbinding aerial display.

"Contact, contact!" Andy yelled over the radio. "We have dozens of Horde pouring out of the eastern compartments. Wait for it. Choose your targets and hold your fire. Let them to come to us . . ."

Sam couldn't help but stare at the intestines and muck hanging from the blades of the fan.

Despite the urgency of the situation, Eddie gawped at them too. Incongruously, the younger man laughed.

"You see?" Sam stated in a matter-of-fact tone. "Sometimes the shit really does reach that high."

The floor beneath them flexed as the first mines exploded, breaking the spell.

"What say we go and lend a hand against the incoming tide?" *And we'll try getting to the bottom of what's* really *going on.*

Chapter Twenty-Nine

Like Diamonds in the Sky

The *Abeille* rolled violently to one side, its engine pitch rising considerably as the pilot fought to keep the drop ship level. Marcus made a conscious effort to control his breathing and keep his face blank.

It won't do for the men to see fear on the face of their commander after the rousing speech I so recently delivered.

To distract himself, Marcus stared at the shimmering waterfall cascading around them outside as uncountable tons of metal and gigajoules of photonic potential combined in a scintillating onslaught of light and flame. Bright flashes indicated when enemy fire strayed too close, almost breaching their defensive perimeter. Then their craft bucked and yawed like a leaf in rapids until the current nudged them back on course.

He was lost in the moment.

Though Marcus was an outstanding example of someone determined to adjust to his fresh life in a strange new world, at times like this his simpler origins came to the fore.

How can anyone survive such a bombardment? Had Rome possessed such might, our empire would have encompassed the entire globe . . . and beyond.

"Thirty seconds until mesosphere," announced Beth Pattison, their pilot. "You know what's coming. Here we go."

Leaning to one side, Marcus opened a channel to the *Shadow of Autumn.*

"Gold Command, this is Silver, confirming that we'll be experiencing communications problems for the next five minutes or so as we pierce the atmosphere. I will resume contact as soon as we're through."

"Roger that," Seraphim replied. "Godspeed."

Marcus initiated a ship-to-ship feed, so the soldiers aboard the *Ballarat*, *Eurus*, and *Orison* could hear him as well:

"We are about to encounter significant turbulence, so hang tight. Jake, Angus? Watch your horses. Men of the Ninth, never forget: today, we make history."

He cut the link and leaned back.

Just in time.

The *Abeille* trembled, and a ruddy glow highlighted the extremities of her stabilizing fins. Marcus felt an invisible hand press against his spine.

He glanced at the temperature, speed, and advance-to-contact indicators.

1226˚F—17, 800mph—300miles.

The shuddering increased; the light outside intensified. Brightening gradually through rose gold, orange, tangerine, peach and then yellow, the glare etched its way up the windows.

A prominent rattle from one of the overhead racks caught everyone's attention.

"Now in the chute, five by five," Beth said, "homing beacon activated."

"Is this normal, sir?"

Marcus stared across at the source of the query and espied the infamous Felix. Strapped to his seat, the poor legionnaire was wide-eyed, white-knuckled, and shaking so badly Marcus thought he might vomit at any moment.

Although he tried not to, Marcus grinned.

Sometimes it's easy for me to forget. Few of my men have made an effort, as I have, to familiarize themselves with so much new technology. Indeed, I am the only one who dares to fly machines such as this. It is only natural for even the hardiest veterans to be unnerved by the experience, especially as this is the first time we have done so under full combat conditions.

"If any of you are feeling queasy, don't worry, there's no shame in it. Our pilot must endeavor to land us as quickly and as brutally as possible to increase our chances of survival. Just ensure you use the sick bags situated in the compartment between your knees." He glanced back at Felix. "And yes, soldier, this is perfectly normal for a tactically controlled descent. Expect the vibrations to increase a hundredfold before they cease."

Marcus had an idea.

"Look at the readout, Felix. What do the numbers tell you?"

Felix craned forward.

"That we're traveling more than ten thousand miles per hour and the temperature exceeds two and a half thousand degrees."

"You've sliced into flesh. You know how hot the insides of a man are, and what resistance the knife experiences as it shears through sinew and muscle. Unless your blade is very sharp, even the simplest fat can present a problem, so you have to hack at it." Marcus gestured to the cargo hold about them. "The *Abeille* is like a big blunt cleaver. She's flat, and she's heavy, and she's doing her best to bludgeon down through the skin of this planet's atmosphere. That's why the going is hard."

Marcus tapped the porthole beside him.

"Now gaze out the window. Tell me, what do you see?"

Felix's eyes popped even wider.

"I see the heavens on fire, sir."

"That's right. And the blaze will get brighter and brighter until you'd think we'd melt. But we won't. In a few minutes that conflagration will be extinguished. When it is, we'll plunge from searing heat into a soaring vista of utter tranquility. The inferno will be replaced by ice, and our ships will look like jewels falling to earth. I tell you, the sensation will be wonderful."

"It will?"

"It will. So make the most of it, for it'll be the last thing of wonder you see before all this is over."

"Aye!"

"Hear, hear."

"To glory."

"Well said."

It wasn't until the chorus of affirmations rang back that Marcus realized the entire crew had been listening.

"Very inspiring, Marcus," Beth teased. "Now prepare your men. We're almost through to cruising height. There's high-altitude ionization ahead, so things will remain a bit bumpy as we punch through, but afterward it'll be plain sailing until we smack down. Range to target, two-forty megs. Speed, two thousand and falling. Lining up for final approach . . . Stand by, stand by."

Marcus noted the difference in his men in their seats as they readied for battle. Fingers opened and clenched repeatedly.

Knees bounced. Many rocked backward and forward. Some muttered feverishly as they crammed in last minute prayers to their favorite deity. Felix vomited at last . . . thankfully into the bag provided.

He'll do.

But their pilot hadn't finished:

"In case I don't get the opportunity once we hit the LZ, thank you for flying with Beth Airways. The temperature groundside appears to be a balmy eighty degrees. Once we land, don't forget to adjust your clocks to thirty minutes until doomsday. Oh, please be sure to take your trash, gum, and stained undergarments with you."

A smattering of laughter broke the tension.

I'd better keep them focused.

"You heard the lady," Marcus bellowed, "as soon as we're clear, unclip your weapons and make your way to the ramp. Remember, before you deploy, allow the *Orison* to complete its sweep to secure the open ground between us and . . ."

*

The boiling mass of concentrated wrath hesitated as the last mines took out at least twenty of their number. An eerie silence descended like a shroud across the room.

Yes, Sam thought, *you're beginning to switch on at last, which is exactly what I want.*

His strategy had worked like a charm.

Although Sam hadn't been there to bear witness, Andy had relayed the initial assault through to Sam's HUD. No sooner did the huge compartment gates open in the main corridor than the preset explosives did their work. The front ranks of the Horde advance simply disappeared, taking most of the bulkhead with them and causing a partial collapse of the substructure.

Undeterred, the rest of the howling mob pressed forward. And sure enough, the majority entered the medi-bay through the doors prepared for them. When the Horde pack ran straight into the next set of traps, the entire reception area disintegrated in a series of implosive concussions that compacted and vaporized the brunt of their charge.

Enraged, the leading grunts followed the natural pathways created by the arrangement of terminals and workstations, only to succumb to another set of cunningly-laid deterrents.

Needless to say, the remainder were now wary. Sam couldn't be sure if this was due to sheer attrition, or the presence of two Controllers standing to one side.

At more than twelve feet in height, both apparitions were sheathed in a purple and blue nimbus that warped the air about them. Their whirling coronets identified them as Lega'trexii, and the lurid crimson sparks skittering through their coronas revealed they were pissed. Extremely pissed.

Okay, let's see what they do now.

Sam glanced down at the bottleneck where three main aisles came together. From his position, he could see that the final gravity compressor remained safely hidden, invisible and ready to detonate.

What a shame we squandered the rest of them upstairs. Still, we weren't to know . . . And waste not want not.

He addressed his squad on their covert channel:

"Assault team, we've attracted the attention of Horde Masters. I don't want them getting suspicious, so the next time their minions press forward, start firing. Short, controlled bursts. Remember: because of our shields they haven't seen us up until now. Consequently, the moment we open up they'll know where to look. So, begin backing off toward the treatment booths. We've seen what this lot is like when they think their food is getting away: they can't control themselves."

And then we'll get a true indicator as to how different these new freaks really are.

Sam surveyed the far reaches of the facility, near their projected exit.

"Bob, have you and Lady P prepared the extraction route?"

"Yes, yes," Bob replied. "We saved one grenade each, and used the rest to create a nasty little den of iniquity over here. Click your heels together three times, follow the yellow brick road, and you'll stay in one piece. Transferring route to your HUDs now."

An overlay of the medi-bay's west wing appeared on their viewers, along with a phosphorous citrine line indicating the safest course through the maze of equipment.

"Nice one. Bob, pay attention to what's going on down here. The next time the enemy rushes us, I want you to remote-detonate the ordinance you and Eddie laid out on the primary tier above this deck. If nothing else, it'll distract the Horde and make them even twitchier. Nervy buggers make mistakes. If they're spooked, it'll be easier for us to slip behind the partitions and make a break toward you. Wait until the last of us is protected by cover before you obliterate the desks in front of us."

"Got it . . . I think. Bloody hell, I hope I remember which button's which."

Wanker!

Giggles, quickly suppressed, revealed how tight Sam's team was, and how—even at times like this—their humor provided a great motivating factor.

Ignoring the banter, Sam kept a close watch on their enemy.

Some of the brutes were fanning out, sidling along several minor walkways.

Oh, these guys are switched on, all right. "Everyone, I suggest you carry out last minute equipment checks. Any second now, our friends are going to charge."

His words proved prophetic:

Out in the eastern thoroughfare, the air shivered and a gray void whirled into existence. Looking much like an elongated corkscrew, it narrowed and stretched until its extremities touched both floor and ceiling.

Memories of the first time Sam had witnessed such an event came crashing back.

I was with Mac out at Rhomane Starport. That's when we saw Angule for the—

A hulking great brute appeared from within the asperity. Blazing forth in gold and silver majesty, it stood close to fourteen feet tall. Its presence ignited the ether around it. Eyes like smoldering lava pits swept the room.

Sam stared at the sizzling halo of stars above its huge head.

Bloody hell!

"We have a Grand Master in our midst. I say again, the entity in the exterior corridor is a Grand Master. Get ready, I've a nasty feeling things are about to cha—"

A piercing shriek rang out. A number of ogres instantly split from the main group and jumped across whatever obstacles blocked their way. At the same time, those monsters already creeping through adjacent gaps gave up all pretence of stealth and leaped forward.

It looked to Sam as if their enemy suddenly knew where to go.

Sure enough, the remaining host chose that moment to charge.

Kalina shook as all the bombs arranged throughout the floor above them exploded. The blast was immediately followed by the report of the final gravity compressor.

"Open fire and retreat," Sam yelled. "We are leaving."

The men in front of him formed up and let rip with everything they had. Andy and Joe to his left, Stu and Tosh on the right. Beside him, Eddie stepped forward, brought his rifle to the shoulder, and calmly dispatched a grunt who tried to take advantage of the weightless conditions by leaping the thirty yard gap between the two parties.

Sam shuffled away, squeezing off short sharp bursts as he went.

Out in the main hallway, evidence of the cataclysm along the upper tier grew ever more pronounced. Air vents popped open; roof tiles burst from their mountings; an opaque cloud billowed from the emergency stairwell. The leading edges broke against the sickbay windows, congealed for a moment, and surged off along the passage like milk-colored magma venting from a volcano.

The Grand Master didn't move, and within seconds it was engulfed within a thickening brume.

Sam dismissed it from his reality, for his entire existence was now dominated by drills. Drills that were as natural to him as breathing or putting one foot in front of the other:

Spot—exhale—hold—fire. Spot—inhale—hold—fire. Check bullets readout:

72.

Spot—exhale—hold—fire. Spot—inhale—hold—fire. Check count:

57.

Spot—exhale—hold—fire—

Over and over, round and round, the cycle extended into one long repetitive test of discipline under pressure. Eventually, his rounds indicator flashed zero . . .

"Changing magazine."

As Sam dropped to his knee, Eddie immediately moved to stand over him and maintained cover until his teammate was ready to rejoin the fray.

Sam used the momentary respite to check on his squad.

Andy and Joe were already more than halfway to the partition, their torsos twisting left and right, up and down as they engaged anything that moved. Adjacent to them, Stu and Tosh, now free of intervening obstacles, were making short work of those bogeys trying to flank them.

Out in the corridor, the thinning cloud had assumed a translucent quality. Its surface shimmered and sparkled as if infused with stardust.

It didn't reach the end of the hall? But—

Then Sam caught sight of the void through which the beast had teleported: *Of course, he must have left it open, as Angule did back at the Starport. The excess pressure here will simply push the mist through into the vacuum.*

Sam had a sudden thought:

Just how far can these big guns travel using the . . . what did Zagam call it, the vext? From what I remember, they cover short distances with hardly any effort and without the need of a portal. So are these gateways a more powerful version of what they can do naturally? And is that how they managed to get to Harper and Stark? If so—

A fresh charge tabled further deliberation.

Leaping to his feet, Sam called, "This is it, guys. Once we reach the room dividers, stand still and empty your current mags into them. It'll give us a bit of space and allow Bob to time things better." He raised his voice. "Bob? Any second now . . ."

"I'm on it, boss." Bob's voice was taut with concentration. "No worries."

Time compressed into a confusing display of blinding illumination and black outlines. Step by torturous step, the team retreated until they were tight against the screens. There they formed an arc, ready to make their stand.

Fluorescent sparks spat death as hundreds of magnetized rounds stitched the air. As each bullet passed through the rarified essence of their howling victims, they impacted floors, walls, and workstations alike, bouncing around to cause further mayhem. But Sam wasn't worried about the danger of ricochets, as these bullets were of softhead design, specially manufactured to obliterate Horde entities before rebounding off soft surfaces without harming other living beings. And they did their job well. Very well.

Scores of screaming demons fell. Soon the room filled with lurid flashes of leaping nightmare effigies desperate to get out of the way, and pyrotechnic implosions as monsters met their end against an impenetrable wall of steel.

The trouble was, the longer the battle continued, the more difficult it became for Sam to ignore the surfeit of odd events caused by the peculiarities of zero-g conditions . . .

A console near the far wall had been damaged; now it blazed. The oxygen-rich environment fed the flames with all the fuel needed to melt resin and plastic alike. Nevertheless, in place of the roaring conflagration Sam might have expected, the workstation was encompassed within a domed nimbus of muted blue light.

The instrument panel next to it also had been smashed. Incorporating a mixture of highly charged gel packs and other fluid-filled components, most of the protective membrane had burst, spilling its scalding contents into the atmosphere. However, in place of a spray of angry bubbles, a seething and misshapen globule continued to squirt from the rupture in an ever-expanding mass. Swelling larger by the second, this glob distended and rippled like a miniature sea in midair.

Even their own weapons were affected.

The quad-column magazines their modified machine guns utilized were capable of holding one hundred bullets. Empty casings were being ejected at a rate of twelve rounds per second. Instead of falling to the floor in a tinkling cascade as they usually did, the expended jackets went sailing off through the air in ranked convoys of glowing-hot metal, a cavalcade that proceeded undisturbed until the intervening bulkhead got in the way. Only then did they shower to the ground, wreaking havoc on any ogre foolish enough to stray too close.

To break the spell, Sam accelerated the timetable:

"Bob, start counting us down. We'll let off a final burst and start ducking behind the partition. Guys? As you go, bring up the exfil route on your HUDs. Follow the path and everything should go smoothly. Once we stop firing, the Horde won't know where we are, so make the most of it. On my mark. Three, two, one . . . *Mark*!"

On either side of him, Andy and Tosh unleashed a deafening final salvo and skipped away.

"Listen in," Bob instructed. "Things will get toasty in, ten, nine . . ."

As Joe and Stu followed suit, Sam cast a final glance along the underside of the triple-tiered nursing station where their departing gift was concealed.

This should be fun

"Eight, seven, six . . ."

Moments later, Sam joined Eddie in a rush along the short hallway.

"Five, four, three . . ."

They cut right at the consultation rooms and picked up the pace.

"Two, one. Showtime. Grenades primed."

Emerging from behind the redundant treatment center, Sam got there in time to catch the show:

The counter had disappeared beneath a sprawling mass of malice. Bristling with gleaming fangs and glittering talons, the Horde roared; snarling, and snapping at themselves as much as at the thin air about them. It was clear they were working themselves into a frenzy in their eagerness to wreak havoc on their tormentors. The psychic wash accompanying their efforts was overwhelming, and the hairs along Sam's neck prickled at its intensity.

C'mon, you bastards.

Just as the leading wave looked as if they would sweep by without incident, eight singularity grenades detonated. Timed to initiate in micro-sequence, their combined mass amplified the total sum of their energy.

The fabric of reality stretched like molten plastic. Everything appeared to sag inward and the mad charge stalled. From Sam's perspective, it looked as if someone had pressed the ultra slow-motion button on a remote control.

He couldn't help it: Caught in the moment, Sam stopped to watch. Beside him, Eddie did the same.

An opaque tear ripped its way across his vision and the distortion increased. For the blink of an eye, everything froze. Then a subliminal snap pulsed through the ether. Those beasts closest to the anomaly simply folded out of existence, while those leaping through the air toward the partitions found themselves yanked backward like overzealous attack dogs on an elastic leash.

An unseen influence tugged Sam toward the developing calamity so irresistibly that he was forced to brace himself against a desk top.

A gravity well. Thank God they only last a few seconds. Just long enough to—

A shimmering force-field coalesced between the trap and those grunts closest to the main corridor.

How in blazes . . . ?

He glanced toward the medi-bay entrance. From what he could see, the Grand Master had grown tired of the carnage and roused his Lega'trexii underlings to action. Working together, they created a powerful protection against the unstable singularity busy eating its way through their minions.

Too late, I think.

When the ogres behind the shield abruptly stopped and hunched down, as if awaiting fresh orders, those unfortunate enough to be caught on the wrong side of the barrier were dragged kicking and screaming into oblivion.

A swirling disc of light bloomed to life around the collapsing singularity. It reminded Sam of the accretion discs around many black holes; only this example loomed horrific, revolting, generated as it was by the macerated remains of living creatures as opposed to interstellar dust.

What a way to go. . .

Still, better them than—Whoa!

The strength of the gust increased, and Sam held tight to prevent himself being swept off his feet. Before he could right himself, the miniature nebula flared and vaporized a section of flooring more than eighty feet in circumference. Sam tried catching a glimpse of what was on the deck below, but a potent shockwave chose that moment to announce the collapse of the unstable vortex, and slapped Sam backward through the air.

Behind him someone cursed as heavy equipment was knocked to the floor.

Glass shattered, unknown items bounced hither and thither, and someone groaned. Each sound amplified the others.

Fuck me! That was far more powerful than expected. I'll have to remember it for future missions . . . if I live that long.

As Sam gained his knees, he discovered he'd landed on top of Eddie.

"Thanks, buddy. You make a mighty fine cushion."

Eddie grunted. "And *you're* heavier than you look. Help me up, will you?" He glanced over Sam's shoulder and cursed, "Shit! I think we'll need to be getting out of here sharpish."

Sam got to his feet, pulled his colleague upright, and peeped around the side of the nearest storage locker.

Things were not good. The Grand Master was already scrutinizing their end of the chamber.

As Sam looked on, it raised one mighty paw, pointed, and roared.

The baying mob split in two. Some ogres spilled back out into the eastern corridor while the rest of the Horde bowled straight at Sam's squad through the confines of the medi-bay. So frenzied was their attack that desks, chairs, and cabinets went flying. The effect reminded Sam of a steam locomotive with a snow shovel on the front, breasting through head-high drifts.

"They've spotted us," he yelled. "Quickly, get to the turbolift area and activate your pattern enhancers."

With no further need for silence, Sam opened a direct channel to the *Shadow of Autumn*:

"Seraphim, we're coming in hot. Scan for our bio-signs and get us out of here. The sooner the better."

"Roger that, Captain Pell," Seraphim replied. "I am monitoring your situation. Stand by for extraction."

The assault team arrived at the open elevator shaft. With nowhere else to go, they formed up around its edge and divided into two ranks. Those in front dropped to one knee, replaced their magazines and dipped their heads to their sights. Behind them, their compatriots adopted the same drill, but remained standing.

"While you still have time, share out your remaining singularity grenades," Sam instructed. "Don't be shy about using them. We'll be out of here in moments and can resupply back at—"

"Boss," Andy interjected, "what the hell are the Controllers doing?"

Seventy-five yards away, at a point midway along the eastern thoroughfare, the Lega'trexii had come together with the Grand Master and enclosed themselves in a sizzling corona of blue and white light. This nimbus steamed and pulsed in shorter intervals, so that Sam could nearly taste the static charge intensifying.

I don't like this.

"Captain?" Tosh yelled. "We've got more bogeys joining us from the stairwell at the end of the north passage. You were right. They must have been lying in wait for us outside the green zone upstairs."

Sam glanced along the adjacent hallway. Sure enough, another undulating mass of glowing eyes, dripping talons and boiling silhouettes swept toward them.

This is getting bloody ridiculous.

"Seraphim?" he called again. "What's the delay? We're in danger of being overrun down here."

"Something is preventing me from establishing a permanent lock," the AI replied without the slightest hint of urgency. "I am attempting to isolate the source and counter it."

Sam's gaze came to rest on the Masters.

As if I couldn't guess. They did something similar during the Battle of the Line when we were trying to evacuate refugees. Only it took lots more of them that time.

Then he peered toward the latest swarm.

A hundred yards out and closing.

Everyone shuffled back toward the space once occupied by the turbolift. More than twenty yards wide, it presented a formidable hurdle.

Forced to think on his feet, Sam turned in place and considered his only other option. He peeked over the edge of the borehole and saw a bright mass shining through the remains of a ruined disc, hundreds of yards below.

That's Exordium. So the core did *blow out? Interesting.*

A plan came together in his head: "Squad, divide and quarter. Overlapping fire." He put a restraining hand on Bob's shoulder. "Not you. I want *you* to find me some fire extinguishers; quickly, before these bastards get too close. Lady P, cover him."

Sam paused to throw a maximum-yield grenade at a cluster of ogres in the eastern gangway who'd dared to sprint ahead of the main pack.

Oblivious to the danger, the brutes surged forward. A pinpoint of darkness blossomed in their midst, followed by a skein of silver-blue energy. Those grunts closest to the incongruity were abruptly wrenched into the air, sucked backward, and crushed. As the singularity closed, a ringing thunderclap accompanied a bright flash.

Seeing their comrades snatched away so easily, the rest of the crowd ground to a halt.

The Grand Master didn't move. Instead, it issued a series of guttural yips and barks. Sam tried to judge the effect of those sounds on each mob.

He's slowing them down and herding them together. At a signal from him, they'll simply rush us and take us out by sheer numbers.

"People, I suggest you remind our hosts why they don't want to fuck with us?"

The opening volleys tore into the advancing Horde, filling both corridors with a rippling series of shockwaves. Thresholds ruptured. Panic ensued as a self-immolating chain reaction ripped its way through those ogres massed too close together.

Some bullets struck the Horde Masters. Their shield flared and sparked, and the creatures inside flinched.

Of course, when they overran Exordium they didn't face this kind of resistance. They're not used to dealing with beings who can kill them.

"Seraphim? How's my transporter lock? Or failing that, where's the EMT shuttle and her escort?"

"The interference adapts every time I counter it," Seraphim replied. "And the transport is waiting off the station's northeastern quadrant."

Sam needed a new plan, and came up with one instantly:

"Maneuver the shuttle until she's directly under the base. Ask her to scan for our life signs in about . . . thirty seconds from *now*. We're going to try a different exit strategy. Send half the flyers with her to keep unwanted attention away. And, Seraphim? Assign two drones to enter and check the ship itself. If someone's managed to stash Smith away, who knows what else might be in there?"

"Understood. And the rest of the squadron?"

"Have them surround the base and take it out."

"Take it out?"

"They can start immediately at the outer ring. Metallic rounds only. But once we're clear, mangle this place out of existence with as many mines as it takes."

“Copy that . . . will do.”

A clunking sound rose above the din of sporadic fire. Sam thought something might be amiss, but at that moment Bob came through the nearest door along the southern passageway’s shattered remains, heading toward him. To Sam’s delight, Bob was carrying and dragging an assortment of six or more fire extinguishers.

“Will these do?” Bob asked. He pushed them down on the deck so they wouldn’t float away.

“That was quick,” Sam replied. “Was there a sale?”

“Just lucky. This is a space station. As well as the automatic precautions threaded through the superstructure, they always have a couple of detachable mobile units at the junction of every major thoroughfare, and inside the main doors to every compartment.” He let go of his treasure trove. “I managed to get a few CO2 models. The rest are dry powder.”

Perfect.

“Assault team, listen in,” Sam yelled. “On my command, the front rank will release a final volley and then throw whatever grenades you have left into the crowd. Once you’ve changed magazines, sling your weapons, team up with a partner, and select an extinguisher from the pile. Jump into the lift shaft and use the propellant to boost you down the tunnel. While you’re doing that, the rear rank will lay down suppressive fire, and then adopt the same procedure while LT and I step into the breach and cover them. Don’t worry. The EMT shuttle should already be waiting at the bottom. Is everybody clear on what’s going to happen?”

“Yes, yes.”

“Got it.”

“Loud and clear.”

“Give the word.”

The others flashed a quick thumbs-up back over their shoulders.

"Okay," Sam called out. "Here we go. Three, two, one . . . *Fire*!"

A hail of steel-washed lead blasted down each corridor, disintegrating the nearest ogres in a blistering firestorm of fury. Moments later, the micro singularities did their work, and every entity within their reach was ripped away into oblivion.

After a brief lull, the murderous scenario was repeated.

Overhead pipes and conduits burst, flooding the halls with gas. Bulkheads crumpled as the exploding and imploding essences of myriad monsters consumed anything in close proximity. Decks gave way, creating a fistula of ruined metal and resin from which Sam could survey the results of his work.

Andy picked up the final extinguisher and prepared to activate it. Sam felt him clip a line to his belt. As they stepped backward into the void, Sam raised the scope of his weapon to his eye and released a final burst, right into the face of the Grand Master.

The swarm of rounds peppered its shield, forcing it to retreat.

Satisfied, Sam flicked the finger. One of Andy's arms appeared from behind and gripped him across the chest. The air filled with a condensed cloud of CO2.

And they were away, punching through an already existing miasma of crystallized vapor, a sure sign that the rest of the team had come this way.

They crossed the threshold of an air-retaining force-field and everything went blissfully quiet.

Sam thought it might be wise to continue firing, to ensure none of the Horde took it into their heads to follow, but Seraphim beat him to it. No sooner had Sam and Andy cleared the edge of the ruined shell of the base than they were surrounded by drones. Several of the outer units took up defensive positions and doused the interior of the tunnel in a heavy spray of solid iron-shot rounds.

Good thinking.

The sentinels continued circling them until he and Andy touched down on the hull of the EMT shuttle.

"Report," Sam snapped.

"The interior is free of infection," Seraphim replied, "and I am currently carrying out a full diagnostic to establish how anyone could to steal away onboard. I would nevertheless be grateful if your men would carry out a final sweep."

"We'd be glad to," Sam replied. "Don't beat yourself up about it. This thing was parked in its own dedicated bay on the *Shadow of Autumn.* Who'd have guessed we had a traitor on board?"

"Traitor?"

"Of course. How else do you think anyone could have managed to sneak inside without triggering an alarm? I tell you, when this is all over, I'll round them up and shoot them myse…?"

He turned to face his men, froze, and laughed out loud.

Each one was glazed from head to foot in a rime of ice fragments. Against the backdrop of space and with the curve of the planet cresting the bow of the ship, they looked like a diamond-coated dance troupe. The sight reminded Sam of an old vidi-clip he'd once seen of a twentieth-century Earth entertainer who never performed unless he was wearing a sequin-encrusted suit.

"Bloody hell," he quipped, "who organized the Liberace convention?"

Chapter Thirty

Just Cause

Va-ákil did her best to maintain a meticulous overview of the events unfolding on the surface and on the destruction of the floating citadel far above—but fate, it seemed, was against her.

Not only had a small flotilla of ships landed on the outskirts of the facility, but one of her finest Prátors, Tadãhk, narrowly escaped with his life when the orbiting bastion was pulverized by the arcane weaponry in the insects' possession.

As if that wasn't bad enough, now that the Houston had been transferred into her presence, she was realizing for the first time just how exasperating its constant fawning could be.

She remained aloof, yet Houston's shallow sentiments continually pattered against the veneer of her mind in a feeble attempt to ingratiate itself—or *him*self.

". . . worked perfectly, Your Majessty. Melgána, the repressentative you tassked with my insstruction, was most forthcoming with many of the more advancced techniquess you employ to manipulate both the vext and the Ixx. With her assistance, I absorbed sufficient essencce from my erstwhile nephew to project a tangible representation to fool their sensorss. An excellent strategy. It's such a pity Melgána's effortss in teleporting Stark and Harper over such a vasst distance killed her. I sstill have much to learn."

Va-ákil wasn't fooled by this projection of false regret.

Keep your opinions to yourself, she snapped, *Melgána was a fool who thought her power and recent elevation to Prátor gave her license to express her own free will. And while she might have eventually regained my favor had she survived, she learned to her cost the price of stepping beyond her station.*

Anxiety leaked from Houston in waves, and Va-ákil found the sensation both delicious and redolent with possibilities.

And if you wish to address me, you'd best learn a more sophisticated form of communication. You have the wherewithal to employ telepathy, so do so. Verbal speech is an irritation I am inclined to punish rather than ignore.

"Of coursse . . ." *Of course, Your Majesty,* Houston simpered, *forgive my naivety. I know I lack understanding, but that is why I have been at pains to prove my resourcefulness. Despite my nephew's interference, my plans have been an unqualified success, yes?*

That is the second time you have used such an expression. What is a . . . nephew?

An outdated fleshly bond that shackles fools to courses of action they do not agree with. I am glad to be free of it now that I am superior and gaining suffi –

Then why is it *still alive?*

The spark of genuine puzzlement radiated by the abomination intrigued Va-ákil.

With the utmost sincerity, Houston replied, *He is alive to facilitate the next stage of my master plan . . . er, with your blessing, of course. I did mention this aspect to you previously. Although my origins lack the technical complexity possessed by your pureblood enemies, my union with Permian Hasanem, captain of the Shivan-Estre, provided me with certain insights that guide my every step. As you will be aware, although his transmutation was halted by the lydium barrier, he was a pioneer of our race, predating even Your Majesty's grace by many, many years and . . .*

Our race? Va-ákil thought to herself. *The presumptuousness of this fool.*

. . . and his acumen furnished me with the knowledge to ensure the flawless—

Va-ákil thought of an elegant solution to her dilemma:

Battlemaster, she called, *it would serve me if you avail yourself of this creature's strategy. Houston has been guided by the vision of one who, it transpires, was first to undergo the expansion toward enlightenment, so I am sure you will quickly see the value (or otherwise) of his counsel. Assist me now in making an accurate determination of our next steps.*

As you wish, Altás replied.

Bristling with indignation, the Prime Catalyct led Houston to one side, and Va-ákil approved the way her mate exuded an air of unconcealed malice.

Regardless, Houston's resolve didn't waver, not even for a moment.

Hmm. It is committed to a course it feels will ensure its survival. Good. That bodes well for us.

At the corner of her eye, the vext shimmered, and Tadãhk appeared from within the rarified substance of hyperspace.

Tadãhk, she called, *you survived, I see?*

Barely, my Queen.

He stomped toward her, and she sensed the mix of outrage and concern proliferating equally in his thoughts.

The vermin possess bane-metal in abundance. Their foul brew disrupts the matrix binding our essence together, and they are liberal in their willingness to share its nature with us. A paradox, for while I was in close proximity to their hive craft, I discerned the thoughts of those undisciplined in the art of guarding their minds. Majesty, despite the horrors inflicted on our fellow Kresh on the nearby world, it may shock you to know they feel they are here to save us.

Save us?

Yes. To them we are a travesty of nature, and they seek to free us from what they perceive is a mutation of our true form. His aura darkened. *However, those we tried to bait into rescuing their lost brethren were . . . they were . . .*

Yes?

My queen, although they wore armor to shield them from my sight and from my probes, their actions revealed their true intent and purpose. They were there to kill Kresh. And in that undertaking they are skilled beyond measure. Never have I witnessed such single-minded determination. Were it not for my presence of mind, I would be among those now gracing the Halls of Vashenta. And Majesty, Tadãhk stepped forward, *I must warn you that this selfsame sentiment is shared by the chattel now streaming from the smaller craft upon the surface. Those within are likewise protected from mental manipulation. Nevertheless, their vocalizations exhibit a united cause. They do not wish to aid us. Instead, they seek revenge for the actions that resulted in the death of a number of their brethren when we defended our kinfolk.*

Then I'd better warn Romũle and Remíle.

Already done. I stopped by on my return. They have assured me our barriers will not fail until you deem they should, and that the other countermeasures have been primed as instructed.

Perfect.

My Queen? Altás lumbered quickly to her side. *You need to listen to what the Houston has to say. I must confess, it is . . . he has . . . just listen.*

Altás stepped aside and a simpering Houston undulated forward.

Thank you, Battlemaster, Houston said. *As I have maintained, I only seek to serve and show how competent my people and I can be.*

Your people? Va-ákil interrupted. *It appears you misunderstand the extent of my benevolence. Should you continue to prove useful, I am prepared to extend mercy for you—and you alone. Your 'people,' as you so aptly put it, will service the needs of* my *people forthwith.*

Then I am happy my former associates will suffice, at least in one aspect of our brief but fruitful union. And as to my usefulness . . . Houston shrugged and committed the further indiscretion of pushing his strategy directly into Va-ákil's mind. *Judge for yourself.*

In that fleeting touch, the Magnate delved into the darkest corners of the abomination's consciousness. What she found there possessed elegance and a cold-heartedness that stayed her anger.

He is like us in so many ways.

Against her better judgment, she pondered the enormity of what lay ahead, and decided to be merciful. *Go then,* Va-ákil decreed, *and take the Prime Catalyct with you. If you can ensure all is in place for when we need it most, perhaps you may yet win a permanent position amongst us.*

As they left, movement on the far side of the cavern alerted Va-ákil that she was being watched. She warmed immediately and extended an invitation.

Don't linger there in the shadows, apart and alone. Anyone would think you regret your decision to return to the path of illumination. Is not survival of the species one of the most noble and just causes any creature could fight for?

Oh, I don't regret it, Caym replied, stepping out into the light. *Subterfuge and withholding of information apart, I'm merely surprised I got away with it so easily.*

Va-ákil was perceptive. Something was on the former Lega'trix's mind.

And?

And I can't help but wonder if my betrayal shall come back to haunt me.

*

Marcus followed his men down the landing ramp.

He'd not felt so alive in a long time, and the anticipation coursing its way through his veins made his heart pound fiercely within his chest.

At last. This *is what we are trained for*. This *is what we do best.*

Crystallized flakes of the re-genesis matrix saturated the ground in a hoary coating of frost. As he stepped onto the soil, it crunched softly beneath his feet like compacted snow. Stirred by the wind, each fleck mingled freely with the dirt of centuries of abuse and decay.

His gaze strayed across the lowland to find a mirrored curve that shone as if a huge glass ball had sunk into the ground until only its top protruded. Extending outward from the promontory, it masked what lay behind with an ease that served as a chilling reminder of all they yet faced.

Mohammed's suspicions were right. That's what the energy spikes related to. The Horde knows why we're here; they're making it obvious they won't go down without a fight. A spark of excitement ignited along his nerves. *Just as we hoped they would . . .*

Flavius, this day is for you.

The *Orison* had done its job well. The entire four-hundred-yard stretch of open ground leading up to the barrier had been totally cleared of enemy presence. The only remaining evidence of resistance was the odd scorch mark here and there, where a number of ogres had been immolated together when death rained on them from above.

Surveying the field, Marcus could see piles already driven into the ground and telescopic rods extended. Moments later, the sizzling blue curtain everyone had come to know so well sprang into being.

Now it's safe, and we're not going anywhere unless we choose to.

Behind him, Walter "Jack" Daniels, pilot of the *Orison*, followed protocol to the letter. No sooner had the beachhead been established than his ship descended in a cloud of ash and dust to join formation with the other drop craft.

As the whine of the engines droned down, Marcus drew himself to his full height. "Ninth Legion," he bellowed, foregoing the convenience of his helmet microphone. "Fall in."

His voice rolled along the valley, and he watched with pride as the instincts and habits of his men manifested. Before the echoes of his order had faded, the milling throng of all three centuriae transmogrified into a tactically-arranged and battle-ready army.

Now for their surprise.

"Legion, stand easy."

They relaxed, but Marcus could see the puzzled glances many of his legionnaires cast toward one another. Some looked disturbed, frustrated at having their backs to the source of peril. Others frowned, perplexed but intrigued by whatever might be so important it couldn't wait until later.

He decided to end their agony.

"Before we prepare to engage the enemy, you should know the significance of the undertaking we have been tasked with. At the Battle of the Line, the actions of the Ninth Legion did much more than save a city. As such, our original eagle now stands in place of honor within the Hall of Remembrance, serving as a permanent reminder to all of the valor, strength, and sacrifice of those who gave their lives so a world and an entire civilization might live.

"The road ahead is no less daunting, for our actions this day may very well decide the fate of the galaxy. To ensure the survival of the human race, the cancer of the Horde must be excised from existence once and for all. So, how could we commit to such an occasion without an appropriate banner behind which to unite?"

Marcus sensed the change in mood as many realized what was about to happen. Before, it had been focused, tense and dark as men prepared themselves to fight or die.

Now it was electric.

He raised his fist, and a drum roll issued from the *Orison*'s belly hatch.

A clatter of hooves on metal, then on dirt, and Tiberius Tacitus, Triari Centurion of the Legion, appeared on horseback. As he advanced, he hoisted their new standard high. A golden bird of prey sat atop an ebony pole, itself inlaid with rose-coral and tourmaline carvings depicting the letters *SPQR*. With wings and talons spread wide and beak agape, the fiery ensign sparked a response the moment the Ninth laid eyes on it.

Thunderous cheering broke out.

Marcus allowed them to vent their pleasure as Tiberius rode back and forth in front of the lines. Eventually, Tiberius came to a halt before him.

"You will note our new banner portrays a targén from the Erásan Mountains, a creature very similar to the eagles of home. You've seen targéns hunt. They are one of the fiercest predators on Arden, whose courage, power, and endurance are second to none. You've seen them in defense of their young. They are relentless, and will battle to their last breath rather than abandon their own. Men of the Ninth, are these not the principles by which we live and fight?"

Another roar ascended to the heavens.

Marcus got a lump in his throat and had to cough to cover his emotions.

"Felix Nerva, stand forward."

The notorious soldier stepped out.

"You might think your deeds of late have earned my derision. Far from it. You are a man of honor who earned his place within the primi ordinis many years ago, and someone who has shown his quality and bravery on many occasions since." Marcus took the Aquila from Tiberius, and then extended it toward the warrior before him. "I can think of no one better. Will you adopt this charge and defend it with your life?"

Whistles and whoops signified the popularity of the selection. Despite his recent gaffs, Felix had been with the first cohort for eight of his twelve years in the legion. And while clumsy at times, he was like a predator possessed in battle; surefooted and lethal.

Felix straightened.

Tall and proud, he answered, "I do."

"Then accept this signum and be our aquilifer."

Once more the atmosphere rang with approbation.

Oh yes. History will remember the day the Ninth avenged their brothers.

Marcus let it ride for a while, for the occasion was serving its purpose.

Then, suddenly businesslike, he bellowed, "What are you waiting for? A kiss from your mothers? Someone to tuck you in and tidy your shirttails? Ninth Legion, attend."

The massed ranks responded instantly, and the ether resounded to the clash of armor and clangor of steel as weapons were brought back to the shoulder.

"Hastati units to the front, cubic formation. Principes, fall in behind. About face."

The ground shook as more than four hundred soldiers executed the required drill maneuver simultaneously.

"Present arms."

Ordnance and booted feet crashed once more, and the army stood ready.

"Aquilifer, station."

Felix hoisted the eagle and took two sharp paces backward to stand beside his commander.

Marcus had kept the strategy of their deployment as familiar as possible, for a legion's strength lay in its ability to meter out its combat power over protracted periods. They did so by adopting formations which allowed the troops to rotate and tactically redeploy to different positions, thereby conserving stamina and extending their fighting efficiency. Veterans all, every man before him was tried and tested.

And now they're all fired up and raring to kill.

"Legion, you know why we're here. Prepare to march."

While he wouldn't be utilizing the usual skirmishing lines, he had something far more flexible. Marcus turned and waved.

And here they come.

A flurry of hooves and snorting of horses signaled the approach of Jake Rixton's new company. As they passed, the mounted columns split into four distinct groups and divided themselves east and west.

"Rousing speech," Jake called. Both he and Angus trotted over. "Orders?"

"Not really. Simply do what you do best to protect our flanks and pick off stragglers." Marcus gestured at the dome. "In view of the circumstances, I'll ask you to stay alert to the potential of observation posts. Get your boys to use their binoculars to scour the hills and high ground for any unusual distortions. As Angule once emphasized, the Controllers will seize any opportunity to gather in isolation, and to monitor and report on enemy tactics."

"High ground?" Jake scratched his head. "There's not a lot of that about."

"Oh, it's there, believe me. Hidden behind that mirror." Marcus seized his opportunity: "If I may, I'd like to keep a section of your men reserved as a flying picket. We now know the Grand Masters are capable of carrying someone with them when they teleport. I'd hate to think what might happen if they got behind us as we left the protection of the permanent null-point barriers. My men are carrying mobile telescopic poles, but will need time to deploy them in the heat of battle."

"Funny you should say that." Jake grinned. "Angus and I discussed the possibility of that very tactic, so we've distributed a couple of emitters between each of our guys. If things get hairy, we can always ride ahead and clear a space for a temporary command post or regroup position. Even if we only get a chance to lay down several rods, it could make all the difference"—he turned to wink at his highland colleague—"as we're hoping to demonstrate."

"Good thinking."

"Anyway," Jake shrugged and edged his horse around in a full circle, "it looks pretty quiet to me, so we probably—whoa, boy!"

Jake's mount crow-hopped and snorted, suddenly skittish. Then Angus's own colt backed away, neighing loudly. Marcus felt the ground shudder beneath his feet. Before him, heads swiveled from side to side as tense and agitated soldiers attempted to locate a source of possible danger.

"You had to say it, didn't you?" Marcus sighed.

"'Ware the shield!" someone called out over the secure net.

Marcus watched as the dome flickered, revealing tantalizing glimpses of a rugged escarpment with buildings and pylons running along its top, and what appeared to be a series of cave entrances below.

Another, stronger quake gripped the earth, so Marcus vaulted up behind Jake to better survey the scene.

From horseback, Marcus spotted a large group of fiends swarming toward what was clearly a power relay station at a point just inside the perimeter of the failing defense.

Gods, what a stroke of luck.

Still astride Jake's mount, Marcus cupped his hands to his mouth, and yelled, "Legion, that building is now your objective. Quick march."

As one, each centuria started their advance.

They passed through the one-way null-point barrier, and Marcus waited for the cadence of their steps to settle.

"Double mark time," he bellowed.

A foot beat later, the army broke into a sustained jog

Marcus checked to ensure his helmet-cam was recording the incident and opened a channel to the *Shadow of Autumn*.

"Gold Command, this is Silver. Are you getting this? We have just experienced an incident of some kind. From the feel of it, originating underground. Whatever the cause, it has resulted in the distortion you are seeing to the Horde barrier along with their instant response. In my opinion, something has happened to interrupt the adequate provision of energy, and they appear keen to regain control. We are moving to engage."

"Yes, yes," Mohammed replied, "we've got that. Seraphim confirms the plans show that facility to be the surface structure of an external power distribution center. While not designed to generate any form of shielding, we suspect the Horde have attempted to incorporate its capacity into their overall defensive capability."

A sizzling retort fried the air, and the reflective sheen of the bubble frittered away. Before Marcus could respond, a different sound distinguished itself, an ascending hum that rose in pitch and transposed into a prolonged howl. Then the top of the escarpment disappeared behind another, smaller, opaque sphere.

The yowling got louder, and a multitude of flaring, snarling effigies exploded from the tunnels beneath.

Marcus judged them to be more than three hundred yards from the Legion's target, and every one of them were grunts.

Backup and cannon fodder. Every second they are exposed to the re-genesis matrix, they become weaker. They must be desperate to keep that—

"Marcus?" Mohammed's voice in his ear sounded urgent. "Under no circumstances are you to allow them to retake that station."

"Understood."

Marcus slid from the horse's back and looked up. "Angus, Jake, you're up. Buy the foot soldiers time to set up an effective defense."

Setting heels to flanks both men wheeled away, shouting instructions over the comlink. The mounted units deployed along the east and west phalanxes surged forward.

The gap widened rapidly and as Marcus fell in behind the first centuria, an image of the men they had so recently lost flashed through his mind. Pale as moonlight, their translucent faces stared out from shadowed depths. Mouths wide, their eyeless orbs conveyed a sense of need, as if pleading for validation or anything that would give their deaths meaning.

Patience, brothers, you will be avenged soon.

Shaking himself free of specters, Marcus activated the internal net and issued fresh orders:

"Third centuria, break left and support the mounted units in capturing that building. Tacitus? Once you have secured the perimeter, move inside and make sure the interior structure is free of infestation.

"Vergilius? Take the Second and engage the Horde reserves rushing to assist their brethren. It will please me if you crush them entirely.

"Tiberius. Divide the first centuria into two. Half are to strengthen the perimeter around the relay post. The rest will act in support of Vergilius. You have your orders, all units advance to contact."

Marcus scanned ahead. Both elements of the cavalry charge were closing on their respective targets. While Jake and his platoon rode directly for the station and those fiends closest to it, Angus and his men made a beeline for the Horde reinforcements.

A sound strategy. If we can prevent them from coming together, it will be easier for us to pick them apart.

Jake's group arrived first. Looping in from the plain, they grazed the leading edge of the initial faction without slowing. As they passed, Marcus saw their arms rise and fall in rhythmic unison along with flashes of muted sunlight on bronze. Even at this distance, the sizzling retort of each stinger snapping home was clearly audible. Sparks danced and lightning flared as monsters died in one place after another. And with nearly fifty troopers to play with, Jake was able to keep his men circling to deliver an almost constant merry-go-round of withering punishment.

To the north, Angus had also positioned his men wisely to meet the challenge. Like Jake, his initial sweep devastated the front ranks of the charge. However, instead of turning and simply trying to deal with superior numbers head-on, Angus adjusted his strategy to suit.

Intrigued, Marcus watched as the leading highlanders sped away from the engagement until they reached a point midway between the stampede and the advancing second centuria. There, the first riders to arrive reined in and jumped from their saddles. Once on the ground, they deployed their personal cache of mobile emitter poles. As subsequent warriors rode past, they dropped their rods for their friends to employ and returned to the fray just long enough to deliver another stinging rebuke. Only then did they join their fellows behind the safety of an ever-expanding series of bulwarks.

Angus's voice crackled over the radio:

"Ye might like to direct Vergilius and his boys toward the corrals. Why have them run all the way when the wee beasties are so eager to come and say halloo? His men will have a chance to catch their breaths and deliver a personal welcome as the bastards try to siphon through the narrow gaps we've left. We'll stay to pick off any crafty buggers who try to circle around—" A poignant scream as someone was unhorsed signified this had been no easy task. "Hurry along now, it looks like our friends are getting a mite feisty."

Marcus laughed aloud at his former enemy's audacity and equanimity under pressure.

Oh, masterfully done.

"Vergilius?" Marcus commanded. "You heard the man. I suggest you get in there before our Caledonian brother takes all the glory."

Orders were relayed, and the second centuria picked up the pace and fanned out toward the barriers.

Confident they would take care of business, Marcus turned to discover Tacitus and his unit had just arrived at the power station and engaged what remained of the enemy. From what he could see, it would be an easy victory. The Horde had been so intent on reaching the building first that Jake had reduced their number by more than half. Now, only a score remained.

A tight knot swarmed the doorway and crashed inside, hotly pursued by a small contingent of legionnaires.

Marcus clasped his centurion by the shoulder and gestured toward the structure.

"Tiberius, Gold Command needs to know why the Horde are so keen to take that building. I'll take a contubernium with me while you carry on and assist Vergilius. Remember our brother, Flavius. Don't leave a single one of them alive."

"I don't intend to." Tiberius growled.

Saluting, the centurion snapped his fingers and dispatched the closest group to escort their general, before hurrying the rest of the centuria along to catch up with their fellow fighters.

Urgent shouting and a series of muffled explosions indicated a fierce battle raging inside the relay station. Then everything went quiet.

As Marcus and his team jogged up to the outer picket, the door crashed open and Gaius Sextus, Tesserarius for the eighth contubernium emerged, closely followed by seven of his men. Sadly, they were carrying several bodies between them.

The sergeant's left arm was blackened and, from the way he grimaced and nursed the limb against his chest, causing him considerable pain. Nevertheless, Gaius retained a fire in his eyes and gripped his sword tightly in his right hand.

Walking directly up to Marcus, he nodded and grinned. "They're all dead, sir. For some reason, once we caught up to them they stopped running and tried to prevent us from reaching a large monolith covered with lots of glowing lights." He cocked his head. "Come, I'll show you."

His interest aroused, Marcus followed the veteran inside.

The interior was far more austere than the exterior suggested.

Most of the space was filled by three huge power lines rising from beneath the ground along the southern perimeter. Each channel bored into a series of static converters and phase transformers, which in turn fed a massive generator. On the far side, a chain of cables and ducts divided off toward all points of the compass before sinking back into the floor via a multitude of heavily-insulated photonic conduits.

A tall, glowing contraption dominated an open area at the exact center of the room. Looking much like an obelisk, its numerous screens and blinking lights revealed that the automated system was both operative and handling extremely high volumes of power.

Next to it, an everyday workstation looked oddly out of place, especially as the decking beneath bore a cluster of scorch marks.

How odd. Why didn't the Horde simply drain it like they've done virtually everywhere else?

"Commander?" Seraphim's voice was insistent. "Please train your camera on the device in the middle of the room."

Marcus did as instructed.

"It is as I suspected," the AI continued. "This facility forms a major part of a power distribution grid. Perhaps Exordium's council elected to compartmentalize the entire system, so that any one station could take over in a crisis. Obviously, such an arrangement couldn't be permanent, since it would severely strain the capacitors. Nevertheless, it would appear that is exactly what has occurred here."

"Why do you say that?"

"Observe the master unit. The top series of lights are extinguished, suggesting something has blown."

Marcus glanced at the pillar. Sure enough, an entire bank of green-colored indicators along the top lay cold and inert.

"I take it that's good news?" he enquired.

"It certainly is. Pan your camera back over to the computer console next to the main processor. *That* is a command-and-control override. Although the mental interlink coronet is missing, the DNA and voice-control recognition system look to be functional. If they are, three Senatum-level officials will be able to shut down the capacitors and divert power away from the substructure beneath the promontory outside . . . once they've entered the appropriate codes, of course."

"So the Horde will have no shields?"

"Correct."

We'll be able to block off every exit and wipe them out. When are we going to get another opportunity like this?

"Then it's fortunate we have three such individuals with us. We'll sanitize the area and ensure all is safe. In the meantime, please apprise Mohammed, Calen, and Shaní so they can make their way here forthwith."

"They are already proceeding to the transporter room."

Marcus turned to his officers:

"Gaius, select your best men and secure this facility. No one is to enter without my permission. Tacitus, you and your centuria are with me. We'll mop up what's left outside, and then prepare the men for the final push."

"And then it will be over?"

The centurion's question took Marcus by surprise.

"Yes, my friend." He clasped Tacitus by the shoulder. "We'll avenge Flavius, return home victorious, and have a chance to grow old and fat at last."

As they walked back out into the pale sunshine, Marcus had to admit:

I can't believe it'll finally be over.

Chapter Thirty-One

Onions

The latest in a long line of obstacles fell, and Marcus waited for the dust to settle before ushering the drones across the threshold. Behind him, the gravity generators were doing their job, ensuring the newly-opened seam didn't collapse on them while keeping the choking cloud of debris from smothering everyone in an all-enveloping pall. Arduous work, but necessary: so far they hadn't suffered a single casualty.

Marcus used the lull to reflect on recent events.

Once Mohammed and the rest of his advisory staff had arrived, technicians were able to drop the smaller, surface bubble to reveal the rest of the escarpment. Comprised of granite and limestone, the colonists had taken advantage of its imposing height to crown it with several large, and a cluster of smaller, ancillary buildings. Spread out in groups along the plateau, those structures still served an unknown purpose. But blueprints suggested the complex had been built to facilitate experiments of the sort which must take place in a large domed chamber situated nearly a mile underground.

Indeed, most of the strangely fluctuating energy transmissions they had been monitoring since arriving here had originated from its subterranean locus. And that area could only be accessed via a labyrinthine web of marmoreal tunnels (a network comprised of naturally occurring and fabricated arteries) which provided admittance to numerous interconnected grottos and galleries.

Marcus couldn't be sure what was hidden within the maze itself, for the passages and chambers were interspersed with dead zones—regions that had obviously been prepared by their "hosts" to slow the legion's advance and divide their number.

After studying maps of the entire cave system and the adjoining aboveground complex, Seraphim confirmed the presence of an insulated set of power lines leading down into their objective. Those conduits originated in a dedicated relay station, similar in design to the one they had recently secured out on the plain. Good news indeed, as this indicated a strong possibility that they'd find another command-and-control interface with an override capability—or some other option to counter the threat presented by the mystery underground pockets.

In response, Mohammed, Calen, and Shaní had ventured topside, under the protection of Sam and his team, to investigate the complex while Marcus and his legion set about gaining entry into the labyrinth. No easy task, for the promontory had six separate adits at ground level, and a further three sinkholes high on the bluff itself.

Although from simpler times, Marcus had a talent for tactics and strategy, and quickly decided that too many access points meant he couldn't divide his forces safely. To counter that problem, he devised a straightforward approach. Using the resources at his disposal, Marcus assigned the *Abeille*, *Ballarat*, and *Eurus* to one of the three cenotes with orders to collapse the subterranean shafts in on themselves. Once done, he instructed them to mine the rubble and remain in situ to cover the exits with their main guns.

Having addressed the threat of a possible counterstrike via those avenues, he then extended that tactic to the ground level caves. Five of the six openings were in close proximity to each other. He ordered those particular entrances destroyed and left under the watchful eye of Jake's company and the *Orison*.

This done, Marcus gathered the legion at the only remaining point of ingress to begin their final march upon the mystery chamber far below.

His methods proved sound. Even so, the going was frustratingly slow, for each dead zone was protected from detailed scans by energy-absorbing barriers which effectively masked everything within a one-hundred-yard radius. And as they had seen, those pockets didn't conceal only the detritus of centuries of disuse. Oh, no. On two occasions the legionnaires discovered isolated packs of Horde grunts waiting to surprise them. Thus they proceeded with utmost caution, resorting to laser cutters to circumvent hazards by carving through bare rock.

Now more than halfway to their objective, they had at last broken through into what the charts indicated was the final major gallery. Beyond, only one barricade remained. After that, Marcus knew the Horde would throw everything they had at them, for they would be fighting for the survival of their race.

A race I intend to exterminate.

As the drones commenced their preliminary scans, Marcus caught a glimpse of the mysteries within. This chamber had been formed over eons by the action of water on porous sedimentary rock. The air was stale and thick with dust. It was also laden with refuse and minerals, evidence that someone or something had been hard at work here in the recent past.

He paused to check his readings.

From what I can see, the Ardenese colonists used to call this area the Cathedral, and I can appreciate why.

Stalactites plunged like crystallized spinal columns from the shadows high above, while stalagmite ghouls rose up from rancid pools below. Where they joined, bleached colonnades glimmered off into the distance, creating a haphazard maze difficulty for his men to navigate on foot. Around the perimeter, tunnels punctuated the glistening walls like silent screams, each desperate to shock their unwanted visitors into a hasty retreat.

Marcus called his centurions forward and expanded his holo-field so they had a better view of the route ahead.

"As you can see, the Cathedral follows the course of the scarp above us and extends to my right, southeast, for nearly half a mile. Numerous halls and cavities lead into it, so we'd best steer clear and keep on schedule. Our objective lies that way"—he gestured to his left—"and if Mohammed and his team do manage to find another command-and-control terminal, they'll hopefully be able to drop the barrier that otherwise awaits us, four hundred yards in that direction.

"Tacitus? I think the easiest option would be to filter your men inside so they can form a null-point wall a few hundred feet to the south . . . *here*." Marcus pointed to an area on his pad where a large cul-de-sac projected away from the main cavern. "This way, you cut off any chance of Horde backup appearing from those side tunnels; and you can keep the road clear for our retreat. As we proceed toward our target, the rest of the Third can follow us for a similar distance to the northeast and adopt the same defensive line *there*, understood?"

"It will be done," Tacitus replied. "The third centuria will keep the door open until you return."

Marcus turned to Vergilius.

"Brother, I want the Second to lead our advance until we reach the Horde's last line of defense. You know as well as I do that they're massed and waiting for us at the other end. So far, it's been too quiet for my liking. Deploy in manipular formation, scutums ready, and expect an ambush at any moment. I don't imagine for one second they'll allow us to stroll up unhindered and simply say hello. When we do go in, expect a tidal wave of resistance to come sweeping down on us. Lock shields, form testudo, and allow them to roll over you. Most will die from simply encountering the nature of the null-point energy, so you will provide a great distraction as Tiberius and I move to counter.

"Tiberius? You form the main part of our thrust into the central chamber, so have your men draw their modern weaponry from the word go. Be prepared." He paused to look at each man directly. "One last thing. Ensure everyone activates their helmet-mounted flashlights. I don't want you stumbling about in the dark if the drones become otherwise engaged at a crucial moment. You have your instructions."

His commanders moved away, passing on his orders. With smooth precision, the legion filed inside and fanned out to take up their respective positions.

Marcus followed. He hadn't taken more than twenty paces when he noticed a soft crackling underfoot. He glanced down and saw a brittle ivory powder covering the floor in a light dusting.

Did the re-genesis matrix manage to percolate down through the barriers? Amazing. It'll make our job a damned sight easier if it did.

Putting that hope out of his mind, he concentrated instead on the hazards presented by their surroundings. Even after the third centuria left for their designated positions, breathing room was tight. So closely packed were the stalagmites and stalactites that he and his men were constantly squeezing between petrified tears, and the endless weave and bob soon grew exhausting. What's more, their only light came from random illuminations cast by the drones or their helmet-cams. When these caught exposed facets of rock, the gloom was transposed by scintillant prismatic aspirations that only served to confound the eye.

Strange, how in a place and at a time like this, beauty can be an unwanted distraction.

Undeterred, they pressed forward, dogged, cautious.

Five minutes later, the telltale gleam of an energy barrier came into view. More than ten yards across and eighteen feet high, the huge blockade loomed at the exact point where the maze ended and the Cathedral narrowed into a natural chokepoint.

And beyond, we finally come to the end of our journey.

Vergilius snapped his fingers and his men deployed, adopting a series of defensive formations in preparation for the assault. Behind them, members of the first centuria completed final weapons checks.

"General," someone hissed, "come and look at this."

A group of soldiers to his left stood by a small fissure. From his position, the entrance was difficult to see, for it was shrouded in darkness and bent back in on itself. As Marcus strode toward them, the crunching sound beneath his feet became louder. He looked more closely, and got the impression that he walked on broken shards of discarded porcelain vessels.

He reached the crevice and peered inside to find a modest-sized antre. Except this was no fairytale grotto. It was full of bones.

Thigh bones, rib bones, pelvic bones. Femurs, fibulae, tibiae. And skulls. Skulls lay everywhere. Some were intact and grinning insanely, as if delighted at the prospect of a friendly face after an eternity of isolation; others lay in ruins, fragmented or crushed into dust. Only then did Marcus realize what they'd all been stepping on.

Of course, they must have fled here in their numbers during the initial outbreak, hoping to escape the madness. But they were found . . . and by berserkers too, from the look of it.

He studied the way the remains had been shattered and strewn about.

Not content to simply devour the essence of their victims, the monsters must have torn everyone apart, perhaps to enhance the flavor of their meal with terror?

In his mind's eye, Marcus tried to reenact the scene.

Even so, it hurt to imagine the insatiable hunger of frenzied fiends as they rampaged, and the inevitable reaction of the helpless colonists as their flight led them here to their doom.

And they couldn't have realized their panic would act like a beacon, drawing that doom toward them like moths to a flame. Except these *moths were hulking great monstrosities driven by a craving so rabid it bordered on delirium.*

Roars of glee, screams of terror. Flashing talons, primal cruelty. Severed limbs, tumbling in aerial display. Crimson orbs, glowering with lust. Ruby entrails, spilling gore. Glittering fangs and punctured jugulars, spraying blood in a fountain wash, staining ancient seams in the splith of human ruin.

An itch wormed its way up Marcus's spine. He backed away and looked outside. The sense of unease was spreading: his hardened veterans glanced nervously from side to side. As they moved, their helmet lights sent peril reeling across the ceiling and cast flickering threats that made it appear as if danger lurked behind each column and within every shadow.

"Can you feel that?" Tiberius called.

The prickling intensified, and soon Marcus's bowels were shuddering.

I've felt that sensation before.

"They're coming," Marcus bellowed. "Notify surface units and stand to."

*

Impatient to press on, Mohammed showed his agitation in a multitude of ways. To no avail. Whatever he did, Sam resolutely ignored him, and continued to do things by the book. *His* book.

I'll just have to grin and bear it, Mohammed admitted. *He's not going to budge.*

The moment they boarded the *Ballarat* for the short hop onto the plateau, Sam turned to him and matter-of-factly stated, "Just so you know, I'm not going to get involved in a pissing contest or anything like that, but down here you're in *my* world. Your safety is in my hands. You may be the boss, but in this environment what *I* say goes. You'll move when I tell you, where I tell you. And just so we're clear. If we run into trouble, expect to be manhandled. My squad is under strict instructions to keep you alive . . ." Then he grinned in a way Mohammed could only describe as evil, and whispered, "At least until the subterranean barrier is down."

To Mohammed's amazement, the armored warrior had then lowered his visor, turned to Calen and Shaní, and coldly added, "That goes for you two as well. So keep your eyes and ears open and obey instructions."

Thus warned, everyone strapped in, and Mohammed was left wondering exactly how serious Sam was, making such a statement.

He soon found out.

Their landing site was once the quadrangle of the facility, occupying a huge open space in the center of four main buildings. Freshly downloaded plans from Exordium's database showed them to include a laboratory and teaching wing to the north, with a combined astrometrics and deep-space observatory overlooking the plains to the south; an impressive administration block to the east and even larger habitat/recreation center, due west, completed the setup.

The *Ballarat* had dropped them off fifteen minutes ago, and Mohammed had been keen to make his way to the power plant some four hundred yards beyond the campus precincts: If another override net-link existed inside, the legion's task would become much simpler.

But Sam wouldn't hear of it.

Leaving Mohammed stewing in his own juices, he held everyone in place while several flights of robot sentries were sent to complete thorough scans of the surrounding faculty.

Time dragged in the interim, but at last the drones were returning.

About time. Marcus and his lot set off well before us, so they must be deep inside the cave system by now.

Seraphim's voice issued from a command unit hovering above their heads.

"Captain Pell. Scans confirm there are no anomalous readings, dead zones, or Horde-sign within any of the main surface structures before you. As an added precaution, I positioned motion and energy trackers around the perimeter, and tasked Gamma flight to remain and monitor this area."

"Thank you, Seraphim," Sam replied. "Please task Delta flight to recce our route ahead." He paused to bring up an aerial view of the entire complex. "The power station is *here*, four hundred and thirty-two yards beyond the northeastern perimeter. *This* will be our route." A red phosphorous line appeared, leading from their current location to a blinking blue dot. "We'll head just north of the admin block and then branch east. I estimate a journey time of at least ten minutes, so I—"

"Ten minutes?" Mohammed gaped in surprise. "Why so long?"

Sam turned to face him.

"Because as you've seen, safety comes first. 'Fools rush in where angels fear to tread.' 'Look before you leap.' Here's a good one, it's an ancient Malayan proverb: 'Do you think there are no crocodiles because the water is calm?' I could quote these all day."

He's right. Mohammed conceded defeat. *I'm so hot to get things finished I've been acting like an idiot. I've got to make an effort to wind my neck in.* "Point taken," he sighed. "Thank you, Sam."

Calen and Shaní glanced toward Mohammed with puzzled looks. The armored warrior merely nodded and resumed his conversation with the sentry.

"As I said, I estimate a journey time of at least ten minutes. So task Delta flight to remain low, and ensure they emit a hard presence. If our Horde friends are hidden away, I want them to know the drones are here. We'll see if they're as disciplined as their buddies up on the Kalina. Have Epsilon flight maintain an overview from six hundred feet. If anything—and I mean *anything*—unusual or out of place appears, react instantly. Agreed?"

"Agreed."

A series of dull reports rang out, followed by a deep rumbling sound.

Around him, Sam's squad instantly raised their weapons, searching for danger. The ground beneath their feet shook as tremors amplified. Alarmed, Mohammed reached out to steady both himself and Shaní.

"Do not be anxious, Captain Amine," Seraphim advised. "You are merely witnessing the results of sinkholes and cave entrances being sealed as per Marcus's instructions. The charges were set to detonate simultaneously."

The vibrations quickly died away, and everyone relaxed.

Eight drones appeared. Four sped away ahead of them, while the remainder cloaked and shot into the atmosphere. As they did so, the Special Forces squad formed up.

Mohammed noticed how Sam positioned himself at the exact center of the group. Alpha team was also close, as if providing a personal escort, one for each VIP. Bravo team, however, extended their position into an elongated box configuration, ten yards out, front and back. Every one of them maintained a constant vigil over the open ground and buildings around them.

Shaní noticed it too. "Are all the soldiers of your world this thorough?" she asked. "It must be very tiring, maintaining such a high level of alertness."

"Not everyone can do it," Sam replied modestly, "but those who can . . . they adapt to it quite quickly. We think of it as creating an anally-retentive fixation for detail: detail that can make all the difference in life or death situations. Don't get me wrong, part of the selection process involves developing an extremely high level of fitness so you can cover vast amounts of ground carrying large quantities of kit in a short time. But when we can, we always prefer to take things nice and slow. More haste, less speed. A methodical approach allows an operator to notice all sorts of little clues that—hello?"

Ahead of them, Lady P's hand punched into the air. She dropped to one knee and everyone froze.

Her head dipped to her sights, and by the way the muzzle of her rifle kept playing back and forth, Mohammed could see she was scrutinizing an area about fifteen feet in front of her—where the quadrangle ended and a major thoroughfare began. Her movements gradually decreased until her weapon remained trained on one particular spot.

She made another gesture.

Sam's head cocked to one side, and Mohammed guessed he was in conversation with his lead scout over their covert net.

He was right:

A few moments later, Bob and Joe sprinted away from their escort positions and fanned out. When they reached opposite ends of the footpath, they converged from different sides on the location their colleague had indicated.

Each operative moved crisply but precisely, scanning the vicinity in front of them thoroughly before taking the next step. Soon, they were poised and ready to act.

At a signal from them, Lady P detached something from her harness and lobbed it gently onto the paved area. Mohammed heard the clatter of metal on tarmac, then on concrete.

A singularity grenade.

Womph!

The air sparked and squeezed inward toward a point of infinite darkness. Miniature plasma tendrils lanced out, working their way along the metal strip lining either side of the walkway. A whirling vortex appeared. With a shriek, the nearest flagstones, ripped from their mounts, were crushed to dust and swallowed whole.

They were followed by a boiling mass of light and shadow as concealed monstrosities were yanked from their hiding place and consigned to the same fate. The screeching reached a crescendo, only to snap off as the bomb imploded.

As the rebounding shockwave radiated outward, it was joined by several strontium-red effigies that leaped from the cavity and charged toward Mohammed's group.

The fact that the ogres had escaped their friends' doom did them little good. Before they had taken a dozen lumbering steps they were cut down in a blistering fusillade of magnetized rounds.

As quickly as it started, the confrontation ended.

The control sentry descended to study the contents of the would-be trap.

Look at the size of the hole.

"Jesus Christ," Mohammed cursed. "What the hell happened?"

Sam grabbed Mohammed's arm and ushered him toward the crater.

"Lady P tells me the pathways here have power conduits running beneath them. We've seen this aspect before in other cities on Rhomane. By incorporating multiple access points into the infrastructure, technicians saved time and hassle when it comes to completing everyday maintenance. The Horde must have anticipated what we might do, and secreted some of their number here to ambush us."

"So why didn't our scans pick them up?"

"Because of this," Seraphim interjected.

The command drone was examining a strange, glowing object that had survived the destruction. Octahedral in shape, it reminded Mohammed of an oversize crystallized bloodstone, due to its dark green and red coloring and lucent texture. He cupped one ear. The gem emitted a low buzzing noise, as if a wasp had been interred within its structure.

"What is it?"

"This is a biomemetic diffuser," Seraphim replied, "it absorbs the energy signature given off by a selected host and mimics it, emulating the entity itself or its surrounding environment."

"Really?" Sam cut in. "Then why haven't we heard of it before and, more importantly, why haven't these been incorporated into our defensive capabilities already? Can you imagine the advantage such a device would give us?"

"Because they're experimental," Seraphim said. "According to Exordium's scientific database, they had developed only a dozen prototypes before the outbreak started, and were still refining their parameters. They operate a bit like the Horde, in that they absorb the essence of whatever it is they're supposed to imitate. Scientists who tried them out reported symptoms of lethargy, nausea, and severe headaches."

"Hmm!" Sam's visor snapped up, and Mohammed saw he was deep in thought. "Then we have more of a problem than we realized. We've seen the Horde reduce themselves into a nearly catatonic state before." He glanced at Mohammed. "Remember back on Arden, out on the Sengennon Strait that time we were experimenting with the chameleon shields? They were hard to spot then. But *this* little beauty would make them nigh on invisible. What's more, it reveals a level of discipline that's a major cause for concern. Think about it. They were sealed inside that workspace with a rich power source: pure ambrosia to grunts like them and yet they daren't touch it, indicating these particular Triarium Tier members are more refined than their cousins, or—"

"Or they're more terrified of the consequences of disobedience," Mohammed said. He turned to Lady P, easily distinguished by the bright pink death's-head logo on her helmet. "So how did you spot it, Katy?"

"Every time I panned across that area my HUD went fuzzy, as if something greasy had been smeared across the projection lens. The trouble was, it was so faint I almost ignored it, thinking it might be a glitch within my optical resolution matrix. Consequently, I used the sights of my G420 to verify it." She shrugged. "Once I'd confirmed something was there, I applied our safety ethic . . . If in doubt, wipe it out."

"Amen," chorused those specialists close enough to hear the remark.

Amen indeed . . . And thank God!

"Well done," Sam added. "Update Seraphim with your digitized record. We can pass the new frequency throughout the entire network to ensure others don't get caught by the same trick."

Lady P did as instructed, and Mohammed used the lull to reflect on a painful and distressing truth. *This strain is most resilient. We are fortunate their queen chose to remain on Exordium, otherwise I fear our sorrows would have been compounded a thousandfold. In fact, I doubt we'd have survived long enough to bring the Ninth through to turn the tide*. He gazed long and hard at the crater. *What else could they possibly have up their sleeve?*

A nagging feeling tightened Mohammed's stomach.

"I know you have your procedures, but can we please press on?" He sidled a little closer to Sam. "These creatures are more formidable than the ones we faced on Arden, and I won't rest easy until I know we've removed the threat once and for all."

Sam considered the request. His visor snapped into place.

"I'm inclined to agree." He raised his voice and turned full circle. "Squad, listen in. We're going to pick up the pace. CQB offensive, VIP shielding. On the double!"

Mohammed noticed the change in mood immediately. Alpha team maneuvered in close. So close, in fact, the specialists were now standing shoulder to shoulder with their charges. Mohammed glanced to his right and saw that Bob Neville had been assigned to him. By the time he looked back, Bravo team had regrouped to form an outer shield around them.

On Sam's signal, everyone moved at once, and Mohammed felt himself propelled forward by the scruff of the neck. Sam shadowed them, constantly checking his arcs and the positioning of his troops.

They left the main concourse behind and skirted the administration block. Around the corner, a covered walkway cut a tangent across open ground. In the distance, their destination awaited them: a squat block of stone that exuded a chill all of its own. About two hundred yards along, their route was broken by a series of low-tiered stones with a strange-looking effigy at the center.

"Avoid that path and stick to the dirt," Sam snapped. "Scan for recent tracks or signs of disturbance."

They hadn't travelled more than halfway to the monument when two robot sentries dropped from the sky, guns blazing. Their 50mm cannons made short work of an area close to the decorative feature. As the footpath fragmented, ear-splitting shrieks cut the air, dragging like nails down the chalkboard of Mohammed's spine.

He suppressed a shiver.

The onslaught was quickly over, and by the time their party reached the scene, the Horde's latest hideaway was a smoldering ruin.

Mohammed had a question:

"Seraphim, can you task one of your units to collect any diffusers we come across? We can't miss an opportunity to take them back for further study."

"Certainly," the AI responded, "I'll have the trailing drone conduct a thorough search."

At that moment their group arrived at the sculpture. Mohammed didn't get a chance to say thank you. Out of breath, he was shoved down to the ground and forced to remain there while Bob stood over him and checked the vicinity.

Once Bob had finished, Mohammed coughed up dirt, scrabbled to his hands and knees and glanced around. He was dumbstruck to realize this feature had once been a flower and water garden, and that the structure at its center was an artfully contrived fountain. Of course, the Horde's presence had ensured the foliage had withered and died long ago. Now only dust eddies thrived here, spiraling across lifeless beds, stirred by winds sweeping across the barren plateau.

"We're halfway there," Sam called. He kneeled next to Mohammed. "Sir, it's obvious they expected us to make a move on the station. And after the day of surprises I've had, *that* makes me suspicions."

Sam's reference to the Kalina mission wasn't lost on Mohammed.

"I agree. What are you thinking?"

"I wish I knew. All these experimental, kick-ass amenities and defense gizmos. Are you telling me the Ardenese couldn't whip up a shield that would work properly?" Sam glanced across at Calen. "Chancellor, do you have an opinion?"

"I must confess," Calen replied, "I'm beginning to feel as if we're being led along the garden path somewhat." A pained expression crossed his face. "Please excuse the dreadful pun."

Around them, their ever-vigilant protectors groaned loudly.

"So tell me," Sam continued, "am I the only one who thinks we're following breadcrumbs toward a trap?"

Everyone fell silent.

He stood up and pointed toward the power station. "Because if we are, there's the box, and we've got to kick the stick away to get inside."

Mohammed curled into a crouch and stared first toward their destination, then back and forth across the space in between.

His own military background provided a possible solution: "Seraphim, how accurate are the Menta accelerators aboard the *Shadow of Autumn*?" Mohammed juggled various scenarios in his head. "And could they strafe this stretch of dirt in front of us without destroying us as well?"

"Taking current orbital and meteorological factors into consideration . . ." The control unit fell silent as its artificial consciousness completed computations. "There is a ninety-nine point nine percent probability that I can sustain a constant rate of fire for over a minute while maintaining accuracy to within one yard."

"No shit?" Mohammed grinned in delight.

"Indeed. Although I would caution you to withdraw to the main buildings."

"That's not in the cards, I'm afraid. We need to get inside, fast." Mohammed considered his options. "Seraphim, whether or not you register anything, I want you to rearrange the landscape before us. Remove any surprises that might be lingering there."

"Received and understood. Commencing barrage in . . . Three, two, one. *Now*."

Bloody hell, I didn't expect—

Mohammed's train of thought was interrupted when Bob grabbed hold of him and threw him roughly to the ground. As Mohammed hit the deck, he became aware of Sam issuing orders, and everyone else sprinting for the center of the garden.

"The walls of this feature will provide a degree of cover," Sam said. "Quickly, deploy your X-shields and huddle down by the fountain. Bravo team, you'll have the luxury of not having to share. You can maintain cover."

Mohammed was surprised. "You have X-shields?"

"We certainly do. When we saw the scutums Marcus had for his legion, we asked for a modified, collapsible-frame version. Ours are telescopic. That way, we can fold them down and carry them inside our packs. Handy bit of kit to have at times like—" He glanced up. "Watch out! Here they come."

Everyone scrambled for cover. Those positioned along the outer sill kept their guns trained on the approaches, while those inside huddled together as closely as they possibly could.

Mohammed wriggled around and looked upward, through the shimmering plane of the null-point barrier. Everything he saw possessed a blue tinge and a slight distortion. Nevertheless, when the first firefly appeared high in the sky, blazing a fiery trail through the firmament, he marked it instantly, for it was as spellbinding as it was heartrendingly beautiful.

Another flared to life right behind it. Then ten more. Then twenty. Gleaming coals that speckled the eggshell vault in burnt umber and cobalt hues of effervescent passion. In moments, the heavens above were ablaze with flames that danced and flickered as if fueled from within by nuclear furnaces.

Something stirred on the breeze, a rustling sound that reminded Mohammed of leaves at play or a prolonged inhalation of breath through closed teeth.

He blinked as the diamond gauze evolved into a raging tempest of metallic shooting stars, incendiary dross which burned and glowed ever hotter as it dared the purifying kiln of the upper atmosphere.

The whistling rush built into a scream. As the first projectiles bit into the ground, the wailing complaint distinguished itself into individual protests:

Zzzzt – Thud.

Zzzzt – Thud.

Zzzzt – Thud.

Mohammed tensed and tried to huddle into an even smaller ball. But the lure of witnessing such an event up close proved too strong to resist. With morbid curiosity, he bent round and craned his neck to gain a better view.

The terrain before him was dancing. To Mohammed, it looked as if dust-jacketed raindrops were exploding across the surface of an earth-colored drum. The rhythm intensified and a thundering tumult saturated everything in steel and phosphorous tears. Sparks spat, and soil and rock exploded upward in a chiaroscuro of expressions that sprayed lampyrid sprites high in the air. But not for long, for each fell prey to gravity and cascaded back to the ground in a slow-motion drizzle of earthen flakes.

The sound was deafening. Amid the clarion call of remorseless death, plaintive howls revealed several locations where avenging angels had found their targets.

Poor bastards. I can't believe I actually feel sorry for them. But to have all this *falling on you must be terrifying.*

A final volley hammered the ground, and silence descended once more.

Expressions of relief or amazement rang out around him.

"Fuck me, but that was awesome."

"Outstanding."

"Jesus H Christ."

"Fuckin' A."

"I think I shit myself."

"Is it over?" That last one was from Sam.

"Yes, Captain Pell," Seraphim replied. "The barrage is complete. It should be safe to proceed."

Mohammed shuffled onto his side. Shaní was lying by him, next to Eddie and tight against the fountain's protective bulk. He could see she was shaking, so he reached out to touch her arm.

"Are you all right?"

"I am now," she mumbled. "That was too intense for my liking."

Mohammed stroked the back of her fingers.

"I know, I know. I've served in the military for most of my life. Even so, it was daunting, being on the receiving end of such punishment. I don't think anyone could ever—"

Their tête-à-tête was interrupted as Sam issued fresh instructions.

"We're good to go, people. Collapse your shields and dust yourselves off. Let's get this over with."

The squad stowed their gear. Bravo team led the way across the ruined terrain. Shaní refused to release Mohammed's embrace, so Bob and Eddie adjusted their positions to compensate.

The open space had been completely destroyed, as if an enraged leviathan had reached down from the heavens and chewed everything to pieces. Solid rock had been blasted to smithereens and coated in layers of liquefied soil. Smoldering metal cooled in slag-tainted gray and black puddles, and the stench of cordite hung heavy in the air. Everything seemed darker somehow, as if the touch of death had added a permanent stain to the ether.

"Pick up the pace," Sam shouted. "Only a hundred yards to go."

Shaní squeezed Mohammed's hand. Together, they clambered up and down across the intervening moonscape.

Less than a minute later they stood outside their destination, a squat bare cube of lydium measuring some sixty feet square. From the outside, it gave no indication of the deluge it had survived, but for the blemishes marring its porch and the scars littering the footpath encircling its circumference.

Sam called his people together.

"Stu, Lady P, take a breather and watch our VIPs. Andy, Tosh, secure the perimeter. Alpha troop will clear the building." He turned to his own team. "Alpha, activate stealth mode, switch to internals, and prepare for hard entry."

The four specialists formed up and walked toward the entrance. As they went, the air rippled and they disappeared from sight. A moment or two later, the heavy hatch blew inward as if crushed by a gigantic unseen fist.

The sound of machine-gun fire and shrieking issued from inside, and for the briefest instant the door panel was highlighted by the lurid glare of muzzle flash. Then everything went dark. Sporadic concussive reports rang out. Every now and then, a series of muted explosions rocked the ground beneath their feet and a smattering of dust or other loose particles that had been thrown onto the structure fell to the ground.

Mohammed couldn't help but marvel at how safe he felt at this moment, and determined there and then to double the size of the Special Forces unit when they got back to Arden.

From what I've seen today, we need more people like this. He glanced about as Bravo team carried out its duties. Although relaxed, they still regarded the vicinity about them with a level of professionalism that made his heart swell with pride. *Ranger Initiative be damned. God, what could I do with an army of them?*

Then he glanced at Shaní and his heart skipped again. *She's a brave woman; she hasn't complained once.*

Shaní saw him looking and smiled.

He returned the gesture, and turned to hug her. *I'm a lucky man.*

"That's more like it," she murmured, coming into his arms. "It's about time you got over that self-conscious streak."

He grinned as Shaní kissed him. "What can I say? I've got a good reason to make an effort now."

Her eyebrow arched in response. She might have been about to reply when the hatchway to the power station collapsed outward with a crash.

"It's only me." Sam materialized before them and waved. "Come and see this."

Leaving their escorts to guard the exterior, Mohammed, Shaní, and Calen crowded forward, drawn by the excitement in Sam's voice.

Mohammed stepped across the threshold, and was amazed to discover an interior far more opulent than the substation down on the plain. As before, much of the space was occupied by power conduits, transformers, and phase converters. However, in this station a plethora of tangible and holographic constructs had been arranged along the outer perimeter and three of the walls. Most of the devices were operational, and filled the room with an ethereal glow of twinkling lights.

Not that they held Mohammed's eye for long. His attention was drawn to a huge shimmering column that had been lowered into a large circular borehole cut through the exact center of the chamber.

Is that the power source?

He looked over the edge of the railing, but couldn't see the bottom.

Bloody hell. Does this thing reach down to the center of the planet?

Up close, the obelisk appeared fluidic, as if its texture was made of liquefied fluorite. So dark was its surface and so speckled in silver and gold highlights that it looked as if a slice of the night sky had been encapsulated in aqueous crystal and rooted into the foundations of the earth. The more he stared, the more Mohammed felt as if the stars were dancing to a waltz he could never comprehend.

Would you look at that? I've never seen anything so incredibly beautiful. Mohammed reached out to touch it, and felt the hairs along the back of his fingers stand up. He snatched his hand back.

"Careful," Sam warned, "its active. From what we can ascertain, *this* is the main power core for every substation across the continent. And if you think that's impressive . . ." He gestured toward something on the other side of the monolith. "Take a look at the interlink."

Intrigued, Mohammed followed the direction of Sam's gaze and saw a connecting span, similar in design to a telescopic arm. Bridging the gap between the monument and main deck, it ended in a large ocular array encircled by pulsing gems. The ring itself focused a host of coherent beams down onto the headrest of a reclining seat that wouldn't have looked out of place in an orthodontist's surgery.

"Calen, Shaní," Mohammed called, "have you ever seen anything like this before?"

Both Senatum members approached from the other side of the walkway.

"Indeed I have," Calen chuckled. "Though it wasn't quite as advanced as this the last time I laid eyes on it."

"Last time?"

"Yes. This is a Paladin Throne, and I devised a rudimentary version of this very tool a few years before the outbreak." The Chancellor moved around the apparatus to get a better view. "Though I must admit, when I sent the schematics off to the boffins here on Exordium, I never dreamed they'd incorporate so many of my suggestions into such an elegant piece of machinery."

"So what does it do?"

"In a nutshell, the Paladin Throne is the most advanced multi-firewall AI-interface you will ever encounter." Calen made a sweeping gesture with his arms. "This facility controls the distribution of power for the entire planet. You can't allow just anyone to come in here fiddling about with whatever they want to, so we have features like this . . ." He pointed toward the chair. "Those lasers create an artificial mentality net, an augmented telepathic link between the user and the machine not only to establish an identity lock, but also to allow the technician to manipulate chaotic energies with stunning precision. The palm reader logs each incident by taking a verified DNA sample." Calen bent forward to examine the annular. "And from what I can discern, the security ring incorporates a combined facial, vocal, and iris recognition system. You can't deceive it. Those foolish enough to try get fried."

Calen then drew their attention to certain features Mohammed hadn't noticed on his arrival.

"As you can see, remote sensors and targeting emitters are incorporated into the walls, fixtures and fittings. Had you actually touched the pillar, you would have triggered the defense system. Anyone who tries to use this apparatus or meddles with any of the contraptions in this room will pay the price."

Mohammed was stunned. "How do you know so much about it if you haven't actually seen it before?"

"These are merely aspects I included in my original ideas." Calen looked equally surprised. "My colleagues appear to have followed my recommendations quite closely."

"Does that mean we can use it?"

"I certainly hope so. Remember, the download Seraphim broadcast included a revised CIC package. Our names, details, and biological profiles should be registered by now."

That's all I need to know.

"Then we really should crack on." Mohammed turned to the control unit. "Seraphim, would you please make the necessary introductions and connect us to the planetary AI mainframe?"

"Certainly, Captain."

The drone lowered from the ceiling and positioned itself above the apex of the column, whereupon a white light lanced out from its belly and played across the surface of its much larger cousin. The alien construct reacted, and a golden pulse flowed back along the beam. This was followed by a series of bubbling squeaks and squawks which became more prolonged and intense by the second.

After a few minutes, the frenzied exchange cut off.

"I am Plagus," a deep resonant voice intoned, "terrestrial guardian for Exordium Magnus. Cognitive RTB system Seraphim, recognized. Database update confirmed. Primary firewall requirements, established."

The surface of the megalith shimmered, and the outline of a spinning crimson-colored polygon appeared within its depths. As it slowed, a ruby light stabbed out and washed across the forms of Calen, Shaní, and Mohammed in turn.

"State your identities."

To Mohammed's ear, the masculine tone of the AI communicated a clear sense of aggression, grating on his nerves. Nevertheless, he submitted to the process along with the others.

"Psi Calen, Chancellor of the Senatum of Arden."

"Gul Shaní, Deputy Magister of the Senatum of Arden."

"Mohammed Amine, Deputy Advisor elect of the Senatum of Arden."

The rotating shape slowed and stopped to form a hexagonal key. Its outline brightened to amber. Mohammed heard a faint *click.*

Three sparkling pins as thick as icicles slid free of the main shaft until they were within reach of the encircling platform.

Mohammed had seen a device very similar to this back on Rhomane, so he knew what was coming next.

"Senatum ranks confirmed against existing list," Plagus boomed. "Verify hybrid disposition."

The trio stepped forward to grasp their respective rods.

No sooner had his flesh made contact than Mohammed became aware of at least a dozen hair-thin fibers. Sprouting from within the crystal itself, they wavered in the air and then dropped down to pierce his skin along the arm, neck and head. He glanced to his side and confirmed the same thing was happening to his friends.

"Psycho-dermal interlink established. Accessing chromosomal templates. Please substantiate."

"Recognize Psi Calen, Chancellor."

"Recognize Gul Shaní, Deputy Magister."

"Recognize Mohammed Amine, Deputy Advisor elect."

"Identities acknowledged. Welcome, Chancellor Calen, Deputy Magister Shaní, and Deputy Advisor Amine. Secondary firewall requirements, verified."

The filaments slid free of Mohammed's body, and he stepped back. As he did so, the glittering slivers retracted into the main column. The hexagon blazed brightly and morphed into a vivid green octagon.

That was quick?

But Plagus hadn't finished.

"Ranking officers, step forward one at a time, and assume a reclined position within the Paladin matrix. Prepare for full DNA and psidentic analysis, and command code interrogation."

Oh, for goodness sake, Mohammed was exasperated. *I knew it was too good to be true. How long is this going to take?*

He soon received a hint.

Calen stepped forward first. As the stately scientist leaned back and got comfortable, an enclosed gravity sheath activated, effectively welding him to the chair. The encircling halo above him bloomed, and the top half of Calen's head disappeared within a corresponding nimbus.

The Chancellor immediately fell still and silent. Mohammed watched intently, alert for any clues that might indicate what to expect. But after nearly ten minutes of not much happening, he'd had enough.

"Sam? Please tell your people I'm going outside. What with the end so close, I can't stand all this waiting around. I'm going to walk about a bit, see if I can't settle my nerves. Let me know when it's my turn." He turned to Shaní. "Care to join me?"

"Thank you, my love, but no. I appreciate your frustrations, but the scientist in me is fascinated by the invasive depth of the process. Although laborious, this chair is a wonder of design. We really ought to be thankful its brainstem wasn't compromised during the initial outbreak; otherwise there'd be no way to get past that underground barrier without a great deal of bloodshed."

Did she say, 'my love?'

Mohammed was taken aback. He glanced around the room, but none of the others appeared to have noticed the simple intimacy of Shaní's statement.

She's never expressed herself like that in public before.

For some reason he couldn't quite fathom, Mohammed suddenly felt very happy.

He waved and, in a bemused world of his own, headed toward the exit.

Andy met him at the threshold. "Everything okay?"

"Fine," Mohammed mumbled, "Still wondering at how many ways life can find to surprise you, is all."

"Tell me about it," the lieutenant replied. "I mean, where else would we even be having a conversation like this? You and I lived centuries apart. We should have gone through life, died, and never been aware of each other's existence. Yet here we are, having the adventure of a lifetime. Makes you wonder what's waiting for us next, eh?"

"Next?"

"Yeah, the guys and I were discussing it the other week. What if there's something special about us now? What if something like *this* happens every time we buy it? I mean, wouldn't that be crazy?" He made an exaggerated, wide-armed gesture. "Welcome to Arden, where death is only the beginning of the adventure."

If only. Now that *would be something I could handle.*

Mohammed shrugged. "I dunno, Andy. We got lucky once . . ."

Both men looked out across the plain and let the silence between them grow. Unable to think of anything else to do, Mohammed selected a relatively clean spot on the ruined pavement, sat down, and let his head fall back against the wall.

A million and one scenarios rolled through his mind.

The day's events must have taken their toll however, for the next thing Mohammed knew someone was shaking him awake.

"Captain? C'mon, they're waiting for you inside."

Mohammed opened his eyes to find Andy kneeling beside him.

"Eh? What?"

"Everyone else has finished." Andy cocked a thumb over his shoulder. "It's your turn."

"How long was I asleep?"

"On the job? Twenty, twenty-five minutes. Not bad, I suppose, for an expedition leader who's keen to set an example." He hauled Mohammed to his feet and tried not to laugh. "Don't worry, we've only told, like, *everyone*. We've got pictures too, enough to provide us with years of happy piss-taking."

"Ha, ha, very funny. We can talk about what it's going to cost me when I've finished. See you soon."

Mohammed brushed himself off and made his way back into the control center. As his eyes adjusted to the gloom, he spied Shaní leaning against a computer terminal, massaging her temples.

"How was it?"

"Nothing a stiff drink or three won't sort out soon enough." The expression on her face changed. "But if you can think of an alternative form of therapy, feel free to suggest one."

Around him, Sam's team made no effort to hide their amusement.

"Er, what about Calen?" Mohammed mumbled, suddenly anxious to change the subject.

"Oh, he's fine." Shaní pointed off to one side of the room.

In a darkened corner sat the Chancellor, up to his elbows in the open access port of an obscenely intricate-looking device. By the glare of its inner workings, he looked like some demented scientist hell-bent on evil machinations.

"Boys and their toys," she continued. "Now Plagus has granted him full access, he's like a child with a sugar fetish let loose in a candy shop."

Shaní stood up and walked past Mohammed, toward the exit.

"I could do with a breath of fresh air myself," she murmured, squeezing his hand as they passed. Over her shoulder, she called, "Get this finished, Mohammed, so we can all get home."

"Don't worry, it'll soon be over." Mohammed watched Shaní leave before he walked over to the throne.

His comment had the ring of truth.

Hey, this is *it. Once I'm done, we really will be able to go home and live the rest of our lives in peace.* He pinched himself. *Just checking.*

"Deputy Advisor," Plagus intoned, "please take your seat and prepare for cerebral-splicing."

Mohammed did as requested and made himself comfortable. As he leaned back, the chair reclined; a prickling sensation skittered along the palm of his left hand; his limbs became heavy. Mohammed found himself enveloped within a cocoon of isolation. His muscles stopped working, and the annulus above blazed to life, engulfing him in solar radiance.

Overwhelming agony ignited every nerve in his body. For a moment his entire existence was lost to blinding brilliance. Mohammed tried to blink the glare away, but all he could see was a swirling vortex, a polychromatic waterfall that plunged toward him, and then through him.

So intense was the sensory overload Mohammed thought he might pass out.

What the fuck? They said it was uncomfortable, but this is ridiculous.

"Mental congruence established," Plagus declared. "Switching to telepathic resonance. Stand by, incoming message."

Message? Is this thing an answer-phone too?

As the bubble of actuality collapsed, his vision wavered again and folded back on itself. It darkened and rippled, sizzled and boiled, as if two opposing elements had metamorphosed into a turbulent mass of permanent contradiction. Echoes refracted to and fro within his skull. Then the plane of his existence turned inside out.

Clarity returned.

Mohammed immediately wished it hadn't, for a sixteen-foot tall titan, adorned with a crown of twelve silver-white stars and swathed in purple and violet majesty, hovered in the ether before him.

Hatred radiated from it in waves, exposing a terrifying fusion of horns, fangs, and talons. The extremity of its aura blazed vermillion. Eyes as black as midnight regarded him with a promise of death.

While one part of him recoiled in horror, the other still refused to accept the reality of his situation.

Is this part of the test? An evaluation perhaps? Or am I just plain and simple dreaming?

The sound of evil personified grated in the air about him.

This is no dream . . . human. Unless you savor the taste of nightmares?

Then, what . . . ?

You already know in your heart who I must be. Don't deny it.

The queen? What he'd just admitted to himself brought lucidity crashing back. Mohammed was appalled. *Wait a minute,* the *queen?*

*I am Va-*ákil*, the first true progenitor of my race, and the architect behind this many-layered trap you have so eagerly walked into.*

But how could you possibly . . . Mohammed was confused. *This is an ultra secure facility protected by multiple safeguards.*

Contempt crashed down on him like an avalanche, silencing his protestations.

Surely you are not so naïve as to imagine your kind, pathetic as it is, are the only ones capable of sophistication? The more enlightened of my ilk are proficient in the most refined intricacies, especially where arcane energies are involved.

The burning effigy motioned, and multiple images representing many of the colony's finest achievements appeared, orbiting Mohammed's position in a twirling testimony to Va-ákil's statement. In one of them a gleaming set of collars and a swirling vortex stood revealed.

And are such energies not the essence upon which these many artifacts are built to operate?

A Gateway? But . . . how? Caym didn't . . . ?

What? Did you think us incapable, kin-slayer, of bending such eldritch might to our will? Of subverting its programming to serve as we see fit?

Mohammed was stunned.

I wouldn't have believed that possible, he thought.

And your admission reveals the depth of your conceit, Va-ákil countered, *for you did not appreciate that others might comprehend more than you do. We are blended, human, I can hear your personal thoughts as clearly as if you expressed them publicly. Did you not realize that? Is this why you neglected to consider the consequences of your actions here this day, or failed to imagine how the desecration of my race might come back to haunt you when you least expected it?*

But we're here to save you from—

Scalding rage crashed against the flickering flame of Mohammed's sensibilities.

Tell that to the teeming hordes of our brethren massacred by your foul and cowardly schemes, or those Kresh torn from us and raped by your diabolical manipulations.

Malevolent intent coalesced about him.

No. Your interference ends here, now. And in the most delicious of ways.

What do you mean? Mohammed's blood ran cold. *What are you going to do?*

Let's just say, my revenge will be meted out in a reciprocal manner. Of course, as the first of those sacrificed on the altar of new beginnings, you won't be there to witness the extent of its gravitas. A pity. I would have delighted in extending your suffering for years.

Mohammed started to struggle, to kick and scream and shout. But it was no use. His exertions only existed within his head.

Farewell, kin-slayer, Va-ákil crooned. *Die, knowing that yours is but a taste of the sorrow to come.*

Her voice hissed off into the night like a zephyr seeking the arid embrace of the desert. As it faded, Mohammed came alert to his change in circumstances.

For one thing, the feeling of dry heat had increased. He caught his breath, only to discover the act caused him great pain.

My lungs are burning!

The temperature rose exponentially, quickly becoming unbearable.

He tried to open his eyes, but they felt as if they'd been glued shut. The stench of scorching flesh assailed his nostrils, then disappeared as an odd sense of detachment swept all sensation away.

All, that is, except his hearing and an overwhelming sense of darkness.

Noises filtered through the bedlam in dribs and drabs.

A popping and snapping of electric circuitry as it melted. The warbling shriek of an alarm system, expressing danger too late for anyone to respond. The clatter of metal as unknown items collapsed. And voices. Voices everywhere, shouting, cursing, contradicting.

". . . you're told or I'll drag your ass out."

". . . can't we try . . .?"

Mohammed rocked from side to side as the floor bucked.

". . . you again. He's welded to the chair. Get the fuck out. It's going to blow."

". . . crazy? We can't just leave him . . ."

". . . an order. Get out, get out, get—"

A hiss of water sprinklers malfunctioning. The whistle of high pressure gas venting. An unknown screech adding its spine-jarring tincture to the maelstrom about him.

Somewhere, someone screamed a name.

"Mohammed, nooo . . ."

The floor tilted, but instead of falling Mohammed was lifted high into the air by the return of a blinding white light. He marveled that it didn't hurt at all this time around. An impossibly distant source of everlasting peace and sweet solace opened wide to receive him. He rushed eagerly to meet it, only to feel a belated tinge of regret.

Shaní . . . ?

*

Are you sure? Altás queried, clearly surprised by the order. *Would it not be wiser to escape with our army intact and use them against whatever awaits us on the other side?*

I appreciate your sentiments, Va-ákil replied, *but there's no time. As you saw, the trap worked better than I anticipated. Since they have lost their leader, their spirit is bound to be crushed.*

Despite her zeal, the Prime Catalyct still radiated concern.

You have doubts? she pressed.

I do. Forgive me, Magnate, but I would be remiss if I did not highlight the obvious. These humans are insects, true. But those we face are also disciplined soldiers. Despite the fear we can all taste, radiating from them in waves, they conquer those feelings and face us with determination. Surely you have seen the skill and ardor they employ in battle? That is something I can appreciate.

Va-ákil recognized something in the deepest recesses of her mate's heart.

You admire them.

It wasn't a question.

I concede, a part of me cannot help but acknowledge their resolve. Altás was unabashed. *No, it is their mental fortitude I respect. I have a terrible feeling this tragedy will achieve naught but to spur them on to greater efforts. Did you not sense the hatred and focus of those shadow warriors that survived? And with the weapons at their disposal, we would be wise to exercise caution if we are to avoid obliteration.*

Then you had best dispatch the Triarium Tier with all haste. If you are correct and the worst does indeed come to pass, we will need a buffer between us and them until our avenue of departure is prepared. Va-ákil allowed her aura to radiate a warning, indicating that the discussion was over. *Do your job, and I will do mine. The continuance of our race cannot be compromised by sentiment.*

Very well, Altás conceded, *it will be done. And I will personally ensure our defenses receive the impetus they need to stand a chance of victory.*

Altás stomped away, and Va-ákil turned to her Grand Vizage.

Do you have something for me?

I do, Ilion replied. *The great machine has been tested, and works as the Houston suggested it might.*

Lightning bolts of pleasure struck throughout the length and breadth of Va-ákil's essence.

You are sure of this?

I am, my queen. Ilion allowed her own excitement to show. *Following Houston's instructions, we were able to employ the specifics of the hybrid's DNA to work in our favor. The process drains him to the point of death, but fear not: we shall keep him alive until he has outlived his usefulness.*

Go on?

One aspect locks onto his newly added Ardenese chromosomes and initiates a stable threshold within the cavern, here.

And the other?

Although we cannot establish a full path into the vext for fear of killing him, it appears his genetic template acts as a lodestone and seeks his point of biological origin. Know, too, that Caym has offered his services. He believes the added impetus of his own recent splicing might boost the signal and increase our chances of success.

Va-ákil was delighted.

Then let us set the final pieces on our board and be away before it's too late.

A tinge of sadness darkened Ilion's persona.

Must we still leave? This place offers such vitality. How will we ever manage?

We have no choice. Altás fears our actions here may result in the eradication of the entire planet. By the time that happens, we must be far away. Va-ákil exuded an air of consolation. *And as for vitality, don't worry. Where we are going, food exists in abundance. We will hunt as we used to do. Feed and spawn. Dominate, until all life has been extinguished or bent to our service.*

She grasped her confidant around the shoulders and led her away. *Come, while there's still time. Assemble the Prátors and Lega'trexii, the Tribuni, and whatever fresh new Praefacti remain to us. We must be away.*

And what of those of the Triarium Tier?

Va-ákil pondered for a moment and made her final choice.

Those who survive must fend for themselves. We cannot remain to hold the gate open and risk our future. A new world waits, and I for one yearn to savor what it has to offer.

Chapter Thirty-Two

Gateway to Oblivion

"What the hell was that?"

Jake Rixton spun his horse in a tight circle and looked up toward the *Orison*'s portside hatchway where Walter "Jack" Daniels was standing.

"Was that an explosion?"

"I'm not sure," Jack replied. "Hang on; I'll go see what the chatter is over the net."

As he waited, Jake grew increasingly perturbed. His "something's not right" bump was itching like crazy. He called to his second-in-command.

"Angus, do me a favor. Get on the radio and start pulling the guys in. It won't hurt to leave the cave entrances unmanned for a little while—they're mined, after all." He bit his bottom lip as the uneasy feeling worked its way down into the pit of his stomach. "I've got the damnedest notion a shitstorm might be rolling our way."

"I'm on it."

The highlander trotted his horse toward the main cliff face, leaving Jake alone to ponder in silence. Jake scanned the ridgeline above.

Nothing. It looks so peaceful . . .

"You were right."

Jake twisted in his saddle to find Jack had returned.

"About what?"

"I've just been in contact with Pat Keeley up in the *Ballarat*. As you know, he dropped Mohammed and the Special Forces team off before flying out to cover sinkhole number three. He says there was a detonation of some kind inside the power station, and now a whole load of thick black smoke is issuing from the doorway. A powerful EMP surge was released at the same time. Fortunately our ships are protected, but some of the smaller handheld devices won't be."

Jake glanced back toward Angus, who was shaking his walkie-talkie vigorously.

Shoot! There goes that option.

"Jack, if you don't mind the suggestion, I think it might be a good idea if Pat gets his ass across to the station to render support and find out exactly what happened. In the meantime, get the *Abeille* and *Eurus* to join us in picking up the rest of my company. We need to be on our toes and in the air. By the way, what does Seraphim say about the situation?"

"Not a thing. Whatever that pulse contained, it's still preventing surface-to-orbit communications."

Jake scratched his jaw. "Have you tried the EMT shuttle? Remember, there weren't any pilots left to evacuate Sam and his team from the Kalina, so Seraphim assisted by providing an AI ersatz which runs on an independent system. We might be able to establish a link through her."

"Good thinking, I'll see what I can do."

"If it works, ask Seraphim to liaise with Pat up on the plateau in case he finds a whole bunch of casualties. And get the drones to provide live-time intel."

Jake's bump was working overtime.

We're probably going to need it, real soon.

His gaze was drawn to one of the sealed entrances.

Shit! I wonder what this means for Marcus and the Ninth?

*

The energy curtain stuttered, and vanished.

A wall of slavering ogres fell forward, gleeful and expectant, eager to be among the first to kill and feast on the abundant life force gathered close-at-hand.

Their leading ranks disintegrated as they ran headlong into a hail of darts. Ignited by the turbulent essence of their targets, each missile became a flaming brand, allowing Marcus to follow their trajectories as they cut a rippling swathe through the demon host.

Those entities that survived the initial volley ignored the dissipating remains of their brethren, only to slam against the negating field of the interlinked scutums.

Yowling in pain, they recoiled, venting their frustration in the only way they knew how: frenzied rage.

Such impotent posturing served no useful purpose so far as Marcus could see.

That's it, keep doing what you're doing.

The second Hoard wave hit. Driving their incensed compatriots forward, they attempted to use the compressed substance of their less fortunate kin to gain purchase and vault over the top.

To no avail. No sooner did they breach the summit than they were impaled on waiting skewers that exploded, showering those in the immediate vicinity with an all-consuming cloud of iron shavings.

"Advance in manipular formation," Marcus bellowed. "Drive these devils back! Scutums to the front, sarissas behind, bowmen in between each pike. Form up."

The sound of shields disengaging, reengaging, and weapons being brought to bear reverberated along the cavern.

Marcus scurried among the stalagmites, surveying the redistribution of his troops. Professional to a man, each fell into place without so much as a missed step.

Good lads.

"Get ready to—"

"General?" someone called out. "Ware the enemy."

He looked to the front. A fifteen-foot tall colossus elbowed its way through the press toward them. Encompassed by a prismatic nimbus of indigo and gold radiance, it glittered fiercely in the gloom, yet somehow managed to create voids of darkness wherever it passed. Marcus couldn't help but notice how the grunts fell over themselves to get out of its way.

An augmented demon lord, here in our midst.

Before Marcus could shout a warning, it tensed its bulk and two incandescent balls of plasma formed, one in the palm of either hand.

Vergilius snapped an order, and a flight of arrows arched through the air. Every single one disappeared in an explosion of flames.

The Grand Master snarled. For a split second its aura solidified; the iridescent halo about its head ceased its dance. Then a visible nimbus radiated away from its body.

Ten, no . . . Eleven? Eleven stars. Gods, it's huge.

When the energy wave swept across him, Marcus's skin bristled.

"Take cover," he yelled.

Just in time.

The beast flexed its talons wide. Tendrils of telestic majesty burst from its fingertips. Yet its efforts were not aimed at the soldiers before it. Instead, each ribbon thundered into the roof of the vault.

A fretwork of cracks fractured the rainbow sheen above them.

The Horde commander doubled its efforts, and this time whole stalactites were blasted free of their roots. Splinters and shards keen as blades hissed down onto exposed flesh. Men staggered, crying out in pain.

Oh, very clever.

"Form testudo, now!" Marcus barked. "Get to cover."

More bolts of lightning stabbed out and boulders rained free, creating havoc amongst those scrambling for shelter. Screams pierced the bedlam. Entrails, brains, and gore marked the places where some hadn't been quite quick enough.

By Pluto's beard. This creature's tactics are inspired. I can't let it gain the advantage.

"Advance," Marcus yelled, "as fast as you can. Don't allow them to get settled. Target their leader."

The second centuria pressed ahead as one, but the giant stood its ground. As the first line drew near, the brute surprised them by lumbering forward. It scooped two shattered stalactites from the floor and then broke into a run. Closing on the scutums, it jumped high into the air and used its bulk to put the nearest shield bearers under pressure.

Fluid blows rained down. The front rank crashed inward like a shipwreck of broken necks and cracked skulls. Pressing its advantage, the Grand Master laid into the milling soldiers, employing the shards to great effect and causing widespread panic. Then it gestured to its minions to join it.

The waiting throng leaped through the gap, and the rest of the second centuria rushed to intercept.

A bloody free-for-all erupted. In the close confines of the Cathedral, the battle took on a ghoulish perspective, so that it was hard to distinguish friend from foe. Sparks etched the darkest recesses with telltale flashes of conflict; disembodied groans marked the lonely graves of the dead and the dying.

Ogres snarled, gnashed, clawed, and howled. Legionnaires stabbed, slashed, punched, and screamed. A steady ebb and flow developed wherein each patch of fiercely contested dirt was marked by little pockets of random illumination.

The demon lord itself, deceptively swift, managed to skip in and out of the shadows, rallying its troops here, dispatching its enemies there. Every now and again it would stop to take on an entire contubernium. There it would stand, toe to toe, swatting arrows, blocking thrusts, and snapping spears while taking merciless advantage of any exposed limbs or unguarded groins or throats.

Faced with the carnage it wreaked, Marcus was impressed.

Now there *is a warrior*. D*espite its power, one mistake would bring its rampage to an end. This monster shames the rest of its kind, for it leads by example—from the forefront. As brave Angule once did.*

Regardless of what respect it earned, Marcus knew the beast had to die. His men obviously felt the same way, for they fought valiantly.

A multitude of wounds and visceral welts covered them from head to foot, but they wouldn't relent. They bore their injuries proudly, as if each lesion or abrasion were a badge of honor. What was more, Marcus could see how well they'd fought: For all their unusual tactics, the Horde was losing ten fighters to only one of his men.

The tide is turning . . . at last.

Shouts drew his attention.

On the far side of the passage, a lone tesserarius had become separated from the rest of his unit and had backed into a small depression in the cave wall. A swarm of grunts surrounded the area. With a cry of savage delight, they descended on him.

Marcus looked on helplessly as his soldier disappeared beneath a boiling mass of fangs and spurs.

Poor fellow, there's no way he—

A swelling report punctuated the sound of battle. As it reached its peak, a shockwave blasted outward, kicking up a cloud of debris and knocking those closest to it to the floor. When the dust settled, Marcus was amazed to see his sergeant still alive.

Sword in hand, the officer could barely keep himself erect. He brandished his blackened weapon before him and stumbled forward to meet the next challenge. The fabric of the uniform along his free arm and legs was badly burned, and a cruel gash flapped open across his forehead, closing the swollen eye beneath.

"C'mon," he taunted, beyond caring now that his end was close, "what are you waiting for?"

A riot of nearby ogres rushed to accept his challenge. Then a resonating snarl tore through the ether and brought them to a grinding halt.

An unearthly silence descended.

The hairs on the back of Marcus's neck stood upright as the Horde commander waded through the press. Every so often, it paused to discipline any lackeys disinclined to obey its order.

Eventually, it came to stand in front of the stricken soldier.

Marcus's heart went out to his man.

He's barely conscious and too far away to help.

Not until the fiend loomed over him did the injured tesserarius realize he faced an opponent. He looked up, blinked, and wove unsteadily from side to side.

"You'll do," he hissed. "I can't . . . I can't think of a better way to die."

The titan regarded the puny human before it for a moment, then manifested its full essence.

Some of the legionnaires looking on couldn't bear to watch helplessly. Those with bows released flight after flight of arrows, but each and every one was reduced to cinders before they had covered half the distance to their target. Several within the first centuria brought their guns to bear, but a command from Marcus prevented a needless waste of ammunition.

"Remember your duty. Save it for where it's needed."

Unless? Marcus clicked his fingers and directed Tiberius to attend him.

"General?"

"Your gun, Tiberius. Quickly, give it to me."

On the other side of the cave, events were reaching a climax.

"Wash the matter, big boy?" The sergeant's voice began to slur. "Scared to fashe me?"

The sword came up.

With infinite slowness, Goliath reached out toward David. One gleaming talon, big as a dagger, raked along the side of the soldier's blade, sending sparks flying and a prolonged shriek gamboling through the shadows.

How in Hades' name is it managing to touch the iron?

The claw reached the handle, and Marcus took aim.

Nobody dared move as they awaited the tesserarius's inevitable execution.

A gonglike boom reverberated along the passageway, hiding the *click* of a safety catch disengaging. Before its bass tones faded, the massed host turned back and fled along the corridor. All but the Master, who continued staring at its victim intently, as if pondering where to strike first.

At least I can spare him the agony of being fed upon.

The shot rang out, followed almost instantly by the sound of a ricochet.

Bang! Zing!

The brute moved unpredictably fast, swatting the bullet away in the split second before it impacted the legionnaire's skull. With a casual gesture, the Grand Master erected a shield about them, protecting predator and prey from further distractions.

Everyone looked on as the Master reached out toward their comrade and touched him on the crown of his head. The soldier became encompassed by a sheath of power. His entire body went rigid and lifted a few feet from the ground. After a few moments, the surge of power cut off and his body crumpled to the floor.

The fiend stepped back, a gray helix gaping open in midair behind it.

It looked directly at Marcus, who was stunned to hear a voice ring in his head:

There is no honor in defeating a weakened foe. I, for one, am glad your brave warrior won't have to face one of my lesser kin again. It would be a waste.

It stepped into the void and vanished.

Marcus stared, too stunned to react.

Around him, his men rushed forward to recover their fallen brother.

Startled gasps drew his attention.

"Augustus?"

"How can this be?"

"Alive, you say?"

Alive?

Marcus pushed through the gathering crowd and bent to examine the fallen tesserarius.

Gone were the burns and blisters that had marred Augustus's arm and legs. Instead, Marcus found only hale and hearty limbs, restored to their prime. He was perplexed to note the skin tone displayed evidence of months toiling under the sun.

It's as if he was never injured.

He looked at Augustus's face.

A thin white line running from the bridge of his nose toward his left temple remained, the only testament to a wound severe enough to put any man in sickbay for weeks.

This new strain has been relentless and without mercy. So why did it heal him?

He thought back to the monster's parting words:

"There is no honor in defeating a weakened foe. I, for one, am glad your brave warrior won't have to face one of my lesser kin again. It would be a waste."

It has a distinct sense of honor. Like Angule it seeks to—

"General," Tiberius interrupted, "something is happening."

Marcus looked around, expecting another attack. But all he could discern was a series of resonant vibrations running through the earth beneath his feet. Dust fell in shimmering curtains, their patterns corresponding to the length and intensity of each sonic pulse.

"Sir, are they trying to bring the mountain down on us?"

"I don't think so. These . . . No! It can't be."

"I, for one, am glad your brave warrior won't have to face one of my lesser kin again."

Thunderstruck, Marcus made a connection.

Again? As in, never *again?*

"Tiberius, Vergilius, reform the lines. Rapid deployment. I don't know how or why, but I think the Horde are seeking to escape. We cannot let them leave this planet alive." He looked around his gathered officers and men. "Whatever it takes. Is that clearly understood?"

"Yes, sir," they thundered.

"Then step to it, and pray that I'm wrong."

*

"Gone?" Shaní's face was white with emotion. "Are you sure he's gone?"

Sam squeezed off another round of well-aimed shots before bothering to reply. "He's dead, Shaní, pure and simple . . ."

He paused as further loud reports rang loud about them, and waited for ogres to stop screaming. "Those bastards really fucked him up. They must have planted a virus or booby trapped the chair somehow . . . and—"

Sickening images superimposed themselves upon his inner sight: strips of blackened flesh oozing foul mucus from a multitude of cracks and sores. Skin stretched tight across the remains of a calcified skeletal frame. Bones, crumbling to ash. And a blistered skull without eyes, weeping smoke into a flame- and fume-filled room.

A cleansing light had purged the reality of such horror from his mind. Now they returned with a vengeance.

"— and then some."

"But how?" Shaní persisted. "*How* did they do that without harming either Calen or me?"

"That's what I hope to find out, once we've evacuated."

Out of the corner of his eye, Sam caught sight of further movement, a blemish in the air undulating furtively from the laboratory's northern perimeter. All thoughts of consolation faded.

"Excuse me, Shaní . . . Heads up, team: fresh targets at eleven o'clock. See, sneaking out from the rear of the academy wing?"

"Got them," Andy replied. "Leave the fuckers to us."

Bursts of fire chattered forth, closely followed by shrieks of pained surprise and the chain-reactive blast of instant immolation.

Sam clasped Shaní by the elbow.

"I'm sorry. We simply don't have time to talk things out in detail. That will come later—when we grieve. For now, we've got to concentrate on staying alive long enough to regroup and hit them back." He gave her arm a squeeze. "Do you understand?"

Shaní's face set in a mask of grim determination. "Oh, I'll make them pay all right."

Standing tall, she unhooked something from around her waist and unfurled it to its full length. "With interest."

A modified Horde mastig.

"Tell your people to focus on what's out there," Shaní continued. "If anything gets close, I'll take care of it with this."

For emphasis she snapped her wrist, and a loud *crack* snapped through the atmosphere.

Good, she's not lost her spirit.

"That's what I want to hear."

Satisfied, Sam left Shaní to her new task and strode over to where the casualties were being treated.

"How's it going, Joe?"

Joe Stark finished inflating a gel restraint around Calen's left leg and sat back:

"The Chancellor's still unconscious, but stable. The burns along his arm are superficial, but the break to his knee is more serious. I think he's snapped his tendons as well. It'll all need treatment, and soon. The medi-wrap will serve until we get him back up to the *Shadow of Autumn*. Thankfully, Seraphim's on the way in the EMT shuttle, and we'll also have the support of the *Ballarat*." He glanced at the readout in his HUD. "ETA, two minutes."

Sam looked beyond him, to see Eddie and Bob wallowing in a semiconscious haze.

"And the guys?"

"They both have concussion, so they're sedated for now, as you can see. Barring any unforeseen developments or symptoms, they'll be right as rain in a day or two." He tapped the side of his helmet. "Their armor took the brunt of the punishment. While they'll have to forgo the rest of today's festivities, they'll be well enough to receive visitors tomorrow, along with the inevitable piss-taking for having missed the finale."

Sam snorted. "Good to hear. Once we've got all noncombatants strapped in and out of the way, I'll see what we can do about getting back into the fight."

Something in Sam's voice obviously gave Joe cause for concern. "What's up, boss? Problems?"

"It's just something Calen mentioned earlier about being left a trail of breadcrumbs to follow." He gestured about them. "I expected much more resistance. Don't get me wrong, I know we lost Mohammed—and the bastards are gonna pay for that, believe me—but . . . I dunno, it all seems a little too easy."

"As in too convenient?"

"Yeah, you know, as if this is just a small piece of a larger distraction?"

"I know exactly how you feel. So what are you thinking?"

"Truthfully? I won't be happy until we've been able to reestablish communications with Marcus to find out exactly what's going on underground."

*

The passage widened into an atrium, and there the massed ranks of the first and second centuriae slowed their charge and ground to a halt.

Scutums slammed into place, magnetized, and linked together. Sagittaria and hastati fanned out on either side and in between. Behind them, modern weapons were brought forward and made ready.

The chamber into which the Horde had retreated was a wonder to behold. Vast and completely smooth, the inverted dome that formed this cavern had evidently been created by a diminishing flow of water over thousands of years. But Marcus didn't have time to admire its beauty: something of more immediate gravity demanded his attention.

Illumination cast by a throng of obscure, mundane, and holographic constructs lining the perimeter walls competed with much richer glory being emitted by a terrifying host assembled around a central dais. There, as nowhere else, the gallery was awash with conflicting currents of light and shadow.

There must be hundreds of them!

It was obvious the Horde were prepared for conflict, for the elite of their kind had gathered together in fighting wedges, a tactic Marcus hadn't seen since the Battle of the Line more than a year ago. Dazzling concentrations of gold and silver, blue and argent, purple and scarlet awaited them like a multicolored isle, safe within a sea of ogres, promising a savage squall of ferocity that would serve as a last line of defense against the Legion's might.

Or is it?

A telltale flicker, like the distortion seen on the surface of a gem, revealed another facet to the Horde's strategy.

Something else is there, and it's virtually indistinguishable?

He peered back to the encircling girdle of grunts.

So their function is to slow us down.

And to the side tunnels adjoining the rotunda.

But to what end?

The subsonic rumbling plaguing them for the last five minutes grew more pronounced. Dust shook free from unseen crevices while some of the lighter workstations and equipment began sliding across the floor.

They're powering something up, that much is clear. But what? Caym made no mention of a portal and this looks nothing like the gate room back on Arden. Unless they're going to try manipulating the . . . what do they call it? The vext? Are they hoping to boost their own strength so they can teleport out of here?

He returned his attention to the platform.

Just above and on either side of the combined clusters of personified evil, a shining pair of floating brackets hung facing each other. Every time Marcus looked directly at them, he could see the air shimmer, as if subjected to some form of heat distortion.

There. That's what the energy is for. But what do those do?

He glanced down, and a flash of yellow on blue caught his attention.

US cavalry trousers?

Marcus fished in his utility belt and brought out a small set of field glasses. Training them on the spot in question, he fiddled with the focus.

The sallow, haunted face of someone familiar appeared in his field of view.

He caught his breath.

"What's the matter, Marcus?" Tiberius Tacitus queried. "You look like you've just seen a ghost."

"I think I have." Marcus handed the binoculars to his friend. "Tell me what you perceive, *there*, where that series of glowing red cables meets the large reclining chair. It has some form of circular array above it."

Tiberius did as he was asked.

"Which one, there are two?"

"Two?"

"Yes. One toward the back of the stage where it's darker, and one to the front that . . . no! By all that is holy." He spat. "That's Wilson Smith."

Several soldiers standing nearby, hearing the exchange whispered among themselves.

In Hades' name, if that's Smith, then who's the other one?

Marcus retrieved his glasses and peered into the gloom.

Sure enough, a second chair lay in shadow at the rear of the dais. The shape upon it was much larger and muscular, and dressed in formal Ardenese-style clothing. That person shifted position as if trying to get comfortable.

In that instant, Marcus thought he saw someone else he'd grown fond of:

Caym?

As he watched, Caym's features disappeared within a blinding halo of light and his huge form relaxed, as if he'd suddenly fallen asleep.

How in the blazes did they manage to capture him? The last thing I knew, he was safely aboard the Shadow of Autumn.

When he checked back on Wilson Smith, Marcus could see the same thing had happened to him.

They must be linked into that contraption in some way. Is it bleeding their life force?

A bank of red lights illuminated along the top of a nearby control station. Its activation was followed closely by a monotone warning indicator:

Beep—beep—beep—beep—beep!

"Anomaly detected," an unidentified voice announced. "Please stand by . . ."

Marcus heard more generators come to life, followed by the steady whine of building potential. On the beds, both captives were encapsulated within coronas, glowing as if an aurora borealis had been plucked from the skies and confined to this one vicinity.

Two projectors stuttered to life. Their beams focused upon a cloud of white mist originating from a hidden vent in the ceiling. Within its field, a long list of scrolling equations worked their way up the page. So taken was he by the distraction, Marcus didn't realize the U-shaped collars were gradually drifting apart. In the space between them, the atmosphere thickened and started rotating.

I've seen enough.

"Ninth Legion," he yelled. "The Horde have captured two of our number and seek to use them as a means of escape. We must prevent it. On my command"—he raised his arm, paused, and let it drop—"*Fire*!"

A first, deafening volley thundered down upon their enemy, drowning out the sound of everything else and forcing Marcus to cover his ears in spite of his helmet.

While the outer ring of grunts was cut to shreds, the defensive barrier behind them betrayed hardly any evidence of the assault.

His centurions saw it too, and looked toward him.

"Vergilius, have your bowmen and javelins apply their skills and target the unprotected ogres. Tiberius . . ." Marcus surveyed the tightly-packed Grand Masters. "Concentrate your fire on the blue and silver contingent standing close to the forward edge of the platform. I suspect they are the ones channeling their combined strength into the shield protecting them."

As their assault recommenced, Marcus took a step sideways to observe the effectiveness of his strategy.

The surrounding Triarium buffer quickly dissolved under a hail of iron-tipped missiles. But as each torrent eradicated more of the Horde's number, others swirled forward like dust devils to fill the spaces occupied by their comrades only moments before. Throaty cries—lost, hoarse, desperate for reprieve—shrieked forth in one place after another as scores met their end.

And yet they refuse to charge?

The esoteric shield proved another matter entirely. Sparks flickered here and there as ineffective bullets bounced away. But for the most part, it continued to rebuff all attempts to violate its integrity.

"Origination point accepted," the same metallic tone announced. "Establishing anchoring cipher . . . *Now*."

Within the expanse of the struts, the cloying white mist revolved about its own axis. It continued to thicken until it formed an asperity. A cool breeze sprang up as air was sucked toward it. The background vibrations increased tenfold, and Marcus was stunned to hear the rock face itself creaking and groaning from the additional stresses brought to bear.

Marcus felt his entire scalp tingle.

It is *a gate!*

A sense of desperation clutched at his loins.

"Grenades," he yelled. "Aim for that same spot along its leading edge."

A shower of silver-gray orbs arched across the intervening gap. Some landed before the podium itself. Others hit the shield and bounced. Regardless, they all detonated as one.

The visible spectrum splintered and puckered. The distortion preceded an inevitable shockwave. Pockmarks littered the floor. A score of miniature ground-zeros the only evidence of the passing of more than a hundred ogres. The crystal ball luster of the barrier bruised yellow for long, lingering seconds before returning to its former translucent purity.

Nevertheless, it held.

We don't have the wherewithal to breach its strength.

As if confirming Marcus's assessment, the speakers announced, "Geophasic coupling established. Quantum leader powering up."

The swirling miasma within the bands clarified into a distinct maw. Staring into it, Marcus's thoughts were swept into a tide of possibilities. A sea of faces circled him in quick succession: the men he'd lost in Caledonia, along with those who'd succumbed to the rigors of life on Arden since their arrival; Angule, and those brave enlightened ones who fought with them at the Battle of the Line and made such a difference; Mac McDonald and Lexington Fox, courageous friends whose sacrifices would count for naught if the travesty of the Horde was allowed to continue; Ayria Solram, whose unearthly supernatural warnings had saved them while she herself exemplified the ultimate expression of love for others.

And, finally, the strange thoughts expressed by the Horde general who had shown such uncharacteristic honor:

"I, for one, am glad your brave warrior won't have to face one of my lesser kin again."

Marcus expressed his concern aloud:

"If we don't do something soon, the ruling elite of the Horde will escape and start this nightmare all over again." He looked to his centurions to see if they recognized the precarious fulcrum on which the future of the universe now balanced. "I can't . . . *we* can't allow this to happen."

Vergilius and Tiberius regarded one another gravely. Around them, the mood altered as others comprehended what their commander was considering.

Tiberius straightened.

"We're with you, General. Hell, we've all of us lived longer than we should have. At least this way our deaths will make a difference." He grinned. "Who knows, perhaps we'll get to do it all again?"

The automated computer chose that moment to intervene:

"Tracking nodes, activated. Seeking suitable candidates . . ."

The broadcast galvanized Marcus's men.

"End them, sir, once and for all."

"Yes, do it."

A united consensus sounded, back and forth.

"We're with you."

"Even Pluto's with you . . . *and* us. Death tried once before to stop the Ninth, remember, *and failed.*"

Laughter, painful to hear, broke out and quickly circulated.

Marcus's heart clenched with overwhelming pride; his resolve stiffened. He was forced to turn away as tears blurred his vision.

"Aquilifer, to me."

Felix came to his side.

"Pass me the secure communication module."

Felix thrust the lydium-tipped pike of the signum into the earth and rummaged around in his backpack. While he did so, Marcus looked up at the bright sheen of their latest standard and reached out to run his fingers along the smooth lines of the proud targén adorning its plinth.

Those that survive will need to fashion a new one. But in that, there'll be no shame—not after what we do today.

"Here you are, General."

Felix handed Marcus an elongated, box-shaped device. Incorporating a camera, radio, and all-in-one scanner, it was insulated against most forms of intrusive electronic warfare and operated on a closed circuit, linked directly to the CIC aboard the *Shadow of Autumn*.

"Seraphim, this is Silver Command, do you copy?"

"Director Brutus," the AI replied immediately, "we are relieved to hear from you at last. We have been experiencing . . . unforeseen obstacles. Is your part of the mission progressing smoothly?"

"I'm afraid not . . ."

The avatar had sounded flustered, if that was possible, preoccupied by something. But Marcus hadn't time to pursue the reasons why that might be. He activated the camera and scanner, and panned the appliance around the chamber.

"As you can see, Seraphim, the Horde has misled us into thinking they were simply retreating behind a series of barricades to make them difficult to reach. They were playing for time . . . time to prepare *this*. Correct me if I'm wrong, but that is a super-gate, yes?"

On cue, the robotic voice made its next announcement:

"Targeting candidates recognized. Selecting prerequisites . . ."

A siren sounded, and the fog of ionized gas within the active field began shimmering.

"Yes, you are correct," Seraphim replied. "Readings indicate the tangible presence of one end of a hyper-bridge. Once the boundary has polarized, it will home in on a suitable terminus and the portal will activate."

"Then you appreciate the urgency of taking *appropriate* action, as per the guidelines laid out in our primary mission briefing?"

"I understand the urgency only too well."

"And would you agree the gravity of the situation warrants a robust response to prevent their escape?"

"From what I have witnessed here and elsewhere, I most certainly do."

The speakers interrupted again:

"Prerequisites met. Target acquired. Broadcasting anchoring cipher . . ." A shrill tone blared out. "Warning, radiation hazard. I say again, radiation hazard."

Marcus glanced toward Tiberius and Vergilius, and back at the lens. He took a deep breath.

"Then in my capacity as the ranking Senatum officer on site, I initiate emergency sterilization protocol Omega One, with your RTB mainframe serving as second. Confirm?"

"Emergency sterilization protocol Omega One. Request confirmed. Verify verbal command code."

"Marcus Brutus, Director. Proteus, Caspar, nine, Gaul, Cathal, five, Romulus, Pluto, one, one, Omega."

The line went silent. In that split second, Marcus realized he would never feel the sun on his face again. Get to hold Angela in one last gentle embrace. Or enjoy the simple pleasures of time amongst friends.

He strangled down a bitter resentment that threatened to overwhelm him, and tried not to let his disappointment show.

"Command sequence correct. Stand by for validation." The AI paused. "Marcus Brutus, you *do* understand the consequences of enacting this procedure from your current locality?"

"That there will be no possibility of escape?"

"Precisely."

"Thank you, Seraphim, I do. But what choice do we have? Please ensure groundside units are warned and given an opportunity to get as far away as possible."

"They have already been notified, and the *Helexia* is standing by to assist survivors."

"Then validate." Marcus glanced toward the waiting Horde Masters who hadn't yet moved a muscle. "We don't have much time."

"Certainly, but before I do, you must understand one more thing."

"What now?"

The holdup made Marcus sound sharper than he'd intended.

"We may already be too late. The planet crushers will take a full two minutes to reach the surface of Exordium. Slightly longer if you hope to detonate them at its core. It is my opinion the jump-gate will activate before then."

The portal's central processing unit obviously agreed:

"Gravity lock established. Sublunary matrix initiated."

The medium within the braces shimmered. A mirrored sheen replaced the gray and expanded to encompass the mounting bands themselves. Marcus felt his teeth ache in time with the energy fluctuations.

Then we must improvise.

Among his people, Marcus had been foremost of those learning as much as possible about his avant-garde new world. His efforts paid off now as a flash of inspiration gave him a moment of clarity:

"Seraphim, try using your photonic weapons to cut a hole from the surface to this site. The danger of a massed spawning will be negated when you teleport the planet crushers along the conduit and into the cavern itself. One thousand enemy or ten thousand, it won't matter: everything will be squashed out of existence."

"A sound strategy. However, you should be aware the Horde have deployed a dampening field about your location that has hindered communication thus far, and made transporter locks dangerous to contemplate."

"Irrelevant, we're not talking about people. If necessary, transfer the Leviathans to the top of the borehole on a brief time delay, and let them drop the rest of the way. They'll still destroy everything in here."

"And you along with it."

Marcus had tarried enough. He didn't want his men suffering longer than was necessary.

"Seraphim, validate Omega Protocol *now*."

"Very well. Validate Seraphim, nine, principle, Java, seven, template, Armageddon, two, corporeal, three."

Marcus wracked his brains to remember the correct reply. The final *three* was the key.

"Principle – ambiguity. Template – disorder. Corporeal – cerebral."

"Omega Protocol confirmed. You have five seconds to negate your command from my mark . . . *Mark*. Five—four—three—two—one. Sterilization locked and initiated."

In a gentler tone, Seraphim concluded, "Prepare your people as best you can."

"Thank you. Please remember what we do here today."

"Oh, we will, Marcus. Rest assured, everyone will hear of the Ninth's sacrifice."

We only have about a minute of life remaining to us . . .

Marcus turned to face his brothers. "Get ready to make our last stand. Fall back to the main passage and form testudo. Let none in here escape their fate."

Everyone rushed to obey.

Soon, a huge shield wall blocked the only exit from the tunnels. The men behind looked grim, indomitable. Eager to carry out their final duty before death demanded its due. Some grinned, others fidgeted. But Marcus could see all were determined to face Pluto as warriors.

Behind the Horde's barrier, red and scarlet streaks arched through the air, a sure sign the legion's maneuver had caught their foe by surprise.

They're worried, and so they should be.

The only one unperturbed by the events unfolding was Exordium's AI mainframe: the looking-glass patina of the geodesic plane softly shimmered and began twisting in on itself. From Marcus's perspective, he felt as if he were looking down upon a giant bathing tub being drained of water. The other end of the tunnel stretched off into infinity, and its rotating walls ignited under the orphic interaction of unknown cosmic energies.

"Temporal sheath deployed. Stand by for final resolution."

Now they've managed to establish a wormhole. Come on, Seraphim, where are you?

One of the beings on the dais detached itself from the group. Only when the creature stood apart could Marcus see that it was decidedly different from the other Masters. Not only was it much smaller, but it was devoid of a crown or any other form of necromantic embellishment. What was more, its body was a strange combination of 'ghostly apparition meets gelatinous goo.'

What is that? Is it undergoing some form of transition?

The parody undulated across to where Wilson Smith lay imprisoned and extinguished the lights encompassing his head. Clearly exhausted and drenched with sweat, the victim exuded an air of sorrow and abject misery.

Marcus watched as the entity waved at him directly—to ensure he was watching. Having captured his attention, it made a gesture, as if doffing an imaginary cap. At the same time, Marcus received a distinct impression within his mind of someone he had once known.

Houston? That's *James Houston?*

Marcus must have subconsciously broadcast his thoughts somehow, for Houston inclined his glutinous head in acknowledgement. Then, with everyone looking on, he reached out and placed a viscous hand on his nephew's head.

Smith screamed and arched upward. Already pale from his ordeal, his pallor blanched yellow through white and darkened to deathly gray. He went limp and collapsed back onto the bed.

Marcus knew with absolute certainty this young man was now dead.

Around him, his men voiced their distaste at such a cowardly act.

"Peace," he urged. "Justice will soon be served, not only for young Smith but for all who have suffered at the hands of these abominations."

If Houston was aware of the curses directed toward him, it didn't show. Instead, he waddled quietly toward the back of the podium where Caym had been incarcerated.

Marcus held his breath and waited for the same grisly scenario to play out. He was astonished when Houston helped Caym to his feet.

The former Lega'trix stood, flexed his neck, stretched, and then calmly made his way to the front of the platform, where he took a position next to the largest group.

A numbing truth struck home.

He's with *them.*

Further deliberation on this latest betrayal was postponed by several things happening at once:

A nearly subliminal hum intruded—one that existed at the edge of Marcus's perceptions but which nevertheless quickly grew to dominate his whole world. As it did so, the quartz veins lacing the cavern's walls glowed red, orange, and then yellow.

Zzzzzzzzt!

Stalactites melted, boiled, evaporated. And for the first time in millennia, sun-bright radiance penetrated the bowels of the earth.

Boom!

Men yelped in pain, forced to turn from the coherent splendor of seventy billion zephyr-joules of power or risk permanent blindness.

The remaining ogres fell to the floor, kicking and screaming in apparent agony. They lay there writhing, and their thresholds swelled and bulged in different directions at once, as if the souls of all those they'd consumed over the centuries were fighting to get free. A tremendous static charge built in the atmosphere. Sparks snapped and crackled along the floors, walls, and worktops.

So that's what the onset of a spawning looks like?

Marcus didn't care.

It's coming.

The background drone of the generators cut off, and the suspended collars above the dais flashed brightly before cooling to a dull silver-gray metal.

"Safety overrides engaged. Quantum pathway established," intoned the system. "You may proceed."

The massed ranks of more than one hundred Masters dropped their communal shield. Leaving their minions where they were, they turned as one toward escape.

And not a moment too soon.

They hadn't taken more than two steps when a muffled explosion from above them turned the world upside down.

Marcus felt rather than saw the detonation.

One moment he was poised on the balls of his feet, fighting to maintain his balance, and the next he was plucked from the ground and hurled into the sizzling hot apex of the dome. A surreal experience, for it felt as if an unseen force were trying to embrace him through the fabric of the intervening rock.

Amazingly, his thermoflex coveralls worked perfectly, protecting him from sudden exposure to searing heat.

It must be one of the planet crushers. Oh, well played, Seraphim, just in time.

Solid granite squealed as it was torn apart and compressed into nothing.

Marcus managed to lift his face free of the stone to peer through a storm of tumbling furniture and equipment toward the portal.

A churning conduit of prismatic reflections waited, as enduring as diamond, yet as fragile as gossamer whispers on an autumn breeze. Through it, a treasure-trove of prismatic aspirations beckoned. Restraining pins shattered and smashed into the ceiling, joining the demon lords who growled and howled in impotent fury.

Without guide restraints, the plane of the cosmic bridge distorted, flexing backward and forward like an elastic band under opposing tension.

"For Flavius," someone yelled.

"And our general," another added.

"For the Ninth," Marcus shouted back.

A twinkling pool of stars coalesced in the air before him. He only had time to glimpse the appearance of a glowing red beacon atop the matte black ceramic casing of a torpedo tube before he was consumed by the contradiction of spacetime collapsing.

The wormhole ripped apart. Shredded, its geodesic threshold expanded to consume the dais, the Horde, and on past the boundary of the cavern itself.

Everything slowed and then froze, caught between an instant of when and how.

Tongues of fire and needles of ice pierced Marcus's skin in the momentary rapture of eternity. Too astonished to feel pain, he watched himself ascend and transpose. He became both human and ethereal, evanescent and eternal, afraid— now that death had finally come to claim him—and yet beyond caring.

For a fleeting instant he lifted on cosmic winds, high into the vault of the heavens, and thought he might soar free of it all.

Then a maelstrom descended upon him, and he was lost to darkness.

Chapter Thirty-Three

Exordium of Tears

Sandi Chang couldn't quite believe the news Seraphim had just delivered.

A trap? Mohammed dead? Calen and a whole bunch of others badly wounded? And now, there's a strong possibility that Marcus will sacrifice everyone on the ground to ensure the Horde menace be eradicated forever.

Still reeling from the implications, she gasped, "So what are you going to do?"

"My duty," Seraphim replied. "Once the final validation sequence is confirmed, I will destroy the planet, along with everything and everyone on—Stand by, one of my avatars is confirming the cipher as we speak . . ."

The channel went quiet.

"Captain Chang, the Omega Protocol has been duly verified. Please withdraw the *Helexia* to a distance of at least one hundred and twenty thousand miles to avoid tidal shearing.

You must excuse me for a while. I have a most unpleasant task to perform."

Oh Jesus Christ no! She's actually going to do it.

"Roger that, we'll stand ready to assist in any way we can once this is all over. *Helexia* out."

Sandi swiveled her chair about and began issuing instructions.

"Helmsman, you heard the lady, get us out of here. Reverse thrust, half speed. And make it one hundred and fifty thousand megs, just to be sure."

"Half reverse. One hundred and fifty thousand megs. Yes, ma'am."

"Serovai, enhance shields and boost forward scanners; split the main screen. I want a lock on the *Shadow of Autumn*, a high altitude view, and a magnified frame of the plateau itself. Maintain rapport with Seraphim so you know what's going on. If things go south, act first and update me after we're clear. Got it?"

"Yes, Captain," the *Helexia*'s AI construct replied. "I have already armed defensive countermeasures and primed a Slipstream window, should we need to make a quick exit."

"Thank you, Serovai. All noted."

Sandi depressed a button on her inlaid control panel. As the backlighting to the stations around her turned amber, she opened a ship-wide channel:

"All stations, all stations, this is the captain speaking. We are now at yellow alert. I say again, we are now at yellow alert. Standby crews, man your posts. Emergency rescue team, report to sickbay. All nonessential services and other departments, secure workstations. Brace yourselves for turbulence."

And pray for a miracle so we don't actually have to go through with this nightmare.

The holo-screen flickered, dividing into three separate perspectives. Sandi leaned forward, her eyes glued on the *Shadow of Autumn.*

Sublight engines aglow, the great bulk of the dreadnaught coursed forward until it encroached upon the planet. For a moment, its huge outline blazed, advertizing its presence as a harbinger of doom. But as it continued its descent, the shields adjusted and an all-encompassing bubble became visible, edged in flame and light.

The plunge continued for less than a minute before coming to an abrupt stop.

Sandi couldn't help but imagine how the *Autumn*'s profile might appear from the ground as it blotted out the sun and crushed all expectations of a last-second reprieve.

Poor bastards. Do the rest of them know what's coming?

A single blade of concentrated plasma flared to life, an ebullient shaft of limitless magnitude lancing downward with the precision of a surgeon's scalpel.

Sandi's gaze flickered to the other side of the display in time to watch as the brilliant needle pierced the earth without so much as a pause. Granite; limestone; rock and dirt: Everything vaporized in the blink of an eye and a puff of smoke.

The beam disappeared.

"Photonic incursion has breached the gate room," Seraphim's voice announced over the speakers. "Captain Chang, be advised I will be deploying the Leviathan planet crushers in close sequence. One will detonate partway along the excised shaft, while the other will be translocated directly into the chamber itself after a five second delay. Prepare your crew for a double shockwave and severe gravity fluctuations."

"Understood."

"Teleporting ordnance in . . . Three, two, one. *Now*!"

Sandi held her breath and dug her nails into her palms.

On the surface, a layer of soil jumped more than four feet into the air in a manner that reminded Sandi of a prospector panning for gold. The disturbance appeared insignificant, but the orbital view revealed the scale of the tectonic disruption, for the entire continental plate was now suffering a planet-wide earthquake, with Barsoonet at its epicenter. Insidious waves variegated away, generating cyclonic winds and sandstorms as they passed. Cloud formations trembled, distending in spiraling fingers down toward an unseen point of infinite pressure.

My God. Just look at it.

Then the ground beneath buildings began falling away. In moments, the entire headland was gone in a scene reminiscent of a giant hourglass emptying, and Sandi could only imagine what it would take to fill the ever-expanding void opening up in the secret depths of the earth.

Dust spumes ejected skyward from one place after another. Bolstered by concussive detonations of purple and yellow-green fury, they blasted high into the atmosphere, obscuring her view.

But something else stirred deep in the heart of the expanding brume, something hungry and malevolent, wild and unrestrained. Something that continued to whisk the boiling cauldron of ash and silica until it was a frothing brew of contradicting savagery.

Serovai adjusted the resolution of the *Helexia*'s scanners so Sandi could watch as a huge wedge of land measuring a score of miles across dropped down into the substrata. She had the distinct impression that a giant fist, having grabbed the entire peninsula, now tried to yank it through to the other side of the planet.

What the hell is going on?

Every time the slab dropped, blinding eruptions raged forth in psychedelic expressions and spiraling eddies which curled high into the thermopause and beyond. Some shattered, spending their essence in wistful expressions and frittering energies; others fell back to their point of origin in great loops of unfulfilled potential.

A pang of recognition made Sandi's jaw drop.

The substance and texture of those tendrils reminds me of the extremity of a Slipstream terminus. Or the lining of a wormhole. But that's not possible. There's no defining boundary to the event horizon. It has to —

"Captain," Serovai's voice intruded on her deliberations, "my instruments are detecting unacceptable gravity extremes and the presence of pockets of severe temporal dilation. I recommend moving us farther away until we are safely sandwiched between Liberty and Vilén. The mass of each planetesimal should protect us from the worst of these effects."

Damn!

"Make it so," Sandi replied. "Full reverse thrust. But keep our sensors trained on what's unfolding."

"Full reverse thrust, aye," the helmsman echoed.

"And Serovai?" Sandi added. "Be sure you warn Seraphim. She might be caught in a riptide of shit and not realize the danger."

"I have already attempted to communicate, but time distortions are degrading the quality of each signal. I must conf—Aha! It looks as if my efforts weren't in vain: the *Shadow of Autumn* is already moving to a higher orbit."

Sure enough, when Sandi checked the holo-cloud, the huge craft was pivoting around to face away from the planet. The injector outlets glowed hot, a sure sign the jump engines were powering up.

FTL inter-atmosphere? Things must be worse than we thought.

The *Helexia* increased speed. Barely in time.

Far below, the raging cycle of all-consuming annihilation reached a crescendo. Exordium convulsed, and the fast moving chain of events appeared to wind down into a teasingly drawn out slow-motion shadow play. Enormous rents like a spiderweb network of silken threads radiated across the planet's surface. Reaching the ocean, they burrowed deep beneath the continental shelf. The trans-global landmass began breaking apart, and the waters were transformed. Seas, squeezed into mountainous aspect, contended against exposed abyssal trenches for dominance. But not for long. Another spasm rocked Exordium from pole to pole, and the contents of her nebulous bowels spilled out into the chill of the void in an expanding broth of boiling gasses and cooling lava.

Along with this came the vortices, fulminous barbs of unknown celestial potential that homed in on anything in which a spark of life resided.

Before Sandi realized what was happening, one of the tentacles snaked out from the billowing haze and scourged the *Shadow of Autumn* from stem to stern. The maelstrom yawned wide, stretched to envelop the ship and its shields whole. Then it snapped shut, and dissipated in a starburst of dissonant energies.

Sandi's breath caught in her throat.

The Autumn*'s gone!*

An unknown force struck the *Helexia*. Thrown from her chair, Sandi experienced a moment of indescribable agony along with a sickening sense of dislocation. She felt as if someone else was being torn in multiple different directions all at once, while she was the one being blighted by the pain. Her tumble across the floor ended abruptly as she smashed into a bulkhead and bounced.

A bright flash blistered the edges of her perception, but the discomfort helped orient her. Sandi flopped back on the floor, the spinning gradually slowed, and her equilibrium returned.

Bloody hell and damnation.

"Serovai."

"I am here, Captain." The air shimmered and an avatar appeared. "Fear not, I assumed control the moment we were hit."

"Thank God for that. What was that thing?"

"We were caught by the trailing edge of an oscillating gravity streamer."

"An oscillating gravity streamer?"

"Yes. Whatever happened down on Exordium, it temporarily deformed spacetime in some way."

"Tell me about it. My guts feel as if they were twisted out of place." Sandi touched the growing lump on her forehead and groaned. "It's lucky for you that you don't feel pain."

"Noted. I do, however, register damage."

Sandi got the point. "How bad is it?"

"We are very fortunate. Only half a dozen casualties reported so far. Our aqua drive engines are stalled. I have assigned three flights of drones to effect repairs to minor damage to the starboard side of the hull. Long-range scanners are offline. The energy streamer was comprised of exotic matter which drained the shields to the point where I must recharge the capacitors. We are currently at twenty-seven percent and climbing."

"How long until we're functional?"

"Hard to say until I have been able to carry out a full diagnostic . . . One moment, medium range optics are rebooting."

The main viewer flickered to life, and a morbid sight greeted Sandi's eyes:

Exordium, or what was left of it, had been reduced to a toroidal ring of ionized matter orbiting a debris field of moon and asteroid-sized extraterrestrial dross.

My God. I didn't expect . . .

"Where's the black hole?" She gasped. "I thought the Leviathans would combine to create at least one distinct void?"

"It never stabilized, Captain. The dynamics unleashed here disrupted the normal functioning of the bombs. Astounding, when you think of the power required to interrupt such a chain reaction once it had started."

"Is anyone still alive?"

"Doubtful. Those discharges appeared to seek out life force. Most unusual."

But everything was going so well. How on earth could it . . . ?

Sandi's brain kicked into gear: "Can you find Barsoonet? Some of those hunks must measure hundreds of miles across. Surely there may be survivors there?"

"Negative, although I am picking up a residual energy reading very similar in nature to the gyre that snatched the *Shadow of Autumn* away. Only *this* imprint is many times larger."

"Larger?"

"Yes, according to the data I have at my disposal, an area nearly thirty miles square simply disappeared."

"As in it was swallowed by the short-term singularity?"

"No, as in *vanished.* The planet crushers may have ripped the threshold of the hyper-gate wide open, creating the vortices in the process. Whatever happened is beyond my ability to accurately determine at this time. All I can say for certain is that some kind of quantum conduit manifested exactly when the planet expired. And although I am still analyzing the data, it looks as if we existed simultaneously in multiple timeframes, albeit it for a fraction of a second."

Sandi winced at the memory of that experience, and turned to gaze back into the oneiric pageant of scoria and sediment encircling the remains of Exordium like a glowering halo of sorrow.

No wonder it cracked under the pressure.

"Are we still in danger?"

"Unknown."

"Then we'd better call in the cavalry." Sandi pulled herself back into her chair. "Serovai, contact Rhomane central and update them as to the balls-up here. Then do the same with the *Paladin* and *Dark Falcon.* Ask them to rendezvous as soon as they possibly can. Once you've done that, withdraw us to a safe distance to make repairs while we await their arrival. When our systems are back online, we'll be in a better position to understand how everything went so wrong."

She drank in the haunting sight before her and fell silent.

Although in all honesty, I don't think we ever will.

Epilogue

Forty Years Later

Saul Cameron crept along one final corridor and peered across a threshold. The interior of the Hall of Remembrance was deserted. And so it should be. It was well after midnight, and apart from those citizens on duty in various parts of the great edifice called Rhomane City, most sensible people were asleep in bed.

But he wasn't "most people," and the Chief Advisor to the Senatum was here to commemorate a special, if solemn occasion.

Although he walked quietly, his footsteps echoed across the open expanse of the great dome and came resonating back to haunt him from all sides. The sound reminded him of voices whispering from the grave, and put him in a reflective mood.

He thought on those who had passed in the forty-eight years he'd lived on Arden. Of the crew of the *Regent*, his ship, lost in the vastness of space on her maiden voyage decades ago in the Earth year, 2345. Of the exceptional men and women from other eras who, like himself, had been snatched away over the centuries and brought here, to fight a losing battle against a relentless foe on behalf of a race lost in all but memory. And, of course, he couldn't help but reflect on those who had turned the tide in their hour of need.

The shining beacon of the Reverence acknowledged his presence as he passed, buzzing louder for a moment in response to his ambient life force. He ignored it, and continued making his way toward his goal, the most prominent of the nine floor-to-ceiling bas-reliefs carved into the fabric of the outer wall.

Shaped like an open book, it served as a lasting testimony to the bitter fruits of endurance, for it contained the names of all those from the ninth intake who had fallen in death.

And look how many there are now.

He slowed his pace and came to a stop in front of a wide-stepped circular dais positioned in front of the monument. A large standard occupied pride of place on a plinth in the podium's center, and its scarlet and gold fabric perfectly accentuated the burnished glow of the eagle atop a highly polished wooden staff.

The letters *SPQR* were engraved into a small tile attached to the pole. Beneath the banner, a larger sign read:

SPQR
Senatus Populus Que Romanus
In the name of the Senate and the people of Rome
Serovak Pluserak Qen Rhomanax
For Security Prosperity and Rhomane

Saul lowered himself onto the top step, and placed a small basket on the ground. Reaching inside, he removed a pair of elaborately engraved quartz goblets which clunked loudly as he set them on the pedestal beside him. With a reverential air, he next selected a squat decanter and poured out two generous measures of a gleaming topaz liquid that encapsulated the rays of the setting sun within its fiery embrace.

He raised a glass in salute.

"To absent friends."

Tossing back his drink, Saul basked in the warming glow of the phoenix rising from the pit of his stomach, and with the other serving in hand, leaned against the rostrum to make himself comfortable.

"Hello, old friend," he murmured. "it's strange to think another year has passed so quickly, eh? Time seems to fly by now that things are safe, but I suppose that's to be expected. Thanks to the re-genesis matrix, the forests and seas across Arden have returned to the way they were before the outbreak. I tell you, they teem with so much life and vitality, it's a wonder the planet doesn't burst. The agri-drones have a job keeping up sometimes, so volunteers help bring in the harvest. Marcus would be proud. His scheme has expanded, and over eighteen thousand citizens manage their own plots outside the city.

"Now the inner colonies are safe we've started to reclaim some of the outer protectorates too. Just small settlements on three of the farthest planets, but it's a great start. It'll certainly help with the way the population is expanding, as Pat Frost's genome project has quadrupled our numbers over the past few years alone.

"And the children . . . Lively, precocious little buggers. Oh, what a delight they are. Do you know, since the mutation matrix has run its course, the only way you can tell purebloods apart is by the color of their eyes? Ours retain a predisposition for variety, while the Ardenese tend to different shades of topaz blue." Out of habit, he glanced at his own amazingly youthful hands. "You probably wouldn't recognize me now. I look like a surefire candidate for the Area 51 museum back on Old Earth . . ."

A sense of melancholy washed over him, and Saul faltered.

Content to sit there in silence, he stared off into space and allowed more than an hour to pass with only his memories to keep him company. Some of them took courage to contemplate.

Eventually, he expressed what was troubling him:

"I miss you, old friend. Don't get me wrong, I knew the day would come when circumstance might part us. Look at the lives we led, after all. But . . . it's just that . . . after we vanquished the Horde and settled down, who would have thought all that shit would flare up again?

"And I feel old, Mohammed, older than I've felt in a long, long time."

Saul's chest heaved. Unexpected emotion caused his bottom lip to tremble and then tighten. He swallowed a lump in his throat.

"I mean, how can we be sure something like that won't happen again? Both Jayden and Alan say not to worry, the monsters have gone for good. Stained-With-Blood keeps telling me the future's what we make it." He shook his head. "I don't know. He hasn't had a vision of doom since you die – since you left, so I'd like to think that what we have is down to you and the others on the *Shadow of Autumn*."

Out in the far corridor, a light blinked on.

Hmm, probably a contingent from the city patrols completing their security checks.

He looked around the auditorium and sighed deeply.

I'd better get going. It wouldn't do for people to start thinking their Chief Advisor secrets himself away in the wee hours knocking back the hard stuff. Talking of which . . .

Saul lifted the second glass high and stared into the honey depths of the drink for a moment.

"Well, if you're not going to raise a toast to what you achieved, I will."

He stood and faced the eagle.

"Here's to you, old friend. Now and forever."

www.ingramcontent.com/pod-product-compliance
Lightning Source LLC
Chambersburg PA
CBHW021622030826
48979CB00035B/1509/J
* 9 7 8 0 9 9 6 4 2 8 9 8 9 *